Don't Walk Away

A Novel

(Book 1 of the Violet Kelly Series)

By:
Avery McCoy

This book is a work of fiction. Any references to historical events, real people, or real places are used fictitiously. Other names, characters, places, and events are products of the author's imagination, and any resemblance to actual events or places or persons living or dead is entirely coincidental.

ISBN: 9798386836320 (KDP)

avery.mccoynovels@gmail.com

Don't Walk Away

For Dad, I miss you everyday.
To my family, thank you for your endless support.

Chapter 1
Violet

The last thing I want to do is get in a car and drive, especially after being on a plane for over 19 hours. I need a shower, a drink and I need to move my body. Drink first. I've never done anything so spontaneous in my life. To get on a plane on a whim and fly across the world to a place I've only heard about is completely out of character for me.

I find an empty seat at the airport bar which is easy because the bar is almost empty. I check the time on my watch, 10:16 PM. That can't be right, the sun is shining outside, I'm still on Boston time. I sift through my bag to find my phone.

"Can I help you, miss?" An older man, late 40s would be my guess, with salt and pepper hair starts to approach me from behind the bar. His tanned forearms twitch as he wipes a white bar towel around the rim of a glass.

"Yes, please. What time is it?" I pull out my phone, trying to turn the location on.

My fingers are not responding to my mental commands, the exhaustion from the flight has turned my brain to mush. I look up and see a smile forming on the barman's face. He, definitely, sees I'm struggling but his smile is not mocking. His smile feels reassuring, like he's seen this a hundred times.

He looks down to the watch on his wrist and responds, "It's one-eighteen. Can I get you something to drink? Would you like a menu?" He sets a square napkin on the bar in front of me. I'm thankful it's after noon and feel less guilty about drinking this early because it feels close to midnight for me.

"Yes, just a drink. I'll have a vodka tonic with a lemon, please." I finally managed to switch my phone off airplane mode and put on the location as I gave my drink order.

Shortly after, the pings and chimes start, 15 text messages, 12 missed calls and 4 voicemails. I groan, knowing I cannot bring myself to check the messages here and now. I need to unwind, I need to figure out my next move. I cannot believe I did this. The feeling of being so far away from home, from everything and everyone I know is setting in. I remind myself not to panic, I can do this. The drink comes quickly and I take two big gulps. I close my eyes and take a deep breath, the cool, crisp drink sets me at ease.

"Thank you, kind sir." I hold up the drink to the barman.

He gives a chuckle and bows his head, "Coming from the states?" He lifts his head and his light brown eyes meet mine.

"Yes, and I think I might move here. Honestly, I don't know if I can do that flight again." I force a smile but think I'm almost serious, his laugh is low and his smile bright.

I have some time off from work, a month if I want. I didn't plan on spending the entire time here but, I think, I need at least three weeks to recover from that flight. I've never been good on planes, between the time difference and the lengthy flight I'm completely exhausted. This place better be as beautiful as people and the internet boast. Looking around the bar I notice a few more patrons have settled in with the same tired, annoyed, jet-lagged look I must have now.

"Welcome to Australia. Give a shout if you need anything else." The barman taps the bar with his palm and sets off to take on the new customers.

I finish the drink in three more large gulps. Thinking of what to do next, I quickly scroll through the text messages. I see 2 from my sister, 6 from my assistant, 2 from my best friend, Beth, and 5 from Sam. Beth was the only one I told about my spontaneous trip to Australia. I called her from the airport with my flight number and told her I was about to board so as to not have to answer her bombardment of questions. Five texts from Sam. A heavy feeling forms in the pit of my stomach, it rolls with queasiness. I definitely can't go there right now. I motion toward the bartender with my index finger up while mouthing, "one more, please". He gives me a quick nod, acknowledging he saw my request, as he pours a draft from the tap. Opening my messenger app I tap on Beth's name.

Beth: You can't spring that one on me and say "I have to go"! Call me AS SOON AS you land!

Beth: Did you land yet??

The last one was sent 30 minutes ago, knowing Beth she probably set an alarm to the time the flight landed and tracked the flight from her phone. I shoot her a quick response and plan to call her once I'm settled.

My second drink comes with a lime this time, I'm too tired to bother correcting the order. Checking the messages from my assistant, Stacy, I see they're mostly brief notes on recent closures and new listings as well as information about a quarterly report that needs my attention. Stacy was a great find, energetic, motivated, smart and no-nonsense. She's been working for me for almost a year while studying toward her degree in real estate law. I trust her, along with my competent staff, while I'm away to keep things running smoothly and keep me up to date.

I take a few small sips and see no distress or concern in the texts from my sister. It's late back home, so I decide to call her in the morning. Or tonight? This time difference is going to drive me crazy. Back to the task at hand, finding a place to stay. Opening the search browser on my phone I pull up nearby hotels. My plan is to drive down the Gold Coast stopping at beaches, hiking paths and explore the national parks. I've never done anything like this by myself and, at the moment, I'm feeling overwhelmed. Sam was the one who always picked the vacation destinations. He picked when, where and how to spend our free time because he thought of it as "his" free time.

I eye the hotel choices, it's just one night to crash and make a more detailed plan. I could stay anywhere right now. Hell, after one more drink, I could crash here on the bar for the night. Then I remember it's the afternoon, the barman might not appreciate some American crashing on his bar. I picked a hotel for one night in downtown Brisbane, it's 20 minutes away by taxi. Finishing my drink I pack up my things and signal the barkeep. He's pouring another draft and nods in my direction. He places the pint down, along with a glass of wine, in front of a young couple. Then he grabs a slip and card from another customer, taking another drink order as he heads to the register, he might be a minute.

I look back at the couple, they're smiling happily and begin to laugh. The woman leans in to peck him on the cheek. She wraps her left arm under his right, resting her head on his shoulder and he kisses the top of her head gently. A stab of anxiety hits my stomach when I see their affection play out in front of me. I don't notice someone's trying to get my attention until I feel a poke on my forearm, it pulls me away from spying on the couple. I turn around and see a young man, tall with white-blond hair, wearing a bright white golf visor smiling widely, too widely. He's leaning against the bar more for support than casualness. There are two other men behind him getting ready to sit down in the empty bar stools next to me.

"Hey, are ya comin' or are ya goin'?" he snickers, glancing at the bartender while putting up his hand in signal. The stench of stale beer and cigar emanated from him. He either started very early or he hasn't stopped from last night. He's American, sounds like it anyway.

"I just arrived but I'm heading out now. My ride is almost here," I lie, I have no ride, I don't know anyone here.

I fidget in my seat to lean away from the smell of the man and to show him I'm not keen on starting a conversation. I look over at the bartender to see where he is on his order of assignments, he's printing a slip from the register. After dropping the slip in front of another customer he comes my way.

"Sorry 'bout that, can I get you another?" He takes my empty glass and places another white square in front of me and one for each of the three men to my right.

"No, thank you. I'll settle up," I say quickly, trying not to look to my right, I hear the man next to me breathing. With every exhale a whiff of alcohol comes my way making me uneasy. I want to make my exit as soon as possible.

"Why, don't you get the pretty lady another, I'll take care of it." He gives me a wink then leans toward his buddies and asks "Whatcha boys having?"

"No, I can't, I have to get going. You boys enjoy yourselves." I take out a few American bills from my wallet and leave them on the bar. I hope what I left is enough for the bill. I start to gather my purse, backpack and suitcase below the bar. I've got to get out of here.

The barman takes the bills, "I'll be back with your change." He smiles at me but it quickly fades as he eyes the trio, assessing their state. "Be right back, boys, hang tight."

I feel a hand grip my right forearm as I swing the backpack over my shoulder and reach down for the handle on my suitcase. I pull away hard from his grasp. I'm jumpy from the flight, lack of proper rest and the vodka but it's also out of instinct. He puts both his hands up in reaction to my withdrawal.

"Oh, c'mon, I'm sure you have time for one more. It's our last drink before our flight! One more, c'mon." His laugh is boyish as if this type of behavior works for him.

He's good looking, with chocolate brown eyes and a perfect white smile but his eyes are unsettling. In his eyes I see something mischievous, impish. I don't want to meet his gaze. I reach for my phone off the bar and throw it in my purse.

"Safe travels fellas." I tuck my stool under the bar and notice the blond stands in front of me.

God damn, this guy won't take a hint. I lean toward the right but he leans with me, it's more of a sway.

"What's the rush? Sit and chat for a while." He flashes his smile but I'm not at all impressed. I don't have the energy to parley with him.

I meet his stare and narrow my eyes, I try to keep my voice level even though I feel myself shaking. "Listen, I don't know how else to say it but I've got to go. Step aside, please." I can feel the heat rising from my chest to my face.

I consider knocking him on his ass, he's inebriated enough, he'd probably be surprised by a swift shove. But I'm not trying to make a scene at an airport, in a foreign country, half a world away.

As I'm debating my next move I hear a deep voice from behind, "The lady asked you to move aside, she's off. Did you not hear?"

I turn around to see a tall, broad shouldered man wearing a crisp white shirt with the sleeves rolled up to his elbows. His tie is loosened at the neck, the shirt is tight around the biceps. It's not until I look up at his face that I realize how tall he is. I stand at 5 feet 7 inches barefoot and this man has got, at least, 8 inches on me. He's unsmiling, a look of irritation sits on his face. However, I can not deny this man is gorgeous with his oval face, chiseled jawline and broad chin. His jaw twitches from clenching it so hard. His hair is a sandy brown with light golden streaks that look natural, like he spends a lot of time outside in the sun. His eyes are bright, a blazing blue, reminding me of the cobalt blue color I wanted to paint my office. I read somewhere the color blue stimulates the mind, creating calmness and productivity. But Stacy pointed out a lighter, smokey blue would be a better choice as to not feel so overwhelming to clients and associates. Now, I wish I had gone with the cobalt. I'm staring at his man but he's not looking at me, instead he's lock-eyed with Blondie behind me. Instantly, I'm brought back to the tense moment I left a few seconds ago.

As I turn back around, I see Blondie is also looking past me to the Adonis standing behind me. Now's my chance for a swift side step and to hotfoot-it out to the passenger pickup outside. I make my move, skirting around him and walk toward the exit. I don't falter, I don't look back, I pick up my stride until I see the exit doors. The effects of the two vodka drinks kick in, my head spins, I feel disoriented. The feeling could also be intensified because of exhaustion and the fact I'm in unfamiliar territory.

I exit the airport and draw in a deep breath of fresh air, the first breath of fresh air I've had since boarding a plane more than a day ago in Boston. The humidity is mild, not what I expected for March in Australia. From the little research I did, this is the Gold Coast's autumn season as opposed to just starting Spring back home in New England. I see a line of taxis in a pick up lane and head toward it leisurely, knowing I left the standoff of testosterone back inside. I'm not at all interested in how that debacle ended, I need sleep.

"Hey, are you alright? You dropped your mobile." The deep voice with a hint of Aussie twang calls from behind me.

I turn to come face to face with the godlike man from the bar, my rescuer. I thought he was another American at first. With a clearer head and fresh air I can hear a faint Australian cadence, it makes him even more beautiful. I don't know if it's the vodka, fatigue or this man but I'm finding it hard to keep my focus.

"I hope that bloke didn't bother you too much back there. Obnoxious American." His eyes widen, he seems to have made himself uncomfortable with his comment, he shifts on his feet. "I mean no disrespect. I know you're American, I'm not trying to offend. He seemed like an ass." He reaches out with his hand holding my phone. "Here's your mobile. Are you sure you're alright? You look a bit in shambles." He rolls his eyes and lets out a strained sigh. "I mean, uh, not a mess, you're beautiful, um, Jesus. Here you go." He shakes his head running a hand through his hair, seemingly, trying to steady himself with a few deep breaths.

He's wearing his suit jacket now and looks like a walking advertisement for some high end cologne or expensive watch. I'm feeling every bit a ragamuffin in my joggers and sweatshirt, I should have stopped off in the ladies room and got myself together. If I had known this gorgeous man would make conversation with me I definitely would have.

"Thank you, I appreciate that. The phone and the assistance back there. It's been a long day." Exhaling deeply, I run a hand down the side of my face. "How do you know I'm American?" I slip the phone in my backpack and zip it closed. I see him eyeing the backpack, a standard issue Marine Corps rucksack.

He points to the pack, “American military pack.” Of course, the backpack is a giveaway. “Can I give you a ride? My car is right around the corner there.” He takes a step back while I swing the heavy pack onto my back and grab my luggage handle.

“No, thank you. I appreciate your help.” I try to look anywhere except his face, I could get lost in those eyes. I feel self conscious now seeing him up close. His towering frame, attractiveness and his ensemble have me feeling inadequate. Not to mention his “shambles” comment.

“Oh, no problem. Here let me take that for you.” He reaches for my luggage handle and I don't know whether to allow it or go with the instinct I had at the bar with the blond and shove him off. He has a gentleness in his eyes unlike Blondie. As he takes the handle his hand brushes the top of mine and I feel a rush of heat. The taxi line isn't far and there are plenty of people around so I concede. “Here on holiday?”

He sets his stride to mine and puts on his sunglasses. Ah, sunglasses. That’s what he must do, sunglasses commercials. I smile and stifle a giggle.

“Yes, an impromptu vacation of sorts. I came here on a whim, trying to be more spontaneous in life. I want to drive down the coast. So, here I am.”

I throw my hands up in the air and give a little chuckle. It's the first time I’ve said that information out loud and it sounds so ridiculous when I hear it. I take a chance and glance over, he flashes a smile, the sexiest smile I’ve ever seen. I feel a rush of heat in my face, I smile back.

“Good for you, hope you have a good amount of time, there’s a lot to see. You're going to love it.” He seems to have regained his composure from the previous interaction. He signals a taxi driver in the lane and I hear the pop of a car trunk. He puts my suitcase in the trunk and heads for the rear passenger door. “Looks like you may be hiking?” He nods toward the hiking boots hanging off the side of my pack.

“I hope to, there seems to be so many trails and paths along the coast. I'm really looking forward to it but first I need about twelve hours of sleep. The flight was something else.” He opens the taxi door as I explain. I'm happy to finally be one step closer to a destination with a bed. I also have a twinge of regret that I’m departing from this attractive hunk.

"Well, then, enjoy your time. I highly recommend the Byron Bay area for hiking and beaching. I'm a bit biased though, I spend a lot of time there." He reaches into his pants pocket and pulls out what looks like a business card. "If you have questions about sights, I'm happy to oblige."

He hands me the card, I'm careful not to let our hands touch. I'm taken aback by the gesture, this guy doesn't know me. He probably thinks, by the way things went back inside the airport, I'm some damsel in distress. I can only guess by my *shambled* appearance he thinks I'm throwing myself to the wolves out here alone.

"Thanks, I think I can manage. I'm winging it but I'm pretty resourceful." I take the card and slip it into the pocket of my sweatpants without looking at it. Realizing my delivery was coarse and cold, I balk on my comment and its hint of annoyance. "I'm sorry if that sounded unappreciative, it's been a really long day." I'm not looking for saving or guidance but I, genuinely, think he's trying to be helpful.

"I didn't mean to overstep," he nods toward the backpack again, "I'm sure you're very capable. Enjoy your visit, Kelly." He steps back from the open taxi door.

I'm thrown by him calling me by my name. It causes me to freeze mid way from sitting down in the cab and stand back up. Why is he calling me Kelly? How does he know my last name?

"Kelly?" I turn toward him leaving the taxi door open between us.

"I saw your name on your pack. I'm Andrew, mates call me Drew." He holds out his hand to shake mine.

"It's Violet, Violet Kelly. That's my brother's pack." I nod toward the backpack sitting on the backseat of the taxi. I take his hand. A shock of heat and electricity from his touch makes me flush again. His hand lingers in mine longer than I expected. When he releases I still feel the heat as if I've held my hand over the flame of a burning candle.

"Nice to meet you, Violet. Enjoy yourself." Hearing my name come from his voice makes my stomach flip and my mouth go dry. He takes the door handle from the outside as I tuck myself inside the backseat. After pressing the door closed he lifts his hand in a wave.

I'm startled by the taxi driver who clears his throat and asks, "Where to, love?" I glance out the window and watch Drew walk toward the parking lot. I flex the hand he held in the greeting and rub it against my thigh.

"The Westin, please." I pull out my phone from the backpack and plug in the directions on the map. I glance back once more but there's no trace of Drew.

Leaning my head against the window, thankful for a dull moment, I rest my eyes. It's not a long drive to the hotel, I don't want to fall asleep but my eyelids are so heavy, I promise myself I won't fall asleep. I hear the pop of the trunk again, waking me 20 minutes later when the taxi pulls up to the hotel. I only nodded off for a bit, I now feel more exhausted which I didn't think was possible. I pay the driver, grab my things and head inside to check in.

After I give all the necessary information at the front desk, I ask for a map of the coast line, information on a nearby rental car service and a recommendation on a dinner location. All things I could have done from my laptop or phone but I'm running on fumes. I don't think I have the mental capacity to do anything for myself right now. There goes the, "I'm no damsel in distress" mantra.

I find my room, open the door and put my bags on the bed. I go straight to the bathroom and start the shower. Looking in the bathroom mirror above the sink, I sigh. My blonde hair is tied up in a high, loose bun. There are flyaways coming from the sides, it looks like I stuck my finger in an electrical socket. Taking out the elastic I shake my hair loose, it falls down to the middle of my back. My eyes are bloodshot, my light complexion looks paler than usual.

"Shambles," I whisper to myself as I look away from the mirror, undress and step in the shower.

The hot water feels like a warm blanket and I start lathering the soap, wiping down my shoulders and arms. I let the water run over my shoulders then my back until I feel some tension release. After shampooing my hair I sit down in the tub, my legs feel like Jell-O. I straighten my legs and stretch, touching my toes, letting the hot water pelt my back as I hold my feet. I stand up after a few moments, wash my face and turn off the shower. Stepping out into a steam filled bathroom, I use the hotel robe and wrap my hair in a towel.

The shower reinvigorated my senses. I'm only here for one night, it seems silly to unpack more than an outfit and some toiletries. I tuck the suitcase, backpack and purse in the closet across from the bathroom but first I pull my laptop from the pack. I trace the name *KELLY* on the backpack with my finger and an image of my brother, James, comes to mind. It was 7 months after he left for the Navy, he was going to surprise me for my high school graduation. I skipped out of school early that day and when I came home I saw his backpack on the bench in the hallway at our house.

I yelled for him, "James! James!" I bounded up the stairs two at a time and he came running out of his bedroom with a terrified look on his face. I jumped in his arms, I can still smell his scent when I think about that day.

He thought something terrible had happened because I was home so early, I guess I was the one who ended up surprising him. That was almost 10 years ago. The evocation is powerful and I feel tears brimming in my eyes. With a heavy sigh, I open the laptop and flop on the bed.

With the computer on my lap, I start reviewing emails and checking the current time in Boston. It's Sunday at 4:50 PM here in Brisbane, making it Sunday at 1:50 AM in Boston. I read through my emails and finished the quarterly report to send back to Stacy. I've owned a real estate company for just over three years. I bought it from my mentor the day after my 25th birthday, shortly after I got my broker license. It was the scariest thing I had done, until now. It has since done well and has made my life comfortable, after two years of eating beans and rice. The company and I have a good reputation around Southeastern Massachusetts. My business is 40 miles south of Boston and close to the New England football stadium. I was able to take on some high profile clients by way of the local professional football sporting team. Along with good investments, property flips and a positive market projection, I finally feel I can take time for myself more frequently.

After I send some emails, I check the time again, it's still too early to call anyone. My stomach rumbles with hunger. I try to remember the last thing I ate, a granola bar on the plane more than 10 hours ago. I go to the bathroom to put on yoga pants and a t-shirt. My hair is almost dry, that's the thing with straight, fine hair, it dries quickly. My sister, Ally, has long, thick hair that's like a mane. I remember when we were teenagers I would iron her hair with a clothes iron. Now we have hair straighteners, not that I need one but I'm sure it's made her life easier. She also has olive skin that tans up nicely in the warmer weather, like my mother. I got my father's Irish genes, light hair, light skin that reddens and freckles with sun exposure. I live with sunscreen all year round, even during the New England winters. I smear sunscreen on my face whether it's snowing or 90 degrees.

I put moisturizer on my face, brush out my hair and put it in a loose braid in hopes to add body to it by morning. Moving back to the bed, I think about finding a cafe or restaurant, my back is stiff and my head starts to ache. Looking through the hotel binder for a room service menu, I find one and call the kitchen with my order.

While I wait for the food I start looking at the map of the coast line, writing down the names of national parks. I'm usually more prepared for something like this, not that I'm the type to strictly follow an itinerary.

There's a knock at the door breaking my focus on the map and list I'm forming on a piece of hotel stationary. As I open the door a young woman hands me a tray, it feels warm and smells good. Bringing the food to the small round table in the corner of the room, I set the tray down. I start on the salad before I sit down as I look out the window. After I eat the salad I reach for my phone. Opening the message app I tap on Ally's text thread.

Ally: We're thinking of heading up north to the cabin for a few days during April vacation. Interested? I'll work out some dates.

Ally: April 16-20th, Wed-Sun.

Ally is a school teacher and a planner, always planning. She's my younger sister by two and a half years but she's always one step ahead of me. Ally does everything by the book, four years of college, a job in her degree field, marriage and recently a new home. I played more of a reactive role during my younger years and sometimes still as an adult. I tried college, it was my first time away from home, I didn't adjust well. I left after a semester, found a job and worked full time. I ended up going back to college, getting a degree in business and my realtor license, it didn't turn out too bad. I'd like to think Ally learned from my mistakes and that's why she's so responsible.

I stare at the chicken sandwich, cut it in half and take a bite. Switching on the TV, I turn to a local news station, hoping to catch a weather report. After a few more bites, my stomach feels full and my eyes get heavy. I slide on the bed and pick up my phone. I still have five messages from Sam, my finger hovers over his name, I can't bring myself to read them. I checked my voicemail instead, a spam call about extending my car's warranty plan, two from clients and one from a nosy co-worker fishing for why I took time off on such short notice. I don’t get too close to co-workers, employees or anyone now that I think about it. I have Ally, Cullen, Beth and Sam. But I don't have Sam anymore and come to think of it, did I ever really have him? My eyes start to feel heavy. I thought about setting my phone alarm to go off in a few hours but the exhaustion overtakes me.

Chapter 2
Violet

I wake to the sound of my phone ringing and turn to my left to reach for it on my nightstand. But it's not my nightstand, my phone isn't there. I sit up groggy, remembering I'm in a hotel room in Brisbane, Australia. It feels like I've been sleeping for days. Not that I feel refreshed but it feels like I came out of a very long, deep sleep. I look at the phone, it's Beth. I swipe it to take the call.

"Hey, Beth," my voice sounds hoarse and is quavering.

"Vi! What's going on? How was the flight?"

She sounds chipper, like she's on her second cup of coffee. I've known Beth since grade school, even though life has taken us in many different directions, we've always kept in touch over the years. Always finding our way back to one another.

"The flight was so long. Ten hours in, I thought I was going to stand up and scream. I'm at a hotel in Brisbane." I check the clock, it's 10:30 PM. I've only been sleeping a few hours, I give a sigh.

"Are you okay? I'm worried about you." Beth's voice gets quiet, she knows this is out of character for me, I hear the concern in her voice.

"Don't worry, I'm fine. I had to get away. I left Sam, I couldn't do it anymore, I couldn't take it," my voice fades with each sentence, the final sentence is barely a whisper.

Beth would never say, "I told you so", still I hold my breath and wait. Beth never remained silent on her opinions about Sam, she hated him.

"Did he hurt you?" I hear her uneasiness in the question.

I'm quick to reassure her, "No." Of course Sam hurt me but not in the physical way Beth's concerned about.

She settles back to her chippy tone. "Well, then, good for you. I'm proud of you! I don't want you to feel you have to run across the globe and be alone. You have me and Ally. We could've done a girls weekend instead!"

I can't help but laugh, why hadn't I thought of that? "We can still do that when I get back. I just need to be alone, get my head together, somewhere with no memories."

"Do you want to talk about it? What was the straw?" she asks.

I don't want to talk about it, mostly, because my head is still buzzing and I want to go back to sleep. Beth's life always seemed so uncomplicated, I always felt I was the one bringing the burdens, the grief, the gloom. I don't want to be that person anymore.

"The straw?" I ask, genuinely perplexed by the question.

"The last straw. The straw that broke the camel's back, that straw." I hear the chiming of her car door.

I let out a heavy sigh, "I don't know if there was a *straw*. I was thinking of all the straws, six and a half years of straws. I asked, what the hell am I waiting for? I kept losing myself piece by piece. Nothing was getting better, it only kept getting worse. I packed my things and that was that. I can't believe it took me this long. I'm sorry, I know you've told me so many times it was going to come to this." I start to cry, not because of the break up with Sam but because my relationship with him has put such strain on my other relationships. Beth stuck it out, she didn't lose faith in me, I lost faith in myself and she's still here for me.

"You did the right thing, it just took you time to do it. He's got a problem and you wanted to help him. Do you need anything? Is there anything I can do from *way* over here?" She's trying to make me laugh and I actually do smile a little.

"No, I need more sleep and to make a plan. I'm hoping to take off in the morning down the coast. I'll keep you posted. Thanks, Beth." I know she's probably wanting to talk more but I don't have the energy right now.

"Oh, yeah, okay. Get some rest, please, be safe over there. Check in as much as you can." I hear her car start up. "Vi, I'm happy for you. Do what you need to do and enjoy yourself." She disconnects.

I text Ally back before I fall back asleep.

Me: Sounds great, I'll call Cullen and let him know. Call me after lunch, I've got news.

I can't say I'm surprised when my phone rings three seconds later.

"Hey, Ally," I answer quickly because the phone is still in my hand.

"Hey. What's the news?" I hear the excitement in her voice, she hates feeling left out.

"Well, first thing is, I'm taking a trip to Australia. The second thing is, I moved out of the condo, I left Sam." I wait with unease for her reply. If anyone is going to say, "You should have done it years ago", it's going to be Ally.

There's only a few seconds of silence, it feels like minutes, then, "Wow, are you okay? How'd he take it?" she asks, each word of the questions slowly and I can tell she's processing a lot right now.

"To be honest, I don't know how he took it. I packed while he was at work and when he got home my car was packed. He actually didn't seem surprised at all. He saw my stuff and he asked what was going on. I told him I was leaving." I pause because there's not really much else.

He didn't yell or scream, he certainly didn't ask me to stay and he didn't apologize for anything. He didn't ask where I was going, he didn't get emotional. He went to fridge and got a beer and said, "Get the fuck out then". But I'm too embarrassed to tell my sister that part. Hearing him say that to me validated my decision, it was the nail in the coffin.

I can hear her breathing, waiting, "And?" she asks expectantly.

"And nothing, he said 'fine' and I left."

It was such an anti-climatic moment for my sister as well as for me in the moment a day ago. Repeating the events is giving me a deflated feeling. Did we both know the moment was coming? Were we waiting for the other to leave first? I have so many questions but I can't go back, I can't give Sam anymore time. I gave him more than 6 years of my life and I refuse to give him a day more. I think about his text messages I haven't read yet, maybe they will give me some answers.

"Well, his loss. I'm glad you finally did it. Now you can move on." Like Beth, Ally also made her opinions known, she didn't like Sam. "What about Australia? When do you leave?"

"I'm here, I left yesterday. I arrived here this afternoon, actually, arrived here in the middle of the night for you. The time difference is frustrating, it's almost eleven thirty at night here." I imagine my sister having a cup of morning tea at her kitchen table, sun shining ready to start the day.

"Gosh! You're already there! Where are you? What's your plan?" The plan. She always has a plan and she knows I never do.

"I'm in Brisbane and going to drive south, down the coast, to do some hiking, camping and beaching. I'm really excited and plan on winging it, ya know?" She doesn't know, Ally does not "wing" things. From thousands of miles away I can feel her anxiety over me not having a "plan".

"Good for you," her response is half-hearted, I know she's not upset with me and needs time to process everything I shared with her.

I decided to change the subject, "I think the cabin is a great idea next month."

"Yes, Nate enjoyed it last time we went up." Nate is my sister's husband, they were married last year. He's a great guy and I enjoy his company. He's easy to talk to and seems to be happy all the time. "I'll let you go and rest but stay in touch. Maybe turn on your 'find your friends' app in case I need to find you." Ally, sweet Ally always playing big sister.

"I'll be in touch even if it's just a text everyday. I'll call you when I can and keep you up to date." I understand her worry. Me being this far away, I know, will bring her some uneasiness. After all it's just us, Ally and me, we have to look out for one another.

"Have a good time, call me, be careful." I hear concern in her voice and know I have to keep my word by checking in with her regularly while I'm here.

"I will. I love you." I disconnect and set my alarm for 6 AM. I have to get this jet lag under control and hope I only need a day to adjust. I drift off fairly quickly.

I wake before the alarm tolls and check the time, 4:07 AM. I get up from the bed and take a look outside, it's still dark but dawn will be on the horizon shortly. I go to the bathroom, brush my teeth and take a look in the mirror. My face looks much better, the dark circles are gone and my pale complexion from yesterday looks a few shades brighter. I take my hair out of the braid and shake it loose waiting for it to bounce with the body I was expecting. Nope, still flat, just a few creases throughout. I give a sigh and run my fingers through the bottom of my scalp trying to shake it full. I put on some light makeup, mascara and a light shade of gloss. I pick an outfit, settling on cropped jeans and a short sleeve green blouse with tiny blue aster flowers speckled throughout.

As I pack my toiletries and clothes from last night, a card slips free from the pair of sweatpants. The card lands on the floor at my feet. I bend to pick it up and turn it over in my hands, it reads: Andrew Harris. Below his name is the title of flight engineer with the name of an aeronautical engineering company based out of Sydney. There's an office number listed along with a mobile phone number. I hold the card for a few moments remembering the handsome man from the day before, piercing blue eyes with a strong build and deep voice. A warm sensation sweeps across the top of my hand where I remember him skimming it with his own as he made a grab for my suitcase. I thought about tossing the card in the trash bin near the desk, instead I placed it in the front zipper of my suitcase. I doubt I will use it but it is a nice token from my first experience with an Australian. How could I forget a creature as gorgeous as him? Trying to refocus myself, I head to the small round table where I spread out a map of the gold coast. I open my laptop and start to develop some kind of organized plan heading south from Brisbane.

After some time outlining and checking the maps I had a vague ground plan for the next three days. My plan is to take a short drive to Southport where I can spend some time on the beach while I gather the supplies I need for the following trip, hiking and camping at a national park in the area. I take a quick look at my phone, 7:22 AM. Wow, three hours of research flew by. I gather all my bags on the bed, take one last look around the room and head to the lobby.

After checking out I head to the rental car company which is walking distance from the hotel. I find a cafe and stop off for a large coffee and a raspberry scone. Realizing I can't walk with the coffee, scone and my bags I find a cafe table to sit down with my makeshift breakfast. I look around as I nibble and sip, watching the hustle of people getting off to work with coffees and cell phones in hand. The sun is reflecting off storefront glass and I feel the warmth of the day beginning. I don't feel out of place here. I'm relieved, at the very least, I picked an English speaking country to travel to. However, at this moment I feel alone. Being alone doesn't bother me much but *feeling* alone is something I've always struggled with.

My parents passed away when I was 16 years old. It was a warm May night in 2002 when we got the call they were in a car accident. It was the event in my life that changed everything, splintering the path of my life. My world shook and suddenly, in a matter of seconds, I was off in another direction. James was about to graduate high school, a young, bright 18 year old. Ally was 14 and in her first year of high school. The three of us orphaned in one night. My brother, realizing he was the responsible party, did what he thought was right. He decided to stay home rather than go away to college to make sure we all stayed together. He became our legal guardian, gave up a scholarship to find a job and take care of his two sisters. A momentous decision for an 18 year old boy. He became a man overnight, he never complained and never brought up the scholarship.

James told us the day after the funeral, "I'm staying here with you both, it's what Mom and Dad would want." But was it?

My parents were proud of their first born. He was so smart and had so much to look forward to, James could have done anything he wanted. He had an affinity for numbers, he made algebra, trigonometry and statistics look like a drop in the bucket. When he told us he was staying home, I felt relieved but at the same time I had a voice screaming in my head, *Go to college. That's what Mom and Dad would have wanted.* But I didn't say anything. I just looked at him with tears in my eyes and got up and hugged him.

The three of us dealt with the grief differently. My brother threw himself into finding and holding a job. He became a responsible adult, paying bills, making sure we went to school and had the things we needed. My sister became quiet and focused on doing all the right things, studying, working as a neighborhood babysitter. I, on the other hand, rebelled against everything and everyone. Up until my parents passed I did well in most things, school, athletics and socially. After they passed I did the bare minimum while clinging to a crowd of misfits. I became a loner and started experimenting with different things like smoking weed and cigarettes, challenging authority, drinking and even experimenting with my body. I was lost and felt alone. I tried to feel something, I tried drinking, drugs, sex and nothing filled the void I felt. Nothing made me feel less alone, if anything, I felt more alone. James didn't know what to do with me, he tried setting boundaries and I barreled through each one, he tried positive and negative reinforcement. I remember him reading books on troubled teens and self-help books on grief. He tried telling me he was there for me and I could talk to him about anything. He tried yelling at me, he tried ignoring me and my behavior but nothing worked.

About six months after our parents death, I had just turned 17 and was a few months into my junior year in high school. I came home late one night after skipping school earlier that day, stumbling through the door smelling like pot and beer. My brother was woken from his spot on the couch, where he spent many nights waiting for me, the phone in one hand and the remote in the other. He stood up, took one look at my disheveled appearance and strode toward me.

“Jesus Christ,” a mix of relief and irritation in his voice, “Can't you see I’m trying my best here, Vi? And you?”

He paused for a moment taking a good look at me. I stepped back leaning against the kitchen island for support and trying to create space in the tension filled room. His voice started to raise and his posture shot up straight.

“You? What the hell are *you* doing? You can’t keep skipping school and doing this shit, you're going to attract attention. Attention we don't need, attention that will get us separated! Get it together, Violet! You’ve got to figure it out with or without us because I can't figure you out,” he exhaled and took another huge breath. “This isn’t some Party of Five drama series, its our fucking lives!”

He threw the cordless phone against the cabinets behind me and it rattled into the sink. He ran his hands down his face giving a loud guttural moan. He turned on his heel and stalked back to the couch, flopping down and putting his head in his hands. I was stunned, instantly becoming stone sober, I was too angry and ashamed to admit any culpability. I stomped past him and ran up the stairs taking them two at a time, passing Ally mid staircase, to my bedroom. I slammed the door and threw myself on the bed. The tears were burning my eyes but I wouldn't let them fall. There was a soft knock at the door.

“Go away, Ally,” I said, stifling a sob stuck in my throat. The door opened slowly and I saw her big blue eyes glistening with tears. We looked at each other, I didn't have it in me to yell at her to go away again. I was angry but not with her and not even with James. I was angry at myself, angry at the world, angry at my parents for leaving us, angry at the driver that ran the stop sign slamming into my parents car.

“Are you okay?” She slowly moved toward my bed rubbing her palms against her thighs as she walked. “Don't be mad at him, he’s just…we’re just…” Her voice shook and trailed off as she sat on the edge of my bed looking down at me, “We’re worried about you.” She extended her hand toward my shoulder then pulled it back when I looked away not being able to hold her stare.

“You have more to worry about than me. I’m fine.” The sharp tone of my voice made her recoil like I poked her with a needle. I sat up against the pillows and pulled my knees to my chest.

"Bullshit. You're my sister, *our* sister. What's more important than you? Violet, it's only us, we're what's left. This is something we have to fight for." She climbed onto the bed, sitting directly across from me, a single tear falling over the bottom layer of her thick lashes. Putting her legs under her, she rested her forehead on my knees. She whispered, "Please, we have to figure this out, it's hard for all of us."

I turned toward the door and rested my cheek on the top of her head. When I opened my eyes I saw James in the door frame, arms folded across his chest, leaning his head against the frame.

"I feel alone," I hiccupped, letting the tears fall. I put my hand out, reaching toward James now stiff in the door. He made his way toward us and knelt beside the bed. "I'm sorry, James." It was barely a whisper and I placed my hand on his shoulder.

"I'm sorry, too." He took my hand off his shoulder and kissed it, "You're not alone, we're here, you're never alone."

James put his other hand on Ally's back and rested his head against her shoulder. We sat there, the three of us, still and quiet.

I broke the silence with a short sob, "They aren't coming back. I can't believe they're not coming back."

Both James and Ally looked up at me then to each other. Of course this was no revelation but grief is an intensely odd experience. One riddled with so many emotions, thoughts and perspectives. Until that moment we had all grieved separately, we may have resolved they weren't coming back to ourselves. We all knew they weren't coming back but we never said it aloud in the presence of each other.

That night Ally stayed in my bed and James slept on the floor. We stayed up talking about them, crying and laughing. It took so many months for us to be able to talk about them, to grieve together, I know it was because I was so angry for so long. Grief is different for everyone, the stages come at different times, the duration of the stages vary from person to person, the sequence of the stages is unique for each individual.

I didn't become an angel after that night but I did go to school and stopped skipping out. I increased my hours at my part time waitress job and cut out some negative influences in my life. I tried to make things easier for James, he deserved that. I wish I could have taken some of those rebellious episodes back, I see how much stress I put on James and Ally but I can't go back. I can only move forward and learn from my mistakes, such a simple lesson but one that's so important.

The scone was finished and my stomach ached from the memories. I took one last sip of coffee and found a bin to discard my trash. I scooped up my things and headed off to the rental car office. After signing a ton of paperwork I got the keys to my rental, a small blue Ford Focus. I placed my bags in the trunk of the car, keeping my backpack with me inside the car. I plugged directions into the GPS for the hotel in Southport. I got behind the wheel and was off to my next adventure.

Chapter 3

Drew

It has been 24 hours since I last saw the American, Violet Kelly, at the airport and since then I can't seem to shake the interaction. I drove home purely on autopilot during the two hour ride south to Byron Bay, replaying the conversation with her the entire way. I watched her arrive at the airport bar, trudging her wheeled tote and backpack. She was stunning even in joggers and a messy, unkempt blonde, bun toppling from the top of her head. She looked exhausted, like many of the travelers coming off of the long flights abroad, but those eyes. Her eyes were a stormy blue, they looked sad, maybe even a bit frightened, they held a radiance that made me want to see inside of her. The backpack she wore looked heavy on her thin frame but she seemed to carry it without issue. I watched her for a while pretending to be engrossed in my tablet. When she engaged the barkeep, Barry, making him laugh with some remark she made, I felt a stab of jealousy for reasons I couldn't comprehend. Then those tipsy frat boys showed up and tried to chat her up. I could see the change in her demeanor instantly, she was incredibly uncomfortable. Her posture stiffened, her limbs became rigid, she leaned away from the red faced blond. How couldn't he see she wanted him to leave her alone? I watched the interaction for a few minutes until I saw her reaction to him grabbing her arm, retching her arm away and frantically grabbing her items around her. I quickly packed up my tablet in my attaché and marched over to the bar. I heard her tell him to move aside and he reacted by blocking her path. What kind of asshole would harass a woman like that? When I approached I could smell the booze on him and it took all I had not to shove him off. I could only glare at him until I saw her slip away in my peripheral.

"Oh, c'mon man, she was starting to warm up," his cackle was followed by the howling laughter of his mates beside him.

He wasn't worth the breath it would take to insult him so I turned to the bartender, "Barry, I think these blokes could use a few Solo's on me." I winked at the three frat boys and threw a note down on the bar. They awkwardly looked at each other trying to figure out what I ordered for them.

By the time they would realize I ordered them lemon flavored soft drinks I'd be in the parking lot. I tipped my head to Barry and headed off to the exit. My pace was quicker than usual, I wanted to catch up to the woman to be sure she wasn't distressed much by the altercation. She was ahead of me, about to exit the airport, when I saw a glint of something falling from her bag. I hastened my approach and saw she dropped her mobile. I swiftly bent to scoop it without breaking my stride and called out to her. When she turned to face me I became completely flabbergasted, seeing her up close with the natural light shining on her face, she was stunning. I fell all over myself trying to regain my composure. Did I really call Americans obnoxious and did I say she looked to be in *shambles*? Even now, a full day later, I slap my hand to my forehead and give a low groan remembering the blunder. I guess to be fair I didn't call *all* Americans obnoxious, just that particular one that was bothering her. My mobile rings, breaking me from the trance I've been in most of the morning. I check the call screen, Davy.

"Hiya," I answer in an exhale.

"How ya doing, mate?" Davy's voice is bright and chipper as always. I hear the faint sound of music playing in the background.

"I'm good, finishing up some paperwork." Papers are sprawled across my kitchen island next to my laptop that has gone to sleep some time ago while I was spacing out on Violet.

"Want to meet me at the beach, bring your board?" he asks. Davy's my younger brother by three years and getting ready to be married in a bit more than a week. He's been trying to keep himself busy now that his fiancé is in full blown wedding prep mode.

"You're not trying to slip out on any pre-wedding preparations are you?" A smile steals across my face.

I know how excited he is to get married and this has been an event in the making since he first started dating Mia in high school. They locked onto one another even as tikes. Our parents farm ran parallel to Mia's family ranch, she was always stalking around the fields picking wildflowers and bringing them to Davy. They were good together, they balanced each other well. I always found it odd that Davy never had to search out his soulmate, she was always right next door.

"No, man, are you kidding? Mia has been planning this since third grade, she's running the show. I'm just along for the ride." He lets out a laugh and I hear Mia laugh with him in the background. "But really, Mia has a dress fitting, about the tenth one so far, I thought we could get out for a bit. You in?"

I think for a moment, work isn't pressing but I'm about to take more than a week off for the wedding and events that precede and follow the big day. I didn't get much of anything done today, I have a meeting back in Brisbane two days from now.

"Drew, you there? C'mon, work can wait. You're ages ahead on everything, I'm sure. Take some time and you can get back on the screen tomorrow." There's a hint of annoyance in his voice.

He thinks I work too much but it's mostly because he doesn't work much at all. Davy was a computer fanatic growing up. When our parents came home with our first computer Davy had disassembled and reassembled it within the first two days. I thought Mum was going to blow a gasket when she entered the living room seeing all the disassembled parts and wires littering the floor. It paid off for him when he developed a few software apps and sold them. Even though he explained to me what he does as a software developer, I can't understand it fully. Whatever it is, it has become very lucrative for him. I can barely make a spreadsheet without wanting to toss the computer out the window.

"Yeah, I'm in. Can we grab a bite first? I'll meet you at the pub in thirty minutes." I shoulder the phone to my cheek as I pack up all the papers, attempting to put them in a neat pile, and I slap the laptop closed.

"Brilliant, see you then," Davy says before I end the call.

I grab my car keys and sunglasses, heading out the side kitchen door to enter the garage. I throw my beach duffle in the backseat of the SUV and strap my surfboard atop the roof rack, checking to make sure it's secure. I open the garage overhead and start the car. Just as I sit inside the car, I hear and feel an intense rumble in the pit of my stomach. I reach in the backseat and grab a protein bar I had stashed in my workout bag. I finish the snack bar and toss the wrapper on the passenger side floorboard. The beach where Davy and I like to surf isn't far, about a 25 minute ride from my driveway. Tallow Beach is close and perfect for this last minute jaunt. Sometimes we go a bit further south to Broken Head Beach but I'd like to make it back in time to wrap up a few things for work.

I pull up to the pub where Davy and I often stop off for a pint or two after our surf. I find a parking spot, shut off the engine and I glance at my mobile screen. A few minutes to spare, maybe more if I consider my little brother's lack of punctuality. I take a few deep breaths of fresh air and feel the warmth of midday. I enter the pub and sit at the corner of the bar so I can see the main door.

I order a pint with the barman and glance at the menu. The pint arrives quickly and I take a long draw. I place a food order now rather than wait for Davy. As I set the menu down on the bar I see Davy enter the pub with a wide grin across his face. He's always smiling, so carefree and positive. He was always pulling pranks and could turn any situation into something to laugh about. He had the ability to set anyone at ease during tense or uncomfortable situations, it was something that couldn't be taught but something innate.

"Drew, you good?" He reaches out to shake my hand, pulling me into one of his firm hugs. He pulls the stool out next to me and claps my back. "Thanks for coming out. Glad you could spare the time." Flashing his smile with a mischievous gleam in his hazel eyes.

"Of course, I needed to get out, clear my head." I take another pull from the pint and hand him the laminated menu I had set off to my right.

"I'm good, Mia made grilled sandwiches before I left." He holds up his hands in front of him not wanting to take the menu, "I'll join you for one of those," his head nodded toward the beer sitting in front of me. The barman came over smiling at Davy with a pint already drawn.

"Hiya, Davy. What's happening?" The barman places the beer in front of Davy on a thick paper coaster as he reaches over the bar to shake my brother's hand.

"Not much, Geoff, meeting my big brother here." He slaps my back again, "My brother, Drew. Drew, this is Geoff."

I don't think there's a soul in all of New South Wales that my brother does not know. I nod my head toward Geoff and shake his hand.

"Lemme know if you need anything, mate." Geoff turns around and starts patrolling the other side of the bar.

My sandwich is brought by the waitress working the floor behind us. Quick service is always good and considering it's a weekday I'm not surprised the place is scattered with only a few patrons. I bring the sandwich to my mouth and take a sizable bite watching a slice of tomato slide off onto my plate.

"Jeez, when was the last time you ate?" Davy's eyes are wide and the corners of his mouth turn up in a closed grin.

"Last night. I had a bar on the way over," I grumble with a mouth full, reaching for a few chips and stuffing them in.

"Slow down, it's not going anywhere," Davy laughs as he draws the glass of beer to his lips. "How was the trip up north yesterday?"

"Ugh, nothing that couldn't have been done over a video or conference call but the company likes to be personable. There was a problem with a transmitter, I was the closest one to the airport so they called me in on a Sunday." I wipe at my mouth with the paper napkin as I explain.

My thoughts drift to the encounter with Violet, I muse it wasn't a total waste of a trip. I'll most likely never see her again, I can't help but hope maybe she'll use the card I gave her to call me and ask about some destinations to see. When I handed her the card she hadn't looked at it as she slipped it into the pocket of her joggers. I sigh, feeling a bit disheartened. I glance over at Davy to see him staring at me with curiosity, his eyes glistening with interest.

"What's got you all befuddled, big brother?" He leans back in the bar stool crossing his arms over his chest. His eyes are scanning my face in search of an answer.

"Befuddled?" I draw out the word and look down at my plate picking up the sandwich but not feeling hungry anymore. Maybe the protein bar kicked in and my stomach is feeling full but I know that's not the reason.

"Yes, befuddled. Adjective, confused, perplexed. Unable to think clearly." He tilts his head to the side after draining the remainder of his drink.

"I know what it means," I leave my response there and take another bite forcing myself to swallow it down. His hazel eyes grow wide and he hoists his shoulders up waiting for me to elaborate. "Just thinking about work, trying to get everything done so I can enjoy the week off before the wedding." My statement sounds completely unconvincing. I immediately get a dramatic eye roll and groan from Davy.

"Ah, I call bullshit. Have you forgotten about my infinite wisdom and ability to read you like a book?" He leans forward, placing his forearms on the bar, turning his head so his eyes meet mine.

"It's really nothing. I met this girl at the airport after my meeting yesterday. She was…" I trail off scratching the side of my cheek, not wanting to go on but seeing Davy lean in closer. "She was gorgeous, I mean, fucking beautiful," I say the last part with an unreservedly deflated tone.

Davy shifts in his seat, his long legs bumping into the side of my thigh. "Alright! That sounds great, why the long face?" Geoff comes and checks to see if we want another pint, we ask for two waters.

"She's an American here on holiday. I don't know, it was a short exchange but, damn," I suck in a breath, "I can't get her out of my head." I take a few more chips from my plate before pushing it aside and reaching for the glass of water.

"I'm still not seeing the problem here? Did you get her number? Call her, take her out, show her around." Davy throws his hands up in the air with a look of confusion on his face.

"I didn't get her number, I gave her my card," I say as Davy lets out a low moan and wipes one hand down his face. "What? What's wrong with that?" I'm confused by his reaction.

"Your business card? C'mon, that's pretty impersonal don't you think?" He rubs the side of his jaw thinking of what to say next. "What was the interaction like?"

I told him about the exchange with Violet from the moment I watched her enter the bar to the moment I saw her off in the taxi. We finished our waters and when I was done I rose from the barseat, pulling out my wallet and fishing for a few notes to pay the tab. I don't look at Davy but can feel him taking in everything I told him, processing it all. I turn toward the exit with Davy close on my heels.

He draws a sigh and follows me through the door. "Well, sounds like there's not much to do but wait, see if she rings you," his discouraged tone matching mine from earlier. He stops in his tracks as we're about to cross the street toward the parked cars. "Listen, I know Lexi did a number on you, I know it was hard. But there are women out there, there's someone out there for you. Plenty of fish in the sea." His cliche draws a puff of a laugh out of me, he gives me a smile in return.

"Yeah, I know. I'm not expecting anything to come of it but, man, I can't explain it. She had me fumbling all over myself, when I shook her hand it was like a volt of electricity." I flex the hand that brushed hers a day ago and feel the heat upon the memory. I look over to my brother and see a tinge of regret he has for me in his eyes. “Alright, alright. Let's move on, it's not like I’m going to see her again. Are you ready to hit the water?” I cross the street and unlock the car from the key fob in my hand.

“Yeah, mate. Let's do it,” his voice rises with excitement as he enters his vehicle parked behind mine. “I’ll follow you,” he shouts as he tucks himself inside his stylish sports car and shuts the door.

After a few hours in the water, my body and mind relaxes and I start enjoying myself. When we exit the water I remove my rashguard and toss it on the towel I laid out before we went in the water. I collapse on the towel and sprawl out in the sun. I feel the warmth of the sand on my back from under the towel.

I hear Davy drop his board on the sand, groaning as he squats down to the towel next to me. “Bloody hell, how can I be sore already?”

“You gotta get back in the gym with me. I’m surprised you haven't been coming with me these past few weeks to get ready for the wedding.” I shade the sun with my hand and turn to look at him as he sits back resting on his elbows.

“Yeah, well, you know how much I hate the gym. Anytime you want to go for a run though, lemme know.” He sends me a sly wink, he knows how much I hate running.

I never understood people who run, they never look happy or comfortable while doing it. When I see people running around the neighborhood, they always look pained and miserable. Davy likes to run though, his long, lean frame supports such activities.

“No, thanks. I’ll stick to the gym, you stick to pounding that pavement.” I answer as I hear the muffled ring of my mobile coming from my duffle bag and shoot up rummaging through the bag trying to get to it. I hear a booming laugh come from Davy next to me. I quickly swipe at the home screen, I can't see the caller ID in the brightness of the sun.

“Hello?” I hold my breath and wait for a response.

“Hey, Drew! Are you with Davy? I've been trying to call him for ages now.” It's the voice of my brother's soon-to-be wife, she sounds breathless but in a cheery way.

“Hi, Mia. Yeah, he's with me. Having second thoughts yet?” I tease her while flashing a taunting grin toward my brother who holds out his hand ready to receive the mobile.

She laughs and replies, “Never a second thought, he's my forever. Now hand me over to him.”

I smile to myself but feel a sting of jealousy. I’m not jealous of Davy marrying Mia but jealous they share so much excitement at the idea of living their lives together forever. They’ve been together since we were kids, over a decade, and they’re still so smitten with each other. When one enters a room the other lights up like a beacon. I submit to her request, handing over the mobile to Davy and lie back down on the towel. I’m almost dry and think about grabbing my shirt from the bag. I look toward the water and watch as Davy aimlessly kicks the waves rolling to the shore while talking to Mia on the mobile, a huge grin on his face. I’m truly happy for him, he’s going to be a great husband and provider for Mia. When they’re ready, he’s going to be an incredible father with his boundless energy and positivity. Mia has been a part of our family for awhile, I have long thought of her as a sister, making it official is a delightful outcome. I see Davy disconnect the call and start jogging toward me. I pull a shirt over my head and bring my knees up resting my forearms on them.

“She’s going to dinner with her mum and sister so I’m free to crash your patio for a barbecue.” He vigorously claps and rubs his palms together.

I laugh as I stand up. “I didn't invite you over for a barbecue.” I throw the towel and rashguard in the duffle and zip it up.

“We’re brothers, dufus. I don't need to be invited to crash your place and burden you with feeding me.” He grabs his board along with mine, holding them under each arm and starts off toward the parking area.

“I have some work to do, you can grill while I do that. It won't take me long but you gotta earn your keep.” I come from behind him and take my board from under his arm and trudge up the beach with Davy by my side.

When we arrive at my house, Davy makes himself comfortable in the living room, sprawling out on the large sectional. “I’m going to finish up the presentation I started and check some emails. Beer in the fridge, you know where everything is.” I wave my arm around the kitchen and saddle up to the island opening my laptop. I pull the mobile from my pocket and place it on the counter next to me.

After an hour and a half of working I feel accomplished. I notice Davy rifling through the refrigerator. He pulls some veggies out of the fridge and places them on the far side of the island from where I am working.

"I'm getting hungry but take your time. I'm gonna start prepping this meat, is this the lamb from Mum and Dad?" He holds up a freezer bag with mum's handwriting. I nod my head in affirmation.

"I should wrap up with this in a few," I say, glancing over my emails and deciding only a few need a direct response.

Davy starts pulling spices and dishes from various cabinets and gets to work on the meal prep. He easily works his way around the kitchen keeping clear of my workspace. After he chops, defrosts and seasons the array of food he moves back to the livingroom and grabs the guitar I have standing in the corner of the room. He opens the patio door, sits in one of the patio chairs and starts strumming. His long fingers move easily along the neck of the guitar, the strumming is soft and subtle. After 15 more minutes I checked the time, almost six. I go to the wine rack and pick a red wine, open it and grab two glasses. I place the wine bottle and glasses on the island and I pack up my computer and papers. Then I cut cheese, fruit and add bread on a cutting board. I bring the snack, wine and glasses out to the patio. When I get to the doors extending out to the patio, I clink the wine bottle to the door signaling for Davy to open it up. He stands, grabbing the guitar by the neck and stalks toward the door to open it. He takes the cutting board from me and I close the door behind us.

"Well done, mate, I'm famished." Davy eyes the food as he puts it on the patio table.

He grabs some cheese with a few grapes and gobbles them up, sitting back in the patio chair. He places the guitar on the empty chair next to him and I pour out two glasses of wine, handing him one. I pick a few slices of apple and swipe them in the soft brie cheese.

"Are we all still having dinner at your place Wednesday?" We have dinner at our parents' ranch once a month but Mia wanted to have another dinner before the wedding at her and Davy's house. I found it a sweet gesture and knew my parents were looking forward to it.

"Absolutely, I'm cooking the meal and Mia is baking the treats." He tosses a few more grapes in his mouth.

"I'm going to drive to Brisbane after dinner. I have a meeting early Thursday morning at the airport so I'm going to stay up there for the night," I explain to Davy as I eat more fruit from the cutting board.

"Well, come back after your meeting, the weather is supposed to turn nasty Thursday night. After the storm we should head back to the beach, the waves will be rolling then!" He sounds excited at the prospect. Davy was always the better, more confident surfer. I find it fun and a good way to exercise but it's not my favorite sporting activity.

When planning his bachelor party I decided to take a different spin and planned a day of activities: surfing in the morning followed by beach volleyball then a barbeque at my house where we can all shower and get ready for the night. When I, tentatively, ran the plans by Davy, he seemed excited and a bit relieved. His reaction gave me comfort, knowing I understood his idea of a guys day out. He's not into the typical bachelor party activities, drinking all night, chasing paid women around, becoming a sloppy mess and passing out somewhere along the way. I would do that for him, if it's what he wanted, but we both wouldn't have found that to be an enjoyable night.

"I'm going to start the grill. Wanna grab me the veggies and meat? Everything's going on the flame." Davy places his wine glass on the table and grabs the guitar from the chair next to him.

"Sure thing. You cook and I'll gopher." I head to the kitchen where I see the meat marinating in a large mixing bowl and a stack of foiled veggies. I grab everything and put it on a large cooking tray. The sun is lowering in the sky so I close the awning attached to the side of the living room exit with the switch by the door. I place the food on the patio bar top by the grill and sit at the table going back to my glass of wine. Davy stops his strumming of what sounds like a Bob Seger song.

"Night Moves?" I tip my head with the question.

"You got it." He stands after playing the last riff. He takes the tray of meat to the grill that he must have turned on while I was inside.

"How are you feeling about the wedding?" I take the last sip of wine in the glass and pour another. I stretch back in the chair and lean my head back to collect the remaining rays of sun as it starts to turn the sky hues of red and orange.

"I'm excited. Mia loves this stuff, party planning and details. I'm happy to finally make it official. We could have got married at eighteen like we planned but there was no rush knowing we have forever." Davy puts the meat on the grill and I hear a sizzle.

Mia was one year younger than Davy in school and wanted the university experience. Then she decided to start her own event planning business, it took her a while to get it off the ground and when she did it took off. She's in high demand in this area and surrounding, she's done well for herself.

"I'm only hoping the day will be everything Mia wants. We're only going to do this once so I want it all for her." The conviction and confidence in his voice pulls at my heart.

To be so sure that you've found your forever is something I can't make a connection to. My last girlfriend, Lexi, and I were in a four year relationship. We met working with the company I'm presently with. After dating for two years we moved in together. All the while together I never felt a forever feeling, not that I was off looking around for another. It was comfortable, we had a lot in common starting with the job. She wasn't an engineer, she did marketing and connecting various airlines with us to work with. We both liked to travel and hike. But on the important stuff, the long term, we never agreed. She wanted to get married and move to the city, she wanted kids. I couldn't stand the city for more than a weekend, I needed to be close to the ocean and mountains. Marriage didn't interest me at 28 or at 29. When we decided to move in together it was because I thought it was the next step. By the time we were 30 she started pushing the issue of marriage, dropping not so subtle hints all her college friends were married or about to be.

"Hello, hello?" Davy waves a hand in front of my face and I'm pulled out of my trance. "There you are, we need plates and utensils. I just put the veg on, it'll only be a few minutes."

I hop up and return to the kitchen for the requested items. I can see my mobile screen light up as I pass by the kitchen island and feel my heart rate rise. I grab it from the counter and see it's a call from my father, I place it in my pocket letting it go to voicemail. I get plates and utensils and head back out to the patio. I hear Davy on his mobile and realize he is talking to my father. I feel bad ignoring the call and hope it's nothing urgent.

"Naw, Pops, you don't need to bring anything, just yourselves. I'm just sitting down for dinner with Drew." There's a short pause as my father talks to Davy on the other end of the line. "Looking forward to it, see you then." He disconnects, dropping the mobile in his pocket and pulling the veggies from the grill. Everything smells so good. He places the tray of food down on the patio table and starts filling his plate.

"Looks great, Davy. Thanks," I grab a plate, pile on the veggies and a piece of meat.

"Sure does. You alright, mate? You seem distracted," he sounds concerned but doesn't look at me.

"I'm fine." I answer.

I don't tell him I'm thinking of Lexi because I wasn't really thinking about her. I was remembering our relationship wasn't what I thought it was. I don't bring her up, firstly, the relationship is over and, ultimately, I have no regrets. Secondly, Davy gets upset when she comes up in conversation. Davy's fiercely loyal and protective of those closest to him and he finds Lexi the antithesis of all the values he holds true. Davy's quick to love but unhurried to forgive.

"Still thinking of that girl? Lily? Rose? What the hell was it?" He thinks on it, shaking his head. "Violet!" He snaps his fingers in recollection and shoves a forkful of green beans in his mouth.

"No, I wasn't." I take a deep breath and sit back thinking about how to word my thoughts. "I'm really happy for you. I see how much you and Mia vibe and in the years you've spent together you both have grown so much. You make each other better, ya know? You're so captivated by each other. I mean, you're still giddy about each other, like teenagers. It's kind of sickening at times." I shoot him a teasing grin to let him know I really don't mind it. "There's probably no more mystery to each other…" I trail off thinking of the right words. "Yet, the excitement and enthusiasm is still there."

"Yeah," he laughs with elation, "She's my world. Sure we know everything about each other and, yes, at times things are so predictable we don't need to speak. But there are times when it's surprising and spontaneous. It's hard to explain but when you have *that* one, you want to be better, you want them to be at their best. When you're with someone who makes you better, who makes you feel like you're the finest chap in the world, why wouldn't you want to make that person the happiest you can? You do everything in your power to make it true to life. She does the same for me." Davy shrugs his shoulders nonchalantly and goes back to the food on his plate. “You’ll find out for yourself one day. You’ll understand it all too well and then you’ll tell me how right I am.” He smiles so wide that I actually have hope I’ll be able to tell him he told me so.

We finish our dinner and the rest of the bottle of wine. It’s dark when the clean up is finished. I see Davy meander into the kitchen with a deck of cards. He shakes the deck at me silently asking for a game.

“Gin?” I ask, pointing toward the small dinette in the kitchen.

“No thanks, I can't drink anything else if I’m expected to drive.” He winks at me waiting for a laugh.

I grab two water bottles from the fridge, making my way to the table. “Grab that scratch pad and pencil.” I point to the pad of paper on the counter.

After a few hands of gin rummy, where I beat Davy considerably in a best of three match, he calls Mia to check in. I grab my mobile from my pocket and scroll absentmindedly. I move from the table to the large sectional in the living room, stretching my long body out on the chaise side. I browse a few news headlines until I hear Davy flop at the other end of the couch.

“I’m going to shove off. Thanks for the day, brother,” he says but he doesn't stand up from the couch.

I set the mobile on my chest and turned toward him.“You good?” I ask, noticing his head is set back and he’s staring at the ceiling. “Are you good to drive? I can drop you off at home.” I sit up from my position waiting for a response.

“I’m fine,” he says, sounding unlike himself. Maybe he’s tired from the day or maybe something was said in the conversation with Mia. “I’m good to drive.” He stands up and moves toward me, outstretching his hand. He shakes my hand, “Great day, mate. See you Wednesday, right?” His question is more of a statement but I give a nod in response.

I watch him through the window walk to his car and drive off. I lock the door and head to the bathroom for a shower before I tuck in for the night.

Chapter 4
Violet

After a day in Brisbane and here in Southport, a coastal suburb, I'm craving a more secluded setting. I want to be surrounded by trees and moss, I want to hear the chirping of birds and creatures. I want to sit with a book and feel nature around me. But for now I'm here on the beach, soaking in the sun and smell of the ocean. The water here is beautiful, unlike the cold, crisp Atlantic Ocean I'm familiar with. The water temperature must be in the mid 70s today, the colors of the ocean here are breathtaking. Back home, the ocean is a dark midnight blue, during low tide you might see lighter blue or green tones. Here the blues and greens of the ocean are vibrant.

I've been on the beach since breakfast and start to feel hungry after swimming. When I see the time is close to 2, I pack up my things. I pull on my sundress and ball hat, a navy blue hat with a red B on the front. It was my brother's old Red Sox hat from his high school years. The hat has definitely seen better days but I can't bring myself to replace it. I've adjusted to the time difference but find myself nodding off at some points throughout the day. After I dozed on the beach for an hour this morning I didn't feel as exhausted as I had the first day here. Returning to the lot where my rental car is parked, I toss all the beach gear in the trunk. I walk around to find a cafe or restaurant before driving back to the hotel.

Along my walk I see a bookstore which reminds me I should get a book for the trip. I enter the shop and the bell clangs against the door. There's a coffee bar upon entrance. The delicious scent of fresh brewing coffee hangs in the air and I hear the sputtering sounds of a steam wand. I go to the bar, order a latte with caramel before I start pursuing the stacks. The barista hands me the small latte and I turn to look at the section headers around the store. I don't want a romance novel. Maybe a thriller? Maybe a travel guide about the area?

Moving toward the main display table in the middle of the store, I browse the new releases. I picked up a few books, reading the back cover and jacket descriptions. Lots of romances, stories of loss and redemption and thrillers. I'm not in the mood for these, as a creature of habit, I head to the back of the store where I see a section devoted to classics.

As I sip the latte I peruse the stacks. Some of my favorite titles illuminate from the shelves. Austen's *Pride and Prejudice,* I've read that at least 10 times. Steinbeck's *Grapes of Wrath, The Pearl* and *East of Eden*, I love his writing. I remember reading *Of Mice and Men* in middle school. The tears blurred my eyes so much I couldn't read the words on the page. When I finished the book my eyes were red and puffy for hours. Maybe something uplifting? I find one of my favorites on the bottom shelf, *Walden* by Henry David Thoreau. I take it off the shelf, flipping through the pages. My father loved this book and read it often. I haven't read it in years, I feel a fondness for it as I skim the pages. I hold on to it, close to my chest and continue looking at the shelf. I see more favorites by George Orwell, Toni Morrison, Franz Kafka, Leo Tolstoy and Jack London. I want them all, I've read and devoured all of them but I want them again and again. Many of these titles bring me back to my childhood, young adulthood and my father. I loved to read growing up, I loved visiting the local library and picking new books every week.

My parents, being teachers, instilled in us the importance of reading. When I read a classic like *The Jungle* by Sinclair or Jack London's *Call of the Wild* my father would ask, *"What part are you at?"* I would answer him and the bombardment of questions would begin. What did you think of this scene? What do you think that means? What is the conflict? It would turn into a literature lesson and I loved it. I loved hearing his thoughts and talking about the stories.

Sometimes when I finished a book, the next day there would be another book on my bed. It was usually a used book with a tattered cover, pages creased with fold indentations, sometimes there were pencil notes in margins or underlined sequences throughout chapters. They were my dad's books, books he read and handled and I loved them.

I remember he left me his copy of *Old Man and the Sea* by Hemingway with a post-it note in his handwriting. It read, *"Man is not made for defeat. A man can be destroyed but not defeated."* He signed it with, "*Enjoy this one, Dad*". He died two months later. It took me a long time to finish that book. Was it coincidental he left me a book with such themes as suffering and perseverance? I don't believe in coincidence, I don't think things happen by luck or chance. I feel life-altering events cannot happen by coincidence.

I have been lost in my own world of memories when I hear a voice intruding on my thoughts, "Can I help you with something?" A small, soft voice snaps me out of the dream state.

I turn to find a short woman with gray hair tucked into a firm bun and the base of her neck. She's holding a stack of children's books and wearing a welcoming smile.

"Oh, no, thank you. I'm just looking. Remembering really, these are some of my favorites." I gesture to the bookshelf in front of me.

"Ah, yes. Nice to see the younger generation has an appreciation for them." She pulls her eyeglasses from the top of her head, setting them on the tip of her button nose. "If you need anything, please, let me know." She glances over the titles on the shelf and walks toward the children's section to the left.

I take a sip of my latte, it's cold now, I drain the last sip. Starting to turn toward the register, I stop when I see a familiar blue binding peering at me from the top shelf. I pull the book off the shelf, Kate Chopin's *The Awakening*, my heart warms for another title I've read countless times. The pull I feel for the book leaves me unable to return it to its spot on the shelf. Placing the book on top of Thoreau's I stride to the checkout.

After waiting in a short line, I checked out with my new-old books. I feel the latte setting in, my hands start to shake and a queasy feeling settles in the pit of my stomach. I'm hungry, I need to find food fast, scanning the street around me I see a pub up ahead. It's late afternoon, well past lunch but early for dinner, the place is close to empty which I'm relieved about. I chose a table by the front window so I can watch the people on the street. I like to watch people, some think it's rude, I like to imagine what they're doing or where they're going.

I'm greeted rather quickly by a very perky, very tanned, young girl, "Hiya, I'm Susie. Can I start you with a drink?" She sets down an obnoxiously large, heavy menu which makes a loud thud when it drops on the table.

"I'll have ice water for now, thank you." I place my phone on the table top and pick up the menu.

"Sure thing." Susie spins around and heads to the filling station, leaving me with the 8 pound menu.

There are too many choices, there's no way the small kitchen in this pub can produce all these options. I check the menu for a salad or sandwich section and study the various items. Opting for a salad and soup combo I close the menu before I change my mind. I check my phone, I still have 5 unread texts from Sam I haven't found the courage to read yet. My finger hoovers over the message tab titled "Sam" but I quickly close the app instead of opening the thread. My water arrives and Susie takes my order, she grabs the menu off the table and is off again.

My salad comes with a huge smile by Susie, she refills my water and I ask if she can bring me the soup to-go when she brings the bill at the end of the meal. I was hungrier than I thought and finished the salad quickly. I place the empty salad bowl opposite me on the table and check the time. I should be back at the hotel around 5 which will give me time to shower and take a look at the emails from Stacy. If I can wait up until 10 PM to call Beth and Ally, I would feel better about being out of touch with them if the campground doesn't have service. Boston is 15 hours earlier than the time here in Southport and connecting with people back home is a challenge. When I call my sister tonight she will be starting her Tuesday while I will be in bed recovering from my Tuesday. Susie comes back with my check and a paper bag with soup inside. I thought a light snack for the hotel room later would be a good idea since I plan on staying in for the night.

Once back in my hotel room, I grab my laptop that has been charging most of the day. I take my laptop out on the small balcony wanting to take in the sunset which will be happening in an hour. I'm on the 8th floor at the hotel, there's a nice view of the ocean. Sitting in the patio chair while balancing my laptop on my knees, I logged into my email and read the three updates Stacy sent me. Everything seems to be going well back home with the business and I take a relieved breath. I answer a few more emails, then get a water bottle from the fridge inside the room.

Back out on the balcony I close the laptop and stretch out, putting my feet up on the railing. The sky is turning orange and red with the sunset. The top of the sky remains blue and the clouds hold tones of pink and purple. It's beautiful, I relax my shoulders and stare off at the ocean. The water starts to turn black, the sky has a sliver of orange remaining for light, as the dark navy of the night sky settles over the ocean. Standing from the chair, I bring my arms over my head to stretch. I feel the skin on my shoulders tighten from a soft burn I have from the sun at the beach today.

I head inside and disrobe leaving my sundress and bathing suit on the bed. I step into the warm shower to rinse the sand, salt and sun from the beach. As I towel off and put on a pair of sweatpants and a blue cotton tank, I take my phone from the charger and check the screen. Sitting on the bed, I open my message app, I guess now's as good a time as any. Without hesitation, without allowing myself to change my mind I tap on the thread that contains Sam's messages.

Sam: Are you having one of your moments? Or is this really you leaving?

The next four are from over three hours after he sent the first, enough time for him to drink and get angry.

Sam: I want your fucking key, drop it off.

Sam: I'm changing the locks tomorrow. Get your shit out of here asap.

Sam: FUCK YOU!

Sam: BIIIIIITCH

My stomach sinks, I want to vomit. I can't believe a 36 year old man, a man I spent over 6 years with sent me these messages. Was I in such denial, did he really hate me this much? How could I have let this happen? Why the hell did I stay so long? So many questions swirl around in my head, the room starts to spin. Being honest with myself, I knew he wouldn't apologize or recognize any wrongdoing. I knew he couldn't see how much he had hurt me over the past year, especially. But to spew so much hate, so much anger toward someone you shared your life with, it was astonishing to me. I fight the tears, I will not allow this asshole to make me cry, I will not shed one tear over this man.

The last year with Sam was brutal, I packed my bag and told myself to leave so many times but something always stopped me. Something I couldn't figure out. It's not that he asked me to stay or said sorry for throwing things or yelling at me. He never offered to get help or ask what I was upset about. I wasn't ready to leave for reasons I may never understand. But I was ready that day. A few days ago, something snapped inside me and I knew I had to leave before this man destroyed whatever was left of me.

Sam and I met at a Halloween party, a month before my twenty-second birthday. He was older and looked out of place there. He was tall, with dark features and hair. He had a huge white smile dripping with slyness and cunning. He and I locked eyes many times throughout the night, exchanging flirty stares and smiles. I asked my friend who he was, she said he was the older brother of one of her friends.

"He's like thirty, Vee. He likes to party and he likes young girls, stay clear of him." Her warning was clear but something drew me to him.

After a few drinks I saw him approaching me. We spent the night talking, I told him about finishing my business degree, he told me he was visiting his sister but lived three hours away in western Massachusetts. He said he drove a truck and delivered to areas from the Berkshires to Boston, sometimes taking routes as far as New Jersey and Pennsylvania. He talked about the small town he was from, where he spent his time fishing and hiking. There was a sadness in his eyes that I hadn't noticed earlier in the night. We talked all night and when my ride was ready to go he gave me his number. He said he was around for a few more days and wanted to see me again.

I should have just left the night at that. I was excited to be able to talk to someone so easily, to talk to a guy that wasn't expecting a kiss or a hookup at a college party. I thought because he was older he must be more refined and thoughtful. We went out two nights later, his last night visiting his sister. We hung out with a few of his sister's friends, drinking at her apartment, it was a haze of excitement and insobriety. He called me everyday for a week after he left and asked me if I would come visit him. I picked a weekend and drove three hours to see him.

When I arrived at Sam's house I found out he lived with his parents in a very small town. A town that really was in the middle of nowhere, I couldn't believe where I was. It was like I took a turn off the highway, drove 40 miles and landed in the Shire or some village in a Tolkien novel. I arrived at dinner time and his parents were bubbly and happy to meet me. We had dinner, his parents offered me wine and asked about me and my family. The wine kept flowing throughout dinner and Sam asked me to go for a walk with him when we were done eating. We walked around his parents' country property. He pointed out various gardens and explained what his mother grew. The fairy lights hanging in the windows of the old barn were mesmerizing at dusk. With a flashlight he took me to the river behind his house. We sat in the woods talking and kissing, tasting the wine from dinner on each other's lips.

By the time we got back to the house, Sam's dad was snoring on the couch and his mom was passed out sitting in the dining chair with her head facedown on the table. I actually giggled to myself when we walked in, I thought maybe they weren't used to so much wine at dinner. Sam shut the music off from the dining room radio. He went to the table and scooped his mother in his arms and carried her to her bedroom, lying her in her bed and covering her with an afghan. I thought it was the sweetest thing I had ever seen.

Had I known what it truly was, I would have run for the hills that night, I would have left and never looked back. It was normal for his family, a nightly ritual. It was something Sam did almost every night, carrying his drunk mother to bed so she didn't try to get up herself and fall. But I didn't know that then, instead of running I took his hand that night. He led me upstairs to his bedroom where I made love to him thinking he was the sweetest son for doing what I thought I had witnessed. The next morning his mother was in the kitchen making a breakfast feast, German pancakes, bacon and sausage. She had crepes warming with fresh strawberries and cream. The music was on again, she was humming and swaying to the music. His father was in the yard pruning back trees and raking up fallen leaves. It was a Rockwell painting, or so I thought. That day we went on a hike and Sam showed me local swimming holes with beautiful waterfalls. The events of the night before didn't raise any alarm.

The second night when we returned from dinner in a nearby town his mom was sleeping on the couch with the TV on, a bottle of wine sitting empty on the coffee table. His father was asleep in the recliner with a remote in one hand and an empty tumbler in the other. Sam turned off the TV and gently took the tumbler glass from his father's hand, setting it on the coffee table next to the empty wine bottle. Again, taking my hand and leading me upstairs.

Leaving after that weekend I felt good about things, he had shown me a different part of the world I didn't know existed. I had lived in Massachusetts my entire life and had never known the beauty of Berkshire County. At that time my sister was attending college in western Massachusetts, very close to where Sam lived, I thought it was ideal that I could visit them both in one trip on the weekends. Why didn't I see that I should have just run?

The bile is burning my throat so I go to the bathroom, brush my teeth and smother lotion on my sunkissed skin. I head back to the bed still feeling uneasy and check the time, 9:30, finally time to make a call. But now I don't want to talk to anyone. I decide to call Ally first, she's definitely up and ready to start her walk to work.

The line rings twice before Ally answers with an upbeat tone, "Hey, I've been waiting for you to call me."

"I know, I'm still getting used to the time difference. I was getting into bed and wanted to call before I turned in." I slip the covers back on the bed and glide under the covers. "First few days have been an adjustment."

"What have you been up to?" she asks excitedly.

"I drove to Southport yesterday, I spent the day at the beach today. I outlined about six days worth of activities and travel." I nestle on the pillow and pull the covers up to my chest already feeling my body relaxing into the bed.

"You made a plan! Well, then, lemme hear it." I hear the eagerness in her tone and can picture her eyes widening in surprise that her big sister, Violet, actually has a plan.

"Tomorrow morning I'm driving to Lamington National Park, where I'm camping for two nights. On Friday I'm supposed to go to a place called Springbrook National Park. There's the possibility of a rain storm, so I will have to keep an eye on that. I found a cute bungalow, in Pottsville, to rent for the weekend by the beach. If I keep moving south, maybe I'll make it to Sydney by the end of all this." There's a pause on the other end of the line, I know Ally's taking mental note of the places I listed so she can do her own research to see what I'm up to. "I'll email you a list of the places I'll be, along with the days I will be there."

After a few more seconds of silence, I can hear genuine surprise in her voice, "Sounds great, send me the itinerary. I've been watching *Dateline* and…"

I quickly cut her off, "*Dateline*? Coming from the girl who would flee from the room when the intro to *Unsolved Mysteries* would start." I laugh, as a young girl Ally hated to be scared. She didn't like scary movies or mysteries, instead opting for *Gone with the Wind* or *The Sound of Music*. "Lemme tell you something about *Dateline*, it's always the husband or the wife or the boyfriend. I have none of those so you don't have to worry."

"And sometimes it's a random wacko looking for a vulnerable victim," her retort sends a chill down my spine. "As long as you're safe and checking in with me, I'm fine. But if you go *one* day without letting me know you're okay, I'll contact the embassy or consulate or whatever they have over there." I laugh and want to tease her about not having that information already on hand but decide against it.

"I will," I stifle a yawn and hear the clattering of dishes from Ally's end. "Hope this call isn't going to make you late for work." Ally could never be late for anything, tardiness isn't in her DNA.

"No, plenty of time. So, how long do you think you'll be over there?" I hear the faucet turn on and what sounds like the opening of a dishwasher and the clattering continues.

"I'm thinking two weeks, maybe three. The coast is long and I want to give myself enough time to take in what I can. Plus, I'm not looking forward to the flight home, I still haven't shaken the flight here yet," I sigh heavily and hope my answer is good enough. Although I have somewhat of a plan, I'm still winging it mostly. Work is carrying on fine without, there is no rush for me to get back for now.

"Okay, that sounds reasonable. Violet?" The way she says my name makes my heart rate speed up, like she might be bracing me for something awful.

"Yes?" I say the word slow and soft then hold my breath.

"You didn't have to go so far away." There's a very long pause, I don't know if she wants me to respond so I wait and she goes on, "I don't want you to feel like you have to run away when things happen. I'm here, you're never alone." I hear James' voice echo in my head, *we're here, you're never alone*. Tears flood my eyes and I slam them shut.

"I know, Ally, I know," my voice cracks, "I'm not running away." The statement doesn't sound convincing.

"Okay, just wanted you to know I'm here. I love you. I've got to get going or you will make me late. Send me that itinerary," she gives a half laugh to break the tension I know we both feel.

"Don't be late. I love you, too." I disconnect quickly and blink back the tears.

Chapter 5
Violet

I wake up sweating, my heart pounding against my chest, I hear the pulsating of blood rushing in my head. I take a few deep breaths and unclench the bedding from my hands. The dream, my dream, I've had so many times. The same dream, sometimes with different people, always the same set of events. This time it was James, it's usually James, sometimes it's my father, sometimes my mother and sometimes the three of them. I'm sitting at a table outside of a restaurant. I turn to see James seated a few tables over, I see him stand to walk away, I try to get up from the table. My legs don't support me and I stumble. When I'm finally able to get to my feet, I see him in the distance walking away from me.

I call to him, "James!" But he doesn't hear me and keeps walking. I try to run but my feet weigh hundreds of pounds. As he gets further away I become frantic. I yell again but my voice turns to a whisper, "James!" I can't get to him, he keeps walking away.

My pulse quickens, my heart pounds, my feet sink into the ground. It's truly terrifying. Sometimes after some fighting I reach the person. When I finally grab their arm to turn them around, it's not them. Well, it is them but their face is contorted or decayed in spots. I try to talk to them but they never talk back, they stare past me with lifeless eyes as I weep in front of them. I beg them to see me, to hear me, but they stare past me as if I'm not there. I haven't figured out which is worse, not being able to catch them or finally reaching them only to find them an unrecognizable shape of their former selves.

I shake my head feverishly and reach for my water on the side of the table. Gulping down the remaining half bottle, I stand from the bed wiping at the sweat beads that formed on my chest. I place my hands on my shaking knees and take more deep breaths. Breathe, breathe, I tell myself. The clock on the radio alarm reads 4:47 AM. I groan in despair, I won't be able to go back to sleep. Sometimes when I go back to sleep I slip right back into the dream, feet sinking, unable to yell as they walk further and further away. I'm up now.

I hurry to the bathroom to rinse my face and try to pull myself together. Removing the damp tank top, sticking to my body, I rummage through my suitcase and find an outfit for the day. Comfortable travel clothes, cropped jeans with a purple cotton scoop neck t-shirt and canvas slip on shoes. I start to pack my belongings, making sure I unplug and pack the charger adapters for my phone and laptop. I pick up my phone and call Beth while I have the chance. No sense in checking out this early. I sit on the loveseat in the sitting area of the room listening to the line trill.

"The world traveler! How's everything?" She answers, my body relaxes with the sound of her voice.

"Everything's good. I wanted to call you while I had the chance. I couldn't sleep," I sigh softly as I finger the rip at the knee of my jeans.

"Oh, yeah? Crazy dreams or jet lag?" Beth knows all about my dreams, she's the only one I feel comfortable discussing them with.

When Beth and I were kids, in middle school, we started dream journals. We'd wake up in the morning and write our dreams down from what we could remember. When we had sleepovers we would read them, trying to decipher our subconscious minds. After many months of journaling I started to remember my dreams vividly, after years of journaling I could remember my dreams every night. Sometimes when I dream I know it's a dream, finding the power to manipulate the outcomes and happenings. I dream I'm being hunted by vampires and I can command my dream self to fly away from them. Other times I can conjure a way out of a burning building I may be stuck in. But never with that dream, that dream is the only dream I have where I feel completely out of control. Once in a while, I regret being able to remember my dreams so well. Some people, for the life of them, cannot recall what movie their brain showed them during sleep. But at times, I see my family in situations where I'm not frantically trying to get to them, it's not very often. I do like to see them in my dreams when they're not walking away from me. I just hate that one dream and that's the dream I have of the ones I've lost most frequently.

"Yeah, crazy dreams," my voice is quiet, I change the subject. "I'm getting ready to head to a national forest for some camping and hiking. I got up early so I'll have an early start on the day."

"Atta girl. How are you holding up? Have you heard from Sam?" I can hear street traffic on her end and picture Beth walking around the city, either on a break or done with her work day.

"He texted me a few times. I didn't respond. He wants me to get my stuff and leave the condo key. I don't think I want or need anything I left behind. I took all the important stuff."

Just then I remembered my baby lemon tree. Shoot, I forgot the stupid tree. I started it from seed a few months earlier, nurturing it under grow lights as a seedling, setting it in a pot outside on warm days. I was so happy to see the progress and have never tried starting a tree from seed. I loved gardening and growing things, how could I have forgotten about that tree?

"What an asshole. Really, Vi, I ever see him again, ugh," she doesn't finish her thought and I feel the resentment coming from her voice, it's palpable.

"Please, he's not worth it. I'm going to move on. I can't give him anymore time or energy and you shouldn't either." My words are calm and reassuring.

"I guess you're right. Moving on. I know you won't be back for a few more weeks but when you do, have you thought about moving back to your parents house or do I need to clear out my spare room?" she asks hopefully.

Beth has a two bedroom apartment outside the city of Boston. It's a nice place. I've stayed there a few times when things were unstable at my condo with Sam.

"Thanks for the offer, I'll have to think about that one. I haven't thought past the next few days." I zip up my suitcase and place it by the door.

"Okay, think about it," she sounds discouraged but then there's an uptick in her tone, "I've gotta get back to work, my break is over. Call me when you can and take lots of pictures!"

"I will. Talk to you soon," I say, disconnecting the call.

Before I leave the room, I quickly draft an email to Ally with the names of the state parks where I will be staying along with the days I'll be at each. I add the site numbers I have from my registration confirmation and give her the address of the house rental I have scheduled in Pottsville. For good measure, one I know she'll appreciate, I sent her the rental car information including license plate and registration. I laugh to myself knowing I'm not doing this for myself but to give Ally peace of mind. It's not a bad idea, considering I'm alone in a foreign country. After closing the laptop I gather my bags and head to check out of the hotel.

When I get in the car I plug in the GPS information, my destination to the campground is an hour and a half away. I'm heading to the Green Mountain area of Lamington National Park. After doing more research on the camping accommodations last night, I started to see that camping here is nothing like the camping I have done in New England. The campground where I booked my site offered safari tents and luxury camping rooms with spa options and dining. Looking at the images on the computer I asked myself, why the hell did I bring all this camping equipment? But I'm going for the tenting option because I want to make the most of the experience and camping brings me a sense of nostalgia.

About halfway through the drive to Lamington National Park I think about the conversation I had with Beth on the phone and what my plan should be when I arrive home. I'm not going to respond to Sam's demands. If he decides to change the locks, he doesn't need me to return my key. I packed all the important stuff I had there, my clothes, pictures and anything I felt sentimental toward. The washer and dryer I bought but didn't need. The bed was a relatively new purchase, I definitely didn't want that back. How could he demand me to come get my "shit"? If I actually had taken what was *mine* he would have slept on the floor and had nothing to wash or dry his clothes with. I laugh out loud thinking about how ridiculous his request was. The laugh subsides when I think about how humorless the situation really is.

Over the last year of our relationship, I can't remember laughing with Sam or feeling any love or affection from him. Sam started drinking harder the past two years. It came to a point where he was drunk every night, passing out most nights, barely able to stumble to bed. It was difficult to watch, it was scary most times. I tried to talk to him about getting help so many times, I tried to help him. I learned you can't help someone who doesn't want to help themselves, I almost destroyed myself trying. Sam always drank frequently, I knew that about him very early in the relationship. The first year of our relationship was long distance, visiting each other on weekends. He didn't like to drive "all the way" to see me. He said he drove for work all week and the last thing he wanted was to drive, 6 hours round trip, on the weekend to see me. I should've recognized right then, he wasn't willing to sacrifice for our relationship. But I yielded to his solicitations and found myself making the 6 hour round trip during my time off.

After a year of visiting him regularly, we came home one night to the most horrific scene I had witnessed with Sam's family. There were broken dishes littered throughout the kitchen. Mashed potatoes clung to the wall and windows, fried chicken was strewn around the countertops and floor. There was a vat of oil on the stove, the gas burner still aflame, the oil sizzling with burnt chicken inside. Sam swiftly moved to the stove and shut off the gas. He went from room to room looking for his parents. A part of me hoped the mess was due to an intruder because the only other plausible scenario was one that frightened me more. Sam found his father passed out on the couch. Sam started shaking his father trying to wake him to ask where his mother was. My heart was pounding as I took the stairs up looking everywhere for her on the second floor. Sam's dad was mumbling something about dinner being ready. We went outside, looking on the wrap around farmers porch for her but she was nowhere. We were calling her name and frantically looking in the barn and cars.

After 10 minutes of distraught inspection outside we found her, lying on a hammock in the backyard, snoring loudly. It was the middle of December. Sam shook her awake, her fingertips and lips were tinged blue. If she hadn't been snoring I would have thought she was dead. After waking her, she walked with us inside needing lots of assistance.

When we got into the house through the kitchen door she turned to us and said, "Are you hungry? Your father made the most delicious fried chicken." It was all slurs and mumbles, I stood there stunned with my mouth agape. Sam took her to bed while I stood in the kitchen staring at the mess, trying to wrap my mind around the events that took place. I started the clean up, sweeping the broken glass, wiping up the potatoes and dumping the vat of oil through the tree line in the backyard.

When I came back inside Sam was sitting at the kitchen table with his head in his hands. I went up behind him and rested my hand on his shoulder.

"Is it always like this? Do they drink like this all the time?" He let out a sob but didn't answer. Then I asked, "How long have they been like this?"

He turned in the chair to face me, his eyes held so many emotions. I saw sadness, fear and anger in his dark brown eyes. "For as long as I can remember. I can't leave them alone. You see it, they could've burn the whole fucking place down or she could have froze to death out there!" He slammed his fist on the table and I jumped back.

Sam and I finished cleaning up and went to bed. That night he told me all about his parents' drinking habit. He told me when he was just 8 years old he would get up in the middle of the night to give his baby sister a bottle, change her diaper, change her urine soaked sheets and clothes. He told me how most nights as a child he was left to his own devices. He recalled the terrible fights, the physical and verbal abuse his parents displayed toward each other. Then he explained when they woke up in the morning they would be fine, acting as if nothing happened. His parents went to work and did well for a living, they were functional at work. Sam sobbed in my arms letting all the memories and resentments spill out with his tears and I silently cried with him. It was a heart wrenching revelation for me, I felt so naive to the family's dynamic. After that night I didn't fight with him about coming to visit me anymore. Instead I decided to try and change my real estate post to a sister office closer to him.

I moved in with Sam a few months later, we had been together more than a year. I moved into that dysfunctional home because I thought, if Sam had to be there for them, I could be there for him. We lived with his parents for 6 months before I couldn't take it anymore, the yelling, the fighting and the constant drunkenness. It was making me a nervous wreck, so I begged him to rent a small cottage a few miles away. We could have our own space and we'd be close enough that he could check in on them if needed. I tried to lure him there with the idea the cottage was on a lake and he could go fishing anytime he wanted. When he said yes, I thought it would be a good stepping stone for us. When we moved into the cottage Sam was drinking daily, mostly after work. I was working long days and taking night classes for my broker license three days a week. When I'd come home after class he was already sleepy and incoherent.

A year after we were living in the cottage Sam would come home with an empty fifth of Wild Turkey, throw it in the barrel outside the house before he came inside and go to the fridge for a beer. One night when he came home, I was cooking dinner, he leaned in for a kiss and I wretched away from the stench on him. I slammed down the wooden spoon I was stirring the pasta with. The smell of whiskey on him was so powerful it made my eyes water.

"Sam, you cannot drive like this. You smell like a distillery, for Christ sake. What if you get pulled over? What if you hurt someone? You could lose your job, your freedom." I stood in front of the fridge to stop him from reaching in, forcing him to listen to me.

"Jesus, Vee, I'm fine." He tried to nudge me aside to open the fridge but I stood firmly in place. "Vee, move away," his voice was low and he spoke through clenched teeth.

"No. You're going to hurt someone or yourself. This isn't healthy." My eyes narrowed on him and in a flash I didn't recognize him anymore. His eyes darkened, his face tightened.

"I said I'm fine, now lemme in the fucking fridge!" His voice rose with each word and hands were on my shoulders as he forcibly moved me aside.

"I can't be here if you're going to continue like this," I tried to sound confident but my voice was quivering.

"Continue like what?" He twisted the top off the beer and threw the cap in the sink.

"Like this!" I yelled, pointing my finger at the beer in his hand. "It's every night. You drink all night and do it again the next day. Does this remind you of anything?" That final question was all it took for him to lose control.

In a sudden move his hand came up, I slammed my eyes closed thinking he was going to hit me. He grabbed my neck and slammed me against the kitchen wall. The force of my back hitting the wall drew the air out of my lungs. He bent down over me, his nose almost touching mine.

"I'm nothing like them. Shut the fuck up," he was spitting on me as he spewed out the words. I started to cry and tried to take his hand off my neck, his grip tightened. "You don't want to be here? You don't want to deal with this? Then go!"

He let go of my neck, my hands instantly shot up covering where his hands had been. He opened the fridge, taking the rest of the six pack with him. As he walked away from me, he took the pan of pasta and threw it against the opposite wall. Then he stomped away slamming the front door behind him. I stood there waiting to hear his car start or the sounds of tires peeling out but there was nothing. Then I heard the sound of him dragging the canoe down the sand driveway to the boat launch across the street. I took a breath and realized I had been holding it the entire time. When I looked around the kitchen I didn't see the spaghetti and sauce sticking to the walls, I saw clumps of mashed potato, broken dishes and fried chicken. I should have run.

After that episode with Sam in the kitchen, instead of cleaning the mess, I packed a bag and drove three hours to my parents house. I had to pull the car over, giving into the tears that blurred the road. I called Beth on the way home and she was there in my parents driveway waiting for me with a pizza.

"You can't go back, Violet. He's got a problem, one that isn't your responsibility to fix. Stay here and if you truly love him, wait for him to get help. And if he truly loves *you* he'll get help. Then he should come groveling back here." Beth held my hand as we cuddled under a blanket on the couch.

"I'm afraid if I leave him alone something bad will happen. He might get hurt or hurt someone else." I twisted the tassels at the end of the blanket in my hands, still shaking.

"If you don't leave him, Vi, the only one he's going to hurt is you," her tone was clipped and matter of fact. Her eyes were burning into mine, trying to read my thoughts. "I'm going to say this one last thing," Beth took a huge breath, "You've been with Sam for two and half years and he hasn't gotten better. The drinking has escalated, how he talks and treats you isn't good. From what you just told me it's not getting better. You work hard and have accomplished so much these past few years, you have goals and make new ones. What does he do? He has no motivation to better himself. Since you've been with him you've lost your spark. What happened to the fun, sassy girl?" Beth squeezed my hand, her brown eyes searched mine. "If you stay you're going to continue to lose pieces of yourself." I removed my hand and turned my head away. "Please, listen to me. You need to take a step back. You're twenty-four, I don't think you want this type of relationship, you don't deserve this." Beth tipped her head back against the back of the couch, letting all she said hang heavily in the air.

The more people told me to leave Sam, giving me solid reasons why I should, the more I wanted to prove them wrong. Why did I do that? These were people like Beth, Ally, Cullen and James who cared for me and loved me, they wanted to see me happy and in a healthy relationship. But I didn't want to take their word on what they saw and thought because they didn't know Sam like I did. They didn't know the torment and restlessness he grew up with. They didn't understand that part of his problem was that he didn't have a chance, I wanted to give him a chance. He was living what he knew, what he saw growing up, I thought I could help him change. But another lesson I've learned: you can't be with someone you think you can change or someone you want to change. Loving someone for who they are, rather than what they might become, is much more healthy. Looking back I see, I didn't love Sam for who he was, I didn't even like him for who he was at that time. For a short time in the beginning I did love him but it was mostly an idea of him.

I spent a week at my parents house after the pasta episode with no call, no apology from Sam. He didn't come after me, he didn't call to see where I might be. After a week I went back to the cottage because I had a busy work week or I told myself that's why I had to go back. Who would have gone back after that? Why did I go back? When I showed up Sam was walking back from the dock with his fishing pole.

"You're back," it sounded more of a question than a statement, he brought me into a hug and kissed me gently, there was no taste of booze in his kiss. "I'm sorry, I'm going to do better but I need you." He closed his eyes and brought his forehead to mine. It was what I wanted to hear and I found myself relaxing in his arms.

I had rehearsed an entire speech on the three hour drive, one that was dissolving quickly but I knew I had to get it out. "Sam, I can't be here anymore, it's too much for me out here, I have no connection to this place. Ally's graduating soon and moving back home. I want to go back to be close to her." Ally planned on moving back to our parents house after graduation. When James wasn't deployed he was home during his leave. I wanted more time with them both.

I had reached out to Mark, the owner of the real estate office I started with before I moved to be with Sam, he said he would love to have me back. Mark was an old family friend that went to high school with my parents, he was always good to our family. When he found out I was going into real estate he welcomed me to his company and taught me a lot. He even mentioned the possibility of me buying into the company at a deal I couldn't refuse. I knew he was gifting me an opportunity. Although I didn't want a handout, it was too good a chance to dismiss.

"I'm going back to work for Mark, he's given me an offer I can't pass up. If you're willing to work on yourself and this relationship you can come with me but I cannot do this," I gestured with my hands from me to him, "here in this place. Think about it, we can talk when I get home from work." He stepped back and looked uncertain of everything I laid out. But I left him to think about it, I got back in my car and drove to the showing I had scheduled.

When I returned, Sam was sitting on the deck of the cottage with a bottle of water on the arm of the chair. I smiled but felt an uneasiness in my stomach.

"Hey," he said as I sat in the chair beside him, he held out his hand in an offering to me.

I took his hand, I actually took his hand at that moment. "Did you have a good day?" I exhaled and I looked over the lake across the street, the sun was almost down.

"I did, I've been thinking a lot. I really don't want to leave this place, my family is here and it's everything I know," he said slowly. "But I think a change would be good. As much as I think of this place as home, there's a lot here that brings…" He broke his gaze from me and looked toward the lake searching for the words, "I think a change might be good." He squeezed my hand.

"Okay, we can try it. Sam, I need you to know something," I took my hand from his and placed it on the arm of the chair, "If you ever touch me like you did the other night, I'll leave. I think you should get help or therapy for the drinking. It might be helpful to talk to someone." I searched his eyes, they were sad and despondent. I searched for the Sam I met years ago. If I could get a quick glimpse of him, if I could see that he was still there, I would've felt better. "I know you've been through a lot, I don't want to end up like them." He knew who I was talking about.

"I know, I'm so sorry. It won't happen again," his tone was serious and I couldn't help but believe him, I wanted to believe him.

The GPS alerts me to make a turn and I stumble out of the memory. I check the GPS screen and see I will be arriving very shortly. I shake out the memories and try to take in the scenery around me to keep from falling back into them. A little while later I'm pulling into the campground. After checking in and getting the site information, I feel excited to set up camp. I arrived earlier than I expected, waking up early this morning gave me a jump start. I find the site and pull into the parking area. I take out the camping supplies, the small cooler and James' backpack. I leave the suitcase in the trunk and turn to scope out the camp site. There's a large square outlined with wooden planks and filled in with some loose dirt and sand mixture. That is where the tent will go, a picnic table sits on the farside of the plot. I place all the supplies on the table and organize the equipment.

I make quick work of setting up the tent. I go to the picnic table to set up the foldable two burner camp stove and check to see what I can eat. I boil water to make oatmeal. The sun is shining and there is a breeze. The trees are similar to the white pine trees back in New England but these are called hoop pines. I eat the oatmeal as I glance over the campground map. I'm located toward the base of the camping area and decided to take a trail called Elabana Falls. The trail head is a short walk from my site, the trail is marked as 4.5 miles. I slip into the tent to change into shorts and a cotton long sleeve shirt. After lacing up my hiking boots I empty out nonessentials from the backpack, wanting to keep it light weight for the hike. From the cooler, I take a few water bottles and put them in my pack along with granola bars. I lather my face, neck and legs with sunscreen and place the Red Sox cap on my head. Next, I go to the trunk of the car to grab my camera. I put the camera in the backpack and zip it up and I set off toward the trailhead with a bounce of excitement in my step.

Chapter 6
Drew

Davy called this morning on my way to the gym, letting me know dinner with my parents would be at 6 o'clock. After my workout I walked through the park enjoying the warm weather before I returned home. Taking a seat on a bench in the park, I looked out at the ocean. The waves were larger than they've been the past few days. The impending storm had made the ocean rough with anticipation. Looking around the park and over the ocean I felt content with my decision to move here. I've lived here just over a year and it was one of the best decisions I made. Davy and Mia live in a small neighborhood near Clarkes Beach. I bought a home close to them but more inland, the neighborhood is more country than the beach community where Davy's lives. The neighbors are further apart, there's more space and privacy, I'm still only a short drive to the beach. Coopers Shoot, where I live, sits on a ridge where there are ocean views along with green fields. After an hour watching the water I decided it's time to head back to the fitness center lot where my car was parked. When I got in my car I started the engine and drove toward my house to shower for dinner tonight with my family.

After a hot shower I stand in the walk-in closet, a towel wrapped around my waist, looking for a suit and shirt to pack for my meeting tomorrow. I pick a navy suit jacket and pants with a pair of brown oxfords, I select a white button up shirt that needs to be ironed before packing in the garment bag. I toss the suit on the bed, place the shoes on the bench near the footboard and go to the spare bedroom where the ironing board is set up. I make quick work of the ironing and go back to the bedroom to pack.

I put on a pair of jeans with a burnt orange short sleeve polo. When I've finished getting dressed I make my way out to the kitchen. I head to the fridge, pull out a bottle of water and walk out to the patio where I draw the awning and sit on the cushioned patio sofa. I exhale when I fall back on the sofa and look at the back garden. It's a large garden with a view of the hills to the west. I have a single lemon tree Mia planted in the garden the day after I closed on the house. She said it was for good luck, the lemon tree represented cleansing and optimism. Mia, always with the details and thoughtfulness. When I decided to move out here Mia and

Davy were thrilled to help me look for homes. I found this three bedroom, two bath, L-shaped ranch style house hidden from the main road by a long driveway with Mia's help. Davy and Mia did a beautiful job helping me plan out the front garden with some trees and plants. After a year, not killing any plants, I'm thinking of expanding the garden to allow for some more fruit trees and vegetables.

I don't think I could go back to living in a city now that I found this place. Lexi loved the city and I let her talk me into trying it out. She liked the business of city life, always having somewhere to go and something to do. I was content to stay at home most nights while living in Sydney. When I did go out on the weekends I was bothered by the noise and crowds of people. I prefer the darkened areas where it's quiet and the stars are visible at night. I tried city life with Lexi and it left me dissatisfied with my decision. I asked Lexi to move to the suburbs or country after a year living in Sydney but she refused saying I was a country boy who needed to learn to appreciate the excitement of a city. But I couldn't because it wasn't who I was.

After a year and half of living with Lexi in Sydney I found out she was screwing around. I was away on a business trip for work. I got back a day earlier than expected, the consultation went so well, the company accepted the contract without needing a second meeting. It was a huge closing for my team and the company. I stopped off from the airport on my way home and picked up a bottle of champagne to celebrate with Lexi. We didn't celebrate much anymore at that point in our relationship but I was excited to share the news with her. When I returned to our flat, I could hear music playing from outside the door, I could smell Italian food. I was confused because Lexi didn't cook while I was away, she always complained cooking for one wasn't ideal. When I unlocked the door and entered the flat, I was hit swiftly by the fact Lexi was not alone. There were candles lit on the kitchen table, I saw a suit jacket draped over the back of the sofa in the living room. A pair of mens shoes and a pair of Lexi's heels were haphazardly scattered in front of the sofa. I wanted to call out to her but her name was stuck in my throat.

I moved toward the back of the flat, glancing to the right peering into the kitchen, seeing two plates on the table with chicken parmesan. I continued through the kitchen to the hallway toward the bedroom, my heart was pounding, my hands sweating. I paused at the door listening for something, laughter, talking, moaning. Hearing nothing, I opened the door. I found the bedding crumpled, the remainder of a man's suit lying at the foot of the bed, a woman's dress was thrown on the sitting chair in the corner of the room. Black lace panties clung to the comforter discarded on the floor, my stomach sank. I picked up the suit pants and a wallet fell out, so I opened it. The photo identification picture jumped out at me, his smiling face staring at me made my heart ache. Michael Wallace, my university flatmate and best friend. I dropped the wallet and turned to leave the bedroom. I was going to leave the flat entirely when I heard laughter coming from the end of the hall past the bedroom. Lexi and Mike were in the shower, steam poured out of the bathroom as I opened the door. The glass shower stall was fogged completely, I was thankful for that. I don't know what I would have done if I had to see them both naked, groping and touching one another.

I cleared my throat and called out, "Lexi?" I heard a sharp scream followed by lots of fumbling.

"Drew? What are you doing here?" She practically fell out of the shower stall, grabbing for a towel on the wall beside the shower door. She quickly closed the shower door behind her, not allowing Mike to free himself from the stall. She covered herself with the towel and looked at me in shock and bewilderment.

I stepped back out of the doorway, a feeling of resentment flashed inside me. "What am *I* doing here? I fucking live here, Lex! Mike, get the fuck out of the bloody shower." I tossed a towel over the shower door and turned back toward the hallway. Calmly walking toward the living room, I heard Lexi at my heels calling my name but I didn't turn to look at her.

"Drew, please. Please, look at me." When I turned to look at her she had panic in her eyes and face. I stopped in the kitchen, standing behind the breakfast bar trying to keep something between us.

"Please, what?" What was unfolding before me didn't need words. It was unfolding in sights, sounds and smells. There were no words needed to explain what was happening.

"I didn't mean for you to find out like this. I wasn't expecting you home tonight." She ran her hands over her sopping wet hair.

"No shit," I couldn't help but laugh, it sounded more like a grunt. I waved my arms around the flat in exacerbation, "I'd hope you didn't plan for this. What the actual fuck, Lexi? *Mike*?" Questions swirled in my brain at top speed and I tried to grab them and get them out as they passed but I couldn't.

Lexi put her head down and her voice was barely a whisper, "I'm so sorry, Drew."

She couldn't even meet my eyes as she apologized. After a minute of silence Mike emerged from the hallway, dressed in his pants and untucked shirt, barefoot with wet hair.

He put up his hands in surrender, "Drew, mate. Can we sit down and talk about this? I think if we…" He stepped toward the table and reached for the chair.

I didn't let him finish his thought, "Shut up, Mike, just shut it." I put one hand up and rubbed the other hand against my forehead, "Just stop talking."

I thought for a second, did I want to hit him? Was it worth it? Lexi snapped her head up and Mike stared at me with uncertainty in his eyes.

"I'm leaving. This obviously…" I couldn't find the words to finish my thought. "Mike," I turned my body and straightened my posture trying desperately to find something to say to hurt him as much as I was hurting from his betrayal, "Fuck you." That's all I had for him, looking back I wish I had more to offer. At that moment I couldn't convey a rational train of thought.

Next I turned to Lexi, "You should have told me, he's my best mate for fucks sake. I'll be back tomorrow while you're at work for my clothes. Don't be here. Best of luck to you two." The last sentence was pure sarcasm, my words dripped with acid. I grabbed the keys off the counter, leaving the bottle of champagne, as I strode out the door. That was the last time I saw either of them.

After the discovery at the flat I went to the nearest pub and drank until closing and taxied my way to a hotel. I called out of work the next day, it was a Friday. I went to the flat midmorning when I knew Lexi would be at work. I collected my clothes and took a flight to Ballina Byron Gateway airport where I called Davy to pick me up.

When Davy arrived to pick me up he was suspicious of my unexpected visit. I relayed to him what unfolded the night before and he was silent for the rest of the ride to his house. The silence was tense but I was grateful for it because I wasn't looking forward to answering questions. Questions, I knew, I didn't have the answers to. When we arrived at Davy's house he handed me a beer which I refused because my stomach was heavy with fermenting alcohol from the previous night.

"I'm sorry, Drew. That's awful." He sat shaking his head on the sofa. "I never liked that bloke, always slithering around. Turncoat, bugger, he is. And Lexi…" He threw his hands up. "She was always vain and snobby. Honestly, she was terrible to be around." His eyes widened when he looked at me realizing his ramble was not what I needed to hear. He started to backpedal, "Sorry, I didn't mean to sound like I saw it coming because I didn't." His eyes filled with sympathy. "I mean you're better than them and you handled the situation like a champ." He smiled weakly and sank back into the couch getting the hint I didn't want to talk about it.

"I should have left a while ago, I knew things weren't great between us. We weren't connecting, I was a coward." I shrugged my shoulders in resignation.

"Oh, c'mon, don't play the martyr. *They* snuck around, they kept it from you. They betrayed your loyalty and trust. Don't blame yourself for any of it." He was right to a point.

"Yeah, man. Let's talk about something else. I've got to get my head together, I need to move forward," I exhaled and I sat back on the couch. Davy and I sat in silence for a while, a comforting silence.

Over the next week, while staying with Davy and Mia, I coordinated with the company to transfer to a different team. They were very accommodating, not asking too many questions and discussed plans of opening an office in Queensland. Those plans are rolling out now, almost a year later. Davy and Mia were excited at the idea of me moving out here close to them. Lexi and Mike both called me many times after I left, along with texts, asking me to talk and let them explain. All calls and texts went unanswered and I eventually stopped receiving them all together. I had questions, I considered, even if I got the answers it wouldn't change anything. It wouldn't take away any of the events that happened and it might lead to more hurt feelings. I lost my bestfriend and girlfriend, other than work, my only connections to Sydney. I made the right decision moving out here. I'm much happier and relaxed. I'm closer to Davy and Mia, the most loyal of comrades.

I checked the time on my watch and it read half past four. If I wanted time to stop off for an errand I would have to leave now. I stood up and stretched, I had been sitting in reflection for sometime and tried to shake loose the disturbing memories. After driving a short distance to town I stop at the floral shop and pick two bouquets, one a native wildflower bouquet with yellow Billy Buttons and desert flames. Complimenting the yellow flowers were white rice flowers and everlasting daisies. Wildflowers always made me think of Mia, she was always picking them as a child and creating these wonderful bouquets. For my mother I picked a bouquet of rock lilies, a Geraldton wax flower highlighted by eucalyptus leaves. When my bouquets were ready I headed back to my SUV and drove to Davy's house.

When I enter the house, Mia is walking to the door to greet me. "I thought I heard you pull in." She put her hand on my shoulder and gave me a peck on the cheek. "How beautiful, Drew. Are these for me?" She asks knowingly, I usually bring flowers for her and Mum at our family dinners.

"Of course." I follow her toward the kitchen and hear music playing from the surround sound system.

"Davy's in the backroom with Mum and Dad. Can I get you a drink?" She waves her hand toward the bar tray in the corner of the kitchen. "There's beer in the fridge." She went to work unwrapping the bouquet and placing the flowers in a vase, walking it toward the dining room table.

"Not tonight. I've gotta drive to Brisbane after dinner." I go to the fridge and pull a water bottle and head back toward the sitting room.

My father sat in an upholstered chair with a tumbler filled with amber liquid. My mother and Davy are seated on opposite ends of the sofa, holding glasses of white wine. I walk in the room greeting all three and bending to kiss my mum on the cheek. Davy and my father stand when I approach, we shake hands and hug. I move toward the other chair across from the sofa where Davy is now seated next to my mother.

"You're late. Not like you to be late." Davy complains flashing me a crafty smile before taking a sip of his wine.

"No, I'm not. You said dinner at six." I open the water bottle and take a swig.

"You two." My mother rolls her eyes, her vibrant smile and energetic eyes moving from each of us. "Everyone's here now, let's enjoy the night." She holds up her wine glass in a mock toast. My mother loves these dinners, having both her boys together.

Mia walks in with a tray of fruit and cheese, setting it on the coffee table in the middle of the room along with small serving plates. She takes a seat in the middle of Davy and Mum. "I'm glad you all could come. It's nice having you here." Mia took Davy's hand in hers.

Ever since Mia lost her father three years ago she has made a great effort to keep the family dinners routine and I'm thankful for her doing so. I've never experienced the loss of a parent and I saw how hard it was for Mia and her family. I'll appreciate all the effort she has put into these nights when, someday, we can't do them anymore.

I smile and shoot her a wink, "Thanks for having us."

Mia flushes a light shade of pink, "Mum and Dad, how's everything at the sables? I've been meaning to take a ride up but the past few weeks have been busy. After the wedding, I want to come stay with you both for a few nights."

"Oh, love, don't you worry about that. You're so busy planning the wedding and still working. We're fine. Of course, we'd love to have you for a visit after things settle down." Mum reaches for Mia's hand and gives it a gentle squeeze, "So, tell us how the planning is going. When are your mum and sister coming into town? Will they be staying with you?"

"Everything's mostly ready, vendors are scheduled and everything is coming along well. Mum and Lauren are coming in a week." There's so much excitement in her voice it's hard not to smile along with her. "We have a small bachelorette gathering Wednesday evening and a spa day Thursday. My mum and sister will be staying in a rental around the corner, so the house is open for you and Dad to stay when you come next Friday." I find it endearing that Mia calls my parents Mum and Dad, she's done so for many years.

"That all sounds so lovely. We can't wait for the big day." Mum sips her wine and gives a longing look to my Dad. My father's a man of very few words, Dad returned her smile and sipped from his tumbler.

"Drew, Dad, should we go outside while I grill the chicken? Leave the ladies to discuss details," Davy says and turns toward Mia and Mum. "Need anything, love? Can I get you some wine?"

"No, thank you. I'm fine with this." Mia holds up a glass of water with a few sliced lemons inside. She stands to kiss him on the cheek before returning to the sofa.

Before the three of us exit the sitting room to the patio, Davy asks, "Need a refill Dad? I'm going to grab the chicken. Drew, need a beer?" Davy pauses at the sliding door as we pass him to take a seat outside.

"Sure, son," I hear my father's gravelly voice for the first time tonight.

"I'm good, just water for me tonight," I hold up my water bottle before setting it on the patio table in front of me.

"How's things? Is work keeping you busy?" My father turns to look at me.

His years working a farm show on his body, his hands calloused and wrinkled. His stance now shows signs of arthritis, his back a bit hunched and slight limp caused by hip and knee pain. His 63 years are showing considerably to me at this moment. My mother was four years his junior, years of riding and farming have kept her fit and lithe. However, with my dad, it seemed to break his body down. I regret not helping them out more over the past years.

"Work has been busy, I've got some time off and I'm looking forward to that." I place my right ankle on my left knee and fiddle with the laces on my sneaker. "How's things at the ranch? Are you keeping up with things? I could come out for a few days next week," I meet his stone blue eyes and he smiles.

"No need, things are slow and we have a few local teens who volunteer with your mother, helping with barn chores and feeding. I'm starting to run out of things to do," he laughs a deep rumble and I know slowing down isn't something he's used to.

"That's great. You'll have to get a hobby soon to keep you busy," he laughs harder at my response.

Davy comes out with a tray of chicken, smiling at the both of us as he enters the patio. "What did I miss?" His eyes shifted to my father then me, wanting to get in on the humor.

"Just talking to Dad about all the time he has on his hands now that Mum has hired some volunteers. He's thinking of picking up a hobby." I shoot my dad a playful smile which he returns.

"Really? Come surfing with us. It's great for the body, low impact." He flashes a devilish smile knowing Dad would never and has never been on a board in his life.

"No, I'll leave that to you boys." He drains the remainder of his drink and picks up the new tumbler Davy brought out to him.

While Davy cooks, we spend the time talking about the imminent storm heading toward the coast in the upcoming days. The women come out to join us shortly after. We laugh about the times Mia and Davy would sneak out to meet each other in the barn thinking no one knew about the rendezvous. Davy would sneak out of his window, taking the roof toward the back of the house where there was a path leading to the barn.

"I'd hear him stomping on the roof over the bedroom. Your mother and I would turn to each other and say, 'there goes Davy'." Dad roared with laughter. Although we've heard it a hundred times it still gets a laugh out of all of us while making Mia blush with embarrassment.

"I still can't believe you were on to us the whole time." Mia laughs, wiping tears from her eyes. "Let's go inside and eat before dinner gets cold." She opens the patio door watching us file in.

We sit at the dining table with the fresh bouquets in the middle and tealight candles flickering. The music is lowered to a faint level, Sam Cooke sings *Cupid* in the background. When dinner is finished I stand to collect the plates and silverware from everyone at the table signaling Mia to stay seated.

"I got this, I'll be back in a few." I collect the plates and head out to the kitchen.

I fill the sink with warm water and check the dish washer to see if it's ready to load with the dirty dishes. It's full of what looks like dirty dishes so I add the detergent and press start.

"I forgot to start that earlier." I don't hear Mia come up behind me until she's standing to my right by the sink handing me dish soap. "You wash, I'll dry." She picks up a dish towel hanging near the stove and stands in waiting.

"Yes, ma'am." I grin at her as I grab the sponge sitting in the cradle by the sink.

She unfolds the drying rack and places it on a thick mat to the right of the sink. "Drew?" she asks, saying my name slowly and in question, making my back shoot up in response.

"Mia?" I reply, saying her name slow and tentatively while showing her a reassuring smile.

Whatever she wants to tell me I see she's struggling, uncertainty reflecting in her eyes. She gives a huff of a laugh and nudges me with her elbow, I react by dramatically sidestepping trying to lighten the mood.

"Alright, I'm gonna come out with it," she pauses, taking a dinner plate and starts wiping it with the dish towel. "Do you think Davy's happy?" her voice is soft and quiet, she doesn't want anyone to hear us.

As if on cue there is a rumble of laughter that comes from the dining room, Davy's being the loudest. I nod toward the dining area and say, "Davy? My brother, is he happy?" I laugh but see concern in her eyes. I shut off the water before my hand grabs another plate in the sink. "Yeah, I'd say he's very happy. What's going on Mia? Is something wrong with Davy?" I turn to face her.

"No, please, I'm just thinking. What if when we get married things change? What if I can't give him what he wants?" Her eyes are trying to silently relay something to me but I have no idea what it is.

"Are you having cold feet or something? Has he said something?" I'm confused by this conversation, I need more details but Mia stands with restraint. "You both have been looking forward to this for so long, hell, you've practically been married for years now, just not officially." I rub the back of my neck searching her face for a clue.

Her hands wrap and unwrap around the dish towel. "Keep washing," she nods toward the sink, "I'm thinking, once we're married he may get bored, like there's nothing more to look forward to." She shrugs her shoulders, I still feel she's not saying what's really on her mind.

"You'll have your whole lives to look forward to. Traveling, building a home, children." When I hand her silverware to dry I see tears forming in her eyes, "Mia?"

I feel my stomach clench. Nothing makes me feel more helpless than not knowing how to react to someone hurting. Mia quickly wipes at her eyes and grabs for the silverware. Her mouth opens but no words come out. I take the towel from her hands along with the silverware and place them in the rack. I hold her hands in mine and make her turn toward me. When she looks up her eyes are dry and there's a forced smile on her face.

"You're right, I know you're right. Just some pre-wedding jitters." She takes her hands from mine, smoothing her hair and takes a deep breath, "Lemme go check on them, I'm going to set out the trifle and lamingtons shortly." She turns quickly, I manage to grab her hand before she leaves.

"Mia, Davy loves you more than any man I know loves a woman. If something's on your mind you should take it to him. I know you'll feel reassured if you discuss your worries with him." That's all I can offer her, I feel it's not enough.

"I will, I'm sorry about that, Drew. Really, everything's good and I will talk to him." She turns and heads toward the dining room.

I finish the dishes, wondering what the hell just happened. After the dishes are put neatly in the drying rack I head to the cupboard and grab a few dessert plates. Looking around on the counters for the dessert Mia mentioned I find a covered patter on the farside of the counter. Pulling back the cover I see a tray full of lamingtons, a sponge cake dipped in chocolate and covered with finely grated coconut. They smell delicious and fresh. Even though I'm feeling quite full from dinner, my stomach fills with anticipation for the dessert. I check the fridge for the trifle and find it.

"What are you doing out here? C'mon back and be social with us. The dishes can wait." Davy folds his arms across his chest.

"I'm coming, just helping Mia with this stuff." I nod toward the desserts sitting on the counter. "Everything okay out there?"

"All good. Mum's excited for the wedding, right? All the questions and wanting all the details, driving me crazy," he laughs and I know he's only half serious.

"Well, you're her baby, she should be excited. How about you? Are you feeling good about it?" I try to sound casual with the question. After the mysterious conversation with Mia earlier I'm half expecting some kind of confession.

"Feeling great. Can't wait to make her mine at last. Mia *Harris*, finally. Has a nice ring to it, doesn't it?" He looks at me, his bright eyes gleam with excitement. It leaves me more confused about Mia's questions earlier.

I decide to let it go, maybe it's Mia having some anxiety before the big day. "It sounds great." I pick up the fruit trifle and signal to Davy to grab the plates and cakes.

We eat dessert in the sitting room and everything is as usual. I glance at Mia a few times trying to figure out what happened in the kitchen earlier. Her eyes aren't sad like they had been, she's laughing and smiling. The bubbly Mia whose laugh and happiness is so infectious sat across from me now. After an hour of chatting in the sitting room I checked my watch, it was close to ten. If I left now, I'd arrive in Brisbane by midnight. I excuse myself, giving Davy and my father a handshake. I give Mia and my mother a hug and kiss, thanking Mia and Davy for the meal. Davy offers to walk me out but I wave him off, telling him to stay and enjoy the conversation. I walk down the driveway to my car hoping Mia will make an appearance and explain the events that happened in the kitchen but she doesn't. I get in my car and begin the two hour drive to Brisbane.

Chapter 7
Violet

Yesterday, I hiked the Elabana Falls trail which led to a beautiful waterfall and emerald green pool. After a few hours on the trail, I explored areas around the park taking in other shorter trails filled with beech trees and evergreens. The park here is diverse with subtropical rainforest as well as woodland forests. I saw so many beautiful, colorful birds and amazing views of mountains and lush valleys. Today I managed a day hike of the Border Trail, 13 miles filled with ancient trees and flourishing vegetation. Stunning views of mountains, a mist in the air caused a hazy view of the scenic overlooks but it was still beautiful. I managed to fill an entire SD card with pictures from my camera.

Last night, I read a bit of *Walden* and was enraptured by Thoreau's descriptions of nature and solitary life. These past two days have centered me. I was so tired last night I didn't dream of lost family members or anything at all. I slept soundly for the first time in a while. Tonight, my body is aching and I'm too tired to move anymore. Looking up toward the sky, clouds roll past, the stars come in and out of view. I can't remember the last time I did this, not just camping but enjoying the night sky. I think about it and remember it was probably over a year ago at the cabin. Thinking about the cabin reminds me, I need to call Cullen and let him know my sister and I will be coming in a few weeks to stay.

Cullen Branton was James' best friend. They met in the Navy and were in the same unit for 8 years, touring the middle east. James and Cullen went in together on a large piece of land in the White Mountains of New Hampshire. Large really doesn't describe it, it's almost an entire foothill. James and Cullen built two cabins on the land, about a half mile from one another. They went there on their time off, hidden away from the world. It brought them peace, solitude and happiness. Ally and I would, occasionally, meet James there to visit him when he was home. The cabin was large and accommodated the three of us easily, along with whoever else James invited to stay. I loved spending time in New Hampshire, especially in the Fall months when the foliage changed to bright shades of red, orange and yellow.

A year and a half after our parents died, soon after I turned 18, James sat Ally and I down and told us he decided to enlist in the

Navy. He was hoping to join the Marine Corp. Ally and I looked at each other with expressions of shock. I thought it had to be some kind of joke, James never voiced interest in military life. He had so much going for him, we certainly weren't destitute. Our parents had paid off the house shortly before they died. They didn't leave us with a ton of money but we were comfortable, we had enough.

"What are you talking about, James? You can't go to the military," I said, half laughing, the idea was ridiculous to me.

"I'm going to go, it's decent money that I can send home. I won't need anything. I'll have housing and food during training, they'll give me a college education and I'll be able to use the skills later when I'm ready to settle into a career." He made his argument sound logical but I couldn't believe it.

"We don't need the money. You can make just as much finding other work. They don't *give* away college educations, you have to sign years of your life to them. If you want to go to college we can make that happen. We could remortgage the house. Hell, we can sell the house if we need to! You cannot leave." I frantically racked my 18 year old brain for a counterargument. I turned to Ally for help, she was always the logical, rational one. But her 16 year old face was blank of expression, I thought she might be in shock.

"No, we can't. Mom and Dad left this house to all of us. It's our home, it's our security. I would never sell this place, not ever." His bright blue eyes burnt into mine, "Promise me you won't sell this house, Vi."

"Well, I can't sell it without all of us in agreement so, yes, I promise you I won't sell it. You know there's a war going on right now, right?" My heart started to pound and my palms sweat.

September 11th, 2001 was just over a year before. There were constant deployments and war was tearing through parts of the middle east. I stood from the sofa where we sat. I moved to stand in front of the wood stove where James had started a fire on the chilly November night. The stove made me sweat more so I started pacing behind the couch.

"Yes, I know. I have basic training first and then more training. After that I'll be assigned a job which requires even more training. It will take over a year before they even think about deploying me. It all could be over by then," he couldn't even look us in the eyes as he spoke.

"It *could* be over by then? And if it's *not*? Then what? You'll go to some war ravaged country and what? Keep your head down and try to make it back. Fuck that. James, you're not going. We need you *here*." I threw my hands up in the air, my voice was raised. I looked at Ally again for something, anything. She kept her eyes downcast, gripping her knees.

"Violet, please, calm down. Let's not worry about things we can't control. Let me focus on the training and go from there." James stood up and walked toward me.

"Well, we *can* control that you're *not* enlisting so there you go." I pushed his chest as he moved closer to me and I walked back toward the woodstove.

"I've already signed," James' voice was barely a whisper.

"*What*?" I spun around hoping I heard him wrong. I moved toward the couch and sat on the coffee table across from Ally.

"I signed up two weeks ago. I leave for camp in a month," he finally met my gaze and the fury in my eyes didn't elicit the response I was hoping for. He broke the stare and looked toward Ally who had yet to utter a single word. "Ally, you okay?" He attempted to lift her chin but she didn't allow her head to move.

The weeks before James left for basic training were tense. Ally didn't say much of anything for a while. I picked up more hours at work, trying to avoid James and my anger toward him. We were scared, all of us. I couldn't believe the decision James made. Especially in the climate of post 9/11, it didn't seem like a smart or thoughtful choice by him. He met with lawyers and took care of important duties. James added me to the guardianship agreement over Ally, it was heartbreaking for me to sign the document. He reached out to extended family making sure Ally and I had someone checking in on us, it made me furious.

"Did you wait until I turned eighteen?" I asked him during dinner three days before he was about to leave. "Did you have this planned since they died? You plan, James, that's what you do. You don't sign away your life without thinking about it. You didn't do this on a whim."

James froze mid bite, his fork hoovering in the air. "I've been thinking about it for awhile, no, I haven't planned this since they died." He looked at me pleadingly, silently asking me not to fight with him, his eyes asking for forgiveness.

"Stop. Stop it, Violet. We are *not* fighting about this anymore." Ally dropped her fork to the table and stared at me. Her usually bright blue eyes darkened with emotion. "James made his decision and we are going to support him. *Stop* fighting with him." Ally said firmly as she took her plate and brought it to the sink.

When Ally speaks, you listen. So, that's what I did. I pushed away the anger and displeasure with the situation and tried to accept what was about to happen. James left for training the first week of December. He seemed nervous but was also excited. He loved being physical, he loved challenging himself. Despite not having any brothers, he was very competitive even with us girls. Most importantly, James was smart. He would do well and he knew it. Ally and I knew it, too. When we came home after bringing James to the airport Ally went to her room, I went to mine. I cried all night and I'm almost positive Ally did the same.

The wind is picking up and I'm feeling a chill. There are no open flames allowed so a fire to warm myself isn't an option. When I stand from the table I feel the pull and ache in my hamstrings and lower back. I'm enjoying the view of the stars but not enjoying the memories whirling in my head right now. I think about bringing Thoreau's book into the tent with me. I could read a few chapters with my lantern or flashlight but I know as soon as I lay down I'll pass out. I groan thinking about what my body will feel like in the morning. If I'm feeling this sore now, I hope I'll be able to move tomorrow.

After watching the weather patterns religiously for the past two days, Springbrook isn't my best bet for waiting out the storm. I emailed the host of the rental I scheduled for the weekend and asked if I could check in a day early. The host, a woman by the name of Emma, was happy to allow me to check in early and I was thankful she was accommodating. Therefore, tomorrow I'll be driving to Pottsville to wait out the storm and maybe have a chance to recharge my body. I'm hoping to get an early start, especially, if the storm is coming early and escalating through the afternoon hours. The storm might be a blessing, after two days of hiking I don't think my body could have taken much more. I'm not used to the trail hiking I have done these past days.

Since my plan has changed, when I get to the cottage rental I want to reevaluate the map of the coast and make another itinerary for the upcoming week. I heard a few other hikers talking about coming from the south, they talked about a beautiful place called Whian Whian National Park. It sounded like a must see. I pull out my phone from the pocket of my sweatshirt, I make a note on my Reminders app to buy a few SD cards for my camera, call Cullen this weekend and the last reminder is to research Whian Whian.

I wake the next morning to the chirping and singing of birds I don't recognize from sound. When I open my eyes I notice it's gray outside, I can't determine if it's really early or a darkened morning because of overcast clouds. I checked my phone for the time, 8:07. Wanting an early start on the day I don't linger in the tent. As I stretch I feel muscles in my legs and back screaming with tension. It's painful to move my body off the bedroll. I unzip the inside of the tent and grab the bedroll as I exit. I feel the dampness and humidity in the air. I break down the tent, collapsing the rods and folding the lightweight material like my father taught me years ago. I quicken my pace, I gather everything I packed up from the campsite, I've slept later than I anticipated.

I take one last look around and notice the trees swaying in the breeze, the humidity has thickened. Satisfied with packing and my stay here at Lamington, I get in the car and pull out of the campground. On my drive exiting the park I see either kangaroos or wallabies bouncing on the side of the road and for a moment wish I had my camera available to me. I can't distinguish between a wallaby and kangaroo but it's something I remind myself to look up later. I take the narrow forest road to the main road heading to Pottsville, hoping I make it before the weather gets too bad.

About an hour into my drive the wind picks up and the rain falls faster, harder. I find myself getting nervous driving in a foreign country, on the opposite side of the road than I'm used to and in bad weather. My hands grip the steering wheel so tightly my knuckles turn white. The wipers of the car slap feverishly against the windshield, only one hour left to my destination. My stomach grumbles along with the thunder outside and I push away the hunger pains by sipping from the water bottle I've stored on the passenger seat.

The GPS directs me to take the next exit off the M1 highway and turn on to Cudgera Creek Road and my heart leaps with excitement to be almost done with the drive. I pull off the highway, finding the main road that brings you to the downtown area of Pottsville, I slow the car to look at the surroundings through the pounding rain. It would be nice to find a grocery market to get a few food supplies to get me through the weekend. Shortly into my drive downtown I find an IGA market. I pull into the lot and take a huge breath. Hunger pains stab my stomach. I get ready to exit the car, psyching myself up for a mad dash to the market's entrance.

When I enter the store I shake the droplets off and run my hand over my wet face. The market is not busy, I'm sure people have already prepared for the storm and are settled cozy in their homes. Soon, I realize I'm the only customer in the entire place aside from the employees. I take a small cart and start browsing the aisles. Everything looks so good, I hate shopping when I'm hungry it leads to impulsive buying. I stick to the basics, I can always come back when the weather improves. Having a full kitchen at my disposal for the weekend makes me happy. I don't linger too long in the store, I'm very anxious to get to the rental where I can shower and slip into a bed. I'm greeted at the checkout by a gentleman with wired-framed reading glasses.

"Didn't think we would have any customers today." His smile is gentle and his tanned skin wrinkles around his eyes.

"It's terrible out there. I just drove in," I kept the exchange simple, gazing outside just in time to hear a crash of thunder.

"Awful day to be traveling. American?" As he rings up the items he places them in a brown paper bag.

"Yes, I'm excited for my visit." I pull out my wallet from my small purse slung across my shoulder, "I'm here for a few days before I head south again."

"Ah, off to Byron Bay? My wife and I take rides down there on the weekends." He puts the last item in the bag and gives me my total.

"Byron Bay? I heard about that place," I say, remembering the insanely good-looking man from the airport.

Drew mentioned Byron Bay, he said it was beautiful and he spent a lot of time there. Did he frequent the area on his time off? Maybe with his wife or girlfriend? I didn't see a ring on his finger but there couldn't be a universe where that man would be single.

My thoughts tear away from that day at the airport when the man says, "Oh yes, it's a popular spot." He takes the bills from my hand and types something on the register's screen. "We like to go to the lighthouse and they have a few breweries, too." He hands me my change and puts two brown bags on the counter in front of me.

"The weather is going to clear, the next few days should be nice for your visit."

"Thank you," I grab the two bags hefting them up and head toward the exit.

I stand at the exit for a moment trying to prepare for the torrential downpour I'm about to face again. Taking a deep breath, I run toward my rental parked in the lot. I quickly and awkwardly open the back seat behind the driver's side, toss in the brown bags and jump into the driver's seat. There's a flash of lightning that lights up the dark clouds above, instantly, a menacing crack rings out making me jump. I look at the GPS and see I have to cross a causeway ahead, my destination is less than half a mile after that. I pull out of the lot and follow the GPS voice commands. When I drive over the causeway lightning sparks in the sky, illuminating the clouds with streaks of purple and yellow, it's absolutely beautiful and terrifying at the same time. Soon, after driving over the bridge, I'm parked in front of a charming pale yellow bungalow with a short sandy driveway.

The host of the tiny cottage, Emma, said there would be a small lockbox attached to the front entry door, the code was 8723. The wind's now howling being so close to the water. I grab one grocery bag from the backseat, the perishables, and sprint toward the door. I remove the key from the box and enter the tiny house. It's adorable with a beach theme, colors of navy and wheat yellow fill the entry room which has a small loveseat and white wicker chair with navy blue cushions. Behind the living room is a compact kitchen, a breakfast counter with high bar stools separating the living room from the kitchen. There's a small white fridge in the kitchen, pictures of sunsets and ocean waves litter the walls. I see a coffee pot, an electric kettle and a microwave resting on the counter to the right of the fridge. There's a two burner stove and a tiny sink across from that. On the breakfast bar I see a bottle of wine with a card with my name on the envelope. I go to the card and open it.

Violet,

Welcome to Australia! I hope you enjoy your stay. Please call with any questions. Checkout list is printed on the fridge. Hope the weather clears in time for you to enjoy the beach.

Thank you for staying,
Emma

I'm touched by her thoughtfulness and thankful for the wine. I could use a glass or five after the white-knuckled ride. I place the soaked grocery bag on the counter and head down the narrow hallway to the back room. A single bedroom with a double bed is already calling out to me. The walls in the bedroom are a pale, powdery blue, the comforter is striped white and yellow. Across from the bedroom is a bathroom with a tiny antique sink, a stand up shower and a two foot wide linen closet. The place is charming with nautical themes. I head back out to the car before I lose my nerve, thunder rumbles above me as I grab my suitcase from the trunk and the remaining grocery bag from the rear seat. When I reenter the house the paper bag rips open, sending the fruit and vegetables scattering to the entryway floor. A small puddle forms under my frame from the water dripping down my body. I step over the mess and bring my suitcase to the back bedroom. Tossing the suitcase on the bed, I rummage through and find dry clothes. I need a hot shower but I'm a little reluctant to shower in the midst of a lightning storm. I go back toward the entryway and pick up all the food that fell from the grocery bag. I'm happy I didn't buy too many things, the fridge is small, I wouldn't have been able to fit much more than what I have.

After organizing the kitchen, I ran back out in the rain to grab the rest of my belongings in the car. I'm officially waterlogged, my fingers are pruney, I strip off the soaking wet clothes. Trembling in my bra and underwear, which are wet as well, I take my chances with the shower. The thunder is a faint roar in the distance, I turn on the shower spinning the knob to the hottest setting. I back out of the bathroom and go to the hallway closet where there's a stackable washer and dryer, everything is dollhouse sized in here. I feel like Alice after drinking the potion that makes her grow. I throw the wet clothes in the washer, leaving the top open to add my hiking clothes from the previous days' adventures.

The bathroom is steaming up from the hot water. The hot water hits my body and I melt under the stream. My muscles throb and I sigh in pleasure. I wash my hair and stand under the flowing shower long enough until I feel the hot water turning lukewarm. Stepping out of the shower I wrap my hair and body in towels, I bundle up in my warm dry clothes. Now, I address my hunger. I make a sandwich, it's quick and simple because I'm starving. I take two huge bites and swallow them down then grab my phone from the charger on the kitchen counter.

The rain lasts all afternoon while I drink tea and answer all my emails from work. I go to the United States Post Office website and complete a change of address form, forwarding all my mail to my parents house address. I also log into the electric company account and request a close out of services in two weeks. Sam and I split the rent each month, the electricity went in my name and the cable and internet went in his name. I'd have to let him know, within two weeks time, he would have to call the electric company and transfer the service to him. My stomach lurches with unease as I think about how to handle that situation.

After all the business end of my work is done, I set to research some surrounding areas like Byron Bay and Whian Whian National Park. Both areas look so beautiful, I want to visit each place. I wrote down the names of some accommodations and sites in Byron Bay. I like the idea of finding another cottage like this, it beats a hotel experience, I like the solitude and privacy of it. Looking at a vacation rental site, I found a studio cottage available across from Clarkes Beach. There are a few other beaches around as well, Belongil Beach, Wetegos and Tallow Beach, they all look stunning. I check the availability of the rental and see it is available this week. With a check in available on Monday, I book it for a three night stay.

Looking at Byron Bay and Whian Whian from the computer I find myself getting excited for the next leg of this journey. I shut down my laptop and went to the kitchen to open the bottle of wine from my gracious host, Emma. I pour a glass of the Merlot and sip while I prepare some vegetables to go with the steak I bought for dinner. I can't use the outdoor grill because the rain continues to beat down. I cut up some potatoes and put them in a pot of water until I am ready to cook. Taking the bottle of wine over to the coffee table I set it down as I continued to watch the wind and rain pelt the window remembering I must call Cullen.

It was last July, 2013, I remember it was a really hot day. I got a call from Cullen at 2:30 in the afternoon. I was at work and thought about not answering, wanting to call him back when my work day was done. But I knew if I needed to call Cullen he would always answer, taking that into consideration I answered his call.

“Hey, Cullen,” I answered, Jamcs was coming home soon, while James was away Cullen would often check in with Ally and I.

“Violet, are you at your condo?” His voice was dull and quiet, the question set me on alert.

“No, I’m at work. What’s up?” I stood from my desk and waited for his response.

“Can you meet me at your parents’ place? Say, 25 minutes?” I was confused as to how he knew it would take me exactly 25 minutes to get there from my office.

“Yeah, I guess. Why? What's up?” I asked again, already grabbing my purse and keys from the coat hook on my office door.

“Alright, I’ll see you there,” he disconnected the call without answering me.

“Damn it, Cullen!” I exclaimed to myself, calling him back. It rang once, going to voicemail. I hurried out of the office to my car. I called over my shoulder to Stacy, my new assistant, I had to run out and I would check in soon.

I frantically got in my car and started the engine with shaking hands. I tried to calm myself down but the panic was taking over. I didn't know anything yet, Cullen could have been there because he was in town waiting for James to get home. Maybe James was surprising us and had arranged to come home early. Ally was getting married in a month, maybe James got some extra leave and he wanted to try to surprise us. I called Ally before I left the parking lot but there was no answer. I called again, nothing. I pulled out and tried to keep within the speed limits as I drove to my parents’ house.

When I arrived at the house I noticed Cullen’s truck parked in the driveway. I pulled my car behind his truck but I couldn't get myself to exit my car. I sat in the driveway for what felt like an eternity. I saw the front door open, Ally stood behind the screen door, arms across her chest looking at me. Taking a huge breath I got out of the car, standing on shaking legs. I walked slowly to the door and saw Ally’s eyes red and puffy, the brightest blue eyes with specks of gold. You could really notice the gold specks in her eyes after she’d been crying. I paused midstep. Over her shoulder I saw Cullen standing behind her. I couldn’t go in, I couldn’t move. The heaviness in my chest stole my ability to breathe and my legs shook more. Cullen placed a hand on Ally’s shoulder and gently moved her aside to open the screen door.

"Violet, come inside," his voice was calm and soothing.

"No. What's going on, Cullen? Ally?" I asked as my voice cracked and Ally's hand went up over her mouth.

I wanted to drop to the ground, the world was spinning around me and the heaviness was taking over. In a few strides Cullen was down the front steps at my side just as I was about to fall. He put an arm around my waist and led me inside the house. Ally was sitting on the sofa in the living room, in the same spot she sat the night James told us he was enlisting. Cullen sat me next to Ally and took a seat in front of me on the coffee table.

"Violet, I'm sorry," he whispered as Ally let out a sob.

Tears filled my eyes, I couldn't breathe. "Sorry about what?" I didn't want the answer but couldn't help but ask, "Sorry about *what*?" I asked again and Ally leaned into me holding her hands across her chest as if her heart was breaking.

"James died on a mission yesterday. I found out this morning and picked Ally up at the ferry a few hours ago and we came right here." He reached for my hand but I pulled away.

"No, he's coming home in four days. He called a few days ago and said he's coming home," I tried to convince myself he was coming home and it was all a mistake, a misunderstanding.

"Vee," Ally stood up and took me by the shoulders, "he's gone. He's not coming home." She wrapped her arms around me but I stood erect and unyielding.

"No!" I yelled as I shook Ally off, "He can't be gone. He's not!"

I tried to gasp for the air that refused to enter my lungs, my head spun and I felt like I was going to vomit. My chest hurt, my eyes blurred not from tears but from overwhelming emotion. I was sweating, my heart was pounding so fast and loud, I couldn't hear anything except the throbbing sound of blood pumping through my body. I was having a panic attack. I felt large hands firmly pushing on my shoulders, guiding me down toward the sofa. Then I felt the same hands rest on the top of my back, between my shoulder blades, guiding my head down between my legs.

"Breathe, breathe, Violet," each word from Cullen was slow and pronounced but sounded muffled as if Cullen was miles away from me. I felt another hand rubbing my back, Ally's hand. I took in large gulps of air. "Short, quick breaths. Breathe."

I listened to his commands because I wanted, more than anything, for the feeling to stop. I felt more in control of my body after a few rounds of the breathing. I lifted my head and looked at Cullen who was sitting on the coffee table right in front of my face. His eyes shifted from my eyes to my lips to my cheeks. He was assessing me, my condition.

"How do you know?" I asked Cullen.

"I got a call this morning from his squad leader. Stay sitting, I'm going to get some water." He stood but I grabbed his hand.

"It could be a mistake," my voice was weak and questioning.

"It's not. I'm sorry, Vi, he's gone." He reached for Ally and guided her down to the sofa next to me.

I looked over at Ally and stared into her eyes for a while examining the threads of gold against the blue of her iris'. Cullen came back with three water bottles and a peach. He handed me the peach but I didn't take it. I took the water with shaking hands, fumbling the cap, unable to grip the cap hard enough to open it. My muscles were weak as the shot of adrenaline left my body. Cullen took the bottle from me and removed the cap. His phone rang, making Ally and I jump. He stood quickly and took the call, turning his back to us.

"Yeah, I'm with the family, they've been notified." There was a pause and then, "Got it, thank you." He turned to us and we sat in silence waiting for him to say something. There was a ringing in my ears from the silence or from the panic attack, I didn't know which.

"What do we do next?" Ally's voice was soft and monotone.

"His body will be here tomorrow morning. I don't think you'll be able to see him," Cullen cleared his throat and looked away for a second, "I don't think it's a good idea to see him. I'll take care of whatever you need. His funeral is already arranged, he had specific instructions in place, he has a plot next to your parents. He'll have a military burial with honors. I'm here for whatever you need." Cullen rubbed the back of his neck and sat back atop the table.

"How did it happen? Where?" I looked up at Cullen and he froze in his spot.

"I don't know if they'll release all the information but from what I know, his unit was hit with an IED and James was...He wasn't in pain, he didn't suffer. I can't say where he was, that's classified, they didn't tell me. Did he tell you where he was going?" Cullen's green eyes searched mine.

"He didn't tell me where he was," I turned to Ally, "Did he tell you?"

"No, I talked to him three days ago, he sounded…" Ally's voice trailed off as she looked off in reflection, "tired."

"Do you know who was with him? Chapman maybe? Kurtis, Hoppy? Maybe Sol or Pete?" I started pulling names at rapid fire. Names of men I've heard James and Cullen talk about, some I'd met over the years.

"No, not any of them. I've talked to most of them today." Cullen shook his head, "What can I do for you two? Ally, did you call Nate? Violet?" He looked to us hopeful that we had something for him to do.

"Nate's on his way, he got a ferry reservation and should be here in a few hours." She picked a torn tissue in her hand. She looked at me, "Do you want to call Sam?"

"I don't," I replied to her question without thinking and the response startled me. "I mean, I should. I will soon." I needed time to process all that was happening around me.

"I can call any family you want, let me know who. James sometimes talked about an uncle." Cullen looked at us and took a drink of water.

Ally and I stared at each other and I knew we were silently thinking the same thing, *it's just us*.

I sit up from the sofa in the small bungalow and realize I drifted off for a little while. The wine, exhausting drive and foul weather was the perfect combination for an afternoon nap. The clock reads five and I'm relieved to know I was only asleep for less than an hour. I get up and head to the kitchen to cook dinner. As I cook, I try to think about all the beautiful places I explored in the past few days rather than the fact that I have to call Cullen tomorrow. Because every time I talk to Cullen I see his face staring at me through the screen door of my parents house, waiting to tell me the one thing I feared most in this world: losing another person I loved with all my soul.

Chapter 8
Violet

Last night the rain tapered off to a light drizzle by late evening. I woke early this morning, I made a large pot of coffee and dressed in jeans and a sweatshirt. I went out to the small porch on the front of the house, the clouds were not as thick as yesterday, I saw the remaining morning stars playing peekaboo from behind the clouds as they passed over. I went inside to refresh my coffee and decided to take a walk to the beach, hoping to catch a sunrise if the clouds continued to dissipate.

As I walk to the beach at 5:15 AM the air is chilly, the sand is damp from the previous day's rain. Slipping off my shoes, I let the wet sand stick to my feet as I walk near the shore line. I find a spot and sit in the sand, watching the dark ocean waves crash to the shore. The sound of the ocean is soothing, similar to the flames of a fire. The clouds are clearing, giving way to a lightening sky. My body is less sore today, I'm thankful to have slept in a bed last night. My thoughts keep wandering to James, I had vivid images from his funeral in my sleep last night. The impending call to Cullen is igniting many of these memories for me. Maybe following through with the call and putting it behind me will subdue the memories. I'm not afraid of Cullen, he's actually a dear friend. Someone James trusted and thought of as family, as a brother. But Cullen is a trigger for me, a trigger that sparks the grief inside me at times. He's also someone who brings me immense comfort.

Grieving is a lifelong process, some people think you work through your grief and leave it behind you. Grief doesn't leave you, it stays with you forever. You learn to grow around it but it's always there. And because it is always there, certain sights, smells, people and sounds bring the grief bubbling back to the surface. Triggers. Sometimes there are good triggers, evoking a happy memory. Sometimes the triggers are traumatic and filled with sorrow. Fear, anger, regret, and questions all ebb to the surface with triggers, you can also find resolve, love and purpose in grief.

Cullen stayed at my parents' house for the week leading up to James' funeral. Ally's fiancé, Nate, stayed too. Sam stayed one night, the night after we found out James had died. He said he felt "too crowded" and elected to stay at the condo. James never liked

Sam, I'm starting to wonder if anyone liked Sam. James didn't like Sam's drinking and knew the toll it took on our relationship and me. I'm sure he discussed as much with Cullen because Cullen was ice cold to Sam during any interaction the two had. Sam never wanted to go to the cabin for family weekends, we didn't spend holidays together either. Sam went back to be with his family and I spent the holidays with James, Ally and Cullen. Looking back now, I don't understand what Sam and I were doing. It was an unfulfilling relationship, even toxic at times, especially in the end. Were we afraid to be alone? Was I afraid of change? I had no idea. Maybe one day I would figure it out. I would need to figure it out to find some kind of closure but not today.

The first night Cullen stayed at the house, he cooked dinner and answered the door when people came with food and sympathies. The little extended family we had, a few aunts, uncles and cousins came over with food and stayed drinking coffee asking if we needed anything. I just wanted to be alone. After the last of the family left, I went upstairs to James' room. I sat on his bed holding his pillow, breathing in his scent. I cried into the pillow for a while before I heard the door open. Ally came into the room and sat next to me on the bed. We held each other for a while, never saying a word. Nate finally came to find where Ally had gone. They left the room together and went toward her childhood bedroom. I was happy Ally had someone she could rely on, someone to share her grief with.

I laid back on James' bed, exhaustion taking over. I was still in my work pants and blouse, still wearing my heels. I slipped off the heels and went to James' dresser. I undressed and pulled on a pair of his sweatpants and sweatshirt. Looking at the pictures on his bureau, I saw one of the three of us. Ally missing her front teeth, on the beach in front of a sandcastle we built. I didn't remember the day and I felt bad about it. There was a picture of our parents holding each other in an embrace while dancing, looking at the camera, they looked young and happy. There were more pictures, Ally's senior photo, a picture from my graduation day with Ally and James flanked at my sides. I went back to the bed and stared around the room. He'd never be back, he wouldn't return to this room. I bent my head down but no tears came, just a feeling of intense sorrow. Maybe I had no tears left, maybe I was dehydrated. I heard the door open for a third time, I didn't look up, as the person approached I could smell Cullen's musky scent. He sat on the bed next to me and put his arm around my back. I leaned into him and the tears came.

"Why? *Why* did this happen?" The anger inside me was rising and I felt Cullen tighten his hold. "Why does this *keep* happening?" I looked at him for the first time since he entered the room.

"I don't know, I can't answer that," he paused, letting his arm fall from my back and crossing both arms across his chest. "You've known me long enough to know I don't believe in much. I don't think there's someone up there pulling the strings. If there was, they have a lot to answer for," he took a deep breath and continued, "I know James didn't want to leave you. I know he was smart and skilled at his job. He was careful and focused. He went into every situation ready to handle his business so he could come home to you both."

We sat in silence for a long time, so many questions swirling in my mind. I broke the silence with another question, "I thought when a Marine died they sent uniforms to the family. You know, like in the movies? They come all dressed up and hand you a folder saying they're sorry for your loss and all that bullshit. Why didn't anyone come?" Cullen's back stiffened and his arms went slack to his sides, he rubbed the back of his neck.

"I was here to tell you." It was all he offered but his body language was different, he knew something. But what could he possibly know and not want to share?

"Cullen, what are you not telling me?" Anger, again, flashed in my voice. "I want to know why we didn't get a call or visit from the Navy?"

"Listen, Violet, calm down. We can talk about this tomorrow after some rest. You need to rest." He wasn't meeting my gaze and I couldn't sit next to him anymore.

I stood up and fixed my frame in front of him. "I don't want to rest, I want an answer."

He was quiet for a long time, it felt like hours. "Damn it," he grunted through his teeth and drew in a breath. "Sit down, Violet, you're making me nervous. I'll tell you but you have to understand James didn't want me to. I'm sure he had his reasons and a plan but he asked me not to let you girls know." Cullen started pacing the length of the room as I sat on the bed.

"Jesus, spit it out. If he didn't want us to know then he shouldn't have gotten himself killed!" The statement was harsh, I flinched from my own remark.

Cullen's green eyes studied mine. "James left the Navy over a year ago." The statement stunned me, I heard the high pitched buzzing in my ears again as the room started to spin. "He left after eight years like most of us did. He started working with a contract company. They do military contracts. He was always in and out, diplomat security, supply runs, the occasional extraction was as spicy as it got."

"Like a mercenary?" I was completely floored by the discovery. How could I have been so oblivious? Why didn't he tell me?

"Some people call it that but he called it contracting." Cullen sat at the foot of the bed as I moved up the bed to rest my spinning head on the pillows.

"Why?" I didn't know if he had the answer but he already knew so much more than me, I thought he could offer me something.

"I don't know, specifically. The money is decent, it's flexible, there's more free time. The food and the accommodations are way better," a low laugh escaped him, he was trying to lighten the mood. "He was good at what he did, Violet. James was one of the smartest soldiers I knew." Cullen went on, "After years of military life he thrived on it, the discipline, the ability to take care of you girls. He was the best at what he did, inside the M.C. and outside. I can't explain it all, James was complex in many ways. But I can tell you he tried to do right by you both and I know he never wanted to leave you."

"Well, he picked the wrong profession for that. He should have become an accountant," my tone was bitter.

I was angry he didn't tell me what was going on. I couldn't say for sure why he did what he did, it always puzzled me from the first day James said he was enlisting. I didn't know what else to say or ask. Cullen gave me a lot to process.

"You can stay in my room tonight or the master. I'm going to stay here," I said, my stare never left the ceiling in James' room.

"I'm fine on the couch. Can I get you anything before I head down?" he asked cautiously.

"No, thank you," I started to cry again although those tears were angry then. I clenched the comforter below me.

"I'm here if you need anything." He stood and turned toward the door but stopped in his tracks when I started talking.

"Because James asked you, right? Because he told you if something happened to him you should take care of his sisters? Some kind of brotherhood code? You don't have to do that, you know, we've done this before," my words sounded aggressive, the anger inside me was intense, the betrayal I felt was oppressing. Tears were rolling down my face and I felt a wave of nausea.

"Yeah, he asked me to watch over you girls if something happened. But I'm here because I want to be. He was my brother and I know that doesn't make me *your* brother. But he was my *brother*, Violet. Even if he didn't ask me to be here, I would be." He took a step closer and sat right next to me on the bed, "You've been through this before, it was hard on all of you. That doesn't make this easier, I know. But you will get through this. You're strong, you won't break. I won't let that happen, more importantly, *you* won't let that happen." He wiped the tears from my face and put his hand on my heaving stomach.

Through uncontrolled sobs I said, "I don't know if I can do this again."

I tried to breathe through the sobs like he had instructed me earlier. With a fluid glide Cullen was beside me in the bed, holding me tightly against his chest while I sobbed until exhaustion overtook me and I fell asleep.

When I woke the next morning, to the chiming of the doorbell, I was half expecting to find Cullen next to me on the bed. Instead it was empty, no indentations or clues another person was there. I was tucked under the covers and the lamp on the side table was turned off. I stumbled out of bed, my stomach muscles ached from sobbing the night before. When I went to the hallway I saw Ally emerging from her room, she heard the bell as well. Her eyes were red and puffy and I'm sure mine looked the same. We descended the staircase, close to the bottom we saw Cullen at the door shaking the hand of a tall dark-skinned man with full sleeve tattoos down his arms.

"C'mon in, can I get you some coffee?" Cullen stepped aside and glanced at us as we stood at the staircase landing. "Hey, morning." He smiled then looked at the man, "This is Theo, he worked with James, he came to see you. I've got coffee if you all want to come back to the kitchen."

Ally and I exchanged curious looks and followed the two men to the kitchen. Cullen poured out four cups of coffee and set sugar and cream on the middle of the table. We all took seats around the six person table. When the coffees were delivered, Cullen sat down across from me.

"Thanks," Theo's low baritone voice rumbled. "I'm sorry for your loss, Violet and Ally. James talked so much about you two." He connected on our gaze with sympathetic eyes.

"Were you with him?" I asked, noticing a fresh bandage taped to the inside of his forearm, my eyes fixed on it.

"Yes, ma'am, I was." He saw my look and took his arm off the table, placing it on his thigh, "I've worked with him for a year now. He was a great guy, super smart, and very professional."

I glanced at his tattoos running down his upper arms and forearms. I noticed the bottom half of a bone frog tattoo peeking out of his polo shirt sleeve.

"You're a seal?" I asked.

"Yes, ma'am. Well, not currently but that's where I started." Theo sat up a little straighter and his brown eyes glanced from me to Cullen to Ally.

"Can you tell us what happened to James? Where were you?" I noticed Cullen looked at Ally and I remembered she wasn't a part of the conversation the night before. She didn't know about James' most recent job venture.

Theo shifted in his seat, "There are some things I can't share. Currently, there's an investigation into the events but I'll tell you what I can."

Ally stood up and took her coffee from the table, "I'm going to go check on Nate."

Ally looked at me and I could read in her eyes, she didn't want to hear whatever Theo was about to say. Theo cleared his throat and looked at Cullen as if asking if he should proceed. Cullen nodded and took a drink from his mug.

"We were on a routine weapon drop, we've done the route before without issue. About ten clicks from our drop point coms went out." He watched my face carefully to see if I followed along, I nodded and he went on, "We stopped to try to figure out what happened with the coms. After a few minutes we came under fire. We tried to get outta there but they were everywhere. One of our guys was hit outside the vehicle and James moved in to offer medical treatment and they were hit with an IED. It was an ambush, they knew we were coming, we barely got out." Theo ran his palms over his thighs and I noticed one of his legs was frantically twitching under the table.

"Can you tell me where my brother died?" I looked at Theo, I could tell by his eyes that was one thing he couldn't share.

"I'm sorry but I can't. I wish I could do more." He took a drink of coffee then turned back to me, "You're Violet, right?"

"Yes." I didn't introduce myself, I guess he had a 50/50 chance of guessing correctly.

"James talked about you a lot. Said how fierce you were, he was very proud of you. He said you never backed away from a challenge." He smiled at me and went to take something from his back pocket.

"Really?" It was a whisper but I smiled, thankful to Theo for sharing.

"Absolutely, he talked about you and Ally so much, I feel like I know you girls." He put a small brown bag on the table in front of him. Ally and Nate emerged from the living room and sat at the table with us. "James gave me a few things a while ago. Sometimes we do this type of thing before we go away. Anyway, he gave me these and asked if something happened…" He held three white envelopes as his voice trailed off. He cleared his throat, "Well, I wish I didn't have to do this but here I am."

He shook out the remaining contents of the brown bag. The rattle of dog tags hit the table, along with a few wallet size photos. Ally let out a long sigh and Nate reached for her hand. Theo handed the three envelopes, one at a time, to me, Ally and Cullen.

Cullen took the envelope with uncertainty, "For me?" he asked.

"It says your name right there. He talked about you a lot, too, I thought you were his brother. I guess you are." The energy around the table was tense. All three of us stared at the envelopes with hesitant contemplation. "I have some other things in my truck, his pack, pistol, KA-BAR and a few other things. I can grab it before I go."

I traced my fingers over the letters of my name written on the front of the envelope. James' block handwriting was one I could pick out from anywhere. He wrote so many letters to us during his deployments, I had two shoe boxes full of letters from him.

“Can you stay for breakfast, Theo?” I didn’t know how to repay the appreciation I felt for him.

“That actually sounds great. I don’t want to intrude on family time.” He sat back in the chair assessing all the faces around the table.

“We’d be happy if you stayed. I don’t know what we have but I’m sure we can manage something.” Ally smiled reassuringly.

“I went to the store this morning, plenty of options. I’ll get started, you guys can go hang out.” Cullen stood up and headed to the fridge, when he opened the door, I saw a fully stocked fridge and my heart swelled with gratitude.

Theo, Ally and Nate filed out of the kitchen after refilling their coffee mugs. I remained seated at the table still clutching the envelope with sweaty hands. I placed the envelope in the kangaroo pocket of the sweatshirt I was wearing and stood to start more coffee. Cullen was pulling eggs, milk, bacon and orange juice from the refrigerator.

“Thanks for getting all this, let me know how much it was and I’ll get it to you.” I moved beside him at the counter helping him gather items from cabinets.

“You don’t owe me anything. I’m staying here until the funeral so I’ll be eating all of it anyway.” He started putting the mixing bowls and frying pans we gathered on the island. “You can go out there with them, I got this.”

“I can help.” I finished adding the ground coffee to the filter basket and pressed start on the machine. “What can I do?”

“You can crack these dozen eggs in that bowl while I start on this bacon.” We worked together in silence for a few minutes. “Did you talk to Sam yet? Surprised he’s not here,” his tone was cold while his eyes stayed on task.

“I’ll call him in a little while. He's on a route coming back from Jersey or Delaware, I’m not sure.” I didn’t want to explain anything to Cullen but I’m sure it was what everyone was thinking. “I’d rather be here with just Ally and you for now,” I whispered my confession and Cullen stopped mid turn of the bacon slices.

He looked me straight in the eye and hummed questionably, “Says a lot right there, doesn’t it?” He withdrew his gaze and went back to flipping the bacon.

The sunrise on Pottsville beach was breathtaking, I watched the sun ascend into the sky lighting up the clouds and ocean with vibrant colors. The shades of yellow, orange and blue in the sky were incredible to discover. The ocean came alive, changing from a harsh midnight blue to lighter shades of aqua and green. The waves, still crashing, looked less menacing in the light of the morning. I've seen many sunsets in my life, spending summers on Cape Cod with my family, I haven't seen many sunrises. I've been waking up so early since I started this trip, I might be able to make a habit of getting to the beach and watching the sunrise. As the sun continues to rise, I notice people coming to the beach, joggers, walkers, dog owners, all enjoying the early morning quiet. I stand and stretch, turning back to the way I came, knowing I need to call Cullen so I can put these memories back in the vault. Pull the trigger and be done with it.

When I return to the cottage, I wash out the thermos that held my early morning coffee and take my phone from the counter. I take a deep breath and tap his contact name on my phone.

Two rings and I hear his voice on the other end, "Hey, Violet."

"Hi, Cullen, how are you?" I'm sitting on the wicker chair, in the sitting area of the cottage, playing with the sleeve of my sweatshirt.

"I'm not going to complain. Are you good? How's Ally?" I hear a door close on his end and figure he is either entering or leaving his cabin.

"Yeah, we're good. I wanted to let you know, we're planning to come up next month. Ally and Nate are going to stay a few days and I'm thinking of staying a week, depending on work." I find myself relaxing as the conversation starts to flow.

"Hell yeah, that's great. I'll open it up and get it ready for you. Text me the dates so I don't forget. Everything else good? Is work keeping you busy?" I hear songbirds in the background on his end and know he's probably outside on his cabin's porch.

"I'm taking a trip right now, I have some time off." I don't want to get into too many specifics right now, just keep it surface.

"Oh yeah, where are you? Hope it's somewhere warm, it's been freezing over here. As soon as I think everything's going to thaw we get another round of snow," he explains and I can hear the frustration in his voice.

"I'm in Australia, it's beautiful, sunny and warm. I spent the last few days hiking in a rainforest. This morning I watched the sunrise on the beach, it was beautiful." There's excitement in my voice and it surprises me.

"Wow, Australia. Who are you with?" He waits for my response and I debate how much I want to tell him.

"I came alone, having some me-time. I left Sam last week." There's a long pause and I wait for a response.

There's a low hum from Cullen on the other end. "Well, it's about fucking time," his congratulatory tone makes me smile. There's another brief pause. "I hope you take the time you need, enjoy yourself. You deserve it."

I can't help but laugh at his honesty, it's probably what James would've said if he were here. "I will, I'm here for two more weeks maybe."

"You're alone?" His question seems to come as an afterthought, as if he's thinking out loud.

"Just me." I know where he's about to go, the same place Ally went. He's going to ask for my plan, if I have proper supplies and so on.

"Jesus, there's nothing like you, Violet. Are you checking in with anyone regularly? Christ, you better be careful. Are you camping alone? Not a great idea." I can practically hear the wheels in his head turning from thousands of miles away.

"I'm fine. I sent Ally all the information about where I'll be and when. I'm being careful, I don't stay in one place too long," I try to use my most reassuring tone.

"Damn, Violet. I'm serious." Now he's worked up and I feel bad. I hear him pacing his porch.

"I'm fine, now stop it. I'll send you those dates," my voice is calm and I hear him take a breath.

"Check in with me every few days, I don't want to be calling Ally all the time. Be careful," his words are a command but more composed.

"I will. I'll see you next month. Good night, Cullen." I get ready to disconnect then I hear him call out.

"Hey, Vi?" He waits until I acknowledge him with a hum, "I'm glad you left him, do me a favor?"

"I guess I owe you a favor," my tone is light but I'm very serious, I owe Cullen more than a favor. He's been there for me at a time I didn't know I would make it back from.

"If you think about going back to him, call me." He sounds serious and then adds, "I'll tie you to a fucking tree on this mountain and leave you there for a week." He laughs and hangs up the phone.

I'm smiling when I hang up, I send Cullen a text with the dates and go to the bedroom to dress for the day. The sun is shining now and there are very few reminders of the storm that went through the area yesterday. I put on navy linen shorts, adding a simple white cotton v neck top. Slipping on flip flops and a generous amount of sunscreen I head to the car to go back into town for the items I wasn't able to get the day before.

After returning from the shopping area, I packed a small bag for the beach. I spent the rest of the day on the beach reading *The Awakening,* taking breaks to swim in the water and eat fruit. I've read the story about Edna many times but reading it on the beach at this point in my life is emotional and thought-provoking. Is it a coincidence I picked this book from the shelf along with Thoreau's book to keep me company on the beach and in the forest on this trip? I don't think it is. I stop myself from finishing the book in one day because I want to read something later in my trip.

When I get back to the cottage I undress and get ready to take a shower. As I peel off my clothes and bathing suit I notice I've got *a lot* of sun. When I take the bikini bottoms off it feels like sandpaper scratching down my legs. I can't believe I didn't feel this burn happening today. I hate sunburns and I'm usually good about constantly applying sunscreen. I must've underestimated the power of the sun here or got distracted reading. When I step into the shower the hot water hurts my skin so I turn the temperature down to just above cool. After the shower I apply an obscene amount of lotion and resolve that I can't spend the day at the beach tomorrow. I'll head into town to look around or do some work on my laptop.

After I make dinner I planned on checking in with Ally with a phone call but between the sunburn, day at the beach and a full belly I just want to relax in bed. I sent her a text letting her know I'll call her tomorrow.

I take a bottle of water with me to the back bedroom with my laptop and watch old episodes of *The Office* until I fall asleep.

When I wake up the next morning I inspect my sunburn and I'm pleased to see it has subsided. I'm still red but not the color of a glowing heat lamp like I was last night. After I brush my teeth and apply more lotion I go to the kitchen and make a cup of tea.

After my tea I grab my purse and car keys. The drive is short, going back over the causeway was a different experience when the rain wasn't pelting down. I arrive in the small downtown area and park my car. After walking around for a while, taking in the shops, I found a small bistro with a sign advertising brunch in the window.

When I walk in I see some open tables in the main dining area, a small bar to the right and in the back there's another dining room. Walking toward the back, I see it's decorated for what looks like a baby shower. There are powder blue balloons, beautiful bouquets of blue and white flowers sit on the tables. About 20 women dressed in sundresses and rompers stand around in small groups talking with each other. This must be a private party, I sit at a table in the back of the main dining area. I can still see through to the private party and notice a woman dressed in a pale blue maxi dress with a steep v split in the back, when she turns I see she's all belly. She looks beautiful and so happy. If she hadn't turned around I would never have guessed she was pregnant. Definitely a boy. My mother would say if a woman is carrying a boy she becomes all belly and you won't know she was pregnant from behind. But when you carry a girl your entire body changes, it was probably an old wives' tale.

After I order from the brunch menu, I drink a cup of tea while I wait for my poached eggs and sauteed vegetables. I continue watching the ladies in the other room. I never thought about having kids because I never wanted a child when I was with Sam. I would never have thought of bringing a child into that relationship. I was so careful not to get pregnant while I was with him. As I approach 30, seeing many of my friends settle into marriages and start trying for kids, it has got me thinking if one day I want to be a mom. My food comes, the mushrooms and tomatoes look delicious, the poached eggs sit on a thick piece of fresh baked bread.

I order one more cup of tea after I finish eating and head to the bathroom before it arrives. The door knob to the bathroom turns but when I pull nothing happens. I pull again but nothing so I give two quick knocks and take a step back.

I hear a faint, cheerful voice call out from inside the restroom, "Be right out."

I take a few more steps back, lean against the far wall and wait. I hear the knob turn and a soft thwacking sound from the other side.

I hope whoever's in there is alright. I take one tentative step toward the door and wait.

"Hello? I can't open the bloody door, anyone there?" I hear the voice again as I see the knob turning but nothing is happening.

"I'm here. Is there a lock inside there?" I ask with my face close to the door frame.

"There's an eye hook but it's not latched. Can you pull while I push, please?" Her voice isn't panicked but anxious.

"Sure, I'll start pulling." I start to pull on the door trying to shake the knob as I do so. I hear more whacking sounds and then the door flies open sending me back until I fall, hard on my butt, on the tile floor.

"Oh my! Are you alright, love? I'm so sorry." A woman in a white pants and a blue blouse bends down beside me on the floor.

"No, don't sit down here. You'll get your pants dirty." I get up quickly from the floor. "I'm fine, I'm not hurt," I look over at her and hear her laugh, it's a wonderful sound.

"Don't be silly, they're just pants! Are you sure you're okay?" She places her hands on my shoulders and inspects my body. Her auburn hair falls down over her chest in loose curls, her eyes are catlike. Her eyes are emerald green with a circle of what looks like amber around the pupil, stunning. She's tall and thin, wearing tall heels. She's absolutely beautiful.

"I'm fine, really." She's still holding my shoulders. I gently step out of her hold.

"I'll talk to the manager about that door, it's lethal. I'm so sorry I knocked you over, please, let me get you a drink." She has genuine concern on her face.

"That's not necessary, I just finished my meal and was on my way out." I rub my hands on the back of my shorts, they feel sticky from the restaurant floor.

"I'm going to talk to someone about that right now." She looks down the hallway hoping to find a staff member, "I'm Mia by the way." She holds out her hand to me.

"I'd shake your hand but it's sticky from the floor. I'm Violet." I give her a wave instead of a shake.

"Pleasure to meet you, Violet. I've got to get back to the party. But I'd love to do something for your help." She looks toward the hallway again and I see she's conflicted.

"Go back to the party. I was happy to help. If I see you again sometime I'll let you buy me a drink. Have a good day, Mia." I watch her walk back down the hall and decide not to enter the bathroom.

Instead I pay my bill and walk around more of the downtown area before I head back to the cottage to pack for my trip to Byron Bay.

Chapter 9
Drew

I woke early Monday morning before the sun was up, unable to fall back asleep. I got up from bed and went to the kitchen to make coffee. I sit in the dark kitchen willing the coffee to drip faster into the carafe. Davy and I went surfing yesterday and spent the afternoon finalizing plans for the bachelor party on Thursday. There were going to be six of us, Davy, four of his friends and myself. Tomas and Sean have been friends with Davy since university and they were flying in early Thursday morning. I arranged a car to pick them up from the airport and drive them to Davy's house. Brian and Ethan were local to Byron, they surfed and ran with Davy. They would meet us at Davy's house in the morning so we could start the festivities. I was in charge of the barbecue, Brian and Ethan were getting the drinks and the rest would fall into place. Davy was looking forward to the day.

I hadn't had time alone with Mia since the conversation in the kitchen last Wednesday night at dinner. She was off working an event in Pottsville yesterday, the time I spent at the house with Davy was just the two of us. I've been trying to disregard the conversation with Mia, chalking it up to wedding anxiety. When I tip-toed around questions about Mia to Davy, he didn't let on to anything that might be bothering her. He was happy and hopeful about the wedding on Saturday. I dropped it, if something was tugging at him, he would have brought it to my attention while we were alone yesterday.

I pour a cup of hot coffee and sit at the kitchen island. I debate opening my laptop and start working on a project but there's nothing to do. Today is the first day of my week off from work. I haven't taken any time off since I left Sydney over a year ago. I didn't know what to do with all the free time I would have this week.

I finish my coffee and go back to the bedroom to dress for the gym. I might as well be productive with my day off, even if it's not with work. As I drive to the gym I watch the sun rise. I spend over an hour in the gym doing various shoulder and chest exercises.

While exercising, I think I want to finalize a plan to put vegetables somewhere in the back of the property. I don't know much about growing food but I'm sure I could find something useful on Google. After I'm done working out and stretching, I hop up from the mats and head back to my SUV. I'm feeling very accomplished at 7:30 on a Monday morning. A hopeful feeling comes over me, today appears like it's going to be a good day.

When I get home I go to the patio and look around the back garden. Most of the garden gets full sun during the day, the shadow of the house shelters a third of the yard in the morning hours. I pace out a three by one meter rectangle and eye the plot. This might be a good place to start. I head back inside to research the best material for a raised bed and see what my next steps should be.

I got sucked into researching garden beds, looking down at my notebook, I outlined three pages worth of notes. I grunt, remembering I'm trying to keep it simple. I'll start with one garden bed and see how I do before I convert my entire garden into a self-sustainable plot. Just then my mobile rings, it's Davy.

"Hey, Davy, what's up?" I close the laptop, sliding it to the end of the island and rub my eyes that are burning from staring at the blue light of the computer screen for so long. I check the time above the stove, it's after noon. "Shit," I mumble into the phone, talking to myself and not Davy.

"Not happy to hear from your little brother?" He laughs over the receiver and I stand up from the island and stretch my back.

"No, I got sucked into the computer and didn't realize the time." I go to the sink and fill a glass with cold water and gulp it down. The cold water hits my empty stomach, it rumbles with hunger.

"I thought you were off this week?" he asks curiously, not waiting for a response before adding, "Are you coming to dinner tonight? Six o'clock, wear something presentable," he laughs again, deviously. I'm instantly confused by his request. Did I forget I made plans with Davy and Mia tonight?

"We're having dinner tonight?" I draw out the question half asking, half stating, to see if saying it aloud will bring any recollection of the night's plans. I spent yesterday with Davy and he never mentioned dinner tonight.

"We are now!" Davy responds in a fit of laughter and I grow concerned for his state. Davy's usually playful but this exchange has got my head revolving like a hamster wheel.

"What the hell are you going on about?" I rub my eyes again, not interested in whatever Davy is playing at.

"Come to dinner at six o'clock," he says slowly before adding, "Don't be late."

"Davy, what's going on?" We've done impromptu dinners before but his cheeriness has me thinking there's something more.

"Jeez, mate. I'm trying to invite you to dinner and by *invite* I mean command you to come over tonight at six o'clock. Got it?" Some of the playfulness has left his tone but a sprinkle of it remains.

"Fine, see you at six." I disconnect without a goodbye. What the hell has gotten into him? I shake the conversation away and pin it up to one of Davy's annoyingly positive, manic episodes.

I look over the scribbled notes about the garden bed idea while I make a quick sandwich. After inhaling the food, I grab my keys. I head to the hardware store to get wooden planks to start constructing the raised bed.

When I arrive in the lumbar section of the hardware store I get the wood that will be suitable for my project. There's only one register open, four people are in the queue in front of me, I feel my mobile vibrate in my pocket. I check the screen, it's Davy again.

"Hey, what's up?" There's a slight hint of annoyance in my voice. This makes two calls in two hours and if Davy starts in with mysterious tones I might lose it.

"I was talking with Mia, going over the list for the wedding. Are you still planning on coming solo or have you found a date?" I roll my eyes at his question, he knows I planned on attending alone. If I had found a date he would've been the first to hear about it.

"It's just me. Is that all, mate? I'm in the queue at the store," I'm short and frustrated with him now. I was having such a peaceful day, now I'm irritated and cranky.

"Oh, well, it's okay. You still have time to find someone. Might be fun to have a date for the night. See you tonight, six o'clock," he disconnects with a nefarious laugh. I cannot believe this guy.

As I put my mobile back in my pocket the cashier calls me to the register. I check out, load the lumber in the back of my SUV and take off for home. Maybe saw work and hammering will displace some of the frustration I feel. I pull around the side of the house, driving on the grass, to the rear patio to unload. After I unload the material, I go to the garage to get the tools. After an hour

I have a new garden bed made. With the frame connected and resting on the spot I chose, I feel excited. Soon I will be able to fill it with garden soil and start planting vegetables. I assess my handiwork for a few minutes and gather all the tools to return them to the garage.

Standing in front of the sink, drinking the glass of water, I check the time, 5;17. There's no way I'll be at Davy and Mia's for six knowing I still need to shower, dress and possibly stop off for a bottle of wine or flowers. I empty the glass of water in the sink and head back to the bathroom for a shower. I strip off my clothes, noticing the smell of sawdust on my shirt and toss the clothes in a basket of laundry outside the closet door. The hot water feels good on my sore muscles.

I dress quickly in the bedroom after my shower, pulling on a pair of faded jeans and a fitted black cotton shirt with a v cut at the neck. I towel off the dampness in my hair as I head to the bathroom to put on cologne and add styling cream to my hair. Standing in front of the mirror I glance down at my mobile on the counter next to the sink, I wake the screen which reads 5:48. I send Davy a text, which I should have done as soon as I realized I would be late.

Me: Running late be there at 6:30. Need me to pick up anything?

The chime dings as soon as my text is sent.

Davy: Running late!? Not like you. Get here ASAP.

I redirect myself to the mirror, my short hair is almost dry. I spray on a puff of cologne and head to the closet to put on shoes. I put on a pair of all black trainers and lace them up. I think about grabbing a blazer to top the shirt but decide against it, it's a warm night and I don't think I'd wear it.

Along the drive, I consider disobeying Davy and stopping off for a bottle of wine but checking the time, I see I only have minutes to spare so I drive straight to the house. When I pull in the driveway, the bungalow is lit up and the side patio has the outdoor globe string lights on. We must be eating outside tonight, I should have brought the blazer. I don't see anyone on the side patio so I head to the front door. Before I reach the top step the front door swings open, revealing Davy with a wide grin. I'm glad he doesn't seem annoyed I'm late, in fact it's the opposite, he looks as if I'm the one person he wants to see right now.

Davy eyes me up and down, “Couldn’t bother with a coat, mate?”

“What the fuck, Davy? What's gotten into you today?” I push through the door, the annoyed feeling from earlier returns.

“Kept us waiting long enough,” he is still grinning and steals a devilish glance at me.

I walk into the kitchen but don’t see Mia in sight, I hear low playing music over the surround sound. A freshly prepared salad sits on the counter next to a tray of brightly colored vegetables ready to be roasted. Davy grabs the bottle of wine sitting on the island along with four wine glasses. Four? Why four? Then the realization of the situation takes hold.

“Four glasses, Davy? Tell me you’re not up to your tricks again?” I ask and remember a few months ago Davy invited me to dinner when Mia’s university friend was visiting.

He tried to set us up but the vibe wasn't there. She wasn’t my type and I didn’t seem to be hers. Although Mia understood the energy wasn’t there Davy kept pushing and pushing. It was an incredibly awkward night, even Mia’s friend could pick up on the tension. I made it an early night, leaving shortly after dinner, saying I had to let my dog out. It was a complete lie, I had no dog waiting to be let out at home. Mia called the next day to apologize and reassured me she didn’t know I was coming to dinner. She would never send me blind into a situation like that.

“You’ll thank me later,” he hands the four glasses out for me to take but I don’t. He follows up with, “If you don’t have a good time you can go home and let your dog out.”

He smiles as if he was reading my mind about the event a few months prior. Instead of taking the glasses, I take a step toward the door.

“Why didn’t you just come out with it earlier? Does Mia even know I’m here?”

Davy stands between the door and me, still holding the bottle of wine in one hand and somehow holding four wine glasses by the stem with the other.

“I promise you, this is going to make your day, brother. If I’m wrong you can write me off. I’m willing to stake our brotherhood on this,” as he finishes his promise, he looks over my shoulder and I hear Mia enter the room.

"Hey, I didn't know you were stopping by. Nice timing though, we're getting ready for dinner," Mia's voice is pleasant and cheerful as usual.

I turn to her and see two figures walking into the kitchen. Mia dressed in a long flowing skirt with a white top. Then I see her, the beautiful blonde, holding an empty glass with a lemon wedge at the bottom. She's wearing a knee length navy sundress with tiny white daisy flowers. Her hair is down, long with loose curls throughout, I think I'm dreaming. It can't be her, she can't be here in my brother's house. She looks even more gorgeous than I remember. My pulse quickens and my stomach rolls over with excitement.

My voice is an elevated whisper, "Violet?" I say her name in a question. I feel an expression of shock registering on my face.

She smiles in a staggeringly alluring way and responds, "Hi, Drew." She lifts a hand in a tentative greeting.

I don't notice Davy's huge Cheshire cat grin as he steals a glance from Mia who looks as if she's the odd man out of this scenario. It's not a dream I'm actually here in this house with the woman I tried to put out from my mind, Violet Kelly.

Chapter 10
Violet

I left Pottsville early this morning, I drove the half hour to Byron Bay. When I pulled into the studio cottage I was renting, I unpacked and looked at the accommodations. It is more open than the previous bungalow where I stayed in Pottsville. This is a true studio, with a sitting room opening to a sleeping area. The kitchen was separated by a breakfast bar much like the previous place. There's a small front yard with privacy fencing around the sides and back of the property. The backyard has a stone patio with a round table fitting four metal chairs. Above the patio there's a wooden arbor, laced with native ivy, small patio twinkle lights wrap within the ivy.

After I finished unloading all my things, I changed into a bathing suit. I put on a long maxi dress as a covering. My sunburn had subsided but I still didn't want to be too exposed to the elements. The walk to the beach was three minutes.

The beach is stunning, the sand is bright, almost white. There were many people on the beach already but it wasn't crowded. The tide appears to be going out, there's a small strip of wet sand becoming more and more exposed. I walk along the shore line for a while, looking out over the ocean. I find a spot on soft, dry sand further up from the shoreline and I sit down. The sun is warm, there's a light breeze coming off the ocean. I reapply sunscreen to my arms, back of my neck and face.

I look around the beach watching families play in the sand. There's a group of young men playing a game of frisbee, down the beach I see a woman walking alone. She's holding sandals and watches the ocean much like I had done on the way here. As she approaches I notice her thin frame and long red hair blowing in the breeze. She's about 50 yards away when I realize who she is. Mia, the woman I encountered yesterday at the bistro in Pottsville. The beautiful woman with the incredible eyes. I thought for a moment about whether I should approach her or not. She's thirty yards away when I know, for sure, it's her. She was so friendly to me and seemed so sincere when I met her yesterday. I tentatively got up and started walking toward the shore, she would approach soon. I watch as she walks closer. Her head is down, she's watching her feet hit the sand as she walks, she looks thoughtful, distracted. Maybe I shouldn't bother her. As I'm about to turn back toward my towel she looks up. Her stare meets mine and after a few more steps I see her face wash over with recognition. The sadness leaves her face and she breaks out in a beautiful smile. She brings her hand to her forehead, blocking the sun shining in her eyes.

"Violet?" She approaches me, stopping a few feet from me.

"Hi, Mia. I thought it was you, I saw you walking back there and I thought I'd say hello." I smooth the front of my dress with my palms.

"Wow, isn't this something? I'm so glad to see you again," she sounds genuine, I laugh at her remark. She didn't know me, why is she so happy to see me again?

"Nice to see you, too. Are you visiting?" I'm trying to put together her connection to Pottsville and Byron Bay, she could be traveling like me.

She gives a melodic laugh as she responds, "I live here, just up there." She points behind me toward the treeline separating the homes from the beach. It looks like she's pointing to the path I took to get here.

"Isn't that something?" I repeat her phrase. "I came here this morning, I'm renting a little studio back there."

She tilts her head to the side, "The little blue one with the white trim?"

"That's the one," I return her smile, "Do you want to come sit? Maybe I can ask you about sights and what to do while I'm here." I gesture toward the large beach towel I have spread on the sand above us.

"Yes, I'd like that," Mia follows me and we take a seat on the towel looking out at the ocean. "Where are you coming from? I know you were in Pottsville. You're from the states, right? When did you get here?"

I quickly run through all the places I've been in the last week, since arriving in Brisbane, she nods enthusiastically and compliments at the right times with ohs and ahs. Mia's easy to talk to and I find myself relaxing in her company. Her smile never fades, the sad girl I saw walking the beach earlier is gone. Her smile and laugh are contagious, I find myself smiling with her throughout the conversation.

"So, that brings me here for the next four days. I want to take some day trips, hiking and sightseeing. I'd like to check out Whian Whian National Forest during or after my stay here. Then maybe go further south and explore more of the coast. I'm kind of winging it." I give a self-conscious laugh as I shrug my shoulders.

"Bravo! That all sounds so wonderful. How long have you been planning this trip? Coming from so far away all by yourself, that's amazing." Her eyes dance with delight.

I laugh at her question then answer, "This was completely impromptu. I got on a plane in Boston last week with no reservations or accommodations, I arrived in Brisbane with absolutely no plan whatsoever." I glimpse at her, her mouth is agape and her expression is inquisitive.

"Wow," she whispers the word, "You've done all of that in a week with no plan? That's amazing, Violet." She stares at me, curiosity written all over her face. "I like you, I *really* like you," she laughs, I really like her, too.

I change the subject and ask her questions about herself not wanting to get into the reasons why I'm half a world away from my home. She tells me she's an event planner and was in Pottsville yesterday working at the baby shower. She also told me she's getting married this weekend to her childhood sweetheart. The way she talks about him, the way her face lights up when she says his name, makes me happy for her. We talk about places to explore here in town, she tells me about her favorite restaurants and pubs. The conversation is flowing smoothly, it's like we've known each other for years. Her vivacious personality and energy is infectious. Our conversation is interrupted when Mia's phone rings.

"Oh, this is Davy, I'll just be a moment," she says.

"I'm going to walk by the water, take your time." I stand up from the towel to give her privacy. As I walk away I hear her singsong voice answer the call.

I put my feet in the water and tie my dress up to my hip so it doesn't get wet. After a few minutes of talking on the phone Mia stands and comes down to the water.

"He was checking in, I didn't realize how long we were chatting. I told him I was taking a quick walk on the beach. He got worried." She turns the phone in her hands.

“If you have to get back I understand, now that we’re neighbors I’ll probably see you again over the next few days,” I smile at the thought of meeting my first friend here in Australia.

“I’m in no rush to get home. I’m off this week and I’m enjoying this beach day.” She lifts the hair off the back of her neck. “I’m getting a little hungry.”

“Do you want to come over and see my rental? I could make some tea. I don’t have much but I have some fruit and cheese.” I thought it would be a nice gesture since I stole her away on her day off from her soon-to-be husband.

“That sounds lovely,” her smile grows wide. I'm pleased with the idea as well.

I gather my bag and towel, Mia and I walk toward the path where I entered the beach this morning. On the walk to my rental Mia points to a white ranch hidden behind tropical trees and bushes.

“That’s our place there,” Mia says when we pass her house. After walking past four more houses we arrive at the studio cottage.

“Here we are. See that? We’re practically next door neighbors.” I walk up the stone path to the front door. As I enter the studio I toss my bag on the bench at the entrance.

“Very nice. A few years ago, they gutted this place to the studs. It’s nice to see what they’ve done with it.” She walks around the studio taking in all the furnishings and stops to look out the huge floor to ceiling windows, “Beautiful.”

“I have water and tea, I meant to get to the store today.” I pull fruit out of the fridge and search the drawers for a paring knife of some kind.

I get two blocks of cheese and half a wheel of brie. I have a small loaf of baked bread I bought yesterday. If I put it in the toaster it could accompany the brie. Mia sits across from me at the breakfast bar.

“You know, I have some sliced meats that would go nicely with that. Do you mind if I call Davy and have him bring it over?” She pulls out her phone from her skirt pocket and dials.

“That sounds nice,” I can’t wait to put a face with a name.

When she’s done with the call she walks to my side at the counter, with a bread knife, and starts slicing the loaf.

“What do you do for work?” she asks as she slices bread.

I tell her about the real estate company I have back home, I tell her about some of the house flips I’ve done recently. We talked about real estate for a while and what it's like running a small business, we have that in common. Then she asks me what it's like living in New England with all seasonal changes. Mia has only been to the states twice for conferences with Davy, both times were to California. She's curious about the fall and winter in the northeast. We have everything plated and start picking at the fruit when we hear the doorbell chime. Both heading toward the door, I place the tray of fruit, cheese and bread on the table as Mia opens the door.

"Hi, love. Thank you for bringing this over." She takes a paper bag from him and leans in to kiss him on the cheek.

"Of course," Davy says stepping through the doorway and I meet them in the entry.

Davy is tall and lean, his eyes are hazel-green. His hair is light brown and he's wearing a loud, colorful shirt with cream colored linen pants. If I saw him on the street I would think he was a tourist. The shirt seems perfect for him, Mia described him as a spirited, carefree guy who loves to have fun. His eyes make me feel I know him from somewhere but I can't place him.

"Hello, I'm Davy. The love of Mia's life," he holds out his hand offering a greeting.

I laugh at the introduction, "I'm Violet, your new American tourist neighbor. Well, for a few days anyway." I take his hand.

"Violet you say? What a pretty name, American?" His head tilts as if he's trying to place me, I nod at him. His face is curious and his smile brightens.

"Mind if Davy joins us for a bit? I don't want to make him exclusively my errand boy," she says with a laugh, reaching around his waist as he takes her to his side wrapping an arm around her shoulder.

"Not at all, come in. Do you want to sit here or out on the back patio?" I turn toward the sitting area looking at the tray of food I placed on the table.

"Here's fine," Mia glides to one of the sitting chairs and removes the sliced meat from the bag, placing it on the tray.

When I turn to let Davy pass, I notice he's still searching my face and smiling. It's not threatening but it gives me pause.

"You look so familiar. I haven't met many people here but I feel like I've seen you before," I say, trying to place those eyes.

"I might have one of those faces," he shrugs as his grin widens.

"I'll make some tea." I head toward the kitchen to start the electric kettle.

"So, Violet. What brings you to Australia?" Davy calls after me while I walk to the kitchen.

"Umm, well…" I try to find the right way to word the response to his question as I fumble with the kettle, "I've thought about coming for a while. Things were slow at work so I thought it might be a good time to take a break and finally get away. I haven't taken a vacation in so long. Go big or go home, right?" I manage a halfhearted laugh and drop tea bags in the mugs I placed on the bar.

"No better time than the present." Davy takes Mia's hand and lands a gentle kiss in her palm as they settle on the sofa.

I hand out the mugs of tea and place mine on the table. "Mia says you both have a big day coming up, congratulations."

"Yes, we're very excited. So, tell me how you two met? On the beach this morning?" Davy sits back in the chair, taking a sip of his tea.

"Remember I was telling you about the baby shower yesterday? I knocked a girl down in the hallway of the restaurant, that was Violet! Then we saw each other on the beach this morning and spent the entire time talking. What a small world." Mia's eyes are full of excitement and I smile at her.

"Extraordinary," Davy's response is an exhale.

"Oh! That reminds me, Violet, I owe you a favor! Please let us host you for dinner tonight. Davy, you can grill while Violet and I drink wine and chat," she laughs and claps her hands.

I can't have her invite me to their home in front of her boyfriend and not give him a choice in the matter. So, I offer an out to be polite, "No, I can't intrude on you guys. I appreciate the offer, maybe another time."

"Another time? Don't be silly, you're only here for a few days," she looks at me then to Davy.

"Violet, please join us for dinner. We'd *love* to have you." Davy sits forward, reaching for some fruit, I feel his request is genuine.

"If you're sure," I say, as Mia gives a hop of excitement in her chair.

"Violet, when did you arrive?" Davy asks as he spreads cheese on a piece of bread and covers it with a slice of salami.

“Last Sunday, I landed in Brisbane and have been driving south for the past week.” I quickly skim over the places I’ve been as I told Mia previously. Davy seems to be hanging on every word.

“Sunday in Brisbane. What a trip! And you still have two weeks to go. Excellent!” He pauses for a moment and checks his watch, “Ladies, I’m sorry but I have to step out and make a call, I forgot to get back to a coworker about something. My apologies, I’ll be back in a jiff.” There’s a bounce in his step as he heads out to the back patio.

“He’s great, Mia. You two look good together,” I say and Mia smiles in agreement.

I ask Mia some details about the wedding and find out it is taking place here in Byron Bay and the reception will be held at a restaurant overlooking the beach. She wanted the ceremony to be small and intimate.

“My dad passed away three years ago. I’m sad I won’t have him here to walk me down the aisle,” her voice cracks, “I’m sorry, I don’t know why I said that. I’ve been thinking about him a lot these past few weeks.” She wipes her eyes and puts on a brave smile. A smile I know too well, it's a mask, her openness pulls at my heart and I know exactly how she feels.

When Ally told us she was getting married I felt awful my parents wouldn't be there to share her day. There wasn’t a question that James would walk her down the aisle in our father’s place. When James died a month before Ally and Nate were married my heart broke for her. If the day ever comes when I wed my heart will break again.

“I’m so sorry, Mia. I know how hard that is.” I twist a paper napkin around my fingers, “Special moments, holidays, especially a day as special as a wedding. I truly understand how you feel. I’m sorry for your loss.”

I look up to see her bright green eyes penetrating me. She waits as if I might say more, I stare back at her and offer her a small smile.

“Thank you,” her voice is soft, her eyes don’t leave mine. “I knew you were like me,” she whispers as if she didn’t mean for it to come out.

“Like you?” My heart quickens and I wonder why she thinks I’m like her.

"I don't mean offense, please, Violet. Don't take it like that," she hesitates and looks toward the back door. Davy still hasn't returned so she continues, "You have sadness in your eyes, I see loss all around you. But I also see strength and determination in the aura you have, it's powerful." She blushes when she finishes. "You think I'm crazy."

I don't doubt she sees the grief and loss in me, it's made me who I am, it's a part of me. Sometimes I feel like there's a neon sign above my head that lights up saying: *anguished soul.* I also think if she offers to read my palm or tarot cards I may have to find somewhere else to stay or leave this beautiful seaside completely.

"No, I don't think you are crazy," I want to comfort the worry on her face. "My parents died when I was sixteen. It was a very terrible time, something I still struggle with. I know how you feel, Mia."

Mia stands and sits next to me on the sofa, she wraps her arms around me. I stiffen in surprise at her affection but give way allowing the embrace.

"I'm sorry," she whispers in my ear.

"Thank you." I hear the patio door open. Davy comes to the living room and stops in his tracks when he sees the two of us in an embrace.

"Everything alright here?" He quickly shifts his gaze to Mia then me then back to Mia.

"Yes. All good, just thanking Violet for being such a good listener," Mia says in an uplifting voice. "How was your call?"

"All set, I was going to head back and finish up some things at home. Violet, I'll see you later. Does five thirty sound good? Do you have any allergies to shellfish?" He turns to me, raising his eyebrows.

"That sounds fine and anything you cook will be great. No food allergies here. Can I bring something?" I planned on going into town to the market, I should get something to contribute to the meal.

Davy waves a hand in dismissal, "Absolutely not. Bring yourself and an appetite."

"I'm going to head back, too. Leave you to take a rest before tonight." Mia embraces me once more, "Thank you, Violet. I'll see you in a few hours."

She clasps her hand in Davy's as they make their way out the door. I watch them walk down the stone pathway through the window, their bodies fused together, walking in perfect rhythm with one another. She rests her head on his shoulder and my heart melts for them. It's already 1 o'clock when I turn around and check the time. I went to the beach early and the morning went quickly. I decided to take a quick ride to town and get some food and wine. With the chance I might have visitors I want to make sure I have something to offer.

I got caught up walking around the town, taking in all the lovely markets and stores. By the time I get back to the house with the groceries it's close to four. I take a quick shower, not washing my hair. I chose a navy blue tea length dress with quarter sized white daisy-like flowers. The flowers remind me of the feverfew plants that grow wild by the cabin. James taught me about the plant and its amazing healing qualities. I found a large barrel curling iron in the back of the linen closet this morning. I try to add some curls to my hair to counter the flatness from being tied up most of the day. I put on a very light layer of makeup and add the final touch, some slingback sandals with braided brown leather straps.

Davy said not to bring anything but I can't go empty handed. I stopped by the bakery and got an assortment of treats and a bottle of wine. I sling a bag over my shoulder, grab the pastry box and bottle of wine and set out for Mia's house. The evening air is very comfortable and there's a breeze coming from the ocean. I smell the salt and sand of the beach only yards away. When I get to the path leading up to Mia's house I feel a ping of excitement in my stomach, maybe it's an indication that for the first time in a long time I'm happy. Whatever it is, it brings a smile to my face as I march up the walkway to the front door.

Mia answers the door in the same skirt she had on earlier but with a different white blouse. "Violet! Welcome," she opens the door to let me inside.

When I enter the atmosphere hits me and I instantly feel comfortable. The smell of fruit blooms cling in the air and the low lighting creates a sense of solace. The house has an open floor design with the kitchen to the right and dining room to the left of the entry. To the back, dropping two steps, is a living area. The back wall of the living room has two sets of large french doors leading to a large stone patio. The post and beam design makes the space seem larger than it truly is. There are two halls on either side of the living room. I assume they lead to bedrooms or other common areas.

"It's so beautiful, Mia. I love the layout, the beams are gorgeous," she takes the box and wine bottle from me while I admire the details of the home, "I never would have thought it was this spacious from the outside. Great job."

"Thank you, we've done a lot of work over the years. Our offices are down the hall to the left side. Two bedrooms, a bath are down to the right with a sitting room leading out to the side patio area. That's where I thought we would eat tonight, if you don't mind being outside." She moves to the fridge and takes out a pitcher of water with lemon slices and mint leaves floating on the top. "Water, wine or whiskey? We like our W's over here," she laughs, shrugging her shoulders.

"Water would be great." I take a seat on the stool next to the island. "Davy around?" I ask as I continue to look around the kitchen.

"He'll be along, he's setting up the patio," she starts to pour the water in a tall glass Davy comes from down the right side hallway.

"Violet! So glad you came," he comes from behind me, entering the kitchen and lands a peck on the side of my cheek as he passes. I blush from unexpectedness.

"Thank you for having me. This is beautiful," I lift my arms around me indicating the house is stunning.

"Coming from a realtor that means a lot. We worked hard to make it what it is now." He kisses Mia on the cheek and heads to the liquor cart under the window against the wall of the kitchen. He pours amber liquid from a crystal carafe into a short tumbler, "Should we head to the sitting room while we wait for the grill to warm?"

Mia hands me the glass of water and fills one for herself. She leads the way down the narrow hallway to the sitting room at the end of the hall. I take a seat in a floral chair with a view of the patio, the sun is setting and the patio lights look dim in the early evening glare. Mia and Davy take seats on the sofa, placing their glasses on the table in front of them. I sip from mine, then place it on the side table next to my chair.

"Mia told me you're here for a few days of sightseeing and hiking. You picked a great spot," Davy leans back placing an arm around Mia's shoulders, it looks so natural for him as if it's more comfortable to have her a part of him.

"That's the plan. Mia told me about places to see while I'm here. I want to venture inland and explore the forests later. This area seems like a good jump off point," I look around the room and see pictures of wildflowers and meadows.

"I thought I could take you to the sushi restaurant I told you about today on the beach. I've been wanting to go back since the last time we ate there. Do you want to go tomorrow evening?" Mia places a hand on Davy's knee and leans back against the sofa.

"Really? That sounds great, I love sushi." I think about it then I backpedal, "If you and Davy are busy with wedding stuff, please, don't let me disrupt your plans."

"It's no disruption," she says with reassurance.

"Well, honestly that sounds great. I'll probably stay close tomorrow and take a look at the places you told me about on the beach today. I'll take your number before I go." I'm happy to have an opportunity to get to know her more.

"Splendid. I hope you like mango and coconut. Davy's making the most delicious shrimp tonight," she squeezes his thigh and sends him a loving smile.

"How did you two meet?" I ask, Mia mentioned they were childhood sweethearts, I'm very interested in their story.

Mia and Davy take turns sharing the story of how they grew up together on adjoining farms. Davy said when Mia was in third grade, he in fourth, she told him on the school yard they would be married someday and she was going to make him the happiest man to ever live. They talked about when they were in high school Davy and Mia would sneak out of their houses and meet in the barn, kissing and doing what teenagers do through the night. It wasn't until a few years ago Davy's parents told them they were on to him the entire time. It was endearing, the way they took turns telling the stories, like they had told the story a thousand times. After the heartwarming tale of their love story, Davy got up to put the grill on.

"You two are very lucky." I'm more than a bit jealous of their story. To have a lifetime of love starting from so young, to know you have someone in your life so solid and sure.

"Yeah, he's amazing," she blushes again and looks at Davy through the patio doors, "Can I ask you something?"

"Sure." I take the final sip of the water in the glass and hold it between my hands rolling it back and forth.

"Do you think it's odd we had that exchange in Pottsville and then the next day we met on the beach?" Her green eyes seem brighter as she asks the question.

I think for a moment and decide I'm going to answer her honestly, "I don't think it's odd. However, I don't think it's a coincidence. When people cross paths sometimes they move on without connection but sometimes paths are meant to cross for a variety of reasons. We don't know the reason until we know the reason," I shrug and realize I'm sounding like the crazy one now.

"I agree, I think for some reason I was meant to meet you. I don't know why yet. It feels like a friendship that has formed somewhere else but we've been handed it here, now, in this place."

"I agree," I echo as we, contently, let the pause fill the room.

"Alright, enough of the heavy," Mia laughs with contagious amusement.

Davy comes through the door and stops between us, "Glad to see you ladies are having a good time. I'm going to get the shrimp and veggies. Should I open a bottle of wine?" He turns to Mia who takes the last sip of water and hands him the glass.

"Sure. I'll be out in a minute to get it. Is wine okay with you, Violet?" Mia asks as Davy continues on down the hall.

"Yes, I prefer red, I brought some if you don't have any." I hope I'm not being a bother but I have a feeling Mia appreciates honesty.

"Red it is," she smiles and I thank her.

"I'm going to use your ladies room if that's alright." I stand and place my empty glass down on the side table.

"Sure, first door on the right, I'll go grab the wine and we can sit on the patio while Davy cooks." She stands and heads down the hall, I follow until I reach the first door on the right.

When I come out of the bathroom I go to the sitting room. I don't see Mia. I peer through the glass doors to the patio, I don't see Davy or Mia outside. I take my empty glass from the table and head to the kitchen. As I enter the hallway I see Mia emerge from what must be her bedroom.

"Perfect timing, I stopped off as well," she laughs as she leads the way to the kitchen.

Before I turn to walk through the living room I hear low voices, men's voices, coming from the kitchen. When we emerge from the hallway I see Davy standing in front of the door. He's holding a bottle of wine in one hand and with the other he's holding out wine glasses for the other man to take. The man is tall, his back is to me. He wears a black t-shirt snug against his back and I can see the outline of traps, deltoids and lats. He's meticulously sculpted and his shirt doesn't hide it. He's wearing faded jeans, he has a well defined v-tapered torso. As I'm admiring his form he turns around, my heart skips, butterflies wake in my stomach and start frantically flapping. It's *him*, the man from the airport.

Our eyes meet and Mia's voice breaks me out of my haze, "Hey, I didn't know you were stopping by. Nice timing though, we're getting ready for dinner." Mia stops and turns to me then back to Drew, she notices we're staring at each other.

"Violet?" he asks, in a voice barely audible. Hearing my name coming from his lips sends my chest leaping with delight, he remembers me.

"Hi, Drew," I lift a hand in a semi wave but my arm feels like it weighs a hundred pounds. Who is this man and why does he have such a mesmerizing effect on me?

I break the stare he has clamped on me and I him. I take a few steps forward and see Davy has the most delighted look on his face while Mia is searching all of us questionably. I want to reach out and touch Drew to see if he's really here. Mostly, I want to feel the lightning current he shocked me with during our first meeting. I take two more steps forward and stand a few feet away from him.

"You two know each other?" Mia is looking at Drew trying to penetrate his line of sight.

"Yes, well, no. We met at the airport when I landed in Brisbane last week, briefly. I dropped my phone leaving the airport and Drew returned it to me. He told me how terrible I looked," I couldn't help the last detail. I smile at him teasingly, hoping I didn't hurt his feelings when I see his face fall. There's a sudden roar of cheerful laughter coming from Davy.

"I didn't say you looked terrible," Drew hurries in response, he puts his hands up in defense.

"No, you said I looked to be in *shambles*," I tip my head and tap my chin thoughtfully. When I saw the discomfort on his face I think I may have embarrassed him so I backpedaled, "It's okay, when I got back to the hotel and looked in the mirror I thought you were spot on." I smile warmly at him and he seems to relax a little.

"Well then. Isn't this a pleasant surprise?" Mia asks in a hesitant tone. She stares at Davy as if she just found something out on him and I'm unsure why.

"It's a very pleasant surprise," I give Drew one more tender gaze before I move toward Davy and take the wine glasses he's still holding out, "I'll take these."

"Thank you, Violet." He moves past me and grabs a tray covered with foil from the counter. "You lot coming outside with me or are you going to stand here in the entry?" He shakes his head and stalks toward the back hall.

"Drew, will you stay for dinner?" Mia asks, taking the salad bowl from the kitchen island.

"Yes, I think I will," he takes the bowl from Mia, "I got this, is there anything else you need me to take out?" He asks her, finally looking a little more relaxed.

"That's it for now, I'll grab another setting," Mia turns toward the cabinet where she starts pulling plates and silverware.

I follow Drew toward the hall, walking behind him, I smell his cologne. He smells of sandalwood with a hint of vanilla. When we get to the patio door Drew opens it and allows me to step through first. I place the glasses down at the table and take a seat on the patio couch in front of the gas fire pit. The flames are low, flickering blue and yellow.

"This is going to be ready shortly, sorry for the delay." Davy turns from the grill to look at me then he shifts to where Drew's standing by the patio. "You good, mate?" he asks in a whisper.

"Great," Drew steps toward Davy and takes the wine from the countertop beside the grill. "Would you like some wine, Violet?"

There it is again, my name, I'll ever not enjoy that sound.

"Sure."

I stand but Drew holds up a hand signaling me to sit back down. Mia returns with an extra place setting and sets the table for four. It doesn't seem Drew's an expected guest, I wonder how he knows Mia and Davy. Mia takes two glasses from Drew, handing one to me, she sits beside me on the sofa.

"How do you all know each other?" I can't help my curiosity.

Mia laughs and sips her wine, "Those two, buggers, are brothers. Drew's the oldest."

I'm shocked but it makes sense now, having the feeling of recognition when I first saw Davy. "Really?" I ask as I take a sip of wine.

Drew comes to sit in the cushioned chair across from me. The sun has set now and the glow of the flames flicker across Drews face. He's the most handsome man I've ever seen.

"Yup, he's the annoying little brother." Everyone chuckles, Drew takes a sip from his goblet then looks up at me. His blue eyes dance over my face with interest, "How's your stay been so far? How long have you been here in Byron?"

"I've been having a great time. I hiked at Lamington for a few days then went to Pottsville, where I met Mia. Then I came here and met her again. This is my first day here, we spent the day at the beach talking, then I came here for dinner." The butterflies in my stomach haven't settled and I wonder if I'll be able to eat anything. Maybe talking will relax me, more wine definitely will.

"Lamington is nice. How long are you staying in Byron?" he asks in an exhale and sits back in the chair. I see the muscles in his forearms twitch as he puts his hands on the arms of the chair.

"A few days, I'm mapping out the next week while I stay here." I look at Mia and I see her studying Drew intently, he doesn't seem to notice.

Mia looks at me, sending me a reassuring smile, "Violet has rented the studio cottage just a few down." She looks at Drew with excitement playing on her face.

"We went there for tea today. Remember when they tore that place down? The rebuild is gorgeous," Davy calls from the grill.

"Yes, it's so beautiful here. I'm excited about the next few days," I lean closer to put my hands next to the flame, it's chiller now and I wish I brought a sweater.

"Do you want a sweater, Violet? I can get one from my closet," Mia asks, getting ready to stand.

"No, no, please sit. It's from all the sun I got, the air is nice." I see Drew lean forward and reach under the fire pit top.

He flips open a metal door and reaches for something. His blue eyes meet mine and he says, "Watch your hands." He turns a knob and the flames jump a bit higher.

"Thank you," I smiled at him appreciatively.

"What do you have planned while you're here?" Drew asks with purpose in his eyes.

“Tomorrow I’ll take a hike, Mia invited me to dinner. I’m still researching things to do while I’m here,” I see discouragement play on his face as I explain.

“Cape Byron is a nice hike, not a full day hike but there’s plenty to do. You could go to the beach after, it's all right there,” Drew explains as he drinks his wine, his eyes are enticing.

This man is going to wreck me, I can’t look away from him. Mia interrupts my trance, “Yes, that’s a great place, I told Violet about it today.” She looks to me then back to Drew and a playful smile extends to her eyes, “You’re not working tomorrow, Drew. That sounds like a lovely day,” she puts it out there for one of us to bite but we both sip our wine instead.

“Dinner is ready, come sit.” Davy sets a huge pile of shrimp and vegetables on the table and we take seats.

Drew pulls out a chair and motions me to sit, my heart races when he takes the seat next to me and sits. I don’t know how I’m going to get through this meal while this man sits next to me.

Chapter 11
Violet

Dinner goes smoothly, I manage to eat a few shrimp and pick at the vegetables on my plate. The energy that is emitting from Drew is magnetic. I have to stop myself from reaching over and touching his hand, his arm, any part of him. Mia and Davy are fun to watch, so much charisma swarmed between the two of them. The way they look at each other is heartwarming, every touch they share is filled with affection. Drew's quiet during dinner. I noticed him stealing glances at me, especially when I laughed. I thought maybe my laugh was distracting or annoying but when I caught him looking he offered me a warm smile. When we finish eating, Davy asks me what I do in my free time when I'm not working. I tell him I like to garden, visit my brother's cabin in New Hampshire and visit my sister.

"What kind of garden do you have?" Drew asks.

"At my condo, I had mostly herbs in pots. I didn't have a yard, it was a shared space. I had a few pots of rosemary, dill, a few types of mint, parsley and such. My father always had a big garden. I still use his space, I plant in the spring, on my days off I go there to water and weed. When I get back home I'll start planting. I grow a lot over there, peppers, corn, cucumber, squash, pumpkin, broccoli, watermelon, you name it I grow it." I see all the faces at the table are smiling at me, I always get excited when I talk about plants. "I grow lots of flowers there as well, lots and lots of plants. I love starting something from seed, nurturing it, seeing it grow to produce something I can feed people with or cut in a bouquet."

"That's wonderful. I bet your parents love having all that growth around," Davy chimes in and I see Mia shoot him a look and poke him with her elbow, not very subtly. "Jeez, woman, what the hell?" He stares back at Mia.

"It's okay Mia, he didn't know," I look at her and give her a smile.

"What?" Davy asks, looking from Mia to me, "I'm sorry if I said something wrong, Violet." He turns to Mia looking confused and takes her hand.

"My parents passed away. I still go to their house, we still have it, I use the garden," Davy and Drew sit up straight and look at me with sorrowful eyes, "I don't like to tell people because I don't like to make people uncomfortable. When I tell people they look at me differently, like they have to feel sorry for me. But you don't, I promise, I'm okay now," I offer a self conscious smile.

"I'm sorry to hear about your parents and why you might not want to tell people," Drew turns to face me fully, "When did they pass?"

"Drew," Mia hisses but I ignore her.

"I was sixteen, they passed away in a car accident, almost twelve years ago. Twelve years this May." The last part is a whisper.

"Sorry, Violet," Davy says as he brushes the top of Mia's hand with his thumb.

"It was hard, it still is. I was angry for a long time," I exhale and put on a forced smile, "I'm here enjoying the most beautiful beaches, the beach was my mother's favorite place. I'm enjoying nature and hiking, which was my father's favorite place to be. I find pieces of them everywhere I've been."

"That sounds lovely, Violet. I'm glad you can find peace here and enjoy your parents even though they aren't here with you," Mia says warmly and takes the bottle of wine to refill her and Drew's glasses. Drew holds a hand over the glass, excusing himself from the refill.

"Were you close with your father, Mia?" I ask tentatively, she must be full of emotion these days leading up to her wedding.

She pours wine into her glass as she answers, "I was. I'm the youngest of two girls, Daddy's little girl. He was one of my favorite people." Her eyes fill as they meet mine.

"I get that, father and daughters share a very special bond. They're our first love, the man we look up to, when you have a great Dad it's hard to lose them." I turn toward Davy. "From what I know of Davy, you had a good example in your father." Davy smiles broadly and Mia kisses his shoulder.

"Thank you, Violet. I really like you," Davy laughs and holds up his glass to me.

"You two grew up on a farm, did you have gardens or cattle like Mia's family farm?" I turn my attention toward Drew and Davy as I shift the conversation to something lighter.

"We had sheep, horses and a few heads of cattle. We didn't grow anything, we harvested the pastures for hay." Drew looks down at his hands as he explains, "I built a garden bed today to try my hand at growing vegetables."

"You built a garden bed? That's great! The farm sounds wonderful, do you all ride?" I can't look away from Drew even though I'm addressing the whole table.

"Nope, I don't ride, never trusted a horse." Davy shakes his head adamantly, "Mia and Drew do though. Mia rides when we go out to see my parents. Drew, when was the last time you were on one of those beasts?"

Drew looks up as if trying to remember. "Last Christmas when we were at Mum and Dad's for the holiday. Mia and I took a ride then."

"I love riding, I haven't been in years. When I was young my dad built a small corral and barn with a stall, very small but perfect. He bought us a horse, that horse was so stubborn. If he didn't want someone to ride him, there was no way you were getting on him. If you did, you wouldn't stay on him for long," I laugh thinking about the horse and the trouble he caused.

"That's exactly why I stay away from them." Davy shutters and I don't know if it's from thinking about horses or the fact the temperature has dropped, with our full bellies the air feels colder.

Mia starts gathering the dishes and I stand to help her. "I've got this. Davy will help me bring them in." She eyes Davy who's giving Drew a sly smile and doesn't seem to notice Mia's request. "Davy," Mia snaps playfully, "help me with these dishes, will you?" She hands him the pile of dinner plates.

"Huh, yeah." He stands and winks at Drew. "I'll take care of these tonight." Mia and Davy exit the patio into the house.

"I usually help Mia with the dishes." Drew turns to me, taking a glass of water in his hand, "I have to say, I'm very surprised to see you again." His eyes are filled with sincerity, "I'm sorry if I offended you at the airport. I was a bit…" He looks away toward the flames of the fire pit behind me before he adds, "flustered."

"Today has been full of surprises. I'm sorry about my comment earlier, when I'm nervous I tend to blurt out sarcasm. I know it's not for everyone." I look down and chill over takes me. I shutter and rub the goosebumps from my arms.

"You were nervous?" Drew looks at me with concern.

"Well, a little when I saw you. But not now, not here." I take the last sip of my wine and place the empty glass on the table. "Mia and

Davy have been great, making me feel welcome, they're easy to talk to. I've enjoyed this night very much." His smile is intoxicating and I have to hold myself back from leaning into him. I want to touch his arms, I want to get closer to smell him again. He's pulling me toward him and he doesn't even know it.

"They're great, my two favorite people." He leans back in the chair and I shrink with regret he has moved further away, "You look cold. Do you want to go inside? Or I can ask Mia for a sweater."

He stands from the chair and I don't think, I react. I stand in front of him and grab his hand not wanting him to leave. There it is again, the shock of heat. I don't need a sweater or to go inside anymore, my body becomes riddled with pulsating warmth and fever. Drew stiffens and looks down to where our hands meet. Why did I do that? I pull my hand away quickly.

"I'm sorry," I mumble, looking down and taking a step back. "I'm going to go check on Mia, see if she needs help." I take a step to the left to loop around him to the patio doors when Davy comes out with a tray of pastries.

"Dessert and tea inside, Mia's worried Violet's getting cold and too polite to ask for a blanket," he laughs and looks toward Drew, "Should have brought a coat, mate."

His smile is mischievous and he cackles with laughter. I can't help but laugh, Davy says whatever he thinks and I love it.

"Thank you, Davy, but I have to get going." I don't even know what time it is but I sense I made Drew uncomfortable. Maybe he didn't feel what I felt, maybe I'm imagining this attraction. If so, I've got to get away before I make a fool of myself.

"Don't be silly, you have to eat sweets with us, you brought them. Come inside." Davy turns leaving the door open for Drew and I to enter the sitting room.

Mia comes into the room with a tray of tea. The steam flowing from the top of the cups is welcoming but I have to leave. Mia and Davy sit in the upholstered chairs leaving the small sofa for Drew and I but I pause.

"Mia, I'm going to head back to the cottage, I've got an early day. Thank you so much for dinner, I had a wonderful time." I look at all three of them, in turns, so they feel my appreciation, "Davy, the food was delicious." I turned to Drew last, "It was nice seeing you again. I enjoyed all the conversation."

"Oh, I understand," Mia sounds deflated as she stands from her chair. "Let me walk you back. I want to give you my number before you leave, so we can make plans for dinner tomorrow. You still want to get sushi, right?" She looks hopeful, I feel I need to reassure her.

"Absolutely, sounds great. I'm going to go on a day hike, I'll be back early in the evening. I'd love to meet you for dinner."

"Mia, dear, let me walk Violet home. I don't want you walking alone in the dark on your way back." Davy goes to stand but Drew steps in front of him not allowing him to make it all the way up.

"I'll walk with you or I can drive you. I'm heading out, too." Drew turns to me, Davy smiles and looks at Mia raising an eyebrow.

"Thanks," I can't meet Drew's eyes even though I feel his stare, I look to Mia instead. "I'll get your number and call you tomorrow," I hand her my phone to input the digits, "Thank you, again." When she's done putting the number in my phone she leans in to hug me.

"I called my phone from yours, so I have your number. Mine is the first one in your call log." She turns to lead us down the hall to the front door. When she gets to the door she opens it for Drew and I. She gives Drew a hug and a kiss on the cheek.

Davy gives his brother a handshake and clapping hug then turns to me, "Violet, it was really great having you. Please, don't be shy, come by anytime." He leans against the open door extending his hand to mine.

"Thanks, Davy." I take his hand before I turn toward Drew, "I'm okay to walk if you want to stay and visit." I give him a chance for an out.

"Let's go," he gestures to the door, signaling me to exit. Davy closes the door behind us and we take the footpath down to the driveway. "Would you like to walk or drive?" He pauses by his car making me think he'd prefer to drive. If this is my last encounter with him, I want to draw it out a few extra minutes.

"Mind if we walk? It's only a few houses down," I step on to the driveway, the tiny stones shift under my sandals. "It's a nice night."

"Sounds great." Drew puts his keys into his pocket, leaving his hand inside. "So, what's your day look like tomorrow?" he asks casually as he looks up at the sky.

"I'll go to Cape Byron like you and Mia suggested. Maybe I'll head to the beach in the afternoon. Then dinner with Mia sounds nice. I really like her, she's so..." I search for the words.

"Delightful," Drew finishes the thought for me, smiling as he briefly glances at me.

"Exactly," I agree.

As we pass the path to the beach I see two men come from the tree line holding a paper sack. One man hands the bag to the other and they turn on the road toward us, walking on the opposite side of the narrow road. Drew nonchalantly steps in front of me to take the inside of the path, between me and the oncoming travelers.

As they pass Drew nods to the men, "Evening, fellas." They nod and mumble a response as they pass.

"Drifters like to walk the beach at night, drinking and smoking. Most are harmless but it's not a good idea to go to the beach alone late at night around here," he says informally but I take note of the warning.

"I'll keep that in mind. Here I am." I point to the next driveway and feel a stab of regret that the walk is so short. I walk up the drive and notice I forgot to turn on the outdoor lights.

"Cute place," Drew observes as he walks by my side up the driveway.

When we get to the porch he allows me to climb the three steps to the landing first. He waits on the bottom step while I riffle through my bag looking for the key to open the door. I find the key with fumbling hands.

"I should've left a light on," I huff, Drew pulls out his phone and turns on the flashlight app as I finish the statement. He holds the light on the deadbolt lock on the door, "Thanks." I slide the key in the lock and turn it, swinging the door open.

"No problem." He steps backward to the bottom step. I think of asking him in but if I do, I might throw myself on him and embarrass myself further. "Violet?" He shifts his weight on his feet putting his hands back in his pockets, forbidding me to reach for them.

"Yeah," I try to sound casual but my voice shakes.

"I'd like to go with you to Cape Byron tomorrow. I don't want to be rude and invite myself. If you'd rather make it a solo mission, I understand." His eyes practically glow in the light of the almost full moon.

"You want to come along?" I'm shocked, again, by this man. I wish I could read his mind, these feelings of uncertainty and desire are giving me whiplash.

He laughs and the sound warms my chest, it's an enjoyable sound, "I would like it very much. If you haven't figured it out yet," he takes the steps up to the landing, standing in front of me, "I'm wholly captivated by you."

I must have misread the encounter on the patio. A huge smile spreads over my face. Before I can answer he takes my hand, brushing the top of my hand with his thumb. He laces his fingers in mine, watching the movements of our fingers as they connect. My heart races and my body fills with a shock of adrenaline. He looks at me and I see the exhilaration dancing in his eyes. I can see pulsating in the side of his neck by the shadow of the moonlight. He then takes my hand by the wrist and gently pulls it toward him. I take a half step forward on shaking legs. He rests my palm on the center of his chest. I feel the rhythm of his heart, a rapid tempo beating feverishly against my hand, same as mine. I take a slow breath in, between feeling the pounding of his heart and his muscular frame, my knees threaten to give way. I try to keep my breaths even, I try to slow my heart rate.

"I'd really like that," the words come out of me in whispered breaths. He removes my hand from his chest, filling me with lust and desire. I want to drag him through the door.

"Excellent. I'll pick you up at eight, is that too early?" He takes a step back, releasing my hand. He continues to watch my hand as it falls to my side.

"Eight is perfect." I take a step back entering the cottage. "I'll see you in the morning. Good night, Drew." I give him a slow, soft smile and grab the door for balance.

"Good night, Violet." He backs away, still watching me and waits for me to close the door.

I close the door and rest my forehead against the panels. My heart is pounding, my hands and legs shake. He does feel it, I'm not crazy. I move to the living room turning on the side lamp and reaching to close the long blinds covering the windows. I lay on the sofa and stare at the ceiling, still smiling. What does all this mean? Meeting Drew at the airport, the connection with Mia, it's not all happenstance. It can't be. But I'm here for only three more days, maybe I'm meant to let go and follow my instincts for the first time in a long time. Maybe I allow myself this brief moment with a handsome, sexy, god-like man and enjoy it for what it is: an alluring magnetic energy that might be worth exploring. I resign myself to follow my instincts but not act foolishly. After all, I'm leaving Australia in two weeks time. I want to get to know him, I want to see him again, I feel a pull to him.

I sigh heavily and stand making my way to the double bed behind the living room. I close the rest of the shades around the cottage, take off my dress and pull on shorts and a tank top. I don't know how I'll sleep tonight. But the sooner I drift off, the sooner the morning will come and Drew will be at my door. I take the suitcase from under the bed and remember I still have Drew's business card in the front zipper. I pull out the card from the suitcase, taking it to bed with me. I turn the card over in my hand several times, staring at my phone sitting on top of the comforter. I wonder if he's an early riser? Not following my instincts but following the desire I feel swimming in my stomach, I pick up my phone and dial the number. After all, you don't get a body like that by sleeping in and lazing around.

"Hello?" Drew's low voice answers.

"Drew, it's Violet." I take a breath and place the business card on the bedside table.

"I thought so, I don't get many calls from U.S. numbers. Are you alright?" There's concern in his question and the butterflies in the pit of my stomach are awake again.

"Fine, I remembered I had your number and I wanted to ask you something," I pause thinking of how to ask my question, "Are you an early riser?"

"Am I an early riser?" he repeats the question.

"Yes, do you get up early?" I start to feel self consciousness but I push it aside when I remember him placing my hand on his chest, feeling the quickening of his heart.

"I do. I was up before the sun today, actually," he laughs and I smile, what a great sound.

"I've been waking up early, the time difference is throwing me off. Anyway, I've been going to the beach to watch the sunrise. If you're awake and want to come with me, I'll be at the beach around sunrise. We could go to Cape Byron after." Not getting any feedback, I start backtracking, "If you're not up for it, I know not everyone enjoys that stuff." I shake my head silently and sigh to myself.

"Who doesn't enjoy a sunrise? I'd like that very much." I can hear a smile on his face. "Do me a favor though?"

"Sure," I wait to hear what favor I might be able to do for him.

"Wait for me to come to the cottage, don't go to the beach alone in the dark. I'll be there at…" There's a moment of silence and then he finishes, "I'll be there at quarter after six. Good night, Violet."

"Great, see you then," I hung up the phone and crashed back on my pillow, kicking my legs excitedly. I'm never going to be able to sleep.

After I calm my beating heart and relax my trembling body I set my alarm to 5:30 tomorrow morning. I don't want to chance oversleeping if I do manage to fall asleep. I turn out the light on the bedside table and turn on my side still grinning ear to ear, feeling my cheeks burning. I relax my face and try to get some sleep before Drew comes back.

Chapter 12
Drew

After hanging up from the call with Violet, I see Davy standing against my SUV in the driveway waiting for my return. Mia is sitting on the front porch, I walk past Davy and take a seat on the top step of the porch landing. Mia sits in the rocking chair behind me to the right.

"How did that go?" Mia asks, wrapping a shawl around her shoulders.

"We're going to Cape Byron tomorrow." I smile slightly, though she can't see my face.

Davy walks toward us with his hands out expectantly. "Well, was I right or was I right? Did I come through?" He's still smiling that sly grin he has had on most of the night.

"You were right," I reply, knowing it will satisfy him.

I'm still reeling from the night's events. The wheels in my head are turning so fast I'm surprised there's no steam coming from the top of my head. I'm still processing the night, from finding Violet in my brother's kitchen to hanging up my mobile a few minutes ago.

"Davy told me about your encounter with Violet at the airport." Mia breaks the silence. "I assure you, I had no idea about what happened that day until he told me fifteen minutes ago." Mia crosses her arms over her chest.

"I'm shocked I came across her again." I turn to face Mia, "You met her in Pottsville yesterday?"

"Yes, then today at the beach. I went to her cottage for lunch and Davy came over. I introduced them and noticed Davy was all giddy, sneaking off to make a call. I didn't put it all together until he told me about last week at the airport." She takes a breath then she breaks out in the most wonderful Mia smile, "She's completely smitten with you, Drew."

"She's beautiful." I run a hand through my hair and stand up. "I don't know, she's leaving in a few days. I don't know what it all means but I can't stay away from her now I know she's here," I look at Davy and Mia realizing I'm talking out loud.

"Yeah, she's beautiful, smart and funny. She's amazing, I really like her." Mia smiles at me.

"I like her, too." Davy looks at Mia then to me, shrugging his shoulders, "I don't see the problem, mate. Why the long face? I thought this was good, seeing her again."

"She's leaving in three days." I feel conflicted. I want to bust down her door, take her in my arms, I want to get to know her. The other part of me wants to let her go because watching her leave in three days might ruin me.

"Yes, leaving Byron in three days but she said she had two weeks left of her holiday. She might be around the area for a while. Why not have some fun? God knows you deserve that. You've been moping about the past year. You've been out on what, three maybe four dates. I've never seen you look at a woman like I saw you watching her tonight." Davy stands up and walks beside Mia, leaning against the porch banister, "Go out, enjoy her company, show her around. Have a blissfully torrid affair. Don't fall in love and there won't be a problem." Davy's so positive, I know he doesn't understand the conflict happening inside of me.

"You're afraid?" Mia leans over resting her forearms on her thighs. She gets it.

"A little." I look into her eyes and see understanding reflecting back on me.

"You could see what happens, the chemistry between you two is palpable." Mia smiles at me as she takes Davy's hand in hers.

"Again, I don't see a *problem* here," Davy throws his arms up in the air in frustration.

Mia stands from the chair, "Leave Drew alone. He'll be fine." She turns to me next, "Go with her to Cape Byron, enjoy the day. Get to know her and be happy with what the universe has given us, an opportunity to meet Violet. She's strong and clever, she might be able to offer us something we didn't know was missing. We might be able to offer her something she didn't know she needed." Mia's so smart, always having a positive outlook on people and situations. My heart is full from her words and I feel better about the situation. I'll take it for what it is, an opportunity.

"I've got to get going, I've got an early day." I smile at Mia and kiss her cheek. I shake Davy's hand, "Thank you, brother."

"Absolutely, have a great day tomorrow. Call me after the hike, maybe we can go to the pub while the girls have dinner." Davy winks at me and walks me down the landing to the driveway.

Driving home, thinking about what Mia said, I became a little more settled and relaxed. Tomorrow will be a great day. Violet Kelly might wreck me but I cannot deny the way she makes me feel. I've never felt the heat of a simple touch like I feel when I touch her. I'm going to go with it and deal with the consequences when they come. I pull into my garage and look around for beach chairs to put in the back of my car for tomorrow. I want to be prepared for whatever the day might bring. I pack some beach supplies in the back of my car then head inside to try and get some rest before the morning.

My alarm blares at 5:15, I slept four hours. I tossed and turned until well after midnight. Thoughts of the previous night's events and anticipation for this morning had me unable to sleep. When I get out of bed I'm not groggy or tired, there's excitement buzzing in my body. I dress in jeans and a sweatshirt, knowing the air will be cool in the early morning hours. I pack a backpack with hiking clothes and swim shorts. In the kitchen I grab protein and granola bars, putting them in the pack along with water bottles. I don't have time to brew a pot of coffee and consider stopping at the cafe in town to get some. As the clock display tells me it's 5:45 I head toward my car with eagerness.

The drive to town is quick and when I get to the cafe they're just opening at 6 AM, perfect timing. After buying two coffees, I get back in the car arriving at Violet's exactly when I said I would. The shades are drawn, the porch light is on and I see a faint glow of interior lights through the windows of the cottage. I grab the coffees and take a breath trying to relax my already racing heart. I ring the bell, waiting for the enchantress to open the door.

The door swings open, revealing Violet. Her long hair is down and damp. She's wearing jeans with a short sleeve white top, dipping down in a v. If I could wake up to this everyday, I'd be a happy man.

"Morning, do you want to come in?" She's barefoot wearing a charming smile, holding the door open for me.

Do I ever. "Sure," I say as I step inside and smell brewing coffee. "I picked these up on my way over," I handed her the coffee and closed the door behind me.

"Thank you, I made some but it's not good." She takes a sip and makes a satisfied humming sound, "Much better than mine."

She lets out a laugh and my stomach flops. I'll never get tired of the sound of her laugh.

"You're welcome. Thank you for inviting me, I can't remember the last time I watched a sunrise."

I reflect back and try to remember. Davy and I went surfing a few months ago in the early morning, as the sun was rising. I was too cranky with him for getting me up so early I don't remember enjoying the experience. I smile to myself, I'm going to enjoy this sunrise for sure.

"Should we head down to the beach?" I ask after I check the time on my watch.

"Yes," Violet puts her coffee down on the entry bench, sitting to slip on her shoes before we leave.

She reaches above the bench to the coat hooks, taking a zip up sweater and a digital camera from the rack. I open the door for her and she files out ahead of me.

"Should I lock the door?" I ask before I close it.

"Sure, I have the key." She taps the front right pocket of her jeans. "Hope I didn't get you up too early to do this. I promise it will be worth it."

It's already worth it. "I wanted to come, it's not too early. If you want to see the sunrise, you've got to get up early, it's part of the experience." I lock the door and we set off toward the beach.

When we get to the beach, the stars are still visible, we sit on the sand watching the small waves roll to shore. We quietly sip on the coffee, the sky lightens to the east, Violet points to the bluffs on the end of the beach.

"It's going to come up right over there," she shifts to face the skyline over the bluffs. "This has been one of my most favorite things to do," she sounds giddy with anticipation.

"It's beautiful out here, it's quiet," as I make the observation, a man with a small dog walks below us on the shoreline.

The man tips his head in a greeting and keeps walking as the dog jumps through the breaking waves. The sun starts to rise, illuminating the sky in yellow and blue hues, it is beautiful. Violet takes her camera and I hear the hum of the lens extending. She snaps a few pictures of the skyline over the bluffs. The rocky bluffs look black in comparison to the bright colors stretching through the sky.

"I usually don't take pictures, I try to sit and enjoy the sunrise. I want something to hang in my office. I'm a novice at this photography thing and nothing beats the real thing," she shows me the display screen of the pictures she just took, leaning into me as she does, she smells like soap and jasmine.

I lean over her shoulder that presses against my chest to take a closer look, "Those are really good, they'd make a great print."

"Do you live close by?" she asks as she puts the lens cap on the camera and places it back in the camera bag.

"I live fifteen minutes inland, Cooper's Shoot. It's nice being close to the beach but a little more private, the houses are more spread out." The sun is up now, we shift or gaze to the ocean.

"That sounds nice. What about your parents' farm? Is it close?" Violet stretches out her legs crossing them at the ankles.

"The farm we grew up on is long sold. My parents live in a rural area about two hours away. Davy and Mia settled here shortly after their time at university. My parents moved closer shortly after. My mum kept the horses and some sheep. She does riding lessons and trail rides at their new space, a small ranch. I moved up here from Sydney a year ago. I didn't like the city and fell in love with the coast after visiting Davy and Mia," I watch her as she intently listens to my explanation.

"I don't like the city much either. Growing up we lived south of Boston. It's rural, a very small town. It was perfect because we were forty minutes from the city and thirty minutes from many beaches. I don't like the noise and bustle of the city, some people love it, I don't like the rush." She buries her hands in the sand, grabbing handfuls and watching the sand fall back to the beach.

"I completely understand, I could never make it my home," I smile at her with appreciation.

"I saw on your card that your business is based out of Sydney. This place seems far from there." She turns back to me still grabbing at the sand. I debated telling her the real reason why I left but it's too early for bad memories.

"The company was working on expanding their client base to northern areas in New South Wales and Queensland. I thought it was a good opportunity to be closer to my family and have more flexibility. Living away from the city was a bonus." It wasn't a complete lie. To deflect what questions she may have next I ask her one, "Would you like to head back and get ready for the hike? It's going to be hot today, so hiking early will be best." I wait for her to respond before I stand.

"Sure."

She shakes the remaining sand from her hands as I stand. I hold out my hand to her to help her off the sand, she takes it and I pull her up. We stand there for a moment looking at each other, hands together, I feel the pull to lean in but I fight it. I don't want to make her uncomfortable this early in our day. I'm hoping to make this day stretch for as long as possible, I want to have as many moments as I can with her. I step back and we start our walk back to her cottage.

When we return to the cottage Violet changes into athletic shorts and a tank top. She packs her hiking pack, the American military sack.

"Does your brother still serve?" I notice she stops packing and stiffens.

"No, he doesn't." She doesn't meet my eyes and she returns to packing the bag.

"You said you had a sister, too. Are you the oldest?" I'm curious about her family and think maybe the loss of her parents put strain on her relationships with her siblings. Death can bring people together but it can tear others apart.

"My sister, Ally, she's the youngest. I'm in the middle. My brother, James, he's the oldest," she continues to pack her bag without looking up.

"You might want to bring a suit, I was thinking of stopping off at the beach on our way back, if you want to." I step closer to her hoping to draw a look from her.

"I'd like that." She turns and smiles but there's a hint of sadness in her eyes.

"Great, I'll have you back for dinner with Mia. She's looking forward to it." I step back again feeling the tension ease.

Violet reaches under the bed for her suitcase, she rummages through pulling out a navy blue two piece and a red one piece suit. I see she's debating which to put in the pack, she eyes them both.

"That one," I point to the navy two piece and give her a wink. She laughs and I'm glad to have broken the ice.

"Oh, really?" She tosses them both in the backpack and laughs again, "I guess you'll have to be surprised." She zips up the pack and puts it over one shoulder.

"All set? I'll take that for you." I reach out for the bag but she shakes her head and goes to the kitchenette.

"I'm going to bring some fruit for the ride." She grabs two bananas and two peaches from the counter and heads for the door.

I put her bag in the back of my SUV. "It's a short ride, just a few minutes. The trail is almost four kilometers, and shouldn't take long. The views are great," I explain as she smiles at me with anticipation, I'm excited to share this with her.

Violet holds up a peach and banana to me as I drive. I grab the peach and take a bite. I reverse out of the driveway, smiling to myself and start the drive toward the hiking path.

"I should have made you a proper breakfast before we left, the coffee probably isn't going to hold you over." She opens the banana and I'm desperately trying not to watch her. "Can I ask you something?" She looks out the window as she asks.

"Anything." My stomach flips and my pulse quickens.

"I assume you're single. I mean, I would hope you wouldn't volunteer to show me around and spend the day with me if you had a girlfriend or wife at home. You don't seem the type to sneak around," she pauses and turns to look at me but I keep my eyes on the road.

"I don't hear a question," I snicker and sneak a glance at her, she laughs again. "If you're asking if I have a wife or girlfriend at home, the answer is no."

"Why? How are *you* single?" she asks with her eyebrows raised. I can't help but laugh at the question.

"I was in a relationship before I left Sydney, it didn't end well. I've been on a few dates over the past year but nothing stuck. I guess I'm picky," I shrug my shoulders.

"I see."

She goes back to looking out the window. I let the pause hang in the air for a while as she searches the scenery.

She breaks the silence, "She must've really hurt you, I'm sorry."

I'm stunned to the point where the air is knocked from my lungs. How can this young woman be so perceptive and knowing?

"Can I ask a question?" I think she knows where I'm going by the considerate look she gives.

"Do I have to answer?" She tilts her head and gives a small smile.

"No." I pause for a moment then continue, "Who's waiting for *you* back home?"

Similar to how she sees me, I see her as loyal and trustworthy. She wouldn't come out with me if she had someone back home, she'd stick close to Mia and would have declined my invitation.

She holds her stare as she answers, "No one."

"Why?" I turn into the parking area, park the car and turn to her.

Sadness and pain fill her eyes as she speaks, "I was in a relationship, it ended before I came here. To be honest, the relationship was over a long time ago. I'm sorry it took me so long to leave him."

She holds my stare, her blue eyes seem brighter than this morning at the beach. I want to pull her into me, I want her to make her forget about whoever was stupid enough to let her go.

"Sounds like he's an idiot."

"That's what people have told me. But it was complicated." Her smile fades and she meets me with a serious look. "I'm complicated, Drew. Honestly, I don't know how to approach this. I'll be gone in a few days and..." She sits back in the seat and sighs, "I don't know."

"You're not complicated, you seem easy going and fun," I reassure her, "Let's see what today brings. I'd like to show you around Byron while you're here, I enjoy your company. We don't have to make it complicated." The last part feels like a lie because I know if things go as well with Violet as I hope, I'll be swimming in complications by the end of the week. "There's no pressure, if you're not having fun I'll take you back." I reach for her hand giving it a reassuring squeeze and wait for her to say something.

"Okay," she opens the car door, "I'm excited for this." I know she's talking about the walk but I'm hoping there's more meaning behind the statement.

We go to the back of the car and I grab my pack. "I'll carry this, I've got plenty of water and snacks. It's a short loop, it won't take long. If you want to take your camera there are lots of worthwhile views."

"Perfect," Violet says excitedly as she takes the camera from her backpack and places the neck strap over her head. "Do I look like a tourist? I don't want to ruin your local vibe." She smiles putting her hands on her hips.

“Locals bring their cameras, too. You look great.” I close the back hatch of the car and open my backpack. I take out a pair of shorts. “I’m going to put these on in the back. I’ll be right out.”

I slip into the back seat and swiftly take off my jeans and put on the athletic shorts. When I step out I see Violet on her mobile typing.

“Sorry, I forgot to call my sister yesterday and again this morning. She’s making sure I wasn’t abducted or lost in the wild.” She rolls her eyes as her fingers move quickly, “All right, all set.” I hear the whoosh of the text being sent. “Mind if I leave this in the car before you lock up?” She holds up her mobile.

“You can throw it in here,” I open the front pouch on the backpack and hold the open bag out to her. She drops it in and zips it closed. “Okay, are you ready for this?” I ask her as the excitement in her eyes spreads to her face.

“Absolutely.”

She sets off to the trail head, I file in a step behind her, letting her set the pace. As we walk the path Violet talks about her sister, Ally, describing her as a calculated type-A. The way she talks about her sister is endearing, she speaks affectionately about her. Ally lives on an island off the coast of Massachusetts and Violet likes visiting her when she can. She talks about visiting in the Spring and Fall months as opposed to the busy tourist season in the summers. I ask a few questions but continue to let her take the lead.

“She’s concerned, I think, with me over here. I came here impulsively and I don’t think she understands. Ally plans and then she has a plan for her plan.” She laughs and looks at me. Her smile and laugh light up her blue eyes sharing the fondness she has for her sister.

“When did you decide to come here to Australia?” I’m wondering how impulsive her decision was.

Violet pauses and looks up for a moment. “Six hours before I left on the flight from Boston.” She turns to face me, reading my reaction.

“Wow, that’s *very* spontaneous,” I say, trying to keep the surprise out of my tone and wait to see if she’ll elaborate but she changes the subject.

“It seems you and Davy are close,” she stops to snap photos of the beach below us.

"Yeah, he's much the opposite of me, like you described with you and your sister. He's very outgoing and carefree, I tend to be more reserved. We balance each other well and if ever I need something he's always there."

We start walking up a set of stairs, the track is becoming busier as the morning pushes on. I check my watch and see it's only 9:30, still plenty of day left. When we reach the top of the stairs, the path starts to wind through a shady area. I'm enjoying watching her walk ahead of me, her long legs, her blonde hair falls to the middle of her back. It's a wonderful view, I'm not taking in any of the scenery other than the beautiful woman walking a few steps ahead.

"This is beautiful, I can't believe you live here," her astonishment for the landscape makes me happy to share it with her.

"Yeah, it is, I don't get out here much. Davy and I surf around here."

I fall into step next to her, the path has thinned out from other travelers.

"You surf? Of course you do, you're Australian," she laughs and nudges my arm with her shoulder, I like it.

"It's not my favorite activity but I enjoy being out on the water."

I feel excitement in the pit of my stomach, I want to reach out for her hand but a group of walkers comes past and I step back behind Violet.

"Do you want to try it?" I ask.

"Surfing? No," she shakes her head adamantly, "I like to stay where I can stand up, I like to see what might be swimming below me in the water. Aren't there sharks out there?" she asks, turning around with a look of dread on her face, it makes me laugh.

"Yes, but they tend not to bother you. It helps if you stay on the board, too," I'm still laughing as I explain, her face continues to show signs of fright.

"No way, absolutely not. I saw *Jaws* as a kid, it completely wrecked me for life. I can't swim past my chest in the ocean," her explanation makes me laugh harder.

"Well, maybe we can work on that later," I offer as we continue on the path.

Violet takes more pictures and we chat about Davy and Mia. Violet and Mia seem to have really hit it off and Violet's excited about dinner tonight. The walk goes quickly, by the time I notice where we are, the walk is almost over. I hear my mobile ping with a message and reach for it in my pocket. It is Mia, asking how things are going, ending the question with an obscene amount of question marks. I laugh out loud.

"Everything okay?" Violet asks when I stop walking.

"Yeah, Mia asking how we're doing. I'll talk to her later."

I go to put the mobile back in my pocket but Violet reaches for my hand.

"Take a picture with me? We can send it to her. She'd like that, right?" Her fingers linger on my hand and my heart pounds.

"I think she would," I find the camera app and Violet stands in front of me, "Ready?"

I hold the camera out to fit us in the frame. Violet leans back against my chest and I smell the jasmine in her hair. I see our smiling faces in the camera and tap the shutter button. I send the picture to Mia with a thumbs up emoji and turn my mobile to silent. I don't want any more distractions.

"You'll have to send me that later, too. When I tell people back home about the strikingly handsome Aussie with the amazing body that showed me around Byron Bay, I want to have photographic proof."

She turns back toward the path and I laugh. I really like this girl. After we get back to my car, I open the hatch and we sit on the boot drinking water. We finish our waters and eat the rest of the fruit Violet brought with us. She lathers up more sunscreen on her legs, arms, face and neck. Her fair complexion is already pink and I see how she might burn easily.

As if she is reading my mind, she turns to me, "I burn easily. The sun is much stronger here than at home."

"I thought about going to the beach but we can find something else if you want to keep out of the sun." I can think of lots of things to do inside with Violet out of the sun. I push away the thoughts when I feel the desire rising inside.

"What are you thinking?" she asks, tilting her head to the side. Her perception is unreal.

I can't help but smile when I answer her, "I was thinking of things we can do that don't involve the sun," I give her a wink, I can't hide the eagerness in my eyes.

"Drew!" Her eyes widened and she laughed loudly, "I don't know what kind of girl you take me for but I can assure you whatever you're thinking…" she doesn't finish, instead she shakes her head, her already pink face turns crimson. "The beach sounds nice. I don't want to take you away from anything, if you have other things to do."

"The beach it is." I step down from the boot and offer her my hand to assist in the drop to the pavement.

Chapter 13
Violet

We backtrack past Clarkes Beach to Belongil Beach. I change into my suit in the back seat of Drew's SUV, the tinted windows give me enough privacy, I put a floral kimono over my navy blue two piece. When I exit the SUV Drew takes my place in the backseat. I checked my phone, it's noon, I got a text from Mia saying she would pick me up at 5:30 for dinner. I'm excited to see her again and get a chance to talk more with her. However, I didn't want this day with Drew to end. Cape Byron was stunning, the views of the beach and cliffs were breathtaking. I took so many pictures, I'm sure I would find a few to print on a canvas for my office. The weather is warm now, the humidity low, I check my bag for sunscreen. Drew exits the SUV, opens the hatch, taking out the beach chairs and a large blanket. I grab my pack and follow him to the shore.

"This is gorgeous," I observe as Drew sets up the chairs and I place the blanket on the sand.

"I like it here. I thought of going to the beach by the lighthouse but it looked crowded."

Drew sits in the chair stretching out his long legs. I can't help feeling disappointed he decided to keep his shirt on. I sit on the blanket and start to sunscreen my stomach, arms, chest, not forgetting the tops of my feet. I lean back on my elbows and watch the ocean. There are a few surfers in the water, kids run by the shore and families walk the beach. It's a perfect beach day. Inhaling deeply, taking in the salt and sand I turn my face up to the sky.

"I can't imagine living here, I would never get any work done, I'd be out exploring all day." When I finish I turn toward Drew and see he's smiling with his hands loosely clasped on his stomach. He's striking, I could not have conjured a better looking man.

"To have the fun, you have to put in the work. It's about balance. Or you could win the lotto and retire here and not have to work."

He laughs and slides out of the chair joining me on the blanket. He lays on his stomach next to me watching the water.

"Do you mind helping me with the sunscreen? I don't want to burn this early in my stay here." I hand out the tube of sunscreen and Drew bolts up to sitting with agility.

"Sure," he squeezes the sunscreen in the palm of his hand and rubs them together.

I can't see his eyes through his sunglasses but I see a sly smile forming on his face. I take off my wrap and turn my back to him.

"Just my lower and upper back, I can get the rest."

He starts at my shoulders, working his way through my shoulder blades then to the middle of my back. The sunscreen feels cool but his hands feel like fire. My heart rate quickens and those damn butterflies are alive inside me.

"What's this?" He rubs a hand over my left shoulder blade where I have a tattoo of three flowers.

"It's a tattoo," my voice is quiet, more quiet than I expected, "The flower on the left is an aster, the one in the middle is a narcissus and the one on the right is a violet."

"They're pretty. Are they your favorite flowers?"

He continues to rub the sunscreen on my lower back, I try to focus on his hands rather than the intruding thoughts entering my mind. The three flowers represent the birth months of my lost family members. My parents are represented by the aster and narcissus and James, by the newest tattoo, the violet. I got the first two for my parents on my eighteenth birthday. The one I got for James was just a few months ago. I don't know how to explain this all to Drew, especially James because it still feels raw. Drew has been honest and sincere with me so the least I can do is reciprocate.

"They're the flowers that represent the birth months of my parents. The aster, for my mom, symbolizes love and wisdom. The narcissus daffodil, for my dad, symbolizes inspiration and forgiveness." I turn to look at him, he's listening and watching me intently.

"The violet? Does that represent you? What does the violet symbolize?" He takes off his sunglasses allowing me to see the tenderness in his eyes.

"The violet symbolizes leadership and strength. That's for my brother."

My eyes burn and I blink, willing the tears not to form with everything I have inside me. Drew's eyes flicker to the backpack on one of the beach chairs.

"Your brother? Is he…" Drew looks back at me, "Is he gone, too?"

"Yes," I whisper and I look away from Drew to the water, "He died last July." The tears come and I can't stop them, I wipe frantically at my eyes, "I'm sorry," I mumble as I stand but Drew takes my hand pulling me back down on the blanket.

"You don't have anything to be sorry about," he says softly as I sit back down on the blanket next to him and pull on my sunglasses.

"I thought I could talk about it but I can't."

I look down at the blanket, I'm still holding his hand. I need to shift this conversation, I feel panic rising in my chest.

"Violet, I'm sorry. That must have been hard for you, it's still hard I'm sure."

He has that look most people have when they find out I was orphaned then lost my brother. The look of not knowing what to say, the look that feels bad for the "poor young girl", I hate that look.

"You don't have to be sorry. You don't have to feel sorry for me. Please, don't look at me like I'm a piece of glass about to shatter," my tone is harsh and jarring. I instantly feel regretful. It's the anger, swelling up from the ball of grief inside, rising to the surface. I shake my head, "I'm sorry. That sounded awful. I'm complicated, like I said." I try to release my hand but he squeezes it harder.

"Violet, you don't have to apologize, ever, for speaking your mind to me. I'm sorry if I made you uncomfortable, that wasn't my intention. If anything it makes me see your strength and resilience more clearly." His cobalt blue eyes attentively connect with mine. I hear the candor in his voice, "If there's ever something you don't want to talk about, say the word and if there's something you do want to talk about I'll listen." He lets go of my hand and I want to wrap my arms around him but I don't.

"Thank you," I rub my hands together, still feeling his touch. "That was wrong of me to talk to you like that, sometimes I get angry thinking about them."

We sit quietly for several minutes, I wait for Drew to ask a question but he doesn't and I'm thankful. He stands up, tosses his glasses on the blanket and reaches down to help me up.

"Let's take a swim," he nods toward the water and waits for me to take his hand.

"Does that mean you're going to take your shirt off? Because me standing here in my bikini doesn't feel like a fair trade." He laughs low and loud, I feel good being the one to lighten the mood.

"I aim to please. You might have to return the favor by putting sunscreen on my back after I swim."

He takes off his shirt to reveal a chiseled torso and chest. This man is a god, his skin is tan from the Australian summer that passed. I'm glad I have my sunglasses on because I feel like my eyes are as big as saucers, similar to those animation characters when their eyes bug out in the cartoons. I clear my throat and force myself to look away, I turn my stare to the water. My knees are shaking and I feel the full body current surging. I walk to the water hoping to make it before my legs give out. When we're close to the water Drew picks up his pace and runs through the shallows, splashing me as passes. He dives in the waves and pops up about thirty yards from me. I make my way slowly through the water, I'm waist high when I dip under an oncoming wave. The water feels good over my warm body. When I come up I see there's still a good distance between us, he waves me toward him.

"I'm good right here," I call out to him as I look at the ocean around me, I move further out, the water is just under my breasts.

"C'mon!" He is laughing now but I don't bite.

"I'm not going out there," I cross my arms over my chest and give him an astute look, "Come here, you're making me nervous."

He dips under the water and I track his shadow through the water. I search around in front of me, seeing his shape coming toward me. When he comes up again he's a few feet from me. The water drips from his head to his shoulders, the water runs down off his flawless chest. He walks closer to me and my heart starts skipping to a wild beat. He's inches from me, looking down at me with a mischievous smile. Without thinking I placed my hand in the middle of his chest, in the exact spot he positioned my hand last night on the porch of the cottage. He places his hand over mine and presses down. I want to run my hand all over his chest and defined stomach but I leave my palm flat against his chest. I stretch on my tiptoes, with my free hand I reach out grazing over his abs through the water. I reach around his side, skimming my hand over his rib cage to his lower back, I hear him pull in a breath. I bring my lips to his as he lowers his head. There are fireworks exploding in my chest, the butterflies have turned mammoth sized and my head is spinning. He parts my lips, gently, with his tongue. I bring my hands up to his shoulders and wrap my hands around his neck. I don't know how long we stand in the water kissing, we're finally broken apart by a wave crashing over Drew's towering frame. I stumble back and Drew grabs a hold of me at the waist balancing himself and me.

"Are you okay?" he asks as he smiles down at me as I wipe the water from my face. I push back the hair the wave left plastered to the side of my cheek.

"I'm great," I smile at him as I dip under the next wave he doesn't see about to crash into his back.

When I come up he's laughing, he reaches for my hand and we walk back to the shore. Sitting on the blanket we let the sun dry us. We sit in silence, reflecting on what just happened in the water. I turn my head to see Drew lying beside me, I see the outline of a small smile in his profile. He must have felt me looking because when he notices he reaches for my hand again.

"What time should I have you back?" he asks as his thumb makes slow movements across the top of my knuckles.

"Around four-thirty, I need to shower and change." I don't want to check the clock but I should be aware of how much time we have.

"What are you doing tomorrow?" Drew asks, turning on his side and supporting his weight on his forearm.

"I don't know."

The last two days have been a whirlwind and I feel I'm playing catch-up to the events happening around me. I haven't thought to make a plan for the next few days. I thought about letting myself enjoy this time with Drew and Mia until I check out Thursday. I could go to the national forest after my time here, I'm content here with my new friends.

"I'd like to take you somewhere. It's a bit of a drive but I think you'll like it," his eyes skim over my face as he explains.

"Where?" I ask as I turn on my stomach to get the sun out of my eyes.

"If I tell you, it won't be a surprise."

He lies back down, stretching his arms over his head. I usually don't like surprises, it's not that I don't like surprises, I don't like the unexpected. Which is why my response startles me. I try not to think too much. Today was a great day and if I can get one more day with Drew I don't care what he has planned.

"Okay," I tell him as I bring my head down to the blanket and close my eyes.

"Really? No other questions?" he asks, sounding surprised by my response.

"I trust you," I say as we share a smile, "I don't know about you but I'm hungry and I'm getting red. Is it okay with you if we pack up?"

"Sure," he says as he stands from the blanket and starts packing up the chairs.

I gather up the items scattered on the blanket and put them in my backpack. Then I shake the blanket from the sand and fold it up. We walk toward Drew's car and load up the back. Drew puts his shirt back on and when I sigh with regret, he laughs. I put a pair of shorts over my bathing suit bottoms and he groans, I laugh. I'm beginning to like the rhythm we're creating. I finish dressing by putting on a tank top over my bathing suit and get in the passenger's seat.

The ride back to my cottage is short, Drew reaches for my hand as he drives and rests our clasped hands on the middle console. When we arrive at the cottage Drew goes to the back of the car and collects my backpack while I unlock the front door. The cottage is dark and cool because I forgot to raise the blinds before I left this morning. I open the blinds to catch the remaining sunlight of the day.

"Can I make you a sandwich?" I go to the fridge and look at what I have.

"I know you don't have much time before you meet Mia, I'll go to Davy's and get something over there," he walks toward me and my heart starts thrumming wildly. He stops in front of me, leaving me backing into the fridge, "I had a great day today."

This man is incredible, my body's reactions to him are involuntary and automatic.

"I did, too. Thank you," I stumbled through a reply. When I look up I see a smile that spreads to his eyes.

"I'll pick you up tomorrow around seven. It will take us a couple hours to get there," his voice, his accent, hits my system like a drug.

“Sounds good, I’ll be ready,” I lean back against the fridge, the stainless steel cools the heat radiating through my back.

“Perfect. Have a good time tonight,” Drew says as he leans in and kisses me lightly.

It isn’t a powerful kiss like we shared at the beach, it’s tender and soft and leaves me wanting more. Drew turns and walks toward the door leaving me pressed against the fridge. When he gets to the door he turns, giving me a smile before he locks the door and closes it behind him. I let out a huge exhale, standing for a few minutes watching the door, hearing him start his car and turn out of the driveway. I shake myself awake and go to the bathroom to take a cool shower. After the shower, I put lotion on my arms and legs. I didn’t get too much sun today but the salt and sand left my body feeling dry. I dig through my suitcase to find the minidress I packed with no intention of wearing. It’s gray with some ruching, there’s a slight shimmer effect, nothing loud or too fancy, it should do for dinner. I dry my hair and curl it with the iron I found days earlier. As I apply my makeup I realize I don’t have any shoes to match the dress. The only shoes I brought with me were hiking boots, a pair of canvas shoes and brown sandals. When I finish my make up and get dressed I see it’s close to five. Mia looked about my size, maybe she had something I could wear for the night. I grab my phone and find Mia’s number in my contacts.

“Hi, love,” I hear the excitement in her voice.

“Hi, Mia. I’m getting ready and I don’t have shoes to match my dress. I was hoping you had something I can wear for tonight,” I wait for a reply while I look in the fridge for a quick snack, I’m famished.

“Of course! Come on by, you can pick a pair. The front door is open, I’m finishing up in the bedroom, come straight in.”

She disconnects and I take a few grapes from the bowl for my walk to Mia’s house. I put on my sandals and take a look around making sure I put everything away. I tuck the suitcase under the bed after I lay out a pair of shorts and a shirt for later. Taking my purse off the coat rack, I lock the door behind me as I walk toward Mia’s. The sun is low in the sky and the breeze is warm. When I approach Mia’s house I see Drew’s car parked in the lower end of the driveway. Mia gave me the green light to enter the house but I knocked to announce myself. I wait and don’t get a response so I let myself in and head back down the right side hallway toward Mia’s bedroom. The bedroom door is cracked and I hear music. I knock on the door and hear Mia call out to come in.

"There you are! Wow, you look amazing!" Mia's wearing a stunning kelly green, halter dress that flared at the waist.

"You look great. That dress is beautiful." I look her over and she spins in front of the bathroom mirror with a giggle.

"Thank you, I haven't worn this in ages. Here, my closet's on the other side. Take a look at the shoes and choose whatever you like."

She walks in front of me directing the way to a walk-in closet. The closet is huge with clothes on one side and shoes and bags against the opposite wall. I can't imagine someone wearing all this in a lifetime.

"Wow, this is…" I look around the closest, shoes line the wall and go all the way up to the tall ceiling.

"I know, I have a problem. But I do lots of events and need to be prepared for anything," Mia throws up her hands looking around with me.

"Okay, I'll take a look here, you go finish up."

I notice the shoes are color coordinated, so I go to the neutral section to look at the black and silver shoes she has. Mia is the same shoe size, it's perfect. After a few minutes I settle on a pair of open toe, black heels with a silver strap that laches across the ankle. The heel isn't too big, I don't like huge heels, I'm too clumsy. I sit on the bench in the closet, put them on and look in the full length mirror.

"Those are perfect," Mia stands in the closet reaching for a pair of leopard print pumps and slips them on with ease while standing, "Let's say bye to the boys and we'll head out."

She heads toward the bedroom door taking her bag off the bed as she passes. Mia and I walk down to the sitting room at the end of the hall. I see Drew on the patio, his back to the door. A tray of sliced meats, cheese and vegetables is on the table. When Davy sees Mia his face lights up and he leans back in the chair. Mia and I step out to the patio, Mia goes to Davy's side kissing him on the cheek.

"You both look great," Davy says as he takes in all of Mia, looking her up and down with a devilish look in his eyes.

"Thanks, we're off. We'll see you later," Mia says as she runs a hand through Davy's hair.

Drew, not realizing I'm here, turns to look toward the door where I'm standing. His eyes widen as he stands up to face me.

"Wow, Violet," he says in a soft whisper.

The way he surveys me makes me blush and I feel a surge of desire in my stomach. He likes what he sees and it brings out a wave of confidence I haven't felt in a long time. Drew finally blinks and clears his throat. He puts his hands in his pockets and shifts on his feet.

Davy laughs and stands from the chair, "You two have a good time. Don't go breaking any hearts out there, be careful."

He kisses Mia and sits back in the chair. It's a short drive to the restaurant and it's early, there isn't a crowd. We sit down at a small table in the back. The lighting is low inside, outside is still sunny, there's a golden glow of natural light coming from the windows.

"This is nice," I say, looking around the half full restaurant.

"Yes, this is one of my favorite places. Davy isn't a fan of sushi," Mia places her small clutch on the table, "So, tell me all about your day. Drew came over this afternoon looking like the cat who ate the canary."

I laugh and wonder what, if anything, Drew told Mia. "We had a great day. The walk around Cape Byron was beautiful, I took so many pictures. Then we went to the beach, we talked and took a swim."

Mia interrupts me, raising her eyebrows, "That sounds lovely, Violet. But I don't want the boring parts of the day, I want to know *how* it went. I know Drew very well and I can tell you he's completely enamored by you."

"Enamored? I wouldn't say that. There's definitely an attraction, he's the most gorgeous man I've seen. How is he single? I asked him and he told me a little about his past relationship but a man like him must be highly sought after."

The waiter comes and we order a mixed drink from the special menu, some fruity vodka concoction. I'm so hungry, I can't drink until I get some food in my belly.

"He told you about Lexi?" Her eyes widen and her smile fades quickly.

"He didn't share much other than it didn't end well. He said he wasn't happy in the city and for the last year he's been on a few dates but nothing has come of them. He didn't tell me her name.

Lexi," I whisper the name trying to put a name with the image I created in my mind.

Mia hums questionably, "Yeah, it didn't end well, that's one way to put it. They weren't a great match, they were very different. Since you've come to town I have never seen him smile so much. It's really nice to see him happy."

I tell Mia all about my day with Drew, about the kiss in the water and holding hands. Sharing with her Drew wants to take me somewhere tomorrow but he didn't reveal much about the plans. I talk to her about how my stomach flips over and my heart rate speeds up when he touches me, laughs or at certain times when he looks at me. I feel like a teenager, gushing to my bestie about a boy I'm crushing on. She seems enthralled with everything I say, she's enjoying me replaying the events of the day. When our food comes we change the subject to Mia's mom and sister coming to town tomorrow and their plans for the next few days before the wedding.

"Sounds like you'll be busy. It must be so exciting getting ready for the wedding and having your family close."

"I'm excited. My sister has been married for a few years and has three kids. Her husband is arriving with my nieces on Friday," Mia says with a beautiful smile but I see sadness encroaching in her eyes.

"Are you okay?" I tilt my head with the question, she doesn't look up from her plate.

"I'm fine," She answers in a whisper and I see tears forming in her eyes now.

"Is it your dad? Are you feeling sad because he's not with you?" I ask, I know how upsetting special occasions can be to a grieving family.

"I'm sad about that, very sad. But I'm nervous about Davy and I." She looks up at me, her face full of worry and despair.

The look takes me off guard because everything about her and Davy seems perfect. I can't imagine a scenario where either would be unsure of the other.

"Nervous about Davy?" I ask, reaching for my napkin.

I haven't spent that much time with Davy, sometimes people are good at hiding things. I read Mia well but maybe I missed something with Davy.

"Mia, does Davy hurt you?" I sit up straighter.

When I ask the question out loud it sounds ridiculous to me but I've been wrong about people before.

Mia laughs through welling eyes, "No, no, never. Davy's great, he's good to me," she looks at me and wipes her eyes with a napkin, "Davy and I have been talking about starting a family after the wedding. We've been together so long, the wedding kind of feels more of a formality. We've lived together since I was twenty-one, eight years now. I wanted to start my business and get settled in that." She pauses for a moment and looks around the restaurant, "Davy's so excited to start a family, I know he'll be a wonderful father."

"That all sounds great," I say reassuringly but half questioningly, I feel there's something I'm missing.

"I was going to surprise Davy and get pregnant before the wedding. I know it sounds devious but that's not how I meant it. I thought it would be a great surprise for him, the best wedding present I could give him. I've been trying to get pregnant for sometime now and nothing is happening." Mia puts her head in her hands. I get up from my side of the table and move inside the booth next to her.

"Mia, it's okay. Making a baby takes time." I put my arm around her and can feel her shoulders shake.

"I've taken all the steps. I went to the doctor and they said my hormone levels are off," Mia put her hands on her lap, looking at me with red eyes, "I got pregnant two months ago but lost it after six weeks."

"Oh, Mia, I'm so sorry. That must have been difficult. Does Davy know?" I try to soothe her. I feel her emotions, fear, sadness, grief, pouring from her.

"Davy knows, he was so good about it. He's trying to be positive but I get angry sometimes. My sister has had three children in five years, it seems like every time she sneezes she gets pregnant. I'm not angry with her, I know that sounds awful." Mia leans on my shoulder.

"I don't know much about making a baby, I mean, I know how to make a baby. But I've spent my whole relationship for the past six years making sure I did *not* get pregnant. If the doctors say it's a hormone issue, it seems like something they may be able to help with. Maybe hormone therapy?" I try to encourage Mia, I feel her tension ease a little.

"I think you should take this time to enjoy your wedding, you can focus on the other things after. Enjoy the time you have with your family over the next few days. Don't stress about anything other than the vendors showing up on time. You're going to be fine. I'm sure you and Davy will be able to have a baby when the time is right. Miscarrying must've been so difficult and discouraging. If the doctors didn't find anything wrong with your uterus then you have a great chance of conceiving and carrying."

Mia sniffles and straightens up, "You're right. I'm sorry to be a mess. It's been on my mind so much. What if I can't? What if I can't make Davy a father? What if I can't be a mother? It's the one thing I want, to be a mum. It's why we're born women, to have babies."

"Not all women have babies. And there are many ways to have a baby and be a mother. I wouldn't worry about all the *what ifs* yet. The what ifs will drive you crazy and will stop you from enjoying the *right nows*," I try to comfort her, the empathy I have for her is strong.

As a woman approaching her 30's I may take for granted I'll be able to have a baby when I'm ready. That's not always the case. It must be heart wrenching for a woman to be told she'll have trouble carrying or conceiving a child. However, there have been so many advancements in fertility treatments, many women who never thought they would get the chance for a child are finding themselves with opportunities.

"Try not to stress, Mia, it's not good. Focus on the things you have and on the things you can control. The rest will fall into place, I'm sure of it. I know you must be scared after the miscarriage but try to remain hopeful." I squeeze her hand and slide away, giving her space to wipe her tears.

"You're right, thank you," Mia runs her hands through her hair and puts on a brave smile, "Enough of this. Let's eat the rest of this and get another drink," She exhales and picks up her chopsticks. I move back to the other side of the table.

"So, you had a long relationship. How long have you been single?" she asks.

I'm not sure I'm ready for this but at least it's with Mia and not Drew. "I've been single for a little over a week now," I laugh weakly, pick up a salmon roll and put it on my plate, "I left my boyfriend before I came here. To be honest though the relationship had been over for a long time. I just wasn't ready to leave until I was ready, if that makes any sense."

"Wow," Mia whispers, "Are you okay?"

"I'm fine. When I finally left him, I felt a sense of relief wash over me. I made the right decision. The last year of our relationship we were disconnected, we barely spoke without fighting. We didn't even sleep together, it was awful really. I felt like I was constantly walking on eggshells."

I tell Mia about Sam's alcohol addiction, about the fights, the verbal and mental abuse I endured over the years, it takes me a while to get through it all.

"I see now he manipulated me in ways I didn't even understand at the time. I don't even think he knew what he was doing. Alcohol addiction is powerful and something I thought I could help him with. His problem was never *his* problem, it was always someone else's including mine. The gaslighting, the put downs, I completely lost my confidence," I put my hands on my lap, "I'm working on getting it all back and it'll take time, I did the right thing. I'm thankful it didn't destroy my relationship with my sister and best friend."

"I'm so sorry you went through that. I'm happy you found the strength to leave. Some people spend lifetimes in those relationships." Mia takes her drink and sips the last of it, leaving the ice and pineapple slice at the bottom of the glass.

"Some people see the red flags right away and don't get into relationships like that." I shrug my shoulders.

I don't deserve any credit for leaving because I stayed so long in a toxic, unfulfilling relationship.

"Oh, no! You can't go back to the *should haves* or *what ifs*. What did you just tell me about that?" Mia puts her hands on her hips in a mocking pose.

"You're right, none of that. I need to move forward and not look back."

When we've finished most of the food, had more conversation and Mia finishes her second drink I look at the clock on the wall.

"What should we do next? Do you want to get back home?" I ask.

"Well, Davy and Drew would love for us to go back and spend some time with them," Mia raises her eyebrows in a knowing glance, "But I'm having a great time getting you all to myself. Do you still plan on heading out of Byron on Thursday? I thought a certain someone might make you want to prolong your stay."

Mia waits for my response, the waiter comes over to ask if there's anything else we need. Mia asks for the check and turns back to me.

"I don't know. I'm having a good time with him but eventually I have to leave. I probably should leave on Thursday before things get…" I search for a word but Mia finishes my thought.

"Complicated?" Mia finishes the sentence for me. "Drew understands you have to leave. He also wants to enjoy time with you while you're here. That doesn't complicate things less, by the way you both look at each other, I think either way it's going to be difficult. I think you deserve to have some fun with a handsome, attentive man while you're here. Why not?" Mia shrugs and looks at me searching my face for an inclination of what I'm thinking, "I've talked to Davy, we know you're supposed to leave before the weekend, we would absolutely love it if you would come to the wedding," she looks at me hopefully.

"You and Davy want me to come to your wedding?" I'm shocked, I've known Mia for 36 hours and she's inviting me to her wedding. "Mia, I don't know. You're keeping it small and intimate, you and Davy don't really know me."

"Of course I know you! I feel more of a connection to you than most of Davy's friends I have known for over a decade! But I get it, I know you have plans on seeing the coast." Mia is sweet and authentic with her explanation, I can't help but feel she actually wants me to come.

"It's not that I don't want to go but it goes back to not wanting to make things complicated, you know?" I see her smiling back at me like she knows she may win this argument.

"Yes, I get it. But again, it's just an extra few days. And why not have some fun, right?" She grabs for the bill when the waiter lays it on the table. When I reach for my clutch she waves me off as she pulls out some Australian bills placing them on top of the paper slip, "Think about it, maybe after another day with Drew you'll want to hightail it outta here *or* maybe you'll want to stay." Mia stands from the table and she reaches for my hand.

"Thank you for the meal. I planned on buying you dinner for all the hospitality you've shown," I say as I take her hand. Mia waves me off again and walks with me toward the exit.

“So, we’re all dressed up and looking fab. Do you want to get a drink? Or do we go back to fluster the men anxiously awaiting our return? Or we could sit and have ice cream?” Mia loops her arm through mine as we stand on the sidewalk outside the restaurant.

Chapter 14
Drew

After dropping Violet off at her cottage to get ready for dinner, I went to Davy's house. I told Davy and Mia about the day, smiling like a school boy the entire time. Violet was making me feel like a love-struck teenager and I had mixed feelings about it. The time I spent with her today, feeling the attraction and connection, was exhilarating. However, knowing she would be leaving in a few days made me want to hold back. I couldn't let myself get wrapped up in this woman knowing she was leaving Byron Bay in two days and then leaving the country. After explaining it to Davy and Mia, Davy was still holding strong on his, "I don't see the problem" mantra. Mia was more helpful, telling me to enjoy the time and see what develops. But I'm afraid of what's developing.

When Mia and Violet appeared on the patio before dinner, I thought my knees were going to give out. I felt as if the air had been knocked from my lungs. She was remarkable in that dress. Seeing her long legs made me want to wrap them around myself. I wanted to run my hands through her long blonde hair, I wanted her. It took all I had not to grab her, take her in my arms and ravish her there on the patio. Violet Kelly was some kind of enchantress, captivating my entire being. A siren with the ability to read my mind and capture me with her laugh, I'd do anything to hear her laugh. I couldn't look away when she was close, I couldn't stop the magnetic pull I felt in my core when she was around. Mia and Violet had been gone for 15 minutes and it's taking all my willpower not to get in my car and find her in town.

"You alright?" Davy asks from the grill, pulling me away from my thoughts of Violet in the gray dress, her long legs, the kiss we shared.

"I'm good. How are you doing with that food? I'm starving," I hadn't realized how hungry I was until I settled in here at Davy's house.

"It'll be about fifteen minutes," Davy says without looking up, "You can go take that shower you were asking about earlier."

"That sounds good. I'm gonna grab my clothes in the car and be out in a few." I stand from the patio table and head to my car to grab the pair of jeans and t-shirt I packed earlier.

When I'm done with the shower, I return to the patio. Davy places the food on the table, filling two glasses with water.

"I thought you could use some water, it looks like you got sun today," Davy hands me the glass as I sit opposite him at the table.

"Thanks," I take a few big gulps then fill my plate with salad and grilled chicken.

Davy digs into his meal then looks up to me, "Feeling better?"

"Shower helped. Have you heard from Mia?" I ask, trying to play casual but know it doesn't sound like it.

"They just left! I guess you do have it bad," Davy laughs as he cuts a piece of chicken.

"Just asking, two girls looking like that, don't want to see them get into trouble."

I know it's a weeknight, things will be slow in town. I can't help thinking of the guys throwing themselves at the two beautiful girls.

"Mia can handle herself and Violet doesn't seem like a pushover. Are you worried about some bloke making a move on your girl? I don't think she would accept any advances if that makes you feel better," he looks back toward his plate, taking a forkful he adds, "You have eyes, you see the way she looks at you, mate."

"I don't know about that."

I think about the way she looked at me at the beach while we were in the water, then in the cottage while she was in the kitchen, desire and hunger filling her eyes.

"Oh, man. C'mon! She wouldn't have spent the day with you, she definitely wouldn't have kissed you, if she didn't want you around," Davy says before he takes a long drink from the glass of water.

"You don't worry about Mia? She's a knockout, you don't worry about the men she might notice?" I ask him.

Mia's a beautiful woman, it's hard not to notice. Violet's just as beautiful, it would be impossible for them not to turn every head if they walked into a pub.

"She can notice all she wants. It's human nature to notice an attractive person. I don't worry about her that way, if she *didn't* notice then I would be worried," he laughs again before he continues, "I trust Mia completely. If someone tried something with her, she'd disengage. She can handle herself, those kickboxing classes she takes aren't for the faint of heart."

Davy downs the rest of his water and refills it from the pitcher sitting on the table. We go back to eating our meal, talking about the bachelor party on Thursday and I tell Davy about the plans I have for Violet tomorrow.

"Wow, she's going to love it. Do you think it's a good idea though? Bringing Violet to the ranch with Mum and Dad? Mum might start to get ideas about you and her," Davy raises a single eyebrow at me.

"I don't think Mum will get her hopes up for anything once she finds out Violet's here visiting. Do you think I should change the plan?"

I hadn't thought about how my mum might react to me bringing a woman home, I probably should have. I thought it would be something Violet would enjoy, when she spoke about horses the other night her eyes lit up.

"No, it's a good idea. If you're lucky Mum and Dad will be busy around the property, you might not have much interaction with them. Just be prepared for Mum, you know how she is."

Our plates are empty, our bellies are full and we sit in silence for a few minutes while our food digests. I take my mobile from my pocket and look at the picture I took of Violet and I today. Seeing the way she leaned against me brought an instant smile to my face. I sent the photo to Violet, remembering she said she wanted to see it. I see Davy staring at me from across the table, his white teeth almost glowing he's smiling so hard.

"What are you grinning at?" Davy asks, standing from the table, clearing the dishes.

"Nothing. What are *you* grinning about?" I ask him dryly.

"Happy to see my big brother smiling."

I follow Davy to the kitchen where he puts the dishes in the washer then goes to the fridge and pulls out a beer offering it to me, I decline. He opens the top and takes a swig. Davy's mobile rings and he pulls it from his pocket.

"Hiya, love," Davy sits on the barstool at the kitchen island. There's a moment of pause where I assume Mia is talking but I can't hear, "Alright, sounds good. Glad you had a good time. See you soon." Davy ends the call and takes another pull from his beer.

"They're having a good time then?" I ask, I can see Davy isn't going to give me anything just to have the upper hand.

"Yeah, Mia said they went out for ice cream. I assume you're going to stick around. Violet might need someone to walk her home tonight."

Davy stands, walking down two steps to the living room, turning on the music. We sit on the sofa waiting for the women to return. I decided to send a text to my dad to give him a heads up that I'll be coming by the ranch tomorrow. If I text my mum it will be followed by a bombardment of questions and most likely a call.

Me: Evening Dad, I'm going to come by tomorrow morning. I'm bringing a friend who likes to ride. Be there around 9:30.

I send the text and two minutes later my mobile rings, checking the call screen I see it's my mum. I groan and roll my eyes. I declined the call and put my mobile on silent, returning it to my pocket. After another minute Davy's mobile starts to ring.

"Don't answer it, Davy," I practically beg him.

"You always have to answer the phone when your mum calls. It's a written code," He smiles at me mischievously as he answers the call, "Hi, Mum. How are you?"

Davy never breaks eye contact and with my eyes I plead with him to keep it short.

"Oh, really. Now that you mention it, he said he was going to stop by tomorrow," he smiles at me and I stand up and walk to the kitchen. "I'll let him know if I hear from him. Good night, Mum. Love to Dad." Davy disconnects then says to me, "You made me lie to my poor Mum."

"I didn't ask you to do that. But thank you. Maybe I should rethink this," I scratch the side of my jaw as I look out the kitchen window to the driveway.

"It's a good idea and she's going to love it. Don't second guess yourself," Davy slaps me on the back, I see headlights appearing in the driveway. "Mum said she'll have breakfast ready for quarter to ten."

I hear the two women laughing as they walk up the driveway to the front porch. Mia enters first holding the door for Violet. Mia tosses her bag on the kitchen island and goes to kiss Davy.

"You're back earlier than I thought. But I'm happy to see you," Davy hugs Mia and takes her hand leading her to the living room. "Can I get either of you a drink?"

"I'm good, thank you, Davy," Violet says as she stands next to me in the kitchen.

"Well, come sit down you two," Davy waves us to the sofa where he and Mia have settled.

"I should get back. I've got an early morning. Mia, I had a really great time," Violet glances at me before she moves toward the living room, Mia stands. "I hope you have a wonderful day with your family tomorrow. I'll see you soon."

Violet hugs Mia and kisses her check. She whispers something in Mia's ear which causes Mia to laugh and squeeze her into another hug. Davy stands and Violet hugs Davy.

"Would you like a ride home?" I ask her as she makes her way back toward me in the kitchen.

"I would, thank you," she turns back toward Mia and Davy and sends them a final wave.

"Good night, guys," I wave and turn toward the front door.

"Good night," they both call in unison.

I walk toward my car I parked at the end of the driveway. Taking the handle of the passenger's side door, I open it and step aside to let Violet into the car. When Violet is settled into the seat, I close the door and head to the driver's side.

"Did you have a good time at dinner?" I ask as I start the car.

"I did. Mia's great to talk to, she's really fun," Violet laughs, I know exactly what she's talking about. Mia is wonderful company.

"I'm glad," I say as I back out of the driveway and turn the car toward Violet's cottage.

As I approach the cottage I regret not walking her, the walk would have taken a few extra minutes. I park behind her rental in the driveway.

"Here you are," I turn toward her and see her blue eyes are alert and looking at me.

"Would you like to come inside?" she asks with an alluring smile.

If I go in there I don't know if I'll be able to stop myself from giving into the desire I've been feeling all day. Her face falls and I feel she can sense my internal struggle.

"I would love to, Violet. But honestly, I don't know if that's a good idea," I rub the back of my neck, "I don't know how casual I can keep things with you in that dress."

I laugh, my hands on the steering wheel tense. When I turn back to look at her, she's smiling with delight.

"I can change if it makes you more comfortable."

She leans over the center console and I feel a flutter of warmth that fills my stomach. This girl is going to kill me. She reaches up to my neck and pulls me toward her.

"I'd really like it if you would," she says as she kisses me lightly on the lips and tries to lean back in her seat but I catch her before she does.

I kiss her again, this time with ambition, I feel my body surge with heat. Violet kisses back, running her hands through my hair, I melt into her. I can't control the impulse, in a sudden swift move, I pull her on top of me. She giggles with the unexpected maneuver but goes back to kissing me. Her hands are in my hair, on my neck, she's driving me wild. I place my hands on her hips and press her onto my lap so she can feel the building yearning between my legs. When I do, she lightly bites my lower lip, I give a low groan.

"Are you sure you want me to come inside?" I ask her, my voice is pure gravel.

"I do," she sits back, searching my face.

The horn from the car sounds, making us both jump with surprise. I pull her back into me so as not to let the horn sound again.

"C'mon, before all the neighbors come out to check on the racket."

I open the door, Violet steps out pulling down the shortened dress as she goes. I grab her bag from the passenger's seat and hand it to her as I exit the car. When she finds the key, she unlocks the door and I notice a slight shake to her hand. We enter the cottage and Violet turns on the light in the hall. She removes her shoes and puts her bag on the coat rack above the bench. She walks toward the kitchen, her long hair flowing behind her.

"Water? Tea? Wine?" She opens the fridge, bending down to look inside.

"Wine would be great," I answer as I sit in the chair and turn on the lamp beside the sofa.

When she returns to me with a glass of wine, I can't help looking at her long legs. They seem to never end in that dress.

"I'm going to change," she says as if reading my mind. How does she do that?

"If you're comfortable you don't have to. I quite like the view," I smile at her and she laughs at my remark.

"I'm actually a little chilly. Would you do me a favor? Could you draw those large blinds over this front window while I change?" She moves toward the bed and takes an outfit that was resting on the pillow, "I'll be right back."

I draw the blinds around the living room. When she comes back in the room she's wearing shorts and a long sleeve shirt with a Boston Red Sox logo. She's just as beautiful in her sleeping clothes as she is in the minidress. I smile at her as she takes a seat on the sofa next to me.

"Can I ask you something?" Violet takes the cap off her water bottle and places it on the table in front of her.

"Anything."

I lean back and put my arm over the back of the sofa. Violet turns on the sofa bringing her right leg up, putting her foot under her left thigh.

"You seem straightforward, you'll be honest with me," she takes a sip from the water bottle, "Mia asked me to go to the wedding this weekend."

I sit up straighter, the excitement inside my chest balloons. I raise my eyebrows at her. I try to keep my excitement in check. She brings her left leg in now sitting cross-legged on the sofa next to me, her knees touching my thigh.

"I just met Mia but since I've met her we have shared a lot. I think meeting Mia in Pottsville over the weekend and then again here on Monday can't be a coincidence and throwing in the fact there is a connection between Mia and you, it all seems too unlikely to chalk it up to chance," she looks at me, probing for something.

"Okay, I'm with you so far," I say not wanting to lead her anywhere, I want to listen to what's going on in her mind.

"So, ultimately I don't know what this all means. I don't think she would invite me just to be polite. I don't think staying here a few extra days until the wedding will set my plans back since I have no plans other than getting to Whian Park at some point," she looks around then back to meet my eyes, "Would you be alright if I went to the wedding? If you have a date going with you, I wouldn't want to cause any inconvenience."

She waits a moment and when I don't respond right away she continues with, "That's all, that's my question."

I think of everything Violet said from the part about meeting Mia, then finding out the link to me. Hearing her say she's thinking of staying the rest of the week here has me elated with the possibility of spending more time with her.

"I don't have a date, I told you earlier I'm not seeing anyone. I think you should do what you want in regards to the wedding. Mia invited you because she genuinely thinks of you as a friend and wants you to be there. But don't let that make the decision for you," I put my hand on her knee, "I would like it if you stayed around a few extra days."

"Okay, I'll think about it."

She smiles and takes my hand still resting on her knee. Violet leads my hand up her thigh to the side of her hip. She continues to lead my hand up her side, placing my hand in the middle of her chest, I feel her rapid heart beat. I also feel she's not wearing anything under the thin shirt and I start to ache. My breaths quicken as I watch and feel the rise and fall of Violet's chest. I pull her on top of me again, I toss her hair back over her shoulder and kiss along her neck. She puts her hands on my shoulders, running her hands down and back up my arms. I pick her up and she wraps her legs around my waist as I stand. She kisses me with intense fervor and eagerness. When I ease her on the bed she reaches for my shirt and pulls it over my head. She looks longingly at my chest and abdomen.

"Your body is…" She trails off running an open hand over my chest before she finishes with, "well formed." She looks up to meet my eyes and I smile down at her.

"You're beautiful," I say before I cover her mouth with mine.

I crawl on to the bed, making sure I don't crush her with my weight. Wanting to ravish her completely, taking her without restraint, I remind myself to be slow and unhurried. I want to remember this moment when I finally have the girl that has occupied my mind since I first saw her in Brisbane a week ago. I sit her up and remove her shirt, watching as her eyes never leave mine. Her eyes darken as they fill with lust. When her shirt is off, revealing her full breasts, I stifle a moan I feel rising in my throat. She sets her hands on my waist and moves them up my stomach to my chest, she stops on my chest and smiles. I move on top of her again, my hands glide along her stomach and up to her breasts, her nipples are hardened peaks. When I take one between my forefinger and thumb I hear her moan with pleasure and it's the most amazing sound I've heard come from her. Taking her nipple into my mouth,

I teasingly flick it with the tip of my tongue and she grabs my head running her hands through my hair. I kiss and tease her breasts until I hear her breath quicken. I stand from the bed and bring my hands to the belt of my pants, unbuckling while I watch her stare at me. She shifts up the bed to rest on the pillows against the headboard. When I remove my jeans leaving my boxer shorts on and hover over her, I see apprehension sets in her eyes.

I pause before I lean into her, "Are you okay?"

I search her face for the hunger I had just seen but it's gone now, it causes me to still.

"I'm fine, it's just…" she shakes her head and puts her hands on my shoulders, "It's just been a long time since…" Her eyes glisten with memories or tears, she doesn't finish her thought.

"If you're uncomfortable we don't have to do anything," I reassure her by backing up and giving her space.

She self consciously covers her chest when I do. I feel a stab of regret for making her feel uneasy.

"No, no," she shakes her head, again, she laughs shakily.

I move beside her and wrap an arm around her shoulder. The feeling of her skin on mine is soothing. I run my fingertips up and down her arm in a reassuring touch.

"I don't want you to do anything you don't want to do," I tell her.

She rests her head against my shoulder and brings her hand to my stomach.

"Is this going to…" she runs her hand over my torso slowly, lightly making me feel chills throughout my body, "complicate things?"

As she finishes the question she looks down not wanting to meet my eyes.

"I don't know," my voice is a whisper and I wish I had more to offer than a lie.

"I'm finding it hard to think straight around you. I can't stop the pull I feel toward you." She presses her hand lightly on top of my stomach, right where I feel the same pull she's describing.

"I feel it," I say as I tighten my hold on her.

She looks up at me and covers her mouth with mine. We submit to all the desire we have felt for each other. It's exhilarating, feeling her skin against mine, hearing her sounds of pleasure and my name coming from her throaty voice. I've reached the point of no return with Violet, I've just crossed the Rubicon.

Chapter 15

Violet

I wake up in darkness and feel Drew's arm around me. I hear his rhythmic breathing and feel his breath on the top of my head. I slowly reach for my phone on the bedside table, 4:12 AM, I have three text messages. I tentatively remove Drew's arm from around me. I quietly get out of bed and reach for my shirt laying on the floor. I slip it on and reach for a pair of my sweatpants on top of my open suitcase. When I'm dressed I tip-toe to my laptop sitting on the kitchen counter. I slide out the back patio door, looking back on the sleeping man-god in my bed and smile. I sit at the patio table and start up my laptop. Last night was shockingly amazing. I had not been intimate with a man in a long time and what happened in that bed last night was well beyond anything I'd ever experienced or expected.

Sam and I hadn't slept together in a long time. A year ago I completely withdrew from him and Sam was always too drunk to even attempt to perform. I knew when Sam went on his trucking routes there had to be women he met up with. I found numbers and texts in his phone shortly after James died. I wasn't even angry, I was hurt of course, I was relieved he didn't have to crawl on top of me stinking like stale beer and whisky. I should have left then, I should have left years before I did. I can't go back, I can only move forward. Last night was, absolutely, what I needed. I needed to feel desired and wanted, I needed to feel I was worthy of a man finding me irresistible.

Drew was careful and attentive. When I told him it had been a while, he looked confused but he didn't ask questions other than if I was okay. He was tender and reassuring. When my computer chimed and opened to the desktop I quickly reached to lower the volume, not wanting to wake Drew. I load the video chat app and click on Beth's contact. She came on the screen a few seconds later.

"Violet! Woman, where have you been?" I see her walking on a street, shops and buildings behind her, "I haven't heard from you in days, I called Ally yesterday."

"I know, I'm sorry. I'm in Byron Bay, I met a few locals who have been showing me around. The days have gotten away from me." I see Beth take a seat on a bench near what looks like Faneuil Hall.

"Why are you sitting in the dark?" she asks as she looks at my background, squinting to see what she can make out.

"I came outside to call you. It's early in the morning here, I couldn't sleep." I bend over to plug in the string of patio lights by the door, "That better?"

"A little. So, what about these locals? They seem to be taking up your time, am I being replaced as your best friend?" Beth teases.

"I met a woman named Mia and her fiancé Davy. They've been great. She's wonderful, easy to talk to and a great host."

I tell Beth about meeting Mia in Pottsville then again in Byron Bay. I circle back to the day I arrived in Brisbane telling her about the man I met at the airport, skipping over the part at the bar. I tell Beth how I dropped my phone and the handsome Australian who brought it to me. I explain the night that unfolded at Mia's when I found Drew arriving in time for dinner. I fill Beth in about the day yesterday I spent with Drew. She listens intently, sharing wows and ohs along the way. I tell her about the events of last night but fail to mention he still lies sleeping in my bed. When I finish Beth stares back at me on the screen, her mouth open.

"Wow, I mean, just wow. No wonder you haven't been in touch. What's this guy's name? I'll look him up on FaceBook or Insta," she giggles with delight.

"Beth, c'mon. I need more than that. Am I being reckless?" I put my hands to my cheeks when I feel them blush.

"Hell no, Violet. Stop that! You're having fun, for the first time in a long time might I add. Enjoy the moment, get laid, for Christ's sake." I gasp in horror at her crudeness but she goes on, "Things with you and Sam have long been over. It's not like this is a rebound relationship. Find your confidence, it could be great for you. Just keep in mind you're leaving in the next few weeks and he lives there," she stands from the bench and starts walking again, "I know you think everything happens for a reason. Meeting Mia and him does seem stronger than coincidence, just don't fall in love and move halfway across the world."

"I would never leave home. I don't know if I'm making a good decision by sticking around here. What if…" I'm interrupted by Beth making a loud shh-ing sound.

"Stop. Right. There. Are you having fun?" she asks, raising her eyebrows knowingly.

"Yes, I'm having a great time."

I feel my cheeks redden with memories of last night.
"There you go, enjoy it, Vi. Stop thinking. I've got a meeting in ten minutes. I wish I had longer, call me when you can. Send me a picture of the hunk," she says, winking at me through the camera.
"Okay, thanks, Beth. I love you." I run my fingers through my hair and send her a wave.
"Love you, now go. Enjoy that Aussie hottie."
I close the computer and reach for my phone. I sent Beth the picture of Drew and I on our walk through Cape Byron. I look at my text and see two from Cullen and one from Ally. I responded to Ally's first.
Ally: Call me when you can, hopefully soon. Haven't heard much from you.
Me: I'll call you in a few hours, around 6 your time.
I then open the texts from Cullen.
Cullen: Haven't heard from you, let me know you're alive.
Then another 6 hours later:
Cullen: Don't make me call Ally.
I text Cullen a response.
Me: Busy few days. Alive and well. Stop worrying.
I place my phone down on the table and tilt my head back looking at the stars through the arbor above me. I'm having a good time here, I'm enjoying the company of Mia, Davy and Drew. I'm definitely enjoying Drew. I take a few deep breaths and look back at my phone, it's a little before five. When I look up I see a shadow by the patio door, it draws a scream from me, I jump up bringing my hand to my mouth. Drew opens the door. He stands in the door frame, shirtless, wearing his jeans from last night. The glow from the patio lights cast shadows over the boundless muscles on his abdomen and chest.
"Jesus, you scared me," I sat down with a feeling of relief.
"Imagine how I felt when I woke up to find the bed next to me empty. Are you alright? Was I snoring?"
He comes out to the patio and takes my hand pulling me to his warm chest.
"No. I couldn't fall back asleep so I thought I'd catch-up with my friend back home." I put my cheek against his bare chest, it's warm.
"It's cold out here, come back inside."

He picks up my phone and laptop, taking my hand and leading me back inside. I close the patio door behind me as I watch Drew place my items back on the kitchen counter. He walks back over to me, taking my hand leading me back to the bed. He covers me with the blanket and walks around to the other side.

"Let's try this again," he gets back under the blankets and turns my body to hold me as he was before I snuck away, "When a man wakes up from an incredible night with a beautiful woman and she's not there, it does something to the man's self esteem."

He tightens his hold and I let out a giggle.

"I didn't want to wake you, you looked peaceful," I say as I relax my body and allow myself to melt into his.

"I'm usually a light sleeper, I should've noticed you sneaking out," he says as his warm hand finds its way under my shirt.

I feel the heat stop on my left breast, I turn around to meet his eyes. I kiss him lightly, running my hand from his shoulder to his hand, lacing my fingers in his. He pulls me on top of him, I feel his stiff erection under me. We stay there for a moment looking at each other until he pulls my face to his. His kiss is warm and commanding, his hands are holding tightly to my hips as if I might blow away at any moment.

"I need a shower," I mumble into his mouth.

"That sounds great."

He sits up and hoists me up, carrying me in his arms. I laugh with amusement as he takes me down the narrow hallway to the bathroom. Drew turns on the shower tap and draws the curtain, letting the water warm. He proceeds to undress me leaving trails of kisses over my shoulders and neck. He then opens the curtain allowing me to enter.

"Are you joining me?" I ask as I step in, the warm water falling over my back.

"Is that an invitation?" he asks, raising one eyebrow. Smiling slyly, he reaches for the button on his jeans.

"It is," I say, my eyes wander down to his jeans as I watch him take them off and step into the shower.

After another sensual tryst in the shower we finally wash up and towel off. I stand by the bed with a towel wrapped around my body looking through my suitcase. Drew dresses in the jeans and shirt from the previous day. He had planned something for today but he wasn't straightforward about what we were doing.

"What am I dressing for today?" I wait for him to turn to me and I wave my hand over the suitcase.

"I'm taking you riding. Jeans will be good, maybe layers on top. There might be bugs out on the trail," he sees my eyes widen and smiles, "Is that okay?"

"Really?" My voice is high pitched with excitement, "You're taking me riding?" I clasp my hands together to keep from jumping up and down.

"Before you get too excited," his tone is a warning and he holds up his hands, "I'm taking you to my parents' farm to ride there."

"A *farm*? Your parents' farm?"

I can't contain the enthusiasm and hop on two feet. He laughs again as I start pulling out clothes for the day.

"Mind if I rummage through your fridge, I'll make us something to eat before we go."

"I should be cooking for you," I call over my shoulder while I take the pile of clothes off the bed, "I'll be right back."

I take off down the hall hearing Drew's low laugh behind me. When I finish getting dressed, I go out to the kitchen to see Drew standing over the stove. I can see his lat muscles flexing through his shirt as he stirs something on the stove. He turns and gives me a smile then goes back to his task. I return to the bed and pack up my suitcase putting it back under the bed. I hear Drew take down plates from the cabinet.

"Breakfast," he calls to me as he places two plates on the kitchen bartop and turns off the stove.

I sit on the barstool and look at the plate, egg sandwiches with spinach and tomatoes.

"Thank you," I say as Drew places a mug of hot coffee down in front of me. "Anything I should know about your parents before we arrive? Did you tell them you were bringing an American tourist that you spent the night with?"

He smiles as he chews, after he finishes his bite he responds, "I texted my Dad yesterday, I told him I would be coming over with a friend who likes to ride."

"Okay. Simple enough."

I start to eat my sandwich and wonder if I should feel more nervous than I do but for some reason I don't feel anything except excitement. Excited to see the farm, to ride and most excited to spend another day with Drew.

"My Dad doesn't say much, you know, the strong silent type. Mum, on the other hand, can talk a dog off a meat wagon, she's great though." Drew looks around the cottage then back to me, "Have you given any more thought to the wedding?"

"Since last night? No, but maybe some fresh air will help me think."

I have been thinking about it, I really want to see Davy and Mia get married. The only thing holding me back would have been if Drew had a date. We finish our breakfast, I do the dishes while Drew makes the bed. We lock up the cottage and head to Drew's car for the drive to his parents' farm.

"Do you mind if I call my sister along the way? I haven't spoken to her in a few days." I get in the car and put on my seat belt. "I told her I would call at about six o'clock Boston time." I calculated the time difference in my head, "So, I'd need to check in with her at about nine."

"That's not a problem. We should be there by then or you can call from the car, I don't know how good service will be out there. You can connect to the WIFI when we arrive at the house, it might be a better connection." Drew starts the car and pulls out of the cottage driveway.

"The time difference is hard to work around, I either have to connect early in the morning or late at night." I take a look at my phone and think about checking my email.

I haven't checked in with work for a few days and I scold myself for getting wrapped up when I should be focused on keeping in touch with things back home. Then I consider, I'm on a vacation. I'm allowed time for myself, if there was something urgent I would have heard about it.

As if Drew can hear my inner monologue he places his hand on my thigh, "Are you alright? If you need to make a call, please, feel free. If you need privacy I'll pull off somewhere and step out."

"No, I'm good. I'm going to check a few emails, make sure things at work are alright. I'm sure everything's fine," I say as I pull up my email and scroll through.

There are four from Stacy, I quickly browse through, a line on the last email from yesterday catches my eye:

Sam showed up at the office looking for you today. He was adamant I get you on the phone. I told him that wasn't possible and asked if I could take a message. He stormed out of the office after our conversation.

I feel my stomach ache, what the hell is Sam doing? He hasn't called or texted me since the first night I left. Now he's showing up at my office demanding to see me. I send a quick reply to Stacy:

Stacy,

Thank you for all the information and updates. I appreciate you stepping up while I take some much needed time away. I'll sign the paperwork you sent over and have it to you by morning. Regarding Sam, I'll let him know he shouldn't contact me at the office. If there is any further issue regarding him showing up please call the police for trespassing.

I'm livid Sam would do that, what's his motive? I take a deep breath and drop my phone on my lap.

"Shit," I exhale as I look out the window and try to relax myself with the scenery outside the car.

"Everything alright?" Drew asks, not taking his eyes from the road ahead.

"Yeah, work stuff but it'll be alright."

I think of my next move as uneasiness settles over me. I have to reach out to Sam and tell him he can't come to my office, I have to tell him to switch over the electricity, I have to do this soon so it doesn't become a problem later. I open my text messages and tap on Sam's thread.

Me: I got a message about you stopping by my office. If you come on the property again the police will be called. This is my place of business, you have no reason to be there. The electricity needs to be switched over to you, I've scheduled disconnection in 10 days. Do not contact me.

I hit send and take another breath. I shut my phone off and hope he doesn't respond. I feel the uneasiness from my stomach rising to panic in my chest. I try to breathe through it. I'm having trouble controlling it. Why did I decide to read my email now? I think about being so far away from home, from my work and it causes the panic to spread.

"Violet?" Drew asks, his voice sounds miles away.

"Hmmm," I hum a response while I close my eyes and focus on my breathing.

"Are you okay? You look rather pale, do I need to pull over?" he asks, taking my hand, it feels warm against the clammy sweat forming.

"No," I take a deep breath and try to look out the window.,"I'm sorry."

"Talk to me, please," he squeezes my hand and I feel the car slow.

"Don't stop, keep driving." I feel a little better listening to his voice. Maybe talking will help, "I had something come up at work. I feel bad being away but at the same time I'm glad I wasn't there."

"Do you need to call them? I can stop," he sounds concerned, his eyes shifting to the road and back to me in quick glances.

"I told you I ended things recently with my ex. I told you things weren't good for a long time. He's an alcoholic, it was really hard being with him, it was hard trying to leave him. I thought I could help him. I thought he could change," I take my hand away from him and take a few steady breaths, "His parents were alcoholics, he knew they had a problem but he couldn't see his problem. Or maybe he did and couldn't help it. I stayed with him too long. He came to my office looking for me yesterday and I have no idea why. He hasn't tried to contact me since the day I left him. I don't know why he would go there."

"Did he hurt you?" Drew asks in a serious tone laced with fury.

"He wasn't physical with me, well, just once. He's manipulative and mean. He would sometimes throw things in a tantrum, he was controlling but at the same time inattentive," I'm finding getting this out is helping the panic but bringing up the anger, "I felt nothing but relief when I packed up and left. I'm embarrassed for staying so long." I'm angry more with myself than I ever have been with Sam.

"You did the right thing and you have nothing to be ashamed about." He turns his head to look at me, studying me.

"The last year we were together, we only fought. He had other women and I wasn't even mad, I was relieved I didn't have to…" I trail off finding the courage to say what has been unsaid for so long, "you know, have sex with him. I still stayed. How can I not be embarrassed about that?" My heart raced with anger, although I felt foolish for saying these things, I needed to hear myself say them out loud, "He didn't want me for anything other than to cook, clean, drive him home from bars and to yell at when he was mad. He wanted a mother and I allowed myself to fill that role."

I put my head in my hands, my elbows resting on my thighs. "I was so stupid. He didn't want help, he didn't want to change. I kept losing myself trying to help him. For what? He's still a drunk and now I have to put myself back together."

Drew pulls off the road onto the shoulder. "You can't blame yourself for wanting to help someone. You can't blame yourself for falling in love with someone and wanting to stick by them during difficult times. I can't imagine how difficult that must have been for you. Watching someone you care about not care enough about themselves, that's hard. Being with someone who doesn't value and appreciate you must have been exhausting. He's an idiot for letting you get away." He takes my hand and holds it waiting for me to look at him.

I turn to look at him and say, "He's an addict, I don't think he could help the way he was."

"Fuck that. Don't make excuses for him."

Drew shifts the car to park and takes his foot off the break. I want to crawl inside myself and die from embarrassment.

"Can I ask you something?" he asks me and I nod. "Are you worried about him coming to your job or house when you get home?"

"No, I'm not afraid of him. I have no idea what he could have wanted when he showed up at my office. The day I left him, I packed up all my stuff and put it in my car while he was at work. When he got home from work I told him I was leaving and he said 'get the fuck out then'. That was it, I left."

The realization I have not shared that piece of information with anyone, not Beth, not Ally, hits me hard. I haven't spoken the truth about what Sam said to me until this moment, the shame takes over, I can't even look at Drew. I look out the window ahead of me. "I think because I left other times before and went back, he might think this is like those times. Maybe he went to my office to ask when I was coming back."

"Asshole," Drew draws from under his breath.

"I sent him a text, he knows now not to come by my office and he knows I'm not going back." I look down on my phone which is still powered down.

"Good." He watches me intently as silence fills the car.

"I'm sorry for unloading all that on you. I was in the midst of having a panic attack." I'm feeling very self conscious and wish the car was moving again.

"I told you, you never have to apologize to me." Drew kisses the top of my hand before returning it to my lap.

"Can we change the subject, please? Or is there anything else you want to ask me?" I ask, hoping we can forget this happened.

"We can talk about something else if you're feeling better. You're not as pale as a few minutes ago, you made me nervous," he smiles reassuringly but concern is still in his brow.

"Okay, let's get back on the road then," I say and feel comforted by the opportunity to move forward from the conversation.

Drew puts the car in drive and pulls off the shoulder onto the road. There's a long while of quiet and I see Drew thinking about everything I told him, about everything he has learned about me since meeting me at Mia's house two days ago. He must be thinking I'm such a case, the orphaned, grief-stricken girl just out of a traumatic relationship with an alcoholic. I must seem pathetic to him.

"Drew?" I ask in a whisper.

"Yeah," he says as he stops at an intersection.

"Would you rather take me back?" I want to give him the chance to get out of this situation if he's uncomfortable. "I wouldn't blame you if you did."

"What? No, why would I do that?" Worry and confusion settle on his features.

"I told you, I'm complicated and I don't think you knew what that really meant until now. I don't want you to feel like…"

I don't finish the thought before Drew cuts in, "Violet, I don't think you're more complicated than any other person might be. I want to take you out today. Please, don't be harder on yourself than you already have. If I didn't want to spend time with you I wouldn't, period."

After I shake off the embarrassment and anxiety, the ride to his parents ranch is filled with easy conversation. Drew talks about growing up on his parents farm as a child. I talk about Beth and our friendship that started in the first grade. As the conversation flows I start to feel better and soon we're laughing again. The clock on the display showed it was close to 9 and Drew said we would be arriving soon.

We pull up a long driveway, I see a herd of sheep grazing in the fields to the right. The front of the property is lined with split beam fencing. Drew pulls up to a light yellow, ranch style home with a wrap around porch. To the left of the house is a large brown barn, behind that are two more smaller outbuildings. The space is beautiful, the grass is lush and green. Drew parks the car between the barn and the house.

"Are you ready for this?" he asks me, opening the driver's side door.

"Yes," I open the door and hop down out of the passenger's seat.

Before we can make it to the front porch, we hear a loud whistle coming from one of the outbuildings behind the barn. I turn to see where the noise is coming from, I see a tall, husky man standing by the side of the barn. Drew veers off of the pathway to the house and starts toward the man, I follow close behind.

"Morning, glad you could make it." The man's voice is deep. He holds his hand out to Drew. As I get closer I see the man's eyes, a dark shade of blue but the same shape and likeness as both of his sons.

"Hey, Dad. This is Violet, she's visiting Byron on holiday," Drew introduces me and I take a step closer to Drew's father when he holds out his hand to me. His hand is rough and calloused.

"Hello, Mr. Harris. Thank you for having me."

Mr. Harris isn't as tall as Drew, he's a few inches shorter. The build of his body and facial features are very similar to Drew's. This man must've been striking in his day. He's still handsome but the years of working outside have left his face hardened with lines and wrinkles. His hair is gray under his hat.

"Please, call me Ian. Mr. Harris makes me sound as old as I feel," he says with a smile that I recognize as a smile Drew wears at times, "My wife's inside the house, hope you're hungry."

Ian starts toward the house, I notice a slight limp to his right side. We enter the mud room on the side of the house. Ian removes his hat, hanging it on the coat rack inside the entry. We walk down a small hallway that opens to a large kitchen. It's a full country kitchen with shiplap flooring. There's a huge stone hearth encompassing an entire wall, its original stone was kept intact. A new range and stove with an oven unit was placed inside the original hearth, it's stunning. Dark walnut cabinets line the walls above and below. There's a huge farm sink with granite countertops. I smell biscuits and bacon in the air, this is my new happy place.

"Wow, this is beautiful," I continue to look around the kitchen and see a large L-shaped island with spindle back bar seats at the far end of the kitchen, toward the front of the house, is a very large wooden farm table with seating for eight.

"Thank you! I told Ian, if we bought this place, I wanted a new kitchen with plenty of space." I'm greeted by a tall, lean, rosy cheeked brunette with a strong resemblance to Davy. Her green eyes and larger than life smile are all found in her youngest son. "Drew, it's been a while since you visited," she kisses him on both cheeks and turns to me.

"Mum, this is Violet," Drew stands next to me. "Violet, this is Clare."

"Violet! What a beautiful name, nice to meet you." She leans in, taking a hold of my shoulders and plants a kiss on each cheek as she had with Drew.

"Thank you for having me. I hope it's not too much trouble," I say as I take a step back, looking around the kitchen again.

"Ah, an American. What brings you to Byron Bay, are you here for the wedding?" Clare moves swiftly back to the stove and turns off the burner. She opens the oven to take out a tray of biscuits.

"I'm here on vacation. I met Mia a few days ago. Then I had the pleasure of meeting your two boys," I say watching Drew as he sends me a discreet wink.

"Oh, that's wonderful. Let's sit, then I'll take you to the barn." She sets the tray on the island where it's lined with a breakfast buffet.

"Who's gonna eat all this food, Mum?" Drew asks as he looks at all the choices. "We ate before we left."

"Pssh, sit yourself down. Eat something." Clare gives Drew a stern look, handing a plate to Ian.

"Thank you, Clare," I say as I put eggs, fruit and a biscuit on my plate.

I follow Ian to the table on the other side of the kitchen. I notice Ian doesn't take a seat at the head, instead he sits so he can look out the window onto the front pastures we passed along the driveway. I pause not knowing where to sit.

Drew comes up behind me, as if reading my mind he says, "Sit where you'd like, there's no assigned seating here."

I still wait to see where Drew will sit. He picks the seat across from his father and I sit next to Drew. Clare comes to the table with a tray of coffee and four mugs. She sets the tray in the middle of the table and starts pouring coffee into each mug.

"Violet, how long is your holiday? When did you arrive?" she asks me as she hands me a mug of coffee.

"I have about ten days left then I have to head back to the States. I've been moving my way down the coast, camping and staying in beach towns. I came to Brisbane last Sunday."

I look at Ian as he watches me explain, he looks at Drew with little expression then goes back to his plate of eggs. Clare, on the other hand, is filled with expressions of curiosity, wonder and excitement.

"Are you here by yourself?" Clare takes a sip of coffee.

"Yes," I try to change the subject from me to something else, "Drew said you bought this place a few years ago. Do you like the area?" I take a bite of melon.

"We like it. It's smaller than our last place but that's what we had in mind." Clare reaches for Ian's hand and gives it a squeeze.

"Mum, Violet has to make a call back home. Do you mind if she uses the study for privacy?" Drew stands up and puts his hand on the high back of my dining chair.

"Oh, it's okay. It can wait until after we eat," I offer.

"You don't have to ask, help yourself," Ian answers, glancing at me, his look is tender and comforting.

"Maybe in a few minutes, thank you," I say to Ian then turn to Drew and plead with my eyes for him to sit.

"How do you like Byron Bay so far?" Clare asks.

"It's stunning, I love the beaches. We went to Cape Byron yesterday. I found the scenery beautiful. I'd like to go to Whian Whian Park to do some hiking for a few days. Maybe after the wedding I'll stop there for a few nights."

I just implied I'll be at the wedding on Saturday. When I look over to Drew he's smiling as if I gave him the winning lottery numbers.

"You'll be at the wedding, splendid. We're so happy for Davy and Mia. You know they've been childhood sweethearts since they were eight years old. Too sweet, watching them run around together all these years," Clare says, placing a hand over her chest.

"Mia told me their story, it is special. I'm very happy for them."

I take a sip of coffee and feel Drew's hand on my thigh. I shake it off, I don't want to make this uncomfortable for anyone. When I move my leg Drew gets the hint and puts his hands on the table, giving me a sly smile.

"You two finish up. Violet, if you need to use the office or the spare room for privacy, please do. Your father and I will be in the barn."

Clare stands from the table and heads to the kitchen sink. She starts to wrap up the food on the island then heads to the mudroom where we entered.

"Coming to a new country alone takes courage," Ian remarks and he finishes off the remaining forkful of eggs on his plate.

Ian's penetrating eyes should make me feel uncomfortable but they bring me a sense of easement.

I shrug my shoulders and put my fork down. "I've wanted to come for some time and finally took the chance." I stare back at him trying to figure out what he's looking for in my eyes.

"We'll see you outside, take your time." Ian smiles and wipes his mouth with a napkin. He stands with his plate and heads toward the kitchen. He places his plate in the sink and heads out of the house.

"You go make your call, I'll clean this up." Drew stands, holding his hand out for mine. I take it and rise from the chair.

I follow Drew down the hall off the kitchen to a room set up as an office. Large windows give way to views of the back pastures and wooded area. The photos on the wall are pictures of horses, sheep and old barns in black and white. Drew points to a sticky note on the corner of the desk where there is a password to the WIFI scribbled on a bright pink square.

"Here you go, password, one, two, three, four," Drew smiles as he reads the password.

"Doesn't get much easier than that. I'll be right out."

I wait for Drew to leave before I connect my phone to the WIFI and call Ally.

"No rush, I'll be in the kitchen."

He gently closes the door behind him as he exits. I take a deep breath and figure out what I'm going to say to my sister. I told Beth everything and her reaction was encouraging, I hope Ally will feel the same.

Chapter 16
Drew

While Violet calls her sister I clean the table and start on the dishes. I'm anxious to get out on the trail and away from the constant questions by Mum. I should have thought this through more. Mum was excited to see Violet walk in, I'm sure she thinks this may go somewhere. But where? Violet's leaving. I was delighted to hear she's going to stay for the wedding, I couldn't control my pleasure. When she said she'd be at the wedding, I reached for her leg under the table and the gesture took her off guard with my parents sitting across the table. I'm starting to put together the picture of Violet's life, after just a few days I've learned a lot. During the car ride here I learned more. I still had a lot of questions but didn't know how to broach them with her. Some questions I had most likely couldn't be answered by her. How could a man let her walk away? How could someone treat her like she wasn't the most amazing thing that could happen to them? What kind of man would take her confidence, love, respect and leave her demoralized? I'm getting angry thinking about it. I couldn't help thinking maybe she came here, so far away from home, because she was afraid she'd go back to him.

Last night in bed, I felt her tentativeness, I felt she was unsure. It surprised me because she was so playful and assertive previously in the day. When things became intimate, I saw her retreat behind a curtain of unconfidence. She had nothing to feel insecure about. Violet was smart, charming and unbelievably attractive. How could she not know how amazing she was? I hear the door creak open down the hall, I finish putting away the dishes and grab a couple apples from the fruit bowl to take to the barn.

"Did you connect with Ally?" I ask as she walks toward me as I stand at the sink.

"I did," she says as she stops in front of me and smiles, it looks forced.

"Everything okay?" I tilt my head trying to read her face.

"All good. Can I help with anything here?"

"All set in here. Do you want to go out to the barn?" I feel the unease of curiosity settling in my stomach.

"Yes." Her smile comes to life now and reflects in her blue eyes.

"I got a pair of Mia's riding boots from her room if you want to use them." I point to the pair of brown leather boots I put in the hall.

"That's perfect, thank you." She walks over to the boots and picks them up. "You ready?"

"Let's go," I say as I walk in front of her to the side door.

I open the door and let her pass before closing it behind me. The walk to the barn is quiet and I try to gauge Violet's demeanor. Has something changed or is it me projecting the thoughts I had in the kitchen? As she walks a step ahead of me, I see her reach back and grab her hair from the base of her neck, she ties the honey blonde hair back with an elastic. I catch the scent of her shampoo when the breeze drifts back to me. It instantly sends a shot of need to my core. When we get in the barn I see Mum in the last stall on the right and Dad in the second to the left. There's a horse racked-up by a halter and lead rope on the side of the stall. The horse is light brown with a blonde mane and tail, Stevie is her name. She's often ridden by Mia when she comes to visit. Dad leads a stallion, by the name of Cash, and ties him next to the tack room. Cash is black with white markings on his back legs and his muzzle.

"You can start tacking, son," my father says to me as he stops next to Violet and turns his attention to her, "You know how to ride?"

"Yes, sir. It's been a few years but I can't imagine it has changed much," Violet offers my dad a warm smile as she takes off her hiking boots and starts to put on the riding boots.

"No, it hasn't. Stevie's her name," he points at the horse Mum is using the curry brush on, "She's got spunk but she's gentle."

"Stevie, for a girl? Like Stevie Nicks?" Violet asks, looking questionably toward the horse. "She's blonde like Stevie."

"You know Stevie Nicks?" Dad asks Violet with surprise.

"She's one of my favorites. Fleetwood Mac is one of my favorite bands." Violet turns to face my father, excitement plays on her face, "I enjoy her solo career as well but nothing beats the whole band."

Violet seems more relaxed since we left the house and it puts me at ease.

"Really?" Dad looks hesitant as if he might not believe her, "How old are you?"

"Don't you know it's impolite to ask a woman her age?" Violet laughs, her tone is full of amusement and playfulness. She gives my father a wide smile then answers his question, "I'm twenty-eight."

"Huh, I hadn't put you a day over twenty-five. What's your favorite Fleetwood Mac song?" Dad asks, quizzing her and I want to step in to save her.

At the same time, I haven't heard my father say this much to someone new, so I let them go. The conversation is also putting Violet in an animated state which makes my chest balloon with pleasure. Although it feels like eavesdropping, I'm learning more about her through this interaction I'm not a part of, I continue to listen in.

Violet laughs and her blue eyes brighten. "I can't pick one! I can give you my top five though. I like *Monday Morning* and *Go Your Own Way*. *The Chain* is a good song for the drum and guitar solos. I know Stevie doesn't lead on those three, if I have to pick a Stevie favorite it would be *Dreams* and *Gold Dust Woman*."

She looks to my Dad for his response. I know most of those songs, remembering how much my mother loved listening to music while cooking or cleaning the house.

There's a pause before Dad replies with, "Sounds like you're more of a Lindsay Buckingham fan." He smiles, I hear a low laugh escape him. I can't help but smile at the interaction I'm witnessing.

"He's one of the best guitarists, completely underrated, if you ask me." Violet starts to walk toward Stevie.

My dad turns to me, raises both his eyebrows, and tilts his head toward Violet. "She's something else."

"She sure is." I say.

I know she is. I also know she just impressed my father with that exchange, a close to impossible challenge. I watch Violet approach Stevie with a closed hand, letting the horse smell her before she reaches to touch her forehead. I start to saddle Cash while I continue watching Violet get to know Stevie. Mum hands off the brush to Violet as she starts toward the tack room.

When she gets close to me her eyes widen, her voice is a whisper, "She's beautiful, Drew."

"I have eyes, Mum," I say without looking up while securing the straps. "She's leaving in a few days," I say more to remind myself.

After last night, I don't know how I'll be able to watch this woman leave. I try not to think about that part of this situation, focusing on the little time I have with this mesmerizing girl who has captivated my mind and body.

"I know, dear. Don't get too attached," she says as she gently pats my arm before she enters the tack room. She comes out with a bridle and takes the second blanket I laid out. "Does she ride western or English?" Mum asks, breaking me from the thoughts of Violet scurrying through my mind.

"I didn't ask. I'm almost done, can you bridle him? I'll help her with the saddle." I take the blanket from her and start toward Violet and Stevie.

"Do you want a Western or English saddle?" I ask, putting the blanket on Stevie's back.

"I've never ridden English," she says concernedly.

"We have both. I'll get Mia's saddle." I walk back to get the saddle and see my mum has finished with Cash.

"I'm going to take him out back for you until you finish up over there." Mum says, leading Cash out of the barn.

I take Mia's saddle off the tack room wall and grab a bridle for Stevie. I see Dad come back in the barn with an empty wheelbarrow.

"You want me to saddle her or do you remember what to do?" I put the saddle on Stevie. It's been sometime since Violet has ridden and I want to make sure the saddle is safe when she gets on.

"I can do it. Can you watch me in case I forget something?" she asks, rolling down the straps and straightening the saddle.

"Sure," I step around to the other side of the horse and watch her work, "So, I heard you say you'd be at the wedding. Have you decided then?" I try not to appear too anxious for her answer.

"I'm going to go. Would that bother you?" she asks as her blue eyes wander to the corner of the barn where Dad is mucking the first stall.

"I told you, I'd be happy if you were there. Do you think I changed my mind in," I pretend to glance at my watch, "twelve hours?" I smile as I look back at her.

"Just making sure." She glances back toward the saddle working on her latigo knot. "Can you come check this? I don't know if it's tight enough, I don't want to end up under her."

I walk over to her side and check the cinch and knot. "Looks good to me, if it starts to feel loose I'll tighten it as we go." I start to take off the halter and hand Violet the bridle with my other hand. "Do you want to do this part, too?"

"Yes, please," she takes the bridle and finds the bit, handing me the reins, she slips the bit in Stevie's mouth.

"Just like riding a bike," I say as I hand the reins back to Violet and we talk toward the front of the barn. "You can mount up outside. Mum's with Cash."

"Cash? A black horse named Cash." Violet smiles and stops outside the stall where Dad's working, "Johnny Cash?"

"Yes, ma'am." He looks up from his work and smiles.

"It happens he's another favorite of mine. You like American musicians, I love it." Violet smiles at my dad and I see his face warm into a grin. "There are too many great ones to choose from with him. *Long Black Veil, If I Were a Carpenter*, *Get Rhythm* aside from the regular favorites." She clicks her tongue at Stevie and we continue out of the barn.

"You like old music, huh?" I'm surprised by her knowledge of the old tunes especially given her age.

"I got into a country kick when I was young, I found a Johnny Cash album in my dad's collection. I haven't shook Johnny since," she explains, I laugh as we approach my mum who's walking Cash in large circles.

"Thanks, Mum," I say as I take the reins from her.

"Enjoy." Mum walks back toward the barn after she gives me a wink.

I watch Violet mount Stevie with ease. "Alright, are you ready?" I ask as I use the saddle horn to swing up on Cash.

"Ready," Violet says with a smile, it fills my chest to see her so happy. "You lead the way, cowboy," she says playfully.

"I'm no cowboy," I squeeze Cash with my legs and loosen the reins, signaling him to walk on, "We're going to follow this path through the back field then take a left where it splits, it gets thick for a little while but will open again. Watch your head when we go through the thicket." I turned back to make sure she heard me.

"Gotcha, watch my head in the thicket," she repeats.

As we ride down the path I find myself wanting to turn around and watch her, I make note to have her take the lead after the grove.

I turn around to check on her once and see she's still smiling and a content affect fills her face.

"Was your sister happy to hear from you? You mentioned it had been a few days." I ask, breaking the silence as we leave the field.

"Yes, she was," she calls from behind me, "I told her about meeting Mia and Davy, I told her about you and what we were doing today."

"Oh, yeah? What did you tell her about me?" I turn around to offer her a smile.

"I told her you were showing me around. I explained to her about how we met at the airport. Then I told her how we met again and we've been having a good time." She lets out a small giggle and it warms my chest.

"You're having a good time?" I ask, I know she is, I don't wait for an answer, "That must have eased her mind."

"I'm pretty sure she's more worried now," Violet laughs, again, which makes me smile.

"Why's that?" I ask.

"Oh, she's worried you might be a serial killer or I'm going to fall in love and not come home. Like those are the only two possibilities, it's hard for Ally to see the gray in the middle."

"And what's the gray?" I ask, I wish I was able to see her face for this interaction.

"I guess the gray would be, we enjoy each other's company for the time I'm here, I walk away unscathed and return home in two weeks." She's quiet for a moment then adds, "Ally sees black and white and I romanticize situations so we balance each other well."

Violet is quiet for a few minutes as we walk the path then in a contemplative tone she asks, "Can I ask you something?"

"Anything," I answer with the single word as I always do when she asks that question.

"What happened with Lexi?"

The question she asks isn't one I anticipated. How did Violet know her name? I don't remember telling her. Then it hit me, it was Mia. Mia must've told her something. I take a deep breath and exhale, I pause while we exit the brush and continue to where the path widens. I slow Cash until Violet catches up with Stevie.

"What did Mia say?" I ask before I launch into an explanation.

"She didn't say anything. I told her what you told me and she agreed it didn't end well."

Violet glances at me apprehensively and I see the confidence in her posture has left her. I should've known Mia wouldn't air out my dirty laundry.

"Lexi and I worked together in Sydney, that's how we met. After over a year of dating we moved in together. I didn't want to live in the city but she loved it so we rented a flat. I don't know when the relationship started to sour but a few months before I left we weren't connecting. We wanted different things, she thought I would change my mind and I thought she might change hers." I look toward Violet and see she's watching me, her blue eyes look to mine with empathy. "Anyway, I went away for work, it was supposed to be a three day trip. I went home a day early. When I arrived back at the flat, I found Lexi in the shower with another man." I give her the details without emotion and wonder if it makes me seem cold.

"That's awful. I'm sorry, Drew," Violet's voice is barely a whisper, if she wasn't beside me I might not have heard it.

"It was, the guy in the shower was my best mate. I don't know how long it was going on but looking back I saw signs for months but didn't recognize them until I had left," I continue, giving her another piece of the story.

I think back to the many phone calls Lexi would ignore with a smile. When I'd ask who was calling she'd give the name of a friend but if it were just a friend she would've answered the call in front of me. There were times when she would come home late and take a shower before bed which was unusual because Lexi would always shower in the mornings. It made me angry, thinking of Lexi and Mike fucking at his flat, her coming home to shower before she got into bed with me. It was infuriating and I could feel my blood pressure rise with the memories.

"Your best friend? That must've been hard. You lost your girlfriend and best friend in one day." Violet's brow furrows, I see a crease form between them.

"Yeah. I should have left her months before but I didn't," I added quietly.

I still hold on to the idea that if I had left her when I felt things weren't getting better I could've saved myself some hurt. If I had left her and she ended up with Mike anyway, I still would've been hurt, I wouldn't have had to bear witness to it the way I had. We walk in silence for a few minutes. I glance at Violet a few times but she doesn't return my looks and I wonder what's happening inside that beautiful blonde head of hers. When I think I can't take the silence any longer, she breaks the silence.

"You must have a hard time letting people in. Trusting people and letting them get close," she seems to be talking out loud to herself, she looks ahead on the path. I keep quiet and she continues, "I have a hard time letting people go, I hold on and hold on. I lost parts of myself because I was more afraid of losing someone than of losing myself. Even if I didn't love that someone. I was holding on to the idea of what I thought that someone could be." She finally turns to me and we lock eyes. "It's hard to lose people close to us. That must've been very difficult for you. I'm glad you had Mia and Davy." She smiles but her eyes are sad.

"Losing someone because they cheated and lied isn't the same as the loss you've experienced," I say.

I watch Violet who doesn't take her eyes from mine. Violet has endured so much sorrow, loss and grief in the past 12 years, I understand why she wants to hold those who remain in her life so tightly.

"Loss is loss. Whether it be grieving death or grieving the living. You lost two of the closest people in your life. I'm sure you went through all the emotions, shock, anger, denial, maybe acceptance," Violet explains.

It never occurred to me that one could grieve a living person. I had experienced many, if not all, of those emotions after leaving Lexi.

"I've never thought of it like that but it makes sense. I can't believe it would be the same as losing a parent or sibling though," I say as we continue on the path.

Violet is kind, beautiful, compassionate, insightful the list ticks on, I hope she knows how very special she is. I hope the guy who stole her confidence gets whatever may be coming to him for taking it from her. I want to tell her she's one of the strongest humans I've encountered. I want to tell her all the qualities I find most appealing about her but I wait. I wait because today I learned I have a few more days with her. There will be another time to tell her everything I feel. Maybe I won't be on top of a horse but instead she will be in my arms when the time comes.

Chapter 17
Violet

After riding the trail behind the house, we worked our way back through the open pasture leading to the barn. It felt good to do something I haven't done in years, something that brought me happiness. Something that evoked delightful memories from my childhood, untroubled memories of my father. I'm smiling when I catch Drew watching me closely. Drew stops at the back pasture gate and leans over to unhook the loop of rope securing the pole to the fence. I click my tongue and pull back on the reins signaling Stevie to back up while Drew opens the gate.

"Want me to hold him while you get that?" I ask as Drew hops off Cash to fully open the gate.

"I got him." Drew nods toward the open gate allowing me to pass through before he walks Cash through and closes it behind them.

"Does she like to run?" I turn to look at Drew, watching the muscles in his forearms twitch as he grabs the saddle and mounts Cash again.

"She loves it, she's fast. You want to run her around this back range a bit?" Drew leans over and rests his arms on the horn of the saddle.

"I would." I readjust myself in the saddle and lean over to whisper to Stevie, "How about you, girl? You want to run with me?"

Stevie's ears twitch and her head bobs almost as if she's nodding yes. I loosen the reins and give Stevie a squeeze with my thighs. Stevie starts off with a trot and I slowly find my rhythm as she continues. When she reaches a canter I ease into her rhythm and feel the familiarity of being on top of a horse again. Just like riding a bike. The forward and lifting motion of my hips become rhythmic as I establish the beat of Stevie's steps. I debate allowing her to start her gallop, I feel a lack of confidence and trepidation in my chest but I try to push it down. As if Stevie can sense my apprehension she gives a snort and shake of her head. She speeds up without me cueing her, I allow her, finding the fast four-beat rhythm. My leg muscles work with my hips, I lean forward and bring my elbows in tighter to my sides. Feeling we're working together as one unit my uneasiness crumbles, I give a giggle as we gallop circles around the pasture. I see Drew from my peripheral watching us as he turns in small circles never taking us from his sight. I start to feel the heat emitting from Stevie's back, I bring her back to a canter and then slow her more and we close the circle closer to Drew and Cash. When I have her down to a trot I start my way toward the center of the pasture where Drew's smiling broadly.

"You can ride!" Drew shouts as we get closer.

My breaths are quick and my heart is racing. "That was fun." I stop when I'm next to Drew, I lean over and pat Stevie's neck feeling the heat and sweat. Cash gives a snort and stomp of his front hoof. I nod toward the black horse and say, "I think he is jealous."

"Yeah, he is," Drew says, looking down at Cash and strokes his neck, "I'll run him back to the barn." He smiles at me devilishly, I see desire in his eyes. "You looked happy out there."

"I forgot how much I enjoyed this. Thank you for bringing me here." Seeing him smile at me brings the swarm of butterflies back to my gut. "Should we head back?"

"Sure."

Drew clicks his tongue and gives Cash a nudge with his heels. Cash bolts off with an excited puff. I watch Drew and feel an untamed hunger rising inside me. Watching his muscular frame ride away from me brings warmth to my hands as I remember touching his body last night. I shake my head trying to subdue the desire and start off toward the barn.

"You ride well," Clare calls to me as I reach the side of the barn. "Drew mentioned you hadn't ridden in a while but you looked as natural as could be out there."

"Thank you," I say as I dismount, holding the reins in my hand.

"There's water and hay in her stall. I'll be inside the house, hope you can stay and visit some." She sends me a warm smile before she turns toward the house.

I enter the barn and see Drew has Cash already haltered, he's working on removing the saddle. I led Stevie toward the rear of the barn where I had tacked her earlier. Taking the halter from the hook outside her stall door, I remove the bridle and put the halter on. Using the tacking ropes, I clip her in and start loosening the saddle. I sneak a glance at Drew as he heaves the saddle off Cash and turns toward the tack room to put it away. I hear rustling behind me and turn with a start when I see Ian filling a bucket with water in the back of the stall.

"Didn't mean to startle you," Ian says, not taking his eyes from the filling bucket.

"No worries," I exhale deeply and slide the saddle off Stevie's back, she twitches with appreciation.

"How'd she treat you?" Ian sets the empty bucket outside the stall door and stands to my right giving Stevie's hindquarter a pat.

"She was wonderful, thank you." I place the saddle off to the side and watch as Drew walks toward us.

"I'll put this away." Drew grips the saddle with one hand and effortlessly carries it back to the tack room.

"You're heading back home soon," Ian says, it's not a question, his dark blue eyes burn into mine.

"Yes." I say the word slowly and shift my eyes from Ian to the blanket on Stevie's back.

Ian gives a low hum in acknowledgment. "Nice to see Drew smile. Nice to have him come visit."

Ian takes the saddle blanket from me and without another word heads toward the tack room. Drew comes back after the equipment is put away and hands me an apple.

"Thought she might want a treat."

"She deserves it for putting up with me."

I move around to the front of her and hold the apple in my palm. Stevie takes it in two bites, I laugh when apple juice drips from her mouth. The sound of the apple crunching is loud and satisfying. I feel Drew's hand at my waist, I take in a breath. Leaning back into his chest I feel him exhale on my neck. He brings his head down and nuzzles the side of my neck, planting a soft kiss close to my collarbone.

"You want to head back soon? I want to take you to dinner," he whispers in my ear, the rumble of his baritone sends goosebumps down my arms and a shudder through my entire body.

"How about I take *you* to dinner? As a thank you for today." I turn toward him and bring my hands around his powerful arms. I see the change in his eyes when I touch him, they darken and fill with want.

"No, I'll take you." He drops his head, his lips are millimeters from mine. I can feel his lips pulling me toward him.

"How am I supposed to thank you for today and yesterday?" I take a step back but Drew catches me around the waist in his grasp. I see the quick pulsating on the side of his neck.

"I could think of a few things you could do to thank me." He places a kiss on top of my head as I let out a laugh.

I feel Stevie nudge my back, sending me stumbling into Drew's chest. We both laugh, Drew reaches behind me to unclip her from the tacking ropes and leads her gently to her stall. As he closes the stall door, I reach around him placing my palms against his chest and my cheek against his hard, chiseled back.

"Thank you, again," I say as I feel him exhale deeply.

Drew places his hands on top of mine, lacing his fingers through mine and gives my hands a squeeze. He unhitches our hands, slowly turning around, moving my hands up to his neck. His kisses are slow and soft but it's not what I want from him. I move my hands up his neck, bringing my fingers through his hair. I kiss him hard and deep trying to convey the desire I feel. Not hesitating, he returns my kiss with matching fervor. He takes my face in his hands, our tongues collide with urgency and an energy that's transmittable. There's a sudden cough heard from behind me, I jump three feet away from Drew. I clear my throat and rub my palms on my jeans, I turn to see Ian holding a flake of hay in his hands. I feel my face redden with mortification, I feel like a teenager who was caught by a teacher making out with a boy in the hallway.

"I wanted to set this inside for her," Ian says, nodding toward Stevie who's drinking from her pail in the corner of the stall.

"Of course," I mumble, awkwardly moving aside and turn toward the tack room, practically running away from the two.

I go inside the tack room to take off Mia's riding boots and put back on the boots I came with. My face still feels flushed, I feel sweat forming on the back of my neck and chest. Scooping up Mia's boots, I tentatively peek out of the room and look toward the back of the barn. I see Drew with his arms resting on the stall door, I hear muffled talking as I sneak out of the room.

"I'm going to return these inside," I call out to Drew, not waiting for a response, I head toward the house shaking my head with embarrassment along the way.

When I get to the house, I knock on the side door but there's no response. I open the door and call out to Clare as I enter. Not hearing an answer I head toward the kitchen and call out again.

"I'll be right there, sweetie," her voice echoes from down the hall.

I take a seat at the kitchen table, looking out the window to the front pasture where the small herd of sheep graze. When I spoke with Ally earlier I told her where I was and some of the events that led me to this day. She took it as I thought, tight-lipped and not giving away much. Ally did say to have fun but to be careful, as she always did. I was hoping she would be a little excited for me, not for meeting a guy, but because *I* was excited. She probably thought my decision making was reckless from the time I boarded the plane to coming here to the farm with Drew today. Ally could never relate to my impulsiveness. If she was visiting a foreign country she wouldn't allow herself to be swept up by a man because it would never be a part of her plan. This wasn't a part of mine either, considering I didn't have any type of plan, I'm surprised it's happening.

I deserve a little fun and excitement, I haven't laughed or smiled this much in so long. But what was the cost? Would I be able to walk away unscathed in less than two weeks? Would I abandon what little plan I did have to stay in Byron Bay for the remainder of my trip? Am I setting myself up for something painful? Am I setting him up for a cruel departure? I see the way he looks at me, me leaving isn't going to be easy for him. Drew has been hurt before. He trusts me, he wouldn't have let me in if he didn't. I feel anxiety and unease creeping in my stomach. What the hell am I doing? The lack of confidence and self doubt I feel now is close to oppressing. I should go before this gets more complicated, continue on with the plan I originally had, continue down the coast and see the country. I was engrossed in my thoughts, I didn't hear Clare return to the kitchen. I didn't hear her slide out the chair next to me and sit down.

"Are you alright, love?" Clare gently touches my arm as she vies for my attention, I almost leapt out of my chair.

"Oh, I'm sorry," I gasp and bring my hand up to my chest, "I was lost in my thoughts, I didn't hear you." I push away the thoughts, turning to Clare with a forced smile.

"Well, I know what that's like," she huffs a sigh and hands me a steaming mug of tea.

I clear my throat, focusing on Clare. "I really appreciate you having me today. I know I said it earlier but today has been really great. It brought back so many memories of my..." I catch myself before I say the word father, "old riding days." I offer a small smile.

"Anytime, love. I'm happy to have my boys visit and I'm always happy to meet their friends," she says the last word with a raised brow.

I take a sip of my tea and don't respond to her fishing. I glance toward the kitchen hoping to hear the door open, willing Drew to walk back through the house.

"I'm sure he'll be back shortly," Clare states, reading my stare. "Were you able to connect with your family back home?"

"I was. My sister likes it when I check in with her every few days while I'm here, to let her know I'm alive and well."

"Ah, a sister, I have two. Thick as thieves, sisters can be," she laughs affectionately. "Is it just the two of you?"

"Yes," I answer in one word, not wanting to go into the explanations as to why it is just Ally and I.

"Are you younger than her?" she asks, holding the mug between both her hands.

The question brings a laugh out of me. "Actually, I'm older but you wouldn't know it if you didn't know us. She was always bossing me around when we were younger. She was, and is, always one step ahead of me."

Clare stares out the window to the herd of sheep. "Your parents must be thankful for you girls. I always wanted a little girl. Don't get me wrong, my two boys are my world," she looks at me with an expression of remorse for sounding as if she wasn't happy with the hand dealt to her. "It's that saying about sons and daughters," Clare tilts her head as if trying to remember, "A daughter is a daughter for life. A son is a son until he takes a wife."

"I've never heard that saying. I don't think I like it," I scrunch up my nose and make a sour face, "You could view it as gaining a daughter."

I hear the door creak open from the side entry and relief washes over me. Drew stalks into the kitchen, smiling when our eyes meet.

"Sorry, it took longer than I thought. Everything good here?" His eyes dart from Clare to me and his brow raises in question.

"Of course, dear. Just talking about family." Clare stands and takes her mug to the kitchen.

"You were?" Drew looks at me curiously, saying each word slowly.

"I was telling Violet how lucky her parents are for having two daughters."

Clare places the mug in the sink and looks at Drew who now has his back to me. I can see by the look of confusion on Clare's face Drew must be giving her a look of his own.

"Jesus, Mum," Drew mumbles under his breath as he turns around and comes to the table. "You alight?" he whispers to me.

"I'm fine. Please, don't say anything," I whisper back to him and see Clare straining to hear what the hushed tones are about. I smile at her and stand up from the chair.

"We were having a nice conversation before you busted in bringing Jesus into things." She raises her eyebrows at her oldest son and puts her hands on her hips.

"Sorry, I have to get back. I need to get some things for the bachelor party tomorrow and I'm taking Violet out for dinner."

"Dinner? That sounds lovely," Clare sounds a little deflated, I think she planned for us to spend the afternoon with them. I feel a tug of regret especially after the conversation we just had. "We thought you both might want to stay here for dinner. Let me make you lunch at least before you run out."

"It's okay, Mum. We'll have dinner together Friday with Davy and Mia. I've really got to shove off," Drew answers with warmth, sensing her disappointment.

"Oh, yes, Friday. Violet, will you be at dinner?" Clare asks me with hopeful eyes.

"No, that sounds like a family event," I step toward her wanting to thank her for the day, "I might see you at the wedding Saturday."

"Might?" Drew calls from behind me with a hint of confusion in his voice.

I try to dismiss his question by offering Clare my hand, "Thank you again, Clare. You have a beautiful home and I appreciate you letting me ride Stevie today."

Clare looks at my hand, she openly scoffs as she wraps her arms around me. "I should be the one thanking you." she whispers in my ear, "For putting a smile on my son's face, I haven't seen that in a long while." She kisses both my checks and gently pats my shoulder.

I smile at her and turn toward Drew, "I'm going to say good-bye to your father. Should I meet you out front?"

His eyes search mine, knowing I heard his question a few moments before. He puts his hands in his pockets, "Sure, see you out front."

As I walk back down to the barn I take one last look around the property, it's beautiful here. I see Ian behind the barn holding empty burlap feed bags.

"Mr. Harris!" I call out and pick up my pace, now jogging toward him.

"Ian," he responds as I get closer, placing the sacks on a pallet behind the barn.

"Ian," I echo, standing in front of him, "Drew has to get back, I wanted to thank you, again. It was great meeting you and your wife. You have a beautiful spot here."

I hold out my hand to him as I did Clare, knowing he wouldn't pull me into him as his wife had done inside the kitchen.

"I'm glad you enjoyed it, come back anytime." His calloused hand takes mine and he squeezes gently. "I'm sure I'll be seeing you again before you leave for home." His statement is more of a question and has me shifting on my feet. When I don't respond he continues, "Well, you best be off." He nods behind me and I see Drew walking to the SUV.

"Yes, have a great day." I turn toward the path leading to the driveway.

"Violet," Ian calls after I've taken a few steps.

I turn back to face him without responding, he takes a limped step toward me and clears his throat. There's a short pause while his dark blue eyes meet mine. He nods toward Drew who's leaning on the passenger door of his car, watching my exchange with Ian. His muscular arms are crossed on his chest, his brow furrowed in curiosity.

"My son hasn't brought anyone around in a long time," he says the words like a warning and I stiffen my back in response. He lets out a low laugh and goes on, "Sure, he's big and strong on the outside but…" Ian lets out a breath, his eyes shift toward Drew in the driveway. I see he's searching for words.

"I know." I take a step toward him, I know the hurt Drew has experienced. Ian doesn't know, I share a similar vulnerability. "Are you telling me to be careful with him?" The question rolls out of me. Although Ian's seems guarded, I feel an openness with him at this moment.

Ian let out a laugh making his eyes sparkle. "I'm not telling you to do anything. You're both adults and I've learned a long time ago you can never tell a woman what to do," he put up both his hands with his palms toward me in mock surrender, "I just thought you should know. I don't mean anything by it."

Ian seems straightforward and uncomplicated. He didn't ask me questions that made me feel he was trying to figure me out, unlike Clare. Not that Clare was unfriendly or intrusive, she was curious. Ian's curiosity is delivered in searching glances not in prying questions. With the thoughts I had while sitting and the kitchen table and now this conversation I feel my head spinning.

"Drew's amazing, you and your wife did a great job with both your boys," I offer him a remorseful smile, "I would never intentionally hurt him, he's been very kind and considerate. But I won't lie to you, Ian. Never have I been a blue calm sea." I search him to see if the last line registers with him, when he smiles, I know it does.

"Well, then, there it is." His smile doesn't fade as he steps back. Ian turns and walks toward the back of the barn and I head toward Drew standing against the grill of his SUV.

"All set?" Drew asks, curiosity written all over his face. He steps toward the passenger side of the car, opening the door for me.

"Yup."

I settled into the seat and put on my seat belt. Drew gently closes the door and walks around to the driver side. I don't think I could ever get used to the driver being seated on the right side of the car and thankfully Drew offered to drive during my time here.

"I've never seen my Dad talk so much to a stranger." Drew gives the same low laugh his dad had given a few moments ago, it makes me smile.

I try to think if I laugh like either of my parents had and deflate at the feeling that I don't really know. Drew makes a wide turn in the driveway and heads down toward the road.

"So, a bachelor party tomorrow?" I try to divert the conversation from his parents. I don't want him to ask what his father and I were talking about on the side of thc barn before we left.

"Yeah, a small gathering. Two of Davy's friends are flying in tomorrow morning and two others are local. Davy and I plan to meet them in the morning."

"You must have a lot to do, if dinner doesn't work tonight I understand." I didn't consider Drew spending time with me may be interfering with his best man duties these few days before the wedding.

Drew reaches for my hand resting on my lap. "I want to take you to dinner. I'll be busy tomorrow, I won't be able to spend time with you." Regret and a hint of annoyance fill his tone, "I have to go to the grocery to get some things for tomorrow but that's it." There's a short pause before he continues, "Can I ask you something?" Drew takes a glance at me before returning his eyes to the road.

"I'm going to the wedding. I'm going to call Mia later and tell her."

I knew what he was going to ask, I knew because the wrinkle in his brow hadn't disappeared since the moment in the kitchen when I used the word "might".

"Do you read minds?" he asks and pulls my hand to his thigh, "Sometimes I feel like you do."

The rest of the ride Drew tells me about the plans for the bachelor party. I'm surprised by the idea of a male bonding day filled with activities and barbecues, not like the typical bachelor parties that happen back home. As the conversation flows I find myself registering how at ease I am with Drew. All my thoughts and doubts, although still in the back of my mind, are not consuming me. I notice how much I'm laughing, it feels really good to laugh. To not be walking on eggshells, to be able to relax next to a man, brings me comfort and relief. Drew doesn't judge my tone or words, even when I answer him with sarcasm his eyes don't cloud with resentment or rage. He laughs and asks me questions about myself, my thoughts, my feelings, it's refreshing and encouraging.

I remind myself to call Mia and the host of the rental to see if I can stay one additional night as I know the rental is booked for the weekend. I'll also need to find a place to stay the night before and night of the wedding. When we arrived at the cottage, I couldn't believe the two hour drive went by so fast. Drew opens the door for me once again and walks with me to the front steps. He waits until I'm inside before he heads back to his car to continue with his errands. After I watch him leave I head to my suitcase tucked under the bed, I lift it up and look for something to wear tonight. After I've chosen an outfit I head to the couch and tap Mia's number on my contacts. She's with her sister and mother today, I'm prepared to leave her a message letting her know I plan on attending the wedding. I'm surprised when I hear Mia's bright sing-song voice calls over the receiver.

"Violet! I was just talking about you," Mia answers, sounding breathless.

"Hi, Mia. Hope your day's going well." A smile spreads across my face.

"Yes, we picked up the dresses and I'm getting ready to take my mum and sister to their rental in Byron. What about you? How was *your* day?" Her questions are filled with interest.

"I had a great day. I know you're busy, I wanted to let you know I've thought about the wedding. I'd love to come if the invitation still stands." The last sentence is greeted by a short but high pitched squeal of delight.

"Yes, of course. We'd be so happy if you came." Mia's enthusiasm is contagious.

"I have your shoes from last night. I was going to walk them back over later." I glance at the entry landing where Mia's heels are sitting under the bench.

"Oh, no problem. Davy's home if you want to drop them off or if you want to pick out another pair for tonight," her voice pitches and I wonder how she knows I'm going out tonight.

"How do you know I'm going out tonight?" I laugh as I ask the question.

"Drew hasn't let you out of his sight. I saw his car there *very* early this morning when I went for a walk. It looked like it hadn't left since last night, there was a layer of dew on the windshield," she laughs, she could be a detective with her attention to detail, "I assume, since he's booked up tomorrow, he might want to do something with you tonight."

"I see," I manage to say between the shock and surprise of her statements.

"I would love to hear all about your day and maybe even last night if you want to get together tomorrow. Do you want to get breakfast or maybe take a walk on the beach? I'm free until I meet up with my family again around one o'clock," Mia talks so fast, I don't know if it's because I'm trying to recover from her all-knowingness or because she's anxious to get back to her mother and sister.

"Sounds great. Call me in the morning." I wait for Mia to say goodbye before I disconnect and drop my phone to the couch with a smile.

After the call with Mia, I look up the number to the host of the cottage and dial the number. There's no answer, I leave a message asking if the cottage is available for one more night. I disconnect the call and head for the shower. As I disrobe I smell fresh air and hay on my shirt, it brings a smile to my face. While in the shower I feel the muscles in my thighs and hips throb with certain movements. I hadn't ridden in a while, the muscles were worked in ways that left them tense. I start to think about the last conversation I had at the farm and continue to wonder what Ian was trying to relay to me. He wanted me to know his son had been hurt, which I knew because Drew told me. What I gathered was, Ian wanted me to understand Drew bringing me there, him spending time with me means something to Drew. It meant enough for Ian to say something about it. It meant enough for Clare to whisper her thanks to me. I replay the conversation over and over again.

My experiences in life were scarring and upsetting. Nothing in my life, from the time I was 16 until now, has been easy or painless. When things start feeling good I'm slammed with a tempest of grief. Sure, I didn't make things easy for myself at times, especially having stayed in a damaging relationship for so long. Drew and I both hold pain and hurt from past relationships but it's not something we can't, or won't, get over with time. Drew's going to be fine. As soon as he learns he can let someone in, not everyone is out to deceive him. Just as I will learn I can't save people from themselves or from the circumstances of life.

I towel off and head to the bed to dress for the evening. When Drew dropped me off he said he would return around 5 to pick me up. I glance at the clock and see I don't have much time. Dressing quickly, I head back to the bathroom to dry my hair. I hear my phone chime with a message, I backtrack toward the couch and pick it up. There's a voicemail and I listen. The host replied saying the cottage is available for one more night but I need to vacate the property by 9 AM Friday morning. Feeling a sense of relief wash over me knowing I have somewhere to stay tomorrow, I still need to find a place for the weekend. After I dry my hair and put on makeup I take one more look in the mirror. There's a brightness to my eyes I haven't seen in a long time. As I finish in the bathroom I hear a knock on the front door. Drew arrived at five when he said he would.

"I hope you don't mind, I changed the plans for tonight," Drew says as he walks inside the cottage after I open the door for him.

"Sure, as long as there's food involved, I'm up for anything." I put my hand on my stomach and felt a little rumble.

"There will definitely be food involved. I went to the market and picked up a lot for the guys tomorrow. You know what they say about food shopping while you're hungry. I think I bought half the store," his laugh hits me and there's a warming in my cold, empty stomach, "I thought I might cook for you at my place. I have to get the stuff I bought in the fridge and I need a shower, I smell like a horse." Drew takes my hand hanging at my side, "If you'd like, we can still go out for dinner. I can drop the food off with Davy." He searches my face for a disappointed look, I don't have one.

"I'd like you to cook for me."

I give his hand a squeeze of reassurance and head toward the entry to put on the shoes I hadn't returned to Mia. Drew watches me as I work the straps over the top of my foot, his eyes give off heat.

"I'm ready if you are," I say as I stand in the heels I just put on and reach for my bag on the bench.

"You're so beautiful," he whispers as he walks toward me, he's inches from me which causes the mammoth butterflies to wake.

I feel a strong need to take him into me. He brings his lips to mine, my knees start to shake as he pulls away leaving me wanting more.

"Let's get outta here before I pull you to the bed and the food spoils in my car."

Chapter 18
Violet

The ride to Drew's house was short, I helped him bring in the groceries he had in the car. He was right, he bought enough to feed a small army. Placing all the bags on the granite island, I look around the house. It's very clean, nothing is out of place, there's no clutter. He had all the basic furnishings, nothing more. Much like Mia and Davy's house, the kitchen led to an open living area separated by three steps. The windows on the side of the kitchen and living room were floor to ceiling. Opposite the windows was a hallway which I assume led to bedrooms. The furniture is rustic, dark leather and solid wood. I notice a few personal touches, a picture of Drew and Davy sitting on the side table by the couch. The brothers have their arms around each other's shoulders, wearing hiking gear while they stand in front of an amazing view of a lush, green valley. Another picture of young Davy, Mia and Drew, maybe in their late teens, sitting on a porch. Davy and Mia sit close together on a porch swing, Drew sits on the top step of the porch leaning back against the railing. I take the picture off the table to get a closer look.

In the picture Mia's so beautiful and young, she still is. The picture here shows her innocence, her untroubled eyes are full of joy. Mia does a good job of hiding her worries and loss but her eyes hint to something now, something you don't see in this picture. Drew looks young, his frame is full but not like he stands today. His piercing eyes stare back at me making me smile, his smile is small but filled with amusement. Drew's forearm rests on his knee as he sits on the step, he's so handsome it steals my breath. Davy sits next to Mia with his hand on her knee. Davy has a wide smile, I've come to know this smile as his signature feature. Mia leans her head against his arm, as they were the other night sitting together on the couch. It stirs something inside of me, these two are perfect for each other. This picture must have been taken ten years ago. Seeing Davy and Mia look as happy together now as they are in the picture gives me so much hope for them and for me. It's possible to find someone to be happy with for years and years. I'm sure it's not easy, any relationship is work. But seeing two people working together to make each other happy, making each other better is encouraging. I don't hear Drew come up behind me until his hands are resting on my shoulders, looking over my shoulder to see what I'm looking at.

"Right before Davy went to university. I was twenty-one, Mia was about seventeen." He gently rubs the top of my shoulders.

"Mia and Davy look so happy, just as they do now. I swear, they were in this same position the other night. Her resting on his arm and Davy with this same smile," I look back at Drew as he leans in closer to peer over my shoulder, "It's great to see them still so happy."

"Yeah, I'm happy for them. I marinated steak, and I made a plate with dip and veggies if you want to snack. I need a shower, I'll be right out. Make yourself comfortable," He motioned toward the plate he left on the table in the middle of the living room, "I'll start dinner when I get out."

I place the picture back on the side table and take a seat on the sectional in front of the platter of food. I didn't realize how hungry I was until my eyes locked on the food. I watch as Drew walks down the hall toward the other side of the house, I assume to his bedroom. As I pick at the vegetables I look out the window to the patio. Standing to take a closer look, I see a stone patio area with a table and chairs. Beyond the patio is a tree with green globes, possibly a lime or lemon tree. Next to the tree, on the ground, there's a wooden garden bed. I grab a handful of baby carrots and head out to the patio. The sun is setting and the temperature has dropped considerably since earlier. I walk on the lush grass toward the back of the yard where the tree stands. I look at the fruit growing, they're small fruits, not ripened yet. The leaves are long and oval shaped, this is a lemon tree. Lime leaves are smaller and more round than oval. I smile to myself thinking about the lemon tree I had back home. I turn toward the garden bed and look at Drew's craftsmanship. He did a great job, not that I expected less. Growing up on a farm and having the background of a mechanical engineer, I wouldn't doubt he's great with his hands. He *is* great with his hands, remembering how his touch felt on my skin last night, the way his touch elicits an ache and hunger for more. I look around the yard and see why Drew likes it here, it's private like he said.

Heading back toward the patio I take a seat in one of the cushioned chairs. The sun is low, spreading out shades of buttercup and burnt orange throughout the sky. The hills in the backdrop of

Drew's yard are darkening from bright tones of shamrock and lime to dark shades of emerald. I hear the patio door open and turn in my chair. Drew steps out dripping with temptation and allurement. His light hair is darker, still damp from the shower. He's wearing faded jeans with a white shirt that hugs his biceps and chest perfectly, accenting his defined build. A shiver shoots through my body and I feel my cheeks blush.

"You okay?" He steps toward me with a sexy smile.

"Yes," I mumble, trying to refocus on the yard but my eyes won't leave his body.

Drew stalks toward the grill, taking off the canvas cover and igniting the flame.

"I'm going to start cooking. Can I get you a drink?" He asks, standing in front of me while I'm still seated in the chair. He towers over me but I don't feel intimidated, I feel secure.

"I'd love some water."

I stand when he opens the door and follow him inside the house. The smell of sandalwood drifts in his wake. Drew opens the fridge, taking two bottles of water and the bowl of meat he had marinating, placing them on the island. He takes out a tray of vegetables he seasoned, potatoes, carrots, beans and squash, setting them on the counter. He starts the oven and places the tray of veggies inside. Now turning his attention toward me, he hands me the water bottle, takes the bowl of meat and motions toward the patio door.

"I'm going out there, you're welcome to join me if you'd like. It won't take long to cook these tips."

"Sure, can I help with anything?" I look around the kitchen, I find an empty serving plate and take it with me for when the meat is done cooking.

"Perfect, thank you." Drew takes the lead and I'm happy to watch him as I walk behind.

As Drew cooks the steak tips he talks more about the events for the next day and about Davy's four friends that plan on joining in on the festivities. Tomas and Sean are Davy's friends from his time at college and Drew seems to know them well. They both currently live in Newcastle which is north of Sydney. The drive from Newcastle to Byron Bay is over 6 hours, the two friends elected to fly in early tomorrow morning. Ethan and Brian are local to Byron, Ethan is married with a young boy. When the steak is done and plated we head back inside the kitchen. Drew sets the small table in the corner of the kitchen. He then takes the veggies from the oven and places the steaming food in the middle of the table.

"I thought about having wine with dinner," he goes to the wine rack near the fridge pulling out a bottle, "Is that okay? We don't have to."

His question is subtle but I know what he's asking. He wants to know if I feel comfortable with him drinking given all that he has learned about my past relationship.

"You can drink whatever and whenever you'd like. You don't have to ask," I give him a reassuring smile as I sit at the table. "I'll join you for a glass after dinner but I need to get something in my stomach first."

"Water it is." He sets the bottle of wine on the counter and pulls out two glasses from the cabinet, filling them with water and adding lemon wedges. When he returns to the table to sit he slides the water glass toward me.

"Thanks, this all looks so good." I take in all the food on the table, the bright colored vegetables and the smell of the steak makes my stomach rumble with anticipation.

"Let's dig in." Drew hands me the serving spoon for the vegetables and he forks steak on to his plate.

We start the meal quietly, we're both hungry and don't say much during the first few bites. The steak is tender with a sweet but smoky flavor, the vegetables have a hint of rosemary and citrus.

"This is delicious," I break the silence before I take a sip of the water, he gives me an appreciative smile.

Drew stands and walks to the kitchen counter where he turns on a small box and plugs his phone into an auxiliary wire. I hear the song *Dreams* come over the surround sound. I smile, he heard me tell his father Fleetwood Mac was one of my favorites. Drew turns the sound down so as to not drown out our conversation.

"I meant to turn that on earlier." He sends me an affectionate smile as he sits back down at the table.

"It's nice. Do you like this music?" I ask him as I take the last bite of steak remaining on my plate.

"I do, I grew up on classic rock like you. I went through a country stage as well, honestly, I haven't listened to music in a while. When I listen to something at the gym or in the car it's usually a podcast or talk radio." He shrugs his shoulders.

"My parents loved music. I remember them playing Van Morrison, Cat Stevens, Bob Seger, Warren Zevon, James Taylor, Bruce Springsteen, and so many more. Sometimes my dad would stop the cassette and ask me what I thought the song meant," I laugh at the memory, "He was always doing stuff like that."

"Sounds like our parents had the same taste in music. I know a lot of those guys, Seger is one of my favorites." Drew leans back in the chair. His eyes penetrate me, awakening the fire in my core.

"I saw him live a few years ago, he didn't disappoint," I say.

I place my fork on my plate and take the glass of water from the table. Drew stands and takes our plates to the sink, I follow him to help with the clean up.

When he sees me next to him at the sink he says, "Go sit, I got this. I'm going to wrap up the vegetables on the table and put these in the wash."

"You wrap that up and I'll put these in," I say, reaching into the sink, I take the plates Drew placed in.

After I put the two plates and silverware in the dishwasher I wash my hands at the sink. I search a few cabinets looking for wine glasses. Finding the bottle of wine Drew set aside earlier, I pick up the corkscrew beside the bottle. Drew passes by me putting the vegetables in the refrigerator, he turns back to me and takes the corkscrew from my hand. When he opens the wine his forearm muscles and biceps twitch as the cork pops out. Drew fills two glasses of wine and puts the cork back in the bottle. Motioning toward the sectional with a tilt of his head I fall into step with him. Before we sit on the couch I remove my shoes so I can curl my legs up without scratching the leather with the spikes of the heels.

"What time do the festivities begin tomorrow?" I ask as I bring the wine glass to my lips, watching Drew over the rim as he sits down next to me.

"Davy's cooking breakfast for us around nine then we'll head to the beach. What about you? Have plans for tomorrow?" He puts his arm around the back of the couch, his body opens toward me, as if calling me into him but I stay on my side.

"I'm going to have breakfast with Mia. I'll go down to Broken Head Nature Preserve and walk around after breakfast. I'll probably spend the night doing laundry and packing. I've got to be out of the cottage Friday morning, it's being rented for the weekend." I readjust on the couch drawing my legs out from under me.

"Do you have somewhere to stay? Will you stay with Mia?" There's a hint of panic in his questions and his brow furrows.

"I'm going to find a hotel." I watch as his shoulders relax knowing I didn't plan on skipping out of Byron earlier than expected.

"I see. Well, you're welcome to stay here." He raises his eyebrows and when I tilt my head to give him a curious look he goes on, "I have an extra bedroom down the hall if that makes you more comfortable." He nods toward the hallway and slides his body toward me on the couch. My breath hitches and my pulse quickens. Why does he do this to me? My body reacts without warning, like an instinct or compulsion.

"I can't, I'll find somewhere tomorrow," I say in whispered breaths, his scent engulfs my senses, waves of desire fill my stomach.

"Can't?" he asks.

"You've already taken so much time to show me around, I can't ask any more of you." I turn my gaze past him to the window, it's dark now, I see our reflection in the tall windows.

"I'm happy to have done all those things, Violet." The way my name sounds from his mouth, his accent, stirs the ocean of longing inside me. "I enjoy all the time I get with you. I'm hoping you'll come with me to the wedding and dinner tomorrow with my family."

I'm shocked at his invitation for dinner tomorrow night. I've only known this family for less than 72 hours, I couldn't possibly go.

"Go with you to the wedding? I'm going already," I process his request while asking the question, sounding confused and hesitant.

"Yes, you know, go *with* me. I'll pick you up and take you home. We go together," he starts to falter after watching my face, "Only if you want, of course."

"And you want me to go to dinner with your family tomorrow night?" I ask with more hesitation and uncertainty.

"I talked to Mia and Davy and they said you'd be more than welcome. My parents really enjoyed meeting you today, I don't think it would be uncomfortable for you." I start sweating with his explanations.

"Drew," I whisper as the apprehension sets in, "I don't know."

Suddenly I feel all the unease from this afternoon sitting at his parents kitchen table flowing back to me. The questions of what exactly I'm doing here with him spin around in my mind. The conversation with his father by the barn, was it a warning? The feelings pulling me toward Drew are strong, the desire is strong. But there's a force almost as equal telling me to go before I hurt myself or this man. As if he can sense the internal conflict I'm waging inside my mind Drew puts down his wine glass and slides closer, our thighs touching now.

"Violet, do whatever you want in regards to the wedding and your visit here. I'm not trying to push anything on to you," he draws a long breath, "I'm fully aware you're leaving soon." He pauses waiting for me to confirm but I can't get any words out so he goes on, "You'll be leaving Australia soon after that. I get it. I'm not going to lie, it's going to be hard to watch you leave but I'm willing to take that chance if it means I get to laugh with you as I have done for the past few days. If it means I get to feel your body next to mine, watch you smile at me, it's worth it. I haven't enjoyed someone's company like this in a *long time*. If I didn't spend this time with you I'd look back and regret it, I think you feel the same way." He takes my hand and rests it on my thigh. "I'm willing to take my chances but I understand if you're not."

I want to say something to reassure him but I can't manage to form words. Even though I feel the same way I can't find the words to comfort him. I watch his eyes dance over my face, searching. With shaking hands I put the wine glass down on the table next to his. Breaking the silence and my discomfort, Drew's cell phone rings. He grunts and pulls it from his pocket, silencing it and placing it face down on the table in front of him. He turns to look at me again, I rub my hands against the side of my thighs. The phone on the table rings again and Drew exhales sharply looking at the screen, he swipes the answer screen after glancing at me once more.

"What?" His tone is gruff and filled with irritation, it makes me stiffen. He notices the change in my posture and stands from the couch. "Not a great time, mate." His eyes flicker past me to the kitchen and he lets out an exasperated sigh, "Alright, fine."

Drew disconnects the call and heads toward the kitchen. He unlocks the front door and walks back toward me

"I'm sorry if I made you uncomfortable with anything I said. Davy's coming by to drop a few things off for tomorrow. He'll be here any moment." His eyes and face look incredibly disappointed, I know it's not because of Davy's impending visit. His disappointment is because I didn't respond to his declarations.

I manage a feeble smile as I pat to the now empty space he had filled a few moments earlier. Slowly walking around the coffee table he takes a seat beside me. I take his hand in mine, I offer him something until I am able to collect my thoughts on how I feel about him.

"I'll go to the wedding with you." As soon as I finish the words his eyes brighten and a smile spreads across his handsome face. "I'll talk to Mia about dinner though, I really don't want to intrude."

"It's not intruding. If I was to have a date for the wedding they would be a part of the dinner. I have a date now." His smile is boyish, it reminds me of the picture I was looking at earlier in the night.

"You could have found a date at any time. I'm sure there are dozens of women who'd happily accompany you," I laugh and sit back into the sectional.

"I don't want any date. I told you I'm picky, remember?" Drew explains as he leans in to kiss me.

The kiss is foiled when we hear a knock on the door before it swings open to reveal a grinning Davy holding two grocery bags in each hand. Drew sighs, this time with contentment and it makes me smile knowing he's not unnerved.

"Pardon, don't mind me. Just going to drop this lot and be off," Davy says, smiling and dramatically trying not to make eye contact. I laugh at his physical comedy.

"Nice to see you again. Are you anxious for Saturday?" I ask as I make my way toward him in the kitchen feeling Drew close behind.

"I'm excited, it's going to be a great party, Mia's more anxious than me. She's doing great, much better after talking with you, Violet."

"I'm glad," I respond as I see Drew give me a curious look as he opens the fridge for Davy who's taking items out of the grocery bags and setting them on the island.

"I got enough for twenty people today. I don't think we need all this," Drew says as he starts stacking items in the fridge to make room for the boxes and containers Davy brought.

"Mia made some treats for us and her mum went to the bakery today for more. I talked with Mum and Dad on my way over here." Davy looks at Drew mischievously, "Sounds like you two had a good day." I blush remembering Ian catching us kissing inside the barn.

"We did," Drew kept his response brief and I think maybe it's because I'm here.

"I'm going to use your bathroom." I say because I want to give them some privacy for the little time Davy plans to stay.

"Sure, down the hall, second door on the right. Or you can use the one in the master, first door on the left," Drew motions toward the hall and I set out that way.

"Don't leave without saying bye, Davy. I'll be right back." I give him a warm smile as I continue down that hall.

I'm intrigued by Drew's bedroom and when I'm out of sight from the kitchen I peek in his room. The smell is intoxicating, his scent hangs in the air and stirs something inside me vigorously. I walk in, peeking over my shoulder as I do. The room is dark, the curtains are drawn. Finding a switch, I flip it up, light comes from the recessed bulbs in the ceiling. The bed is huge, sitting on a platform with a shiplap headboard. His long bureau holds more pictures of his family. I turn and see a picture of a farmhouse with a wrap-around porch, much like the one from the picture in the living room, it must be his childhood home. I step toward the bed and feel the soft brown comforter. I find the door to the bathroom next to a closet door. I enter the bathroom, looking at the neat and organized sink counter. I pick up the bottle of cologne, take the top off and take in a deep breath of the scent of seduction in a bottle. Reading the label, I expect to find the scent named Panty Dropper or something similar. After I use the bathroom, wash my hands, I turn off the lights and head back to the kitchen where I see Davy and Drew talking in hushed voices. I don't want to interrupt or sneak up on them so I make my presence known with a, not so subtle, cough.

"Davy, would you like a glass of wine?" I take the two wine glasses from the coffee table as I pass and head toward them standing by the island.

"Oh, no. I can't, I've got to get back to my empty house," Davy's explanation drips with sarcasm.

I move toward the cabinet where I found the wine glasses earlier. I pull one down and fill it with wine, placing it in front of him. Davy puts a hand to his chest.

"Well, if you're going to twist my arm," Davy says as he holds up his glass and clinks it to the one I pick up from the island.

I laugh, looking toward Drew and see the irritation drain from his face when he returns my stare. I place my hand on Drew's forearm and give him a gentle squeeze.

"Let's go sit while you have your *one* glass of wine," Drew warns as he leads the way toward the sectional.

The music is still playing. I know the album well enough, there are only two songs remaining on this recording. When all three of us are settled on the couch, Drew next to me and Davy on the chaise lounge, Davy lets out a sigh.

"It seems you left quite an impression on our folks today, Violet," Davy confesses looking at me then to Drew.

"They're lovely. You guys are very lucky," I say with sincere honesty.

"Yeah, we are," Drew and Davy say in unison which brings a huge smile to my face.

"You must be looking forward to tomorrow. Drew told me about your plans."

I watch Drew as he takes a sip of his wine, his Adam's apple bobs and the small movement sends a shudder through me. I take a big sip of wine trying to calm the urge to trace my tongue down the tautness of his jawline.

"It's going to be fun. Mia mentioned you two are getting together in the morning. You're both welcome to have breakfast with us before we leave, then the house will be yours." Davy grin widens when I turn my stare from Drew to him, knowing he caught me staring at his brother with lust filled eyes.

"That sounds nice," I say, feeling my cheeks redden and I drain the last of the wine in my glass. Davy sends me a wink, making me blush more.

"Alright, you two. I'm off," Davy stands abruptly, clapping his hands together which causes me to jump, "Big day tomorrow, gotta get my rest so I can beat this bugger in volleyball."

Davy leans toward Drew to shake his hand. Drew stands and draws his brother into his arms. After the brothers say goodbye Davy comes to me and kisses both my cheeks.

Davy whispers, “Thank you.” in my ear. When I give him a questioning look he shrugs his shoulders and says, “For talking with Mia, putting her mind at ease.”

“No need to thank me.” I squeeze Davy’s shoulder before I return to my seat on the couch.

I watch as Drew follows Davy to the kitchen, locking the door after Davy leaves. Drew comes back to the couch with the bottle of wine in one hand and a water bottle in the other. He holds them out to me in question, I point to the water and he hands it to me.

“What was that all about?” Drew asks as he sets the bottle of wine on the table.

“I think he wanted to have a drink with us,” I say teasingly, I know what he’s asking. He wants to know why Davy thanked me for talking with Mia but it’s not my place to share Mia’s worries with anyone.

“Yeah, there's that,” Drew smiles as he searches my face. He realizes I won’t disclose my conversation with Mia or what was implied by Davy’s comments earlier. “Well, whatever it was, I thank you too. I know Mia was upset about something but she couldn’t disclose it to me last week. I’m glad she found reassurance and comfort from you.” He takes my hand, entwining his fingers in mine, placing a gentle kiss on top of my hand. “Mia means a lot to me, they both do. And she means everything to my brother.”

“They’re going to be fine. They’re going to make each other happy for a very long time.” I feel it, Mia and Davy have something most people dream about.

I stand, taking his hand and pulling him up from the couch. He smiles and when I look in his eyes I can see his entire soul. I see his happiness, I see the love for his family, below that I see the trust he’s giving me despite the pain and hurt he experienced.

In my bare feet, my head falls below his chin, I look up at him. He takes my face in his hands and glides his thumb along my bottom lip. I quiver with anticipation, an image of his huge bed flashes in my mind. I bring my hands up to his waist, moving them behind his back, up to lats that feel so firm and solid. An unyielding desire swells inside and I can no longer hold it in. I stand on my toes and kiss him with an eagerness I have no authority over. Drew wraps his hands in my hair and tilts my head back kissing me with an intensity that commands my surrender. The heat rises from my stomach to my chest. My head spins with euphoria as I pull him into me. The music stopped some time ago, the only thing I hear is the pounding of my heart.

"I'd like to take you to my bed," Drew whispers against my lips breathlessly.

I nod, not trusting my voice. Drew takes my hand, leading me down the hall to his bedroom. He turns on the lights, dimming them to the lowest setting. He never lets go of my hand until we reach the side of his bed. Sitting me on the bed he removes his shoes, without bending over, while taking off his shirt and my pleasure cannot be contained. A smile so wide comes over my face, I lean back on the palms of my hands as I watch him toss his shirt toward a basket in the corner of the room. When he sees the look on my face he smiles down at me, his blue eyes shine with excitement. I could watch him take off his shirt, put it on and take it off again, on repeat all day. Drew moves over me pressing me against his bed, kissing my neck and jaw. I run my fingers down his face and tilt his head back to find his mouth. His hands move to my hips, he unbuttons my jeans and gently pulls down the zipper. I place my hands on his chest to feel the ripples and mounds of muscle. I hear him exhale a groan, it sends a shot of warmth between my legs. His hands move beneath my shirt, skimming over my breast through my sheer bra, his hands are warm and comforting. I sit up slowly and allow Drew to remove my blouse. My hair tumbles over my shoulders and chest as it falls from the neck hole of the shirt. He sweeps my hair back, kisses my collarbone, sending chills down my arms. With one hand he deftly unhooks by bra, pulling it over my shoulders and down my arms. My breasts fall free and he hums with appreciation, I smile and stifle a giggle at the look on his face.

"You're beautiful." The change in his voice sends my insides into a chaotic tilt-a-whirl, his voice is rough with wanton pleasure.

I stand up as Drew takes a step back, I run my hands down his chest to his washboard stomach and land on the buckle of his belt. I unbuckle the belt and unbutton his jeans, when I look up I see he's watching me intently, his smile is gone and in its place is a look of carnal want. I reach my hands into his pants and feel him harden in my hand, he puts his head back and exhales with satisfaction. I slip his jeans down and he steps out of them. He pushes me back on the bed to remove my jeans.

Drew presses his body to mine but is careful not to crush me. His skin against mine is full of heat, his warmth is soothing. His kiss this time is gentle and forbearing, he turns onto his back bringing me on top of him. His hands rub up and down my back, he places his hands on my waist.

"I want to watch you," he whispers in my ear, I kiss his neck as I had wanted to do earlier in the night.

"Okay," I reply as I kiss him and grab his bottom lip between my teeth.

Drew opens the drawer of his bedside table pulling out a condom, he rips the wrapper and puts it on. I bring my knees up to his sides hovering over his length. When I sit down on him, he slips inside me with ease filling me with heat. I moan as he fills me and he lets out a sigh of satisfaction. His hands land on my hips, I feel a slight ache in my hips and thighs from riding earlier in the day. I find a slow rhythm as I had done while riding in the pasture. Drew's hands move up my stomach to cup my breast, holding firmly. Feeling his hands on my body makes me quicken my pace. His stare is resolute and captivating. His blue eyes darken, his pupils widening, I feel him grow harder inside me. I feel my body edging toward an apex, my tempo increases, I can't control the desire to allow my body to fall over the edge of pleasure. Drew's hands move back to my hips gripping them with powerful restraint.

I know he's close when he calls my name. "Violet." He says my name in a guttural resonance, sending me into a free fall.

I tilt my head back and let out a moan of pleasure as my body shakes. Under me Drew lets out a lust filled groan and wraps his arms around me pulling me down into him. I crumble to his chest and feel our hearts slamming in a wild cadence against one another. Drew moves my hair off my shoulders once more, planting gentle kisses as his fingertips trail down my back.

"That was…" he sighs and I feel his warm breath on the base of my neck.

"Incredible?" I finished for him, hoping it was for him as it was for me.

"I was going to say phenomenal. But was that a question?" Drew slides out of me and turns us on our sides, looking nervously into my eyes.

"It was for me. I couldn't hold out very long, you do things to me that make me want to explode quickly," I laugh nervously, feeling my face redden.

"Well, next time I'll be sure to take my time," he says while he nuzzles my neck and I laugh from the feeling. "And when I say next time, I mean in five minutes."

"Do you mind if we get under the blankets? I'm feeling a chill now that I'm not moving."

Chills from the air and Drew's touch send a shiver down my body. Drew quickly moves off the bed pulling the blankets back and I laugh at the abruptness of his movements.

"Do you want a sweatshirt or pants?" His glorious naked body moves toward the bathroom to clean up.

"I don't think I'll need them if you're going to be taking them off in five minutes." I giggle as I call to him from the bed.

When he exits the bathroom I draw the blankets back to welcome him beside me. Drew stops when he's a few feet away and dives into the bed which makes me laugh louder.

"I love that sound," he says as he turns my body to spoon me, wrapping his arms around my waist and pulling me into him.

We lie in silence for sometime, skin to skin, I want to cry with contentment. I can't remember a time I felt so desired or adored by a man, the feeling is overwhelming. After a few minutes I fully relax, my muscles ease and my eyelids close. I drift off in the solid arms of a man who has given me his trust and allowed my confidence in myself to grow.

Chapter 19

Drew

I'm woken by Violet yelling something I can't make sense of, a mix of mumbles and sobs. I peel my arm from around her body, feeling a layer of sweat on her back and I sit up resting on my forearm. Her feet thrash under the blankets kicking my shins. I call her name softly but she doesn't respond. After one more kick she stills, I place my hand gently on her shoulder, her breaths are rapid and heavy. I see a shimmer under her eyes, tears, her long lashes are wet. When I'm about to lie down beside her she shoots up gasping for air.

"Violet?"

I sit up with her and try putting my arms around her in comfort but she pushes me away. She runs her hands over her face, then down her arms. When she opens her eyes, taking in her surroundings, a flash of awareness steals across her face.

"I'm so sorry," her voice is shaky, she pulls the sheet up over her bare chest and looks around the floor beside her.

"Are you alright?" I reach out a hand to put on her back but pull back not wanting to cause her discomfort.

"I'm fine, I need…" she frantically searches the floor around the bed, "I need something to put on."

I reach down to the floor and grab my boxers and hastily put them on before I go to my dresser to get a shirt from my drawer. Pulling out whatever is on top I walk over to her and hold out the shirt. Her breathing has steadied but her hands shake as she reaches for the clothing.

"Put this on," I say softly and then take a few steps back.

She slips on the shirt as she stands up from the bed. The shirt comes down to the middle of her thighs, she tugs at the hem. She runs her hands through her hair, her face white with fear or panic.

"I'm sorry," she whispers again as she shakes out her arms.

"Stop saying that," I say slowly, trying to figure out what the hell to do to help her. I watch her as she rubs her arms then the back of her neck. "Do you need water? Tea?" I start to move toward the door when her hand bolts out to catch my arm.

"I'm okay, I need to move around. Don't leave, please, don't walk away." Her eyes beg me, still filled with tears.

“Okay,” I say, taking a seat on the edge of the bed as I watch her slowly walk to the window against the wall.

“I have this dream, a recurring dream,” her words come out slow and soft, I strain to hear her from five feet away, “It’s awful, I can’t get to them. They keep walking away from me and I can’t get to them. It’s incredibly frustrating,” her voice is pained with hints of frustration. When she turns to face me I see some color has returned to her face. It doesn’t fully set me at ease, I’m still rigid with tension.

I stand from the bed and walk over to her. I want to hold her until the hurt and fear is gone but I’m not sure she wants to be touched. When I get within reaching distance, I stop not wanting to cross any invisible line Violet may have drawn.

“I feel sweaty and gross right now,” her laugh is forced and weak but when she looks up at me her smile is wistful. “Can I take a shower?”

“Absolutely, of course.” I walk to the bathroom and open the linen cupboard showing her the towels. I turn on the tap for her and leave the shower door open, “Take your time. I’ll be right out there.”

I motion toward the bed with a nod and leave her to her shower. I don’t go back to bed. Instead I grab another shirt and pair of shorts for Violet. I take the clean clothes back to the bathroom when I know she’s in the shower, quietly placing them on the counter. In the kitchen I start the kettle and grab a mug from the cupboard. Checking to see what I have for decaffeinated tea, I settle on chamomile. Tossing the tea bag in the mug, I stare at the kettle begging it to boil faster. I don’t know the exact situation of her dream, seeing how it left her I can imagine the terror of trying to reach someone only to be left deserted. It crushes me to see her pain stricken. The grief and sadness is something she has talked about but to see it flowing unrestrained, uncontrollable, from her shook me. I want to hold her, I want to be the one to make her feel safe from the terror trespassing on her.

The kettle whistled pulling me from my unreasonable thoughts of protecting a woman, who I’ve come to adore, from powerful evocations leaving her afflicted and saddened. I turn off the stove, pour the steaming water into the mug and set off to the bedroom. When I enter the bedroom, I hear the shower tap turn off. I place the mug of tea on the table beside the bed. I picked up the scattered clothes from the floor we casually tossed aside before we fell asleep after, what I consider, the best sex of my life. Violet did something to me, she provoked a longing and desire I didn't think was possible. Seeing her naked on my bed made me want to claim her in ways I knew were unattainable. I was falling fast and hard for Violet, I had succumbed to the realization, I couldn't stop myself. If any woman was going to ruin me it was going to be her, I wholeheartedly resigned myself to accepting this. I toss my clothes in the bin next to the closet door, and delicately fold Violet's skin tight jeans and blouse. I put her clothes on the top of the bench, finding her bra already tossed there. Positioning myself on the bed, resting my back on the pillows, I anxiously await Violet's return to my bed. Checking the clock I see it's past one in the morning. The selfish part of me is relieved I still have eight hours with her before I have to head over to Davy's for the bachelor party. I plan on savoring every minute. Hearing the bathroom door open I look up to see Violet in my t-shirt and athletic shorts. It brings an amused smile to my face.

"I made you tea, it's chamomile," I gesture to the tea on the other side of the bed. Her eyes widen and her face falls causing me to sit up straighter. "If you don't like chamomile I have ginger, lemon and chia. But the chia is caffeinated."

"You made me tea?" she asks, each word has a pause between.

"Yes," I say slowly, trying to see if there's a problem here.

"You made me tea." This time her words come together and it's not a question.

"I made you tea?" Now, I'm questioning because I have no idea if there's a problem or not.

I freeze in bed waiting for her to share what the complication is. She walks toward the bed and pulls back the covers alleviating the unease settling in my core. Violet gets under the covers, smelling like my soap and shampoo, making me the happiest man on the planet right now. Taking the mug from the table she breathes in the steam.

"Thank you."

When she turns to me I see appreciation in her eyes. Her eyes have specks of white and gray which I never noticed before. I understand now it's what makes her eyes seem to glow at times, they can look gray or bright blue depending on the light or what color she wears. I smile knowing I learned something else about this amazing woman.

"It's not a problem." I tentatively put my arm around her as she holds the mug between her hands. "Feel better?" I ask hesitantly.

"Much better. Again…"

Before she can finish I hold up my hand knowing what she's about to say. Knowing she's about to apologize for something she shouldn't have to, she doesn't need to.

"Don't apologize," I say softly.

I want to know why she feels the need to apologize for her thoughts or feelings, why she feels the need to apologize for a dream she can't control. If it has anything to do with the guy who took her confidence and certainties, I want to upend the earth to find him and bury him in my wake.

"I appreciate the tea and the shower."

She settles in against my chest still holding the mug. I hold her firmly against me wishing I could stop time to enjoy this moment of Violet in my bed, in my clothes, sipping tea I made for her. I lean down and kiss the top of her damp head.

"What time is it?" she asks, looking around the room for a clock.

"It's half past one or close to it." I turn to read the clock on the bedside table next to me. "It's one twenty-four," I say as I place it back down.

Violet lets out a pleasing hum, "I guess five minutes turned into almost three hours."

She sets her mug down and turns to me with an enchanting smile. I laugh at her cheeky comment.

"Yeah, well, when you started snoring I decided to let you rest," I say, I squeeze her when she tries to pull back against my hold.

"I do *not* snore," she confidently asserts while narrowing her eyes on me.

"No, you don't. But you do hum, short little hums. It's adorable." I kiss her forehead and she scoffs. "Do you want me to shut off the light?" I ask, wanting to make sure she's as comfortable as possible in hopes it will help her have an undisturbed sleep.

"Do you have to get up to do that?" she asks, I feel her fingers push into my chest.

A laugh holds in my chest. "Yes, I have to go to the switch over there." I point to the switch on the wall next to the door.

"Then no, I don't want you to shut the light off yet."

Violet draws her right leg up over my thigh and it feels like heaven as she wraps herself around me. I pull her closer, wanting her to crawl inside me because she has already imprinted on my soul. We sit in silence for a while before Violet tells me she dreamt about her brother. Describing the dream to me in detail, I understand how it would affect her physically and emotionally. I listen without interrupting, letting her get it all out. The dream sounds frustrating, as she described earlier, infuriating and also heartbreaking. As she replays the dream I don't hear her cry but I feel dampness building on my shirt beneath where her head rests. I understand why she didn't want me to leave her when I offered to get her water. She didn't want to watch me walk away, the idea warmed and broke my heart simultaneously.

I continue to hold her, occasionally stroking her long blonde hair and her back. She talks about her brother, telling me he enlisted in the military after her parents passed. At first she thought he wanted to provide for her and Ally. Then she thought he needed to get away from home, away from the memories and grief, away from her. Violet thought she might have been too much trouble for James, constantly having to deal with her rebellious behavior which drove him crazy with worry. Ultimately, it seemed she didn't blame herself, it sounded like she was searching for answers as to why he left. Since he wasn't around to ask, she was pulling out any and all possibilities. My heart breaks for this young woman who has lost so many people she loved.

I could feel her anger when she said, "There are some parents who are horrible to their children and yet they're still there. And my parents who were so loving, caring and nurturing were ripped from me." It wasn't fair, she knew it and I knew it.

"Is that the house you grew up in?" Violet changes her focus, pointing to the picture on the wall opposite the window.

"Yeah. Mia took that picture before her mum sold their house." I run my finger tips down Violet's arm from under the blankets. "My parents had already left by then. Her father passed away a year after my parents sold the house. Mia's mum tried to keep up with the house but it was too much, she sold their property a year ago. Mia went to help her mum pack up and took the picture while she was there."

"That's really sweet," Violet says, bringing her hand across my chest.

"That's Mia," I affirm.

I don't hear anything from Violet for a few minutes and when I peer down at her I see her eyes are closed. She looks peaceful and calm, I don't want to disturb her. After waiting several minutes, listening to her breathing and feeling the rise and fall of her chest against my torso, I gently moved away and settled her against the pillows. I turn off the light and quickly return to the bed, not wanting to leave her for a second more than I have to. As I settle into the bed, pulling her into my chest, I close my eyes as I breathe her in.

When I wake in the morning, I feel greedy hands scouring my body. Warm, soft hands running down my sides from under my shirt and back up to my neck. I moan with amusement, hearing a soft giggle in response. Feeling Violet slide her warm body on top of me before I've even opened my eyes makes me consider this may be a dream. I feel her soft kisses trailing along my shoulders to my neck, I smell my soap mixed with her scent. A shot of lust fills me, I wrap my arms around her.

"Good morning," she whispers in my ear, she nibbles my earlobe as my pulse rate soars. I smell mint from her whisper, feeling the coolness on my skin.

"Did you brush your teeth?"

I didn't feel her leave the bed, I would have sensed her get up. Then I remember how she slipped away from my grasp yesterday morning at the cottage.

"I did. I found an extra toothbrush, still in the package, in one of the drawers," she giggles again.

"You sneak out of bed for a second time and poke around my bathroom while I lie here alone?" I mock annoyance and flip her under me which causes her to release my favorite sound, her laugh.

I pin her arms above her head with one hand and kiss her neck as I tickle her side with my other hand. She shrieks with laughter and tries to pull away but my grip is strong.

"Am I supposed to just lie in bed listening to you snore?" she asks through fits of laughter.

"I don't snore," I state as I loosen my grip and allow her to wiggle free.

"Yes you do, not loud but when you sleep on your back you snore." Violet looks up from under me smiling, reaching up to put her hands in my hair.

"I hope it didn't bother you, I'll take note to keep on my side."

I bend my head to hers and kiss her gently. Our kissing becomes more torrid as our hands roam over each other. When I take Violet this time, I make sure it's slow, attentive and unhurried. This time when she's close to her climax, she whispers my name in my ear and next to her laugh it's the second best sound I hear from her. After a pleasurable wake up I check the time on my mobile and see it's almost 7 AM. I don't want to leave this bed at all today. I want to ravish Violet over and over until we're too hungry or exhausted. As if she's reading my thoughts she turns toward me, her blonde hair tousled.

"We have to get up soon." As she finishes her sentence my mobile rings.

I groan as I pull her in to me again and pull the blankets over us, shutting out the world around us. "I think we should stay here all day," I whisper to her under the blankets.

"Can't," she replies, she flips the blankets back and steps out of the bed.

She goes over to the window and opens the curtains, casting beams of early morning light over her naked body, I eye her with wonder. She turns around toward me, smiling as she takes my shirt from the floor and slips it over her.

"Get up. I'll make coffee," she says from over her shoulder as she walks out of the bedroom.

I begrudgingly get up, take my mobile from the table and head to the bathroom. I checked the screen of the mobile to see it was Davy. I start the shower as my mobile rings again. I swipe the answer icon and put the call on speaker while I wait for the water to run warm.

"In the shower, mate. What's up?" I say over the noise of the shower spray, noticing a lightness to my voice.

"Making sure you're awake and still coming over with Violet for breakfast," Davy's whimsical voice isn't fooling me, he's fishing as to how things went last night with Violet.

"I'll be there around nine. I'll see you later."

I disconnect before Davy can pry for any more information. I place the mobile on the counter and step in the shower, hot water slides down my back and chest washing away the feel of Violet's fingers and hands. After I've finished in the shower, I wrap a towel around my waist and check in the mirror. I definitely need a shave, the stubble on my chin is noticeable. I quickly foam my face with the shaving cream and shave the stubble away. When I've cleaned up the sink area I head to the closet, thinking of the items I need today before we come back here to barbecue later this afternoon. As I'm zipping up a bag I see Violet enter the bedroom and my heart soars. She's wearing the same skin tight jeans from last night that make her legs go on and on, she has my t-shirt on and it's tied up on one side in a tight knot above her hip. Her hair is down and flowing past her shoulders, her blue eyes are alive with purpose.

"I made you coffee." She extends her arm, holding a mug of coffee. "I'm not gonna lie, it's probably not very good. I either make it too strong or too weak," she gives a nervous laugh as she forfeits the mug.

"Thanks."

I take a sip and try not to cough on the bold, thick liquid. Wow, that'll wake you up. I smile at her with appreciation trying to hide the fact this coffee is undrinkable.

"It's awful right?" Her shoulders sag and her stare goes to the floor.

"No, it's not. It's strong, but good," I lie and feel bad doing it but if I can save her from whatever feeling of discomfort is creeping into her I will.

She takes the mug from me and sips, her eyes widen and color creeps into her cheeks, "Wow, that's awful!" She shakes her head. "I'll make tea."

She turns and marches off to the kitchen, I laugh. When I enter the kitchen I'm hit with pure delight, seeing Violet reaching on her tiptoes to gather a mug from the cabinet. Then hearing her pad around the kitchen in her bare feet, it sounds like home. These are the sights and sounds I was unaware I've been longing for. How was I supposed to go back to my life before her? I wasn't, I couldn't, I'd never be the same after having slept in the same bed with her for two nights. Seeing her in my house, in my t-shirt, watching her sleep in my bed. My world has been titled on its axis forever changing my perspective on life, love and happiness. How could my entire life change in four short days? Violet stills mid step when she sees me watching her from the hallway.

"What's wrong?" she asks as worry steals across her face and I make my way to her.

"Nothing," I place my hands on her hips and kiss her forehead, "I like seeing you in my shirt, in my kitchen." I whisper against her brow. I feel her body stiffen and I wonder if I should have kept the thoughts inside.

"Drew" she whispers my name in anguish and remorse.

"I was telling you what I was thinking. I know you're leaving, we've discussed all this. Please, don't worry about me." I give her a stoic smile, one she returns. Changing the subject before she has a chance to put up a wall I ask, "Do you want to come with me to Davy's? I can bring you there for breakfast. Or I can drop you off at the cottage?" She relaxes in my hold.

"You can drop me off. I need to change and get a new pair of shoes." She nods toward the black heels she put by the entrance to the garage door.

"Alright, I'll pack up and we can go."

I release her, turning back to the bedroom to get my bag. After gathering the last of the items I need for the day and making the bed I walk back into the kitchen and see Violet drinking tea. She's talking on the phone, a smile of enjoyment on her face. I bring my bag out to the car, put it in the back seat and open the bay door. As I'm about to start the car I see Violet enter the garage.

"You're not leaving without me, are you?" She raises her brow and hands me a travel mug of what I assume is tea she made.

"No, I was giving you privacy to chat."

"That was Mia. I'm going to meet her after I change. I feel like I'm doing the walk of shame," she laughs as she waves her arms down her body.

"You look great." I say, closing the car door as I eye her.

"Well, not a good look for breakfast." She takes the two steps down and walks toward me. "Should we go? I don't want you to be late."

"I'm ready."

I move around to the passengers side and open the door for her, when she's tucked inside I close the door and get behind the wheel. When we arrive at the cottage Violet insists I go to Davy's without walking her inside. I wait until she opens the cottage door before I pull out and drive to Davy's.

"Big day!" Mia exclaims as she opens the front door. "How was your night?" Her eyes are full of eager interest, she hasn't moved from the doorway.

"If you let me in I might tell you." I raise one eyebrow at her.

"Of course." Mia moves aside allowing me entrance. I see Davy standing over the stove shifting pots on the burners.

"Drew! You're early," Davy says as he grabs at the kitchen towel hanging over his shoulder. "How was your night?" He echoes Mia's question and I wonder when my free time became so interesting to them.

I take a seat at the island while Mia pours a cup of coffee. She sets the mug in front of me, standing on the opposite side of the island. She puts her elbows on the island resting her chin in her hands, staring at me, her eyes burning into mine.

"Start talking before everyone comes over," Mia talks fast, her tone giddy.

"I'm not going to gossip and I don't kiss and tell. You already know that." I take a sip of the coffee and smile thinking of the cup of mud Violet made for me earlier.

"I'm not a gossip," she playfully slaps my hand and turns toward my brother, "Davy, help me out here." Mia has her hands on her hips, although I can't see her face, I know she's glaring at Davy in a plea for help.

"Oh, let him be. I'm sure you'll hear all about it from Violet." Davy sends me a wink when Mia spins back around toward me.

"Okay, okay," Mia holds up her hands in exacerbation, "I'm going to finish getting ready." She stalks off to the bedroom with an aggravated sigh.

Davy watches her walk away, when she's out of ear shot he moves closer. "So?" he asks as he starts cutting fruit on a cutting board between us.

"No." I stand up and grab another knife from the butcher's block to help him slice the melon.

"I assume it went well after I left." Davy's eyes don't leave the countertop as he continues slicing.

"It did and I'm not going to say anything more. Let's enjoy the day, it's about you today."

Davy and I work in silence cutting pineapple, melon, kiwi and rinsing berries. I continue helping Davy prep, I let him boss me around the kitchen, grabbing whatever he needs from the fridge or pantry. It's not long after we start the food prep when we hear a knock at the door. I drop the knife and head toward the entry hoping it's Violet. When I open the door I see Davy's friends, Ethan and Brian. Ethan's tall and lean like Davy, he wears circular glasses with a green frame in front of his hazel eyes. Brian's shorter with middle eastern features, dark hair, brown eyes and tan skin, his smile is bright.

"Hiya, boys, I say as they enter the house.

"Hey, Drew, thanks for setting this up," Brian says, lifting his hand to shake mine.

"Glad you could make it." I gesture toward the kitchen where Ethan is already greeting Davy.

"Going to be a great day," Ethan says with enthusiasm, stepping aside to allow Brian to shake Davy's hand in a greeting.

The two men stand in the kitchen for a moment before taking a seat at the island where Davy has cleared the chopped fruit. I move to the counter when Mia suddenly appears at my side. She gives both men a greeting, kissing their cheeks and giving them a warm smile. The five of us stand in the kitchen chatting for a few minutes when the front door swings open, Tomas and Sean enter with suitcases in hand. When the last two men arrive, Davy starts cooking omelets, Mia and I set the dining room table. The kitchen is loud with laughter and conversation. I'm enjoying a conversation with Sean when I notice the room quiets and Sean shifts his gaze past me, his eyes widening. When I turn to see what he's looking at I spot Violet walking into the kitchen. I look around and see four of the men staring at her as she greets Mia with a hug. I guess it's not just me that's captivated by Violet Kelly.

"Guys, this is Violet. She's visiting from the States," Mia introduces Violet.

As the men close in on Violet it makes me want to pull her into me, letting them know she's mine. But she isn't mine, I have no claim on her. I watch each man take her hand as Mia introduces each one by name. Violet greets each one, repeating their names, offering them a beautiful smile. I feel an assertiveness rising in my chest but I press it down as I make my way toward her.

"Good morning," I say when her eyes meet mine.

"Hi, there," she says. I notice a flush on her cheeks.

"So, Violet, where do you live in the States?" Sean asks, making Violet's stare shift from me to him.

"I live on the east coast, outside of Boston, Massachusetts." Violet takes a step back and to the side, moving out of Davy's way as he pulls food off the stove.

"Everyone sit down, food's ready," Davy says, motioning toward the table with the spatula he holds.

Mia and Violet are the first to sit, they sit side by side. As I take the fruit platter from the island I see the men fumble for positions next to Violet, I want to laugh but I stifle it. Davy places two trays on the table, one filled with omelets and one with pancakes.

"We're going to make a plate and head out to the patio. We'll leave you boys to it," Mia says as she places an omelet on her plate with a helping of fruit.

"Don't be silly, stay and eat with us," Davy says as he puts a carafe of coffee down on the table, kissing the top of her head as he passes.

"How do you know Mia?" Brian asks Violet as he sits directly across from her.

"We met last weekend in Pottsville. We crossed paths, again, here in Byron a day later." Violet smiles at Mia.

"Violet met Drew, first, in Brisbane when she arrived on holiday." Mia looks across the table to me, I send her a thankful smile. "You boys have quite the day planned. I hope you all got plenty of rest last night," Mia says as she holds my eyes.

"What do you girls have planned for today?" Ethan asks as he fills his mouth with pancakes.

"I've got the afternoon with my mum and sister," Mia replies as she pours coffee into a mug. "Violet, you're more than welcome to come along, my family would love to meet you."

"Thank you but I was planning on going to Broken Head to find a few trails to explore. I might go to the beach after." Violet looks at me, sending me an alluring smile.

"Ethan, how are Sarah and the baby?" Mia asks, turning her attention to her guest.

"They're good. Louie started sleeping through the night, well, most of it anyway. Most nights we can get a solid six hours before he rustles," Ethan laughs, running a hand through his hair, "Sarah's mum is coming to stay with him Saturday, we're looking forward to a night out. Sarah especially, I think this will be her first night away since we had him." Ethan looks up in reflection, "We tried an overnight last month but Louie came down with a fever, so we had to cancel the plans."

After Mia focuses the attention and questions away from Violet I feel more at ease. I don't like the way Davy's friends are showing such interest in Violet. I understand the intrigue, she's beautiful, mesmerizing and charming. Foolishly, I thought that pull was meant for me alone. I'm hit with the realization Violet could be scooped up at any moment. Mia told me to think of this as an opportunity to get to know Violet, to allow myself to have a good time with a beautiful woman. I tried to keep the idea of her leaving out of my mind, as I sit here watching these men practically throw themselves at her, I'm realizing she'll leave and move on. We're from two different worlds, we literally live half a globe away from each other. From what I've learned about her, I know, she would never leave her home. Her sister is all she has left of her family, she'd never leave her. Violet's successful in her employment, she wants to gain independence from a terrible past relationship and I don't fit into any of it. As much as I tell myself I knew the consequences, feeling those consequences is different. I'm getting my first feelings of those consequences now, it doesn't feel good. I couldn't help but fall for this woman. I fell hard, fast and without looking down for a safety net. My stomach feels heavy, the food I managed to eat isn't settling well. I have to get up from the table, I stand with my plate in hand. When I do, Mia looks at me registering my expression. She takes her plate and follows me to the kitchen.

"You okay?" she asks when we arrive in front of the sink, away from earshot.

"Fine, not hungry." I take her plate from her hands and place it, along with mine, in the sink.

"You don't look fine, you look upset." She stands with her back resting on the counter, her arms folded across her stomach.

"Mia, I'm fine," I try not to sound aggravated, it's not her fault, the swarm of feelings and emotions are charging inside of me.

"I'm sorry." she whispers and takes a step toward me.

"Don't be." I force a smile but there's no life behind it.

Mia looks as if she's about to say something, her mouth opens but no words form. Violet comes into the kitchen, empty plate in hand. She smiles warmly at us and I melt inside as the tempest of emotion continues. She places her hand on my lower back and presses a kiss to my shoulder. I turn and take her in my arms, squeezing harder than I anticipated, for longer than I anticipated. She lets out a laugh as I nuzzle into her neck, taking in her smell. I smile through the fear and angst, I smile through the unknown. When I finally break away from her, holding her hips, I look up and see Sean and Brian staring at us as they walk into the kitchen. I place a kiss on top of Violet's head before I let go of my grip and turn back toward the sink to wash the dishes. Violet brushes past me to stand with Mia.

When the men approach with their empty plates Brian whispers, "Well done, mate." He smiles, handing me his plate. I glance at Sean when he extends his dish to me, he's not smiling, I see a hint of challenge in his eyes.

Mia picks up on my mood or the tension. "Violet and I are going for a walk. You boys enjoy your day." She links her arm in Violets and walks toward the dining room to say goodbye to the rest of the group.

I go outside and wait on the porch for them. It's only a few minutes when they appear outside. Mia kisses my check, giving me a knowing look as she continues down the steps.

"I hope you have a great day. Davy's friends seem nice, I'm sure you'll have a good time," Violet says as she stands in front of me, smiling, her powerful gaze holds mine.

"Should be fun." I'm crestfallen that I don't get to spend the day with her. I looked down at my feet, "They seemed to really like you." When I look up, amusement crosses her face.

"It's only because I'm foreign," she laughs then goes on, "I'm different and they're curious about the American friend." Her smile leaves her when she sees my disappointment.

"That's not it, you're beautiful, smart and funny. You're unbelievably attractive." I don't mean to sound as dejected as I do. "If you could see what we all see, you would know." I take her hand and place a kiss in her palm. "Can I call you later?"

"Sure." Confusion and curiosity fill her expression, she takes a step down then turns to look up at me. "I had a great time last night."

I feel awful, she feels like she did something wrong to cause the change in my disposition.

"Best night ever," I smile and I mean it.

It was the best night and morning of my life. Not just the sex but seeing her in my bed, waking up to her in my house, rummaging through my kitchen. It brought me hope and contentment. I try to remember those feelings, not the feelings of doubt and dread filling my chest and head now. I turn back inside the house as Mia and Violet head to the beach. When I get inside the table is cleared and the guys are standing around the living room laughing. Davy looks at me, furrowing his brow in question. I shake my head, letting him know I'm fine. I'm not fine.

"You boys ready to shove off?" I ask, looking at the group.

"Sure," they answer in unison.

After packing up my SUV and Brian's sport utility we divide into two vehicles and head to the beach. Along the drive I psych myself up to make sure Davy has the day he deserves. I push out all remaining unease about Violet and try to focus on making today about Davy and the boys.

Chapter 20
Violet

As Mia and I walk to the beach I can't shake the feeling Drew is upset. I replay the events of the morning in my mind to think if I said or did something to upset him. I don't think I did. Maybe I'm reading too much into it. I was feeling really good this morning and I don't want to lose that feeling.

"Are you okay?" Mia asks me as we pass through the path opening to the beach.

"I'm great, just thinking." I want to ask Mia if she noticed anything that was off with Drew.

"How was your night?" she asks with excitement and I giggle. I'm actually giggling, it's surprising.

"Honestly, it was amazing." I smile so big I feel it in my forehead. She laughs and claps her hands. "Mia, he's *so* good," I say then she gasps and laughs. "No, I mean, not like that. Well, yes like that. He's kind and gentle, he makes me laugh. I haven't laughed like I have in a long time." I feel the happiness travel from my chest to my belly.

"It's nice to see him having fun and enjoying someone's company." Mia stops to remove her shoes, "It hasn't been easy for him since he moved out here."

"I don't know why, he's so handsome, he's sexy. Women must notice him, honestly, you'd have to be blind not to notice him," I say, knowing Drew could have any woman he wanted, he could have a line of women.

"It's hard for Drew to let people in. As much as he tried to hide the hurt he was devastated." Mia shakes her head.

"He told me about his best friend and her." I feel my heart ache knowing two of the most important people to Drew hurt him in the way they did.

"He did? Good, I'm glad he can talk about it. He never wants to talk about it to me or Davy." Mia walks close to the shore, a wave rolls over her foot. "Did you have a good day at the farm? Clare must have been all over you with questions."

"It was nice, they're great people. I really liked talking with his dad, he didn't ask too many questions." I think of Ian catching

Drew and I kissing in the barn and my face reddens with the memory.

"He's usually very quiet, he must've really liked you." Mia went on, "I know he really liked you. They called us last night, they were happy to see Drew. They were happy to see him content, untroubled."

"Did Drew seem upset to you? Before we left just now." I wasn't going to ask but I can't help circling back. When Mia sighs I know I was right.

"Violet, can I be honest with you?" When she finishes the question my back straightens.

"I hope you can," I say, Mia appreciates honesty and I want her to know I do too.

"Drew has been completely enraptured by you. I've never seen him look at a woman like he does when he looks at you. I wouldn't doubt he's falling in love with you," her statements are deadpan, they're bold statements but she says them with little emotion.

I stop walking, "What?" I look in Mia's eyes, her face serious.

"Really, Violet?" She tilts her head, a faint smile on her lips. "You must be able to see the way he looks at you. You must feel what's happening here."

My head is spinning, I feel hot. "We're…" My palms are moist and I run them against my shorts. "We're enjoying each other," I finish the sentence and I realize how ridiculous it sounds.

We are *thoroughly* enjoying each other but there's a lot more there as well. Drew tells me I'm beautiful, he makes me laugh, he shares his feelings and listens when I share mine. He makes me feel confident in my body which I haven't felt in a long time. He makes me feel confident when it's time for me to make a decision or choice, something else that was stolen from me. Drew looks at me like I'm the only person he can see, even on a beach full of people. But it's only been four days, you can't fall in love in four days. My mind frantically pulls images of the last few days, his smile, the way I caught him staring at me this morning while he watched me in his kitchen. The way he tried to comfort me when I woke from a nightmare leaving me crippled with anxiety. Just a little while ago, when he hugged me tightly and kissed me gently on the top of my head. My hands start to shake, when I look back at Mia she's smiling. Why is she smiling?

“Mia,” I say her name to make sure this moment is real. “What do I do?” My voice trails off and I sink to the sand. Mia sits down beside me.

“Have you thought about when you have to leave? What's it going to be like for you?” Mia asks the questions as she takes my hand, I’m thankful because her touch is allowing the chaos in my body to focus on something else.

“I haven't really thought about that, I try not to think about that part. I thought I would go home and be thankful for this time. Being with Drew has boosted my confidence and given me hope that I can have a functional relationship someday. He’s helped me see I’m worthy. I don’t want to hurt him, Mia, I really don’t.”

I hadn’t thought much about going home because when he’s with me there’s nothing on my mind other than being in the moment with him. I keep the feelings toward Drew from fully forming, I don’t like thinking about what would happen if they did. Why won’t I let the feelings fully form? Maybe I’m afraid, maybe I haven’t forgiven myself for allowing someone to hurt me for years. Am I being fair to him? To myself? I’ve been lying to myself about what’s happening here. I thought I could disconnect when it was time to leave but I’ve never been able to do that. Why the hell did I think I could do it now?

“You must hate me,” I say, Mia lets out her musical laugh.

“Never. I could never hate you, Violet. I’m so thankful for you.” She wraps an arm around me, “Drew’s a great guy. He’s like a brother to me, I love him very much. I don’t want to see him hurt or upset. Unlike you, Drew knows what he’s in for and he’s willing to take the punch at the end of all this. I admire him for it but it’ll be hard. However this plays out, he’ll be better for it.” Her outlook is depressingly optimistic and I can’t help but feel like a heel.

“I don’t think you can fall in love in four days,” I say but it’s more of a question.

“I fell in love with Davy the first time I saw him, I was eight years old. He was covered in mud and had a terrible haircut,” she laughs wildly and squeezes me tight, I couldn’t help but laugh with her. Her face turns serious when she says, “I didn’t tell you this to upset you, I thought you should know.”

“Almost everyone I love has been taken from me, suddenly and without warning. The one person I had to let go, I didn’t even like and it took me years to leave him. I'm not good at letting people go."

I don't know if I love Drew, I appreciate him, I love the way I feel when I'm with him. I love feeling heard, wanted and adored.

"Are you sure you don't want to come with me to meet my family?" Mia breaks the long silence and I realize I've been staring at the ocean with absolutely no thoughts running in my mind.

"I can't, I have to pack and clean up. I want to check out Broken Head today. I have to find a hotel, I have a lot to do." I smile at her, an appreciative smile for her honestly and for listening.

"Stay with us, Davy has a futon in his office. Ian and Clare will be staying in the guest room, there's plenty of space." She looks hopeful, it's hard to decline her offer.

"No, I can't. Thank you, but I can't." I couldn't possibly stay at Mia's house while Ian and Clare were staying there.

"You could stay with Drew." Her eyebrows raise as a cunning smile takes over her face.

"I'll find a hotel," I state with finality and Mia gets the hint I don't want to talk much more.

"Okay. I've got to get back." Mia stands, brushing the sand from her bottom and the back of her legs.

"I'm going to stay here for a little while," I say, looking up at her, giving her a reassuring smile.

"I'll see you tomorrow night, dinner at our place." She bends down picking up her sandals before she leaves.

"Mia, I think…"

Mia holds up her hand before I can finish. "You're coming to dinner, everyone's looking forward to seeing you."

I find her comment endearing because it's *her* wedding we're celebrating. Everyone's looking forward to seeing her and Davy, not me.

"I'll see you tomorrow." I wrap her in my arms after I stand up from the beach. "Have a good day. Thank you." I want to cry for a reason I can't fathom. Mia holds me for a few more seconds then steps back.

"Smile, Violet. You're so beautiful when you smile." With that she turns her back and walks down the beach toward the path to her house.

I sink back to the sand and I do smile. I'm happy to have made a friend in Mia. I'm happy to be on a beach in Australia, somewhere I never would've imagined I'd be just a few months ago. I'm happy I met this family and found this beautiful town. I continue to watch the ocean before I feel the urge to get up and finally start my day. I reach the cottage, I survey the house and see I don't have much to clean. I didn't spend much time here. I put the clothes, I started earlier, into the dryer and headed back to the kitchen. Seeing it's close to eleven it would be a good time to call someone back home. If I call Ally I know she'll give me practical advice, Beth will tell me to jump in with both feet and worry about the consequences later. Such opposite ends of the spectrum. I turn on my computer and go to the FaceTime app, I dial and wait. After a few rings her face pops up on my computer screen, I let out a thankful sigh.

"Hey, sis," I say as I slump down on the sofa.

"Hi, how's everything down under?" The sides of her mouth twitch with a grin.

"Great. How's everything there?" I miss Ally, suddenly wishing I wasn't so far away.

"Cold and raw." I notice she's bundled under a thick comforter, I see her adjust her head on the pillows beneath her. "How was your day at the horse farm?"

"It was fun." I smile at her and she smiles back.

"How's the beefcake? Beth sent me a picture of you two." Her eyes sparkle playfully.

"That's why I'm calling. I need you, well, I need you to be you."

I take a deep breath and I unload on Ally. I tell her everything that has happened the past 24 hours, I tell her all the details without holding anything back. She stops herself from cringing at times but she remains stoic. Then I tell her about the conversation I had with Mia on the beach this morning. When I'm done with my rant, which took close to 8 minutes, I sink back on the couch and cover my face. Ally doesn't want to think about her sister falling into bed with a stranger, I could see the details about some events that made her squirm with unease. If she were to share specifics about her and Nate I would cringe with discomfort as well.

"That's all of it." I watch Ally digest the information, I'm anxious for her reply.

"That's a lot, Vi." Somewhere along the conversation Ally must have gotten up because I notice she is no longer in her bed, instead she's sitting on her staircase. "I'm not going to tell you anything you don't already know. You're leaving soon, you have to decide when you're going to rip the band aid. Whether you get outta dodge after the wedding or spend the rest of your time there, that's up to you. Ultimately, you're coming home and he's staying there. You don't think you love this guy, do you?" Her question is cold and almost patronizing. She continues, without waiting for my answer, I understand her question was rhetorical. "It seems like this guy understands what he's getting himself into, you're both adults. He appears to be a smart guy, you're not stringing him along, he has a good understanding of the situation."

After Ally is done with her analysis I feel a little better but I don't think there's anything she could say to make me feel content with the situation. As if Ally's reading my thoughts she adds, "Violet, if you're not comfortable maybe you should leave. You went there to relax and unwind. If you're getting stressed then maybe you should be on your way."

Ally's review of the case makes sense if the situation didn't involve people with actual feelings. Mia's counting on me to come to the wedding, I want to see Davy and Mia wed, I would regret it if I didn't go. When I look at Ally on the screen she tilts her head.

"You have to do what you feel is right. You know what to do, you don't need me to tell you. If you're worried falling into bed with this guy was too soon, rest assured, it wasn't. You've been over Sam for a long time and you shouldn't feel bad about that. If this guy's treating you the way you deserve, if he's giving you confidence like you say he is, go with it." She pauses briefly before adding, "Just know you don't need a man to do those things for you. You don't need a man to tell you you're beautiful, or smart, or funny. You're all those things. It's nice to have someone tell you and believe those things but…" Ally shrugs her shoulders and smiles softly, "I love you, Vi. Just come home when you're ready, I miss you."

There's a lump in my throat, Ally's sweet under her armored exterior. I swallow the lump and blink away the tears forming.

"I miss you, too. I'm going to go for a hike. I'll talk to you tomorrow." I wait for Ally to say goodbye then I disconnect and close the laptop.

Chapter 21
Violet

The hike at the nature preserve in Broken Head this afternoon was what I needed. Fresh air and scenic views were the perfect combination to rest my racing mind. Between talking with Ally and Mia I gained some perspective, considering Ally knew me best and Mia knew Drew well. Like Mia and Ally said, Drew seems to have a full understanding of what's going on here. I may not but the consensus is unanimous, Drew's willing to deal with the consequences of my departure when the time comes. He's willing to put himself out there to spend time with me because it feels good. Whether I'm ready to deal with those consequences is up to me, I've started and continued this relationship with Drew so I must be willing to deal with it later. Here I am, again, playing a reactive role to the decisions I've made.

While I was out today I came across a lovely antique shop where I found a wedding gift for Mia and Davy, it's an old horseshoe. I cleaned it with help from the shop owner who recommended a place to have Mia and Davy's initials engraved in time for the wedding. I found a shadow box to put the shoe inside. I hope the horseshoe will bring them luck but I know they won't need much of it. They have a love, I know in my soul, that will last beyond their lifetime. I spent so much time away from the cottage today, when I returned the sun had set and the stars were beginning to come out. I thought about going out to eat but after the physically and mentally draining day, all I want to do is take a hot shower and lay on the bed.

As I finished packing I realized I didn't have a dress to wear for the wedding, so I texted Mia asking for the name of a dress shop where I could browse. Her response was: Mia's Closet. I thought for a split second Mia's Closet was the name of an actual shop then I laughed. She gave me the code for the alarm and told me where the spare key was hidden. She said I could go over anytime to try on whatever I wanted. After I shower and eat, I plan on stopping by, maybe she'll be home by then.

In the shower I could smell a hint of Drew's soap, regretfully, I washed it away with body wash of my own. I felt re-energized after the shower, I pulled on my sweatpants and long sleeve shirt. I made a light snack with the remaining cheese and fruit from the fridge, taking my laptop from the counter I sat on the couch. I started on all the electronic signatures Stacy needed for a variety of contracts and paperwork. One of the files I emailed Stacy is time sensitive so I remind myself to check my email in the morning to make sure there are no issues. When I look at my phone I see a missed call from a number I don't recognize, it has a Boston area code. The time of the missed call was 2 PM today, that would have been 11 PM in Boston. No voicemail was left, it could be a wrong number. I don't know of anyone that would call me so late at night, it had to be a wrong number.

Before I walk over to Mia's, I make sure I leave the outdoor lights on and have my key for the cottage. It's a cool night, even with my long sleeve and sweatpants, I feel the chill. I find the spare key where Mia said it would be, under a planter on the side of the driveway. When I unlock the door and punch in the alarm code I set off to Mia's bedroom.

Like the shoes in the closet, the dresses are lined by color. I glance over the rainbow of colors, I pick a few bright dresses but they're too loud for me. Back home most of my closet is black, gray and blue. I would love to have the confidence to wear bright orange, red or yellow but those colors don't suit my pale skin or personality. Looking over the pinks and reds I find a deep red, knee length dress. Then I go to my safety net of blue, finding a beautiful satin, sleeveless v-neck. It's so soft and beautiful, the color matches my bright blue eyes perfectly. I take the two dresses over to the full length mirror and start to undress. I tried on the red one first, it's tight on the waist, it's cute but not wedding cute. I return it to the hanger and place it back on the rack. I put on the blue one, it's comfortable and stunning. The long skirt has a slit to the thigh, the material crosses on the back. I take my hair from the ponytail and shake it loose, I could work with this. The blue is the color of sapphire, the satin material makes it shine. I snap a picture of myself in the mirror and send it to Mia, making sure this dress is okay to borrow for the night. Of course I'd be returning it but I want to make sure Mia's alright with me taking it. Still wearing the dress I go to the wall covered in shoes and start my search. I've tried on three pairs of shoes trying to find the right match when I hear my phone ping with a message.

Mia: Stunning! Definitely wear that!

I guess this is the dress. I'm checking a pair of rose gold shoes when I see a shadow behind me in the mirror. I inhale sharply as I whip around, eyes darting around the closet. I walk slowly to the closet door and peer out. The bedroom is dark, I didn't turn on the light. I try to remember if I locked the front door, I look to the bedroom door and see a light on in the hall. Straining my ears for any sounds, I walk quietly to the bedroom door. My heart races, I can't hear anything but I get a whiff of something. A man's smell, aftershave maybe. With shaking hands I call Mia but there's no answer. I text her asking if she's expecting anyone, no reply. Then I hear something heavy drop to the floor as the front door closes. Shit. I didn't lock the door. I try to look down the hall to the front door but there's no way to see the entry from here. Panic rises, my hands sweat. The only other exits, other than windows, are down the hall which would make me visible to anyone who might be out there. I slink back into the bedroom, very gently closing the door and locking it. I tried Mia again, still no answer. I text Drew.

Me: Is Davy with you?

There is a response within 10 seconds.

Drew: Yes, of course.

Me: Can you ask him if he is expecting anyone at his house?

As I send the text I hear shuffling in the hall passing the bedroom door. I'm in full blown panic mode, shaking from head to toe. Nausea floods my stomach, I'm sure whoever walks by can hear my heart pounding through the door and space between us. Do they have 911 in Australia? Or is it something different like 111 or 000. My phone rings and I practically scream, I silence the ringer instantly and head to the closet. I answer the call without looking at the caller, it must be Mia.

"Hello?" I whisper, I look toward the bedroom door and see a shadow stop across the crack under the door.

"Violet?" Drew says on the other end of the line, I have never been so relieved to hear his voice.

"Drew, there's someone in the house." I hear the bedroom door knob turn but not release because it's locked. I feel tears in my eyes and I try to keep a whimper from escaping.

"What do you mean? Violet, where are you?" I hear the panic in his voice, he shouts Davy's name.

"I'm in Mia's bedroom, in the closet," my voice shakes, my hands tremble. Every muscle in my body is rigid with tension and fear. "I heard someone come in. They're right outside the bedroom door."

I'm frantic, I hear Drew talking to Davy asking him if someone is supposed to be at the house. There's a knock on the bedroom door and I jump, letting out a hiccup. I cover my mouth with my hand trying to muffle the whimpers leaving me.

Then a voice calls out from the other side of the door. "Davy? Mia?"

"Are you okay?" Drew asks as I hear a door slam on his end.

That voice calling out, I know that voice, gruff and gravel. It's strong but comforting. I stand on shaky legs and open the closet door.

"Hello?" I call out through the door.

"Mia? Who's in there?" The voice calls back.

"Violet, what the hell is going on?" Drew pleads over the phone.

"Hold on, I think, oh God. I think it's your father." A wave of relief settles over me when I connect the voice to a face.

"Davy, call Dad," Drew commands.

I hear a phone ringing from the other side of the door, I slowly open the bedroom door as Ian pulls a phone from his pocket.

"Jesus, it's him. It's your dad, I'm sorry," I say into the receiver as I feel the heat rush to my cheeks.

I lock eyes with Ian and offer an incredibly weak smile. The relief that washes over me is short lived and is replaced by embarrassment.

"Davy," Ian answers.

"I'm sorry, Drew," I offer when I see another figure step into the hall, Clare.

"Don't be. Do you want me to come there?" I hear the change in his tone from panic to relief.

"I'm fine. Enjoy your night." I disconnect without waiting for a response.

Clare stands next to her husband as Ian explains to Davy, on the phone, they came a night early to have the entire day with the family tomorrow. I feel even more embarrassed when Ian explains he used his own key to Davy's house to enter. I'm the intruder here, I'm the one that doesn't belong and I want to disappear into the shadows of the bedroom.

"Violet, are you okay? You look white as a ghost," Clare says, pushing her way into the bedroom and turning on the light. The sudden brightness and her voice shake me out of the moment of stillness.

"I'm so sorry. I thought you were a burglar or someone trying to break in. I wasn't expecting anyone." I raise my hand to my chest finally able to steady my breaths.

Clare clicks her tongue, "Oh, you poor girl. I'll make you tea."

"No, thank you. I've got to get back." I start after her down the hall wanting to get as far away from this situation as possible.

Clare turns around with a smile, "The dress is beautiful but you can't possibly walk back in that." She eyes me up and down.

I look down remembering I still have the dress on and I flush with embarrassment, again. I let out a sigh and turn toward the bedroom when I slam into the broad chest of Ian.

"I'm so sorry, Ian." I steady myself by grabbing his forearms.

He has a playful smile, his blue eyes alive with humor. "I'm sorry to have startled you."

"I'm fine." I take a step back from him and motion toward the bedroom, "I'm going to change and be on my way."

"Hmm, not if my wife has anything to do with that," his low laugh reminds me so much of Drew it instantly puts me at ease.

I give a small laugh and step into the bedroom, closing the door behind me. Leaning back against the door I sigh in relief and anxiety, is that even possible? I'm relieved I didn't meet my demise by an intruder and anxious because now I have to get through Clare to leave the house to get back to my quiet cottage. I take the dress off and pull my sweatpants and shirt back on, looking in the mirror I groan. I'm practically in pajamas and I have to go out there and have a cup of tea with Clare and Ian. I sent Drew a text to let him know I'm fine and apologize again for causing him alarm.

Me: I'm sorry if I worried you. I'm fine. I'm about to have a cup of tea with your mom.

Again, within seconds there's a response.

Drew: Never apologize to me. Enjoy the tea.

I pack up the dress and shoes, trying to hold my head up, I walk out to the kitchen where Clare stands over a kettle at the stove.

"Just be a minute, love. Have a seat." She doesn't look at me, she puts tea bags in three mugs she has out on the counter.

I hang the dress on the coat hook by the front door and take a seat at the island. I hear Ian limp up the steps from the living room behind me. He takes the seat next to me and I smell his aftershave. The smell that scared me earlier is bringing me comfort now, I turn to offer him a smile which he returns.

"That was a beautiful dress you had on. Is that for the wedding?" Clare asks as she pours steaming water into the mugs.

"Yes, Mia said it was okay if I came over tonight and looked through her closet. I didn't pack anything suitable for a wedding." I shift in my seat as Clare places the mug in front of me.

"Mia's sweet." Clare takes a seat directly across for me.

I softly blow on the steaming tea before I take a sip. Chamomile, the same kind Drew made me last night after my nightmare. I like chamomile, it's my favorite tea.

"I'm happy to have met her," I say, trying to be brief, I have a feeling Clare is an expert inquisitor. Or maybe I should take the offensive and ask questions of my own. "How was your drive?"

"It was fine." Clare sips, her green eyes stare at me from over the rim of the mug. "We're happy to come and spend some time with the boys." Clare's phone rings, she stands up to retrieve it from the counter by the stove.

"Now's your chance to scoot if you don't want to answer all the questions she's lining up in her head. She means well, she's a sweetheart but I know she can be tough on new people. Especially when her son takes interest in said new people." Ian raises a brow and I'm incredibly thankful for his openness. I don't want to be rude but I really want to get back to the cottage and decompress from this exhausting day.

"I don't want to be rude. I…"

Before I can finish Ian holds up a hand reassuring me there's no offense taken here. Clare's still talking on the phone when I stand from the island.

Just as I do Clare turns to look at me. "I'm sorry dear, I have to go." She places her phone back on the counter and turns her attention to me.

"I didn't notice the time, I should be on my way. I've got an early morning," I say. It's not until now I realize I never booked the hotel room.

"Are you sure?" Clare asks, shifting her gaze to her husband.

Before she can be offended by my haste I move to her and kiss her cheek. "Good night, Clare. I'm sorry for the commotion earlier. I'll be seeing you tomorrow."

"Okay, love. It was so nice to see you, I wish we got here earlier so we could chat more." She moves aside as I pass her.

"Good night, Ian." I send him a warm smile thanking him for the opportunity.

"See you tomorrow, Violet." His tips his head and I scurry out the door with Mia's dress and shoes in hand.

I speed walk back to the cottage trying to outpace the embarrassment and awkwardness behind me. When I finally reach the cottage, I toss the dress on the back of the couch and face plant on the bed. I lie there, facedown on the bed for several minutes when my phone rings. I check the display and smile before I answer.

"Hi, Mia," I say as I turn to my back on the bed and reach for a pillow to clutch.

"Violet! I'm so sorry, I had no idea they were coming. Are you okay?" Mia asks.

"I'm fine, I was a little surprised." I put a hand over my face as the tiredness settles over my mind and body.

"Davy called me. They were so worried, I'm glad you're alright." I hear her car door shut, she's either home or leaving her visit with her family.

"Thank you for letting me shop your closet. You have so many amazing things," I stifle a yawn as I stand up to draw the blinds over the windows.

"That dress is gorgeous on you, you wear it well. You're going to have Drew on his knees, maybe a few others, too," she laughs that amazing Mia-laugh.

"Thanks. I'm about to turn in, I'll see you tomorrow. Drive safe." When the blinds are down, I take the dress off the couch and hang it by the entryway.

"Good night, Violet." Mia disconnects as I make my way back to the bed.

I pull the covers back and slide into the bed, the sheets feel cold and rough tonight without Drew lying next to me. Just as I pull the blankets up over my shoulders I hear a ping from my phone, I read the message and send a response.

Drew: Hope Mum isn't bothering you too much.

Me: Back at the cottage, under the covers. It was fine. Have fun tonight.

There's another instant reply.

Drew: Good night, Violet. Sweet Dreams.

I smile and hope tonight is filled with sweet dreams or no dreams. I lower my head to the pillow and drift off in minutes.

There's a bang that startles me from sleep. I bolt up and that's when I feel the vibrating under my pillow. I take the phone from under the pillow to answer the call, my vision is blurred from sleep.

"Hello?" I look toward the door but I don't hear anything. Was I dreaming?

"Violet, I'm at your door." Drew's voice is rough and low.

I look at the door again, hearing a soft knock. I end the call and head toward the door, my hand hovers over the knob. Checking the time on my phone, it's close to 2 in the morning. Apprehension swells inside me. Is he drunk? His voice sounded hoarse but not slurred. I'm hit with a memory, the smell of stale beer and whiskey waking me in the middle of the night, rough hands grabbing at my body. But that's not who's on the other side of the door, I trust the man on the other side. I unlock the door, turn the knob, I see Drew standing on the landing of the porch.

"Are you okay?" I ask as I open the door wider.

"Yes."

He takes a step forward and when I don't move from the doorway he stills with a look of confusion. I search his eyes for a glassy, glazed-over look, I search his frame for swaying. I look at his car parked in the driveway, it's not crooked or haphazardly parked. I don't know why I'm doing this but I do.

"Are you drunk?" I ask softly, I'm ashamed I feel the need to ask.

Drew steps back as if I pushed him, he stares at me with words on his lips but his lips don't move. I tentatively step out onto the landing waiting for an answer.

"I'm not," he looks down to his feet with a hurtful expression, "I've been lying in bed for an hour trying to sleep." He looks up apologetically. "My pillows and sheets smell like you, I couldn't fall asleep." Drew takes another step back, retreating from my cutting misgivings.

"I'm sorry, I thought maybe…" I can't finish the sentence, I should not have compared Drew to anyone from my past. "I'm sorry, come in." I step back gesturing to the open door. Drew doesn't move a step but looks toward the doorway.

"It's okay, I just wanted to see you." He steps back down the last step and I feel a sinking in my chest. I hurt him with my question, it's written all over his face.

"Come inside, please. I'm cold out here." I offer him a smile and see his mouth turn up on one side but no smile forms. I walk over to him and reach for his hand leading him up the stairs.

When we're inside Drew pauses in the entryway, closing the door behind him. I reach up to his neck and wrap my arms around him, his body is warm as always. He rests his chin on my shoulder and I feel him inhale deeply. His arms squeeze around my sides. We stand in that embrace for a full minute before he pulls away.

"I'm sorry if I scared you." A look of realization takes over the wounded look he had on a few moments ago.

"I'm sorry for thinking…" I try to finish but Drew interrupts me.

"Don't be sorry, I've told you, you never have to apologize to me." He leans in to kiss me. It's barely a kiss, his lips brush over mine. There's no alcohol on his breath, there's no smell of another woman, it's just Drew. "I was the driver tonight, I stayed sober so the boys could let loose."

"You could have gotten a car for the night. Do they have Uber here?" I tilt my head with the question and Drew laughs which brings me comfort.

"Yes, we have Uber. We're not an archaic country," his laugh continues, his smile spreads to his eyes.

"Well, then if that's the case, I'm returning my rental car tomorrow." I lean back into him, listening to his laugh through his chest. I take his hand and lead him to bed.

"I don't have to stay, I wanted to check on you." Drew starts toward the bed and motions for me to get in.

"Are you hungry? Do you want some water?" I go toward the fridge when I feel his hand on my wrist.

"It's two in the morning, I don't want food. I wanted to see you." Drew sits on the bed and pulls me in between his legs, looking up at my face.

"Here I am," I say, giving him a wide smile. "How was your night?"

"It was fun but it was a long day. I dropped the guys off at my place an hour ago, they're a mess. Passed out all over my house." Drew shakes his head then rests his forehead on my stomach.

"You left everyone at your house?" I run my hands through his hair and he lets out a pleasure filled groan.

"I'll be back before they wake up." Drew pulls me on him as he lies back on the bed. "Are you okay after the run in with my dad?" He swipes the hair back out of my face, tucking it behind my ear.

"I was mortified but your dad was great about it. I hope I didn't worry you." I place a gentle kiss on his forehead.

"I was only slightly terrified. I'm relieved I didn't have to call your sister and tell her you were abducted or murdered at my brother's house."

We both laugh hard and long at that. When the laughter fit is over, we reposition ourselves at the head of the bed. Drew's arms around me while my head rests on his chest. We're only in that position for a few minutes before I hear Drew's breathing transition to slower breaths, he's asleep. I look up and see he's still fully dressed with his sneakers on. I wait a few more minutes then get up to remove his shoes. I place the sneakers by the bed and take the throw blanket from the back of the couch. I cover Drew and slip under the blankets while Drew sleeps on top of them on the other side of the bed. I gently kiss his cheek, placing my hand on his chest and my head on his shoulder. I drift off for a second time tonight.

My phone alarm sounds at 6 AM, I quickly take it from the bedside table and mute the alarm. I turn to see Drew is asleep in the same position he took four hours ago. He's snoring lightly when I slip out of bed. I have to call Stacy, it shouldn't take very long, I'll be back in bed before he realizes I'm gone. I dial my office number as I, quietly, open the front door. Taking a seat on the chair on the porch, I listen to the line trill.

When Stacy answers there's surprise in her voice, "Hey, Vee." The office line has a caller ID, she knew it was me.

"Hi, Stacy, how's everything? Did you get the Browning and Miller files I sent?" The sky is still dark, I could get to the beach after the call and watch the sunrise.

"I got 'em, I sent them over around ten this morning. Everything's good here, nothing to worry about." I hear Stacy shuffling papers as she explains, I hear a sharp click of a stapler.

"That's good, thanks again. You've been great these past two weeks." I always try to let Stacy know how much I appreciate her, she's a hard worker and I want her to feel valued. I don't want to lose her as an assistant.

"There's one thing, a woman stopped by today. Her name was Emily, hold on I have it here. Emily Hunt, she wrote her contact information. She said she's a friend and needed to reach you. I told her I'd take the message but you would be out of the office for the week." Stacy waits for a response from me.

Emily? I don't have any friends named Emily. "Huh, I don't know an Emily. What did she look like?" I ask Stacy, searching my brain for a woman named Emily.

"She was short, my height, with curly, dark hair and light brown eyes. She drove a sports utility, it was loud, I remember hearing it pull up," she relays. I'm thankful Stacy's so observant but I still can't place this Emily.

"That's not bringing anyone to mind. Did she have a property to list or was she looking for something?" Sometimes people will come in, saying they know the family or someone in the office, thinking they'll get some kind of friends and family deal on real estate.

"I took her info, her name and number, I can email it to you or text it," Stacy offers, I hear a desk drawer open.

"It's okay, you can put the info on my desk, I'll figure that out later." I see the sky start to brighten. "Has there been issues with any other visitors?" I ask the question attempting to be vague but Stacy knows exactly what I'm asking. I want to know if Sam crept his way back over there.

"No issues," her voice is sure and clipped.

I'm glad, for whatever reason, Sam seems to be getting the hint. I haven't heard back from the text I sent him two days ago.

"Good, I'll be available if you need me. Thanks, Stacy." I wait for her to say goodbye before I get back to the sleeping god-man in my bed.

"Just doing my job. Have fun, Violet," her words are sincere and encouraging.

I disconnect from Stacy, standing from the steps, I stretch my arms up over my head taking in a deep breath of the morning air. I have to accomplish a few things today, starting with checking out of here. Just as I'm about to relax my arms and body from the stretch I freeze. There's a figure stopped on the road in front of the driveway looking up at me. Clare. She's waving and smiling a Davy-like smile. The smile comforts me, then I glance to Drew's SUV at the bottom of my driveway and I instantly blush. We didn't even have sex last night, we just fell asleep but I know what his car in the driveway this early in the morning relays to her. She starts walking toward me. Shit. I fumble with the phone in my hands, taking the three steps down from the porch.

"Good morning, Violet, you're up early." She stops in front of me while glancing at the front door behind me.

"I had a work call to make," I say, holding up my cell phone.

"I was going for a walk." Clare glances at the SUV and I feel the need to address the elephant between us but I can't find the words. Drew and I are both adults, there should be nothing to be embarrassed about. "Is Drew awake?" she asks, glancing at the door.

"No, he's asleep." I shift on my feet, this is so embarrassing.

Just as I finish the sentence Clare's eyes flash toward the door. I turn around to see Drew leaning on the frame crossing his arms over his chest. If his mother wasn't standing next to me I would think it was the sexiest thing I have seen, it is the sexiest thing I've seen.

"I guess he's awake." I turn back to Clare and I feel the blush in my cheeks. Drew descends the steps in his socks, jeans and black shirt.

"Morning, Mum." Drew stands at my side and puts an arm around my waist. Then he turns to me and says, "Sneaking off again?" His brows come together in disapproval but a smile ticks up on one side of his mouth.

The gesture causes me to fluster. "I had, uh, I was, um, I called the office. I had some things to talk to Stacy about." My hands shake as I hold up the phone.

"How was the night with your brother?" Clare asks, leaning in to kiss her son.

"It was a fun day, they won't be up for a few more hours." Drew turns to me when he says the last part, making me want to fold into myself because I know what he's implying.

"Well, I'm going to finish my walk, you two have a good morning. I'll see you later." When Clare turns back down the driveway, Drew places an arm under my knees, another hand behind my back, and scoops me off the ground causing me to yelp with surprise. Clare turns back to see Drew carrying me up the steps, she laughs and shakes her head.

"Oh. My. God," I say as we enter the cottage, still in Drew's arms. "Just when I think I can't possibly embarrass myself any further with your parents, something like that happens." I sink my head into his chest as he walks me toward the bed, tossing me on top of the blankets.

"Embarrassed about what? That wasn't embarrassing." He stares at me with a look of genuine question on his face causing me to sit up.

"Drew, your mom walked by my place at," I glanced at the clock, "six twenty in the morning, seeing your car in the driveway. What do you think her take away was?"

"Violet, I'm a thirty-three year old man. They know I'm not a virgin, if that makes you feel better." I see he's holding back a laugh as I watch him through the fingers covering my face.

"Oh. My. God." I fall back on the bed, still covering my face.

"She's not judging you, if that's what you're worried about." He pries my hands off my face and lays a kiss on each hand.

"Of course she is! She's your mother, you're her first born son. It doesn't matter how old you are." I laugh at the fact he can say his mother's not judging me with a straight face.

"She likes you. She wouldn't have made you tea last night if she didn't like you. She wouldn't have stopped by this morning if she didn't like you. If she didn't like you, believe me, you would know." He plants kisses along my neck and jaw sending a shiver of pleasure through me. "What time do you have to leave here?" he asks as he slides his hand under my shirt, letting all the thoughts of Clare and the awkwardness of the driveway interaction melt away.

"Eight-thirty." I close my eyes and concentrate on the feel of his hands on my body. I feel Drew pause above me, I look up to see he's looking at the clock, he smiles back down at me.

"We have two hours," he says before his mouth covers mine.

"No, we have forty-five minutes. I need to pack up the car and clean out the fridge," I say through his kiss. I push on his chest but it does very little to create space between us.

"Five minutes to clean the fridge, five to pack the car, shower at my house. One hour, fifty minutes." He kisses me through my laughter. "If you had stayed put this morning and not snuck away then we wouldn't be having this problem." He looks amused. "When will you learn you should never leave a man in bed alone?"

He takes his shirt off and repositions himself on top of me again, if this is my punishment for leaving him alone in bed I'm perfectly fine in dealing with the consequences.

Chapter 22
Drew

I reluctantly departed from Violet this morning after I helped her clean up the cottage and pack her rental car. There was still some time before she officially had to be out but she had to do a few things before the day got away from her. She mentioned dropping off Mia and Davy's wedding gift for engraving, when I asked what the gift was she deflected my question so I didn't push. I somehow convinced her not to check into a hotel, telling her I had something planned for after dinner tonight. It didn't take much to convince her, much like the day I told her I wanted to take her somewhere, she nodded and said, "okay". The way she puts her trust in me is satisfying, I hope she enjoys this plan as much as she enjoyed the horse riding day. When Violet said she was going to the wedding I booked a villa at the resort where the wedding was taking place. I had booked a room for myself for the night of the wedding months ago, last night during the bachelor party I called the resort to see if I could book it for tonight as well. After some schmoozing, offering to upgrade the guest that was supposed to stay there tonight, I managed to arrange the same villa both nights. It was worth it, two more nights with Violet, I would have paid whatever they asked. Hell, I would have upgraded every guest in the resort if it meant I'd have a two night stay with her.

When I arrived back at my house the men were starting to stir. Davy was in the shower, Ethan and Brian were still asleep in the guest room. Tomas was making coffee in the kitchen, Sean was sitting on the sectional with his head in his hands. I grinned to myself, their boozed filled day and night was showing on all of them.

"Morning, mates," I say to Tomas and Sean as I head back toward my bedroom.

"Where the hell did you go?" Tomas calls after me but I don't respond, I keep walking to my room.

I had packed an overnight bag and the suit for the wedding last night while I couldn't sleep. When the packing was finished I tried to sleep again but the scent of Violet was all over my bed, driving me mad. I knew I wouldn't sleep, so I called her but there was no answer. It was close to one in the morning when I called her the first time, she had texted me saying she was going to bed hours before. Between the smell of her and the fact she had my heart racing when she called me, full of fright, thinking there was an intruder in the house I wouldn't have been able to sleep until I held her. When I collected the items for the wedding Davy appeared, a towel wrapped around his waist, looking very pale. I laughed.

"Please, don't yell," Davy says, squinting in the morning light.

"I didn't yell, I laughed." I set the bags by the door and headed to my bureau to pull out something for Davy to wear.

"My clothes are in your wash, they stunk." He shrugs his shoulders and moves toward the bathroom after I hand off clean clothes.

"At least you didn't get sick," I say over my shoulder as I leave the bedroom.

"Stop yelling," Davy calls back, slamming the bathroom door.

Back in the kitchen three men huddled over mugs of coffee, looking every bit as pathetic as Davy. I was glad I decided to take the role of chauffeur for the night. Even if I hadn't been the driver I wouldn't have gotten myself into the state these men were in.

"I was going to make some eggs." As soon as I say the last word all three men groan in disgust, shaking their heads, I laugh again.

"So, where did you go?" Sean repeats the question Tomas asked earlier.

"I had something to take care of." I leave it at that as I pour a mug of coffee.

"And was that something a beautiful, leggy, blonde American?" Tomas asks, raising a brow.

I didn't answer, it was none of their business, I didn't like hearing Tomas' description of Violet. Of course she was all those things, all those things were noticeable about her and for the most part unoffending. I didn't like the way he said it, he was fishing and I wasn't going to take the bait.

"So are you two a *thing*?" Sean asks, resentment dripping from his tone.

Sean had asked a lot of questions about Violet last night to Davy, I overheard him. He asked how Davy knew her, if she was single, if she was attending the wedding alone. All the questions made me want to do something to make him stop asking about her. Davy did a good job of keeping the answers simple and trying to deflect. Violet was single, even though during her time here we've spent the majority together, nothing was going to become of us after her stay here. She's returning to America and I'm staying in Australia. We'd have this time together and most likely nothing more. I thought of keeping in touch with her, I even fantasized about her giving everything up and coming to live here. She would never do that, she'd never leave her home. I would never allow her to do that. I thought about following her home but I didn't even know how she really felt about me and I don't think that's a part of her plan. I never thought about leaving my family to live halfway across the world. Violet Kelly was making me rack my brain trying to find out how to make her a fixture in my life. The only options were one of us giving up everything for the other. Considering the losses she experienced, she would never ask someone to give up their family for her. She wants everyone with a family to cherish each other, remain together because this world can be cruel and you never know when someone will be taken from you. After five days of Violet I was seriously considering giving up everything to find a way to make this work. Was that absurd?

"I had some things to do in town before dinner tonight." I set my stare to Sean, my eyes telling him to back the fuck off. He sees it and goes back to aimlessly staring at his coffee mug.

"Thanks for the night, Drew. I've never seen this place, it's great," Brian says, making an effort to ease the tension filling the kitchen.

"Anytime, mate. Davy and I were happy to do it." I go toward the fridge and start pulling the fruit salad and pastries Mia made, sugar should help their hangovers.

Davy comes from the hallway and I see some color has returned to his face which makes me feel better. I don't want to drop him off looking as wrecked as he was a few minutes ago. Ethan is the last one to emerge, with a huge smile on his face.

When he sits down at the table he says, "Best night of sleep I've had in months." We all laugh, Ethan had a few beers last night but wasn't in the condition the rest of the guys were in.

We all sit around the table eating refined sugar with a side of natural sugar. Davy seems happy to see all his mates again, I notice he keeps checking the time, he's anxious to get back to Mia. Ethan and Brian are the first to leave, Brian drove to my house after the beach day yesterday. Shortly after the first two men leave Sean and Tomas gather their things, Davy and I would drop them off at their hotel where they'd stay until the wedding. Then Davy would finally be reunited with Mia and I could continue on with my day before dinner tonight with the family.

"I'm going to put this in the car, I'll be out there when you all are ready," I say as I bring my bags out to my car.

Shortly after I load the car Davy, Sean and Tomas come out to the garage. After packing all the suitcases we leave the house. The ride to the hotel is quiet, everyone says their goodbyes and thank yous and the next stop is Davy's house.

"Don't worry about Sean. He's not used to a girl ignoring him." Davy laughs when we get back in the car and pull out of the hotel drop off.

"I'm not worried," I reply, Sean's good-looking, young and athletic. I'm sure he's used to getting a lot of attention, that doesn't mean I have to like him nosing around about Violet.

"So, what's up for you today?" He lets out a loud yawn, "I've got to take a nap before dinner."

"You just woke up," I laugh, "I'm going to get a haircut then meet Violet for lunch."

"Wow, I'm surprised she's not sick of you yet." Davy puts on his sunglasses and reclines in the passenger's seat.

"Not yet." I smile, knowing she definitely isn't sick of me, not by the way she reacted to my touch this morning in bed.

When we arrive at Davy's house Mia, Mum and Dad are sitting at the dining room table laughing over a cup of tea. Mia rises from her seat at the table when we come into the dining room, frowning at Davy.

"Are you alright, love? You look a bit peaky," she questions as she runs a hand down the side of his face.

"I'm fine, some tea would be lovely." With his request Mum bolted into action, going to the kettle and pouring him a mug.

"Don't be a baby," I say, shaking my fathers hand as he stands from the table. "How are you, Dad?"

"Good, son. Did you boys have a good night?" he asks, nodding toward Davy who's basking in the attention he's getting from Mia and my mother.

"We did. He's playing for attention." I say, both my father and I laugh as Davy shoots us an annoyed glare.

"And your morning? How was your morning, Drew?" Mum asks with her eyebrows raised so high they're practically on the top of her head.

"It was great," I reply, not breaking eye contact with her, I see Mia smile at me from the corner of my eye. "I've got to get going."

"What? You just got here," my mother says as she feigns shock.

"I've got an appointment for a haircut," I say as I bend to kiss Mia and walk toward my mother as she hands Davy a cup of tea.

"We'll see you tonight," Mum says as she allows me to kiss her cheek. "Tell Violet we say hello," she whispers in my ear as she gives me a hug.

I shake Davy's hand and he thanks me for hosting his friends and for planning a great day, I tell him to get some rest and then I'm out the door. As soon as I get in my car I call Violet.

"Hi," she answers, sounding happy to hear from me.

"Hey, I'm going for a haircut, then I'm free for lunch. Do you want to meet me at my house around noon?" I originally thought I would pick her up but considering she doesn't have a residence at the moment I thought leaving her rental at my place would be the best idea.

"Sure, I can be there around noon. Can you text me the address? I don't remember how to get there." She sounds distracted, her voice has very little inflection.

"I'll text now. Are you alright?" I ask, wondering why she sounds distracted.

"I'm trying to parallel park. I'm not used to driving from this side of the car, ugh. I've got to go, I'm causing traffic." Before she disconnects, she unleashes several curse words which makes me laugh.

After my haircut, I went to a few shops to get the rest of the items I would need for dinner with my family and for the villa tonight. Violet had called me, around 11:45, saying she was at my house. I gave her the access code for the garage and told her the kitchen door, through the garage, was unlocked. Knowing she was at my house, waiting for me, made my chest puff a bit and made me anxious to get home. After dropping items off with the resort staff and checking in, I headed back to meet Violet. I arrive home at half past twelve, later than I anticipated. Violet lies asleep on the sectional with an afghan draped over her bottom half. Her arm is raised over her head, covering half her face. Her blonde hair is splayed around her, she looks angelic, I don't want to disturb her. It takes all I have not to go over and kiss her, I want her to rest, so I head to my bathroom to take a shower.

Just as I'm about to shut off the tap, I hear the shower door open. I turn to see Violet standing watching me with sleepy eyes. I reach out to her and try to pull her in, she laughs gesturing to her clothes. I watch as she undresses, my mounting yearning becomes difficult to hide. When she steps inside the shower I reach out, not able to get her against me fast enough.

"You didn't wake me up," she said, bringing her under the shower spray.

"I didn't want to wake you." I plant a kiss on her shoulder, I turn her around to feel her back on my chest.

I hold her for a moment before I take the soap, lather it in my hands and rub her shoulders and back. She presses her body into mine, letting out a sigh of contentment and I can't hold back the demand I feel to take her. I turn her around, our lips meet, our mouths become greedy, our hands eager. Her hands are all over my body, she's unrestrained. I find myself wishing she was this uninhibited with her thoughts and words as she is now with her body. Our breathing becomes short, ragged breaths, the kissing intensifies. When her hands travel down to my pulsating erection I have no restraint remaining. I turn her around, she places her hands against the shower wall, I widen her stance by pushing her feet apart with my foot. I kiss her neck and shoulders, tasting the soap on her skin. Violet reaches back and grabs the back of my neck, pushing me into her. I grab her hips and slide myself inside of her. Her back arches, I bring my hands to her breasts as I pump within her. I hear her moan with satisfaction bringing a carnal hunger that takes over my entire body. I'm not gentle, I felt her inhibitions melt away minutes before. I pump in and out of her with powerful thrusts, filling her completely with my length. She calls out my name, I continue a punishing rhythm until I feel her body quiver and cave. I thrust hard as I hold her hips, her slick body trembles. I hold on for a few seconds before I slide out of her. I let out my release, with a harsh groan, onto the shower floor. Taking a few deep breaths I turn Violet toward me and hold her under the warm stream. Coming down from the euphoria, I suddenly feel apologetic for the harshness of the encounter.

"Are you okay?" I whisper in her ear.

"I'm great. It was…"

"Too much?" I finish repentantly.

"I was going to say phenomenal," she corrects as she looks up at me, her bright eyes dancing with delight.

I sigh with some relief and squeeze her harder in my arms. "I'm going to get dressed. Take your time." I exit the shower to get dressed.

Violet appears in my bedroom as I'm finished dressing, wearing a towel on her head and one wrapped around her body. She eyes me up and down, smiling with curiosity in her eyes.

"Well, you look nice," she says, eyeing my outfit. I'm wearing a pair of navy blue trousers with a white polo.

"So do you." When I turn toward my closet to get a pair of shoes I see her roll her eyes.

"I forgot my bag in the car." She looks at me hopefully.

"I'll get it. The suitcase?" I ask as I put on my brown oxfords.

"Yes, please." She sits on the bench at the foot of my bed, as I head out the bedroom door I brush her lips to mine.

After bringing Violet her suitcase I sit on the couch and wait for her to get dressed. I lean back with my hands behind my head relishing in what happened in the shower. When I went to get the suitcase from the car I saw a beautiful blue dress hanging from the hook on the back seat and now I'm picturing Violet in it. The idea of her in the dress brings another wave of desire to my core, I feel like a hormonal teenager around this woman. Violet steps out of the hallway in a long, linen dress with short sleeves and a deep v line. Her hair is in a loose braid hanging over her left shoulder. She looks like a bohemian goddess, the blue and white paisley pattern brings out her eyes. How am I ever going to be able to watch her walk away? Although I'm smiling at her, feeling as if I'm the luckiest man on earth to have Violet in my house and to have had these days with her, my heart was breaking.

Chapter 23
Violet

Drew took me for lunch at a beautiful resort by the beach where Davy and Mia were getting married. We ate outside on the patio of the restaurant in the resort. When we finished the meal Drew walked me to one of the villas using a key card to open the door. There was a bottle of wine and a bouquet of flowers on the dining table when we walked in. I'm astonished by his surprise. When he said we could stay here tonight and tomorrow if I wanted, I wrapped my arms around him. I'm taken aback by his gesture, I had been fully prepared to find a place to stay and I certainly don't want to make Drew feel he has to do this.

"You didn't have to do all this," I start as I walk around the villa taking in the charm.,"I want to pay you back, please, let me pay for one night." I look at him and my face reddens when I see the incredulous stare he gives me.

"I want to do this, I planned on staying here tomorrow night. I got an extra night when I knew you were planning on attending the wedding. Please don't insult me, Violet." He sends me a reassuring smile as he sits on the sofa, motioning me toward him.

I sit next to him and we look out the picture window to the native trees separating the property from the beach. We sit in silence as we watch the light breeze move the leaves on the trees. I rest my hand on his chest, Drew wraps an arm around my shoulders, I feel the steady, content rhythm of his heart. When I tilt my head to kiss his neck lightly, keeping my hand on his chest, I feel the beat quicken inside his chest. I do that to him, just as he does it to me. Is this normal? I haven't been with anyone who has this effect on my body, I wonder if Drew has. Have I deprived myself of a normal romantic relationship for so long I can't decipher what's normal from what's special? Is there any other man out there that could have this effect on me? Maybe a man that doesn't live 10,000 miles away? My stomach sinks with the thought, 10,000 miles is so many miles. I lower my head to his chest when I feel the tears stinging my eyes.

"You okay?" Drew asks as he gently passes his hand down my arm.

"Fine, this is wonderful," I say in a shaky voice, Drew's body stiffens at my side.

"Are you sure?" He gently pulls his shoulder forward trying to make me bring my head off him to look at him.

"Can I ask you something?" I ask as I shift my body to an upright position. When he smiles at me I know what he's going to say.

"Anything," he says, voice low and soft, his eyes brightening as he smiles.

"Do you think someone could fall in love in five days?"

He's startled by the question, I notice him straighten as he brings his arm down from the back of the sofa. He doesn't pause, there's no hesitation with his answer.

"Yes." His eyes hold mine and I know he's wondering if I'm asking about him or myself.

"Mia thinks you're falling in love with me," I say the words slowly and evenly, Drew glances back toward the window pausing for a long time. I don't know if I should continue or wait for a rebuttal or confirmation. I continue, "I'm going to be honest with you, Drew, I was in a very dysfunctional relationship for so long and the relationships I had before were brief because I didn't allow myself to get attached to anyone. I can't discern what a normal relationship is. I don't know if I'm falling in love or finally understanding what a safe, romantic relationship is like. I'm probably sounding so naive, I'm trying to be sincere."

I shift my eyes around the room feeling self conscious over my confession. I'm 28 years old, for Christ's sake, I shouldn't sound as if I have no idea what to make of a romantic relationship. I feel emotionally stunted when it comes to intimacy.

"The feelings I have when you're close, the emotions that take over when you touch me, the connection I feel when our bodies touch, I don't know what to make of it. I don't know if I could feel this intensity with another person and it completely scares me but also gives me so much hope." Drew smiles as I explain my thoughts. "In the short time I've been with you, you've given me confidence and trust in myself and in someone else. You've helped me see past some of my insecurities, I'm very thankful for that." Drew kisses my hand then returns it to my lap. "Ten thousand miles. Did you know Boston is *ten thousand* miles away?" My eyes grow wide and Drew lets out a huff of a laugh.

"It's nine thousand seven hundred miles," he says with a laugh and I roll my eyes.

"Have you felt this way with someone before?"

Again, there's no hesitation, no pause when he gives me his reply.

"No," he says as he leans back into the sofa holding my stare. "I've never felt a force that pulls me toward someone like this ever before." Drew takes a deep breath before he continues, "I see the way men look at you, Violet. You're beautiful, charming and alluring, I'm not the only one that notices. It shocks me that you haven't noticed how people, not just men, are drawn to you. I don't know if it's your experiences in life or if it's a part of you but you make people comfortable, you're compassionate and warmhearted. You might not know if this is love between you and I but I have never felt so sure about loving someone as I have you. I'm prepared to endure whatever comes after this week because when you love someone you have to be willing to let them go. I've said it before, if I didn't allow myself this time with you I'd look back and wonder what if."

I'm stuck on the fact Drew said he has never felt so sure about loving someone as he has me. He loves me? He didn't say, "I love you, Violet" but it was there. My heart does a movement while it palpitates, it rises and falls. My heart soars then sinks. I'm going to hurt this amazing man when I leave. I should've been more careful with him and his feelings. I've been selfish and because of my selfishness a wonderful person is going to have to deal with the consequences.

"And you? You're successful, incredibly handsome, with a body that looks like it's been designed by the gods. How do you think women look at you? You could have your pick of women," I say as I watch him shake his head.

"I know how women look at me and I don't care. I want the right woman, I'm picky, remember?" He explains and I feel the heaviness of the conversation lighten when he winks at me.

Drew confessed his feelings the other night while at his house but I needed time to process. Now we both put what was on our minds out into the universe, even though we didn't have answers, we had understanding. I could relax knowing, hopefully, he had a better awareness of where I am.

"I'm going to get our bags, then we can get ready to go to Davy's." Drew stands and heads toward the door.

"You took my bags?" I ask, remembering I left the suitcase in his bedroom, I thought we'd go by his house later for it.

"I packed while you were in the bathroom getting ready. I grabbed your dress and backpack from your car, too." He sends me a smile and I'm able to fully relax now.

"Thank you," I say as I sprawl across the couch sending him an affectionate smile.

Dinner at Davy and Mia's was not only delicious but very enjoyable. Mia's sister, Lauren, came with her husband and three girls. They had flown in earlier in the day and the little girls were enthralled with my "accent". The older girl kept asking me to say certain words while we played on the patio. Mia was a wonderful, attentive aunt. I met Mia's mother, Carmen, who was excited to meet me. Ian and Clare were very pleasant and comfortable around Mia's family. Since they had been neighbors for years, they'd already had a strong connection to each other. Davy's smile was endless all night and Mia looked very relaxed and ready for the day tomorrow. I didn't get much time to talk with the adults because the little girls had taken to me early in the night. I was happy to distract them so the adults could have conversations and relax without having to entertain the children. The girls wanted me to braid their hair like mine. Even the youngest, who had short baby hair, wanted a braid and I was happy to oblige. I always liked children, full of wonder and amusement, they were unapologetically honest as well. There's no filter on a four year old's thoughts and I found it hilarious when one of the children asked Drew if he turned green when he was mad because he had such large muscles. I found Drew's response more hilarious when he said it happened once, when a little girl spilled a cup of milk on him during dinner. When it was time to sit for dinner all three girls asked for water, instead of the milk Clare poured for them, Drew sent me a humorous smile.

Drew and I left after coffee and tea were served. Drew said he was tired from the night before and wanted to make sure he was rested for the day tomorrow, no one believed him. Still, we made our exit. Drew held my hand the entire 25 minute ride back to the resort. It was close to ten when he unlocked the door, as soon as we crossed the threshold Drew's hands were on me. They were in my hair, on my arms, on my back, his hands were feverishly working the material of the dress, trying to pull it over my head. His mouth, like his hands, was all over me as well. His lips kissed my neck and shoulders, his mouth found mine before he explored a new spot on my body. I shook with excitement and anticipation. When we finally had each other undressed Drew kissed me all the way to the bed. Successfully getting me into bed, his frenzied touching slowed.

Drew fell asleep almost instantly after he gave me the most mind blowing orgasm of my life. It left me reinvigorated, turning to look at Drew, it seems to have left him exhausted. Coupled with the long day and night he had yesterday he barely had energy to pull the blankets over himself before his slow deep breaths took him into a dreamstate. His eyelids were already twitching with REM sleep. I silently got up from the bed to use the bathroom, not wanting to wake him. After I clean up and wash my face, I go to my laptop. I started researching Whian Whian National Forest and I want to write a few more details down. I take my notebook out of my backpack and open the page to where I took notes in the days prior.

After some research I check the clock and see it's close to one in the morning. I have things to do tomorrow before the wedding, I should have gone to bed a while ago. I've got to pick up Davy and Mia's gift and I arranged to get a little something for Drew as a thank you for showing me around this past week. I'll be leaving Byron soon, I might be able to squeeze in a few more days or nights with him but my plan is to go camping after the weekend. Before I get in bed I check my phone, thinking I should set an alarm so I don't oversleep. I see a missed call from the same unknown number that called me yesterday. This time there's a voicemail, I set the alarm. I'll check the voicemail in the morning, the tiredness suddenly takes over me. As I get under the covers I feel Drew shift, he turns on his side and pulls me into him. I settle into his chest, feeling his strong arms surround me, he covers me with his warmth. I'm breathing him in as my breaths begin to match his and I drift off into darkness.

My alarm wakes me at 8 AM, I reach for my phone and shut off the chiming, I notice the bed next to me is empty. I reach over and feel the sheets are cool, Drew must've gotten out of bed a while ago. I yawn and sit up straining for sounds of the shower or movement around the villa. Nothing. I get out of bed and look in the living room then the kitchen, there's coffee made. I touch the pot, it's warm but not hot. I head to the bathroom, it's dark inside, the lights are off and the shower doesn't show signs of being used. There are no droplets clinging to the sides of the wall, there's no moisture on the shower floor.

Returning back to the bed I reach for my phone, when I'm about to call his number I hear the door open. I look up and see Drew balancing two to-go boxes on top of each other and holding a large bottle of orange juice. He's wearing workout gear, black athletic shorts and a black shirt that clings to him, damp with perspiration. It's clinging to him in all the right spots, my mouth goes dry as I look at him. He sees me eyeing him up and down and he lets out a low laugh.

"I went to the gym and got us breakfast." He walks toward the kitchen and sets the food down.

"I woke up and you weren't in bed. Don't you have a rule about that?" I tilt my head with the question.

"I left you a note," he gestures toward the coffee table in front of the sofa, "I got up early, I slept very well."

Drew sets up the table for breakfast, omelets, french toast and bacon. He pours orange juice in two glasses and pulls out the chair for me to sit. The food is still hot, he must've gotten it from the restaurant here at the resort.

"I've got to go back to my house to meet Davy, you can come with me. I know you have errands. We can go get your car or you can drop me off and take mine." He winks at me as he puts a large bite of omelet in his mouth.

"What time should I meet you for the ceremony?" I ask before I take a sip of juice.

"I'll be back here around three."

He brings his plate to the sink and then peels off his shirt. My fork almost falls to my plate, I catch it in time so it doesn't clatter.

"I need a shower." He sends me another wink, I know it's an invitation.

After Drew showers and dresses for the day, he calls Davy. Davy spent the night at Drew's house and I felt bad thinking Drew should have been there with him.

"Is Davy upset you didn't spend the night with him?" I ask when we pull out of the resort parking lot to go to Drew's house.

"No, he was fine. He enjoyed the night, Sean and Tomas stopped by to have a drink with him." Drew's jaw twitches when he mentions Sean and Tomas which makes me think he might not like Davy's university friends.

"They seem nice," I pry but try to play it off as casual.

"Tomas is great," his response is clipped and I want to ask if something happened at the bachelor party with Sean but I don't.

The rest of the ride to Drew's house is quiet but not uncomfortable. When we pull up to the house Davy greets us at the garage door. He's smiling his signature smile, with his hands in his jean pockets. I step out of the car, give Davy a hug and tell him I'm excited for him and Mia. Davy shakes Drew's hand and we file into the house. If I want to get into town, get the items I have waiting for me and get back to the resort in time to get ready, I can't stay long. I tell the boys to have a good time, Drew moves in to kiss me on the cheek before I go. Davy gives me a huge hug and kisses my cheek as well. I love this family, I'm so excited for today.

Drew hands me the keys to my rental that hang from a key rack by the garage door and it makes me pause. For a moment I think about my keys hanging on the rack, my car in the driveway, how when I walked into Drew's house I was shot with a sense of comfort. My heart falls and my eyes well up, I'm leaving soon. The chances of me being in this house after this week are extremely slim if not nil. I'll stay in touch with Mia, I know that with my entire soul. I want to follow her love story forever. I want to know when, in time, she becomes a mother. I want to hear all about her and Davy's honeymoon, I want to know how her business grows. But Drew? Will I be able to keep in touch with him? Will it be hard for me to hear about his heartache when I leave? Will I want to know when he moves on and with who? I could never have a causal relationship with Drew, I know with certainty he could never have a casual relationship with me. Drew senses my shift as I slowly reach for the keys in his hand.

He lifts my chin to meet my eyes. "Are you okay, Violet?"

My name from his lips brings nausea to my stomach and my heart sinks more. How many more times will I hear that?

I force a smile and answer, "I'm fine." I'm lying, his disappointed look tells me he knows I'm lying.

I reach up to kiss his cheek and I without warning, without my brain telling me to do it, my body reacts by throwing my arms around him. I hold back the sob in the back of my throat.

"I'll be in the bedroom," I hear Davy's voice from behind Drew, it's soft and full of confusion.

Drew's arms tighten around me and I never want this moment to end. He whispers in my ear, "What's going on?"

"I'm going to miss you." The sob rips free and I hate myself for ruining this moment. This day is supposed to be about Davy and Mia. It's supposed to be a celebratory day filled with happiness and I'm ruining that.

"I'm going to see you in a few hours," Drew tries to joke but I hear the heartbreak, hell, I feel his heartbreak as he holds me against him.

We stand holding each other for probably a full two minutes, I let out three more sobs and allow the tears to fall while I count to 20. When I reach 20, I collect myself and step back. I see Drew's eyes are glistening and he draws a huge breath. He kisses my cheeks, still damp with tears, he kisses my forehead, he kisses my lips.

"I'm going to get going, I'm sorry for that," I say as I look down at my feet. "This is supposed to be about Davy and Mia today, I didn't mean to be selfish."

"You're not selfish," he offers me a half smile, "And stop saying sorry."

"Do you need anything while I'm out?" I ask, regaining enough composure to look at him.

"No, be careful. I'll see you at three." When he kisses me, I feel pain, his pain.

I exit through the garage and when I settle into the driver's seat I look up and see Drew watching me from the garage. He smiles but before he smiles I see a look of desperation. As if he forced himself to watch me walk away trying to anticipate how it will feel the next time he'll watch me walk away. It must be the same look of desperation I have on my face in my dreams when I try to get to the ones I love. I force a smile and wave.

Chapter 24
Violet

I'm pleased with the engraving of the horseshoe, it was simple, MH & DH with the date 22.3.2014. The shop owner helped me secure the horseshoe inside the shadow box, which I was thankful for, I didn't know how I was going to manage that part. I picked up Drew's gift as well and put it in the trunk of the rental. I didn't want to show it to him until I was leaving. I thought about leaving it with Mia and having her give it to him after I left. That way if he didn't like it he wouldn't have to fake pleasure. When I pull into the resort parking lot I check the time on my phone, 1:18. I smile, the exact time I asked the bartender when I landed in Brisbane. I notice I still have a new voicemail from the unknown number. Inside the villa, I place Mia and Davy's present on the table and go to the bathroom. I place the curling iron I bought on the counter, take my makeup bag out from under the sink and place it on the counter as well. After everything is set up I sit on the sofa, I have some time to relax before I have to start getting ready. I go to my voicemail and listen to the message.

"Hi, Violet, it's Emily. I stopped by your office, uh, I called the other day. I left a note for you at your parents' house, um, just wondering if you got it. Could you, please, call me as soon as you can. It's about James, uh, I want to talk to you about James."

My heart races, I'm frozen to the sofa. Who is Emily? I rack my brain thinking of an Emily I might know. An Emily that knew James. An old school friend? A wife of a fellow soldier? Emily, Emily. I say the name over and over in whispers. I listened to the voicemail three more times. Emily. James. *Hi, Violet, it's Emily.* She says as if I should know who she is, she says my name as if she knows me. *I left you a note at your parents' house.* My parents' house, I haven't been there since the day I left for Australia. *It's about James, I want to talk to you about James.* What about James? He's gone, why does Emily want to talk to me about James? I check the time again, 1:37. I call Ally. It's 10:37 back home, I know she's not awake but I have to ask.

"Violet?" she answers in a sleepy voice, I exhale with appreciation. "Are you alright?"

"Ally, do you know an Emily?" My heart is pounding, my voice shakes.

"What?" she asks in a breath, she sounds annoyed. "I know a lot of women named Emily, it's a common name. What's going on?"

"Do you know an Emily that might have been a friend of James?" I hear the panic in my own voice and I don't know how she doesn't pick up on it.

"No, I don't think so. What's going on?" she asks, again, sounding more awake.

"I got a voicemail from Emily, she wants to talk to me about James?" There's a long pause. "Ally, who is *Emily*?"

"I have no idea. Maybe an old friend who may have heard about his death." There's no panic or concern in her voice. But why? Why isn't she full of panic like me? "Call her when you get home, I guess. Do you want me to call her?" There's resistance in her voice, she doesn't want to call Emily. Who the fuck is Emily?

"No, I'll take care of it. Sorry to wake you, I'll call you tomorrow." I wait as Ally yawns a goodbye and hangs up the phone.

I listen to the voicemail again, pausing it after every sentence, hoping her voice stirs something in my mind. I go to my contacts and make one more call. The line rings twice.

"Violet?" I feel my body relax when I hear his voice. His voice is rough and deep but not sleepy.

I didn't wake Cullen. Cullen never sleeps. If I had woken him, he would make sure I didn't know I had. I've called Cullen dozens of times, if not a hundred, over the years I've known him. He answers at midnight, he answers at 4 in the morning, he answers at 3 in the afternoon. The only time he didn't answer was the day he told me to come home, he told me to meet him at my parents' house so he could tell me my brother was dead. I called him back but he didn't answer, I called him back again and he didn't answer. Every time I've called him after that day he's always answered. It's as if he's trying to make up for that day.

"Cullen?" I choke out his name in question as I think about him not answering that day, I'm forgetting why I'm calling him now.

"Violet, are you alright?" his voice is firm in question, he senses I'm anxious.

"I don't know. Who is Emily?" I put his call on speaker, with shaking hands I placed the phone on the coffee table in front of me.

"Emily?" he asks, sounding confused.
"Yes, *Emily.*" I'm aggravated, does anyone know Emily?
The adrenaline has been pumping in my body since I first listened to the message but it's slowing now. Cullen's making it slow, his voice is soothing. I think about the time I was having a panic attack, hearing his voice over me telling me to breathe. I breathe.
"I don't know an Emily. What are you talking about, Vi? Breathe and tell me what's going on," he tells me to breathe so I do, again.
When I'm collected I go on, "Emily called me, she left a voicemail. She said she left a note at my parents' house for me. She wants to talk to me about James. Who's Emily?" I wait and I wait, the wait is too long. "Cullen?"
"I don't know. I can't think of any Emily. Could it be an old friend, from high school or something?" His words are slow, I can tell he's more concentrated on thinking than talking, "Have you asked Ally?"
"I called her before you. Are you being honest with me?" I have to ask because Cullen has held secrets for James before. Secrets that made me hate James for a time. Is this another secret? Is Cullen keeping this secret, too?
"Christ, Violet, of course I'm being honest. I told you I would never keep anything from you again."
He did tell me, he told me in the kitchen the day after James died. We were cleaning up from breakfast, I asked him if there was anything else James kept secret that I should know about. He looked me in the eye and said, "I will never keep anything from you again".
There's a long silence, both of us thinking, Cullen finally breaks the silence, "She said she left a note? What else did she say?"
I told him exactly what she said in the message. There's more silence which he breaks again, "I'll go to the house and look for the note. I can call her if you want."
I do want him to go to the house, I want him to call her. But I don't say that, instead I say, "No, it's fine. I don't want you to drive all that way, I'll get the note when I get home. I have plans tonight, I'll call her tomorrow."
"It's less than an hour and half away, that's not far," his voice sounds calm again, he wants to help.

He wants to help me because my brother made him promise to watch over his sisters if something happened to him. James made him promise to keep us safe. Cullen owes me nothing, James was wrong to make Cullen promise such things.

"No. It's okay, really. I'll deal with it," I make sure there's conviction in my response. I make sure it's a believable lie, Cullen can't see me, my voice can lie better than my face.

"Alright, let me know if there's anything I can do," he sounds defeated. He wants to know who Emily is and what she wants as much as I do.

I hear a female voice call to him from the other end of the line, "Hey, are you coming back?"

Shit, he has company. He has someone over, I took him away from something.

"I'll let you know. Bye, Cullen," I rush through the words and disconnect before he has a chance to respond.

As soon as I hit the red icon, ending the call, my phone rings back. It's Cullen, I silence it by sending it to voicemail. It rings again, I ignore it. It rings again. I turn the ringer off, and place it face down on the table. I stare at the phone on the table. Emily. Emily. I let out a frustrated grunt, then I screamed. It's not a shrill scream, it's a scream filled with frustration, fear and anger. But then I remember I don't know anything yet. Emily could be who Ally and Cullen assume, an old friend wanting to extend her condolences. She might be someone who wants to share a story about him because she found out he's gone. But my gut tells me this is something bad, this is something I need to address sooner than later. This is something that's going to bring back all the grief and sadness for James.

"James, you and your fucking secrets," I say out loud, I know Emily is a secret.

James didn't tell me about Emily but he told Emily about me. She knew my name, she knew where my parents' house was. Emily knew a lot more about me than I knew about her. I run my hands down my face and count to 20 as I had done in Drew's arms. I push thoughts of Emily and her voicemail down. I push down the anger I have for James right now. I push down thoughts of Cullen. James has only kept two secrets from me, enlisting in the Navy and taking a job with a military contracting company. Both secrets have come with painful consequences, I push that down too. If this is one of

James' secrets I don't want to comprehend the fallout. I push it all down. Today is a day to celebrate Mia and Davy, my new friends. I go to the bathroom, taking Mia's dress from the closet by the bed, I need to get ready.

Chapter 25
Cullen

I hung up the phone with Violet, rather, she hung up on me. She hung up because she heard the voice calling to me in the background, my stomach sank. She thought she was interrupting something, she wasn't. Now that I've heard Violet's voice I can't go back to the woman in my cabin. Jenny? Jeanie? What the hell is her name? I call Violet back, one ring and it goes to voicemail. I call again, two rings then voicemail. She's ignoring me. I call again, it rings eight times now. I call again and again. Five calls with no answer, I grunt in frustration.

"Hello? I asked if you were coming back?" Jenny calls, it's Jenny right?

"Something's come up, I gotta take you back to town." I don't meet her eyes, I can tell by her sigh she's disappointed.

"You don't have a few minutes to finish what we started?" she asks in a sultry voice.

"No," I simply say, walking toward the kitchen, taking my keys from the drawer. When I look up, I see anger and rejection pouring from her every fiber, "I'm sorry, I am."

I lie, I'm not sorry. I would have been more sorry if I had taken her back to my bedroom and had sex with her just to bring her to town two hours from now. She probably would've given me her number and I would've never called her. She would've been more disappointed by that than she is now.

"I can't make you change your mind?" she asks, standing in my bedroom doorway in her black lace panties and bra. She still can't change my mind.

"I'm sorry, Jenny. I have to go, I've got an emergency." I see the instant change in her face, it goes red, the anger and rejection turns to pure hatred.

"It's Jeanie, you fucking asshole." She turns into the bedroom grabbing her clothes from the floor.

Fuck. It's Jeanie, not Jenny. I run a hand down my face and take a deep breath. When she emerges from my bedroom she's back in her jeans and tight pink top, the top's inside out but I don't tell her. She grabs her jacket off the back of the couch and marches out the door, slamming it behind her. I wait a few seconds until I hear the car door slam, I take another deep breath and head outside. This is going to be the longest 15 minute ride of my life.

I dropped Jeanie, not Jenny, off at the bar where I met her two hours ago. She was there by herself, she sat at the bar alone, begging for someone to notice her. I saw her glance at me a few times from the corner of my eye. I overheard her saying she moved here to be closer to her parents, she was just divorced I assumed. After a few rounds of liquid courage, she sat down across from me in the booth. Jeanie told me exactly what she wanted to do tonight and asked if I was interested. I would've been fine with continuing to drink my beer and calling it a night. But a man has needs and my needs hadn't been met in a while. It's hard to find a woman who wants what I want: sex without commitment. I told her, flatly, if she wanted to come home with me she shouldn't expect anything more than tonight. Then Violet called.

Now, I'm driving to the Kelly house to find out who Emily is and why she's reaching out to Violet. Violet said not to go but she was lying, she wants me to go because she won't be able to take the unknown for another week or so while she's away. I can't either. I need to keep Violet and Ally safe from anything that might want to hurt them. I promised James years ago I'd look out for his sisters if anything happened to him. Even if I hadn't made that promise to James, I'd still want to keep Violet safe from anything wanting to hurt her because I love her. I loved a woman who had no idea how much I cared about her. I loved a woman who might never choose me because she would always think of me as her brother's best friend.

A year after we built the cabins Ally and Violet came to visit for James' birthday. It was a cold February night, we made a fire in the backyard of James' cabin after dinner. As we sat around the fire, the three Kelly siblings talked about their parents and how much they would've loved the cabin. They had reminisced about their time in the mountains of New Hampshire when they were kids. Their father, Matthew Kelly, had taken each of his children to climb Mount Washington the summer they turned 13 years old. The man climbed Mount Washington three times with each of his children. I doubted my father even knew when my birthday was. They each spoke about their weekend trip with their father, where they stayed, how the hike went. I noticed Violet and Ally's eyes would well up with tears, their voices would crack sometimes when they talked about their parents. It was touching and made me love this family more. Ally went inside as soon as she started getting cold, as soon as the memories became too much.

Violet, James and I sat outside for a long time, looking at the stars, talking about everything and nothing at the same time. Violet sat next to me, when the cold breeze blew I could smell her shampoo from the shower she took after our hike. She'd looked at me and smiled when I told a story about visiting my grandfather's wheat farm for the first time as a child, a few times she laughed. I loved her laugh, it wasn't something I heard very often but when I did it was hard not to smile. Violet was cold, I saw her rubbing her hands together and she brought her legs into her body on the chair. I got up, put more wood on the fire and took the blanket Ally had left on the chair before she went up to the house. I put the blanket on her as I sat back in my chair. She thanked me, pulling the blanket around her.

When I sat down I glanced at James, he was watching me closely with a knowing stare. I knew James better than anyone, he knew me better than anyone. We had worked side by side in the Navy for 8 years. We met during basic training and had been together through it all. When we were out in the field we sometimes had to communicate without words, without gestures. We learned each other's looks, we read each other's eyes. There were no secrets between us, except for one and it had just been uncovered.

"Violet, can you go check on Ally?" James asked her, taking the last sip from his bottle.

"She's fine. I'm going to go up in a minute," she sounded annoyed, she was looking up at the sky. "Do you remember Dad taking us to the observatory?" she asked, not taking her eyes away from the sky. James gave a hum letting her know he remembered. "We were so annoyed we had to go, it was late at night. There was some kind of meteor shower happening, we thought it was so boring, we complained the entire time."

"We were kids, that's what kids do," James replied, regret filled each word.

"I always wanted to go back to that night and listen to what he was trying to tell us. I wish I could look at the stars with him again, I wish I had appreciated it," her voice was soft and full of anguish as she continued staring at the sky.

"It sounds like you do appreciate it," I responded, Violet dropped her head looking in my eyes.

I felt bad for interrupting the moment she might have been trying to have with her brother. She smiled faintly at me, thanking me, her blue eyes glistened in the fire light. She stood up, said good night and walked into the cabin with the blanket still wrapped around her. I wanted to be that blanket. I continued to watch her walk away until she was inside the house, I stared at the door where she entered until James was ready to hit or scold me. It didn't take him long.

"I've gotta talk to you about something." James sat forward in the chair and I leaned back ready for him to tell me to keep away from his sister.

"Nothing's going on, I haven't touched her." I put my hands up in the air in submission.

"I know, man. This isn't about that," James said with a laugh, his smile faded as his face took on a serious stare. "I got a job offer."

"Oh, yeah?" I sensed there was more but he needed time to collect himself.

"It's with a contracting company out of Virginia." He paused again, I leaned forward putting my hands close to the flame of the fire for warmth.

"Military contracting?" I asked.

James and I had six months left before we were done with the Marine Corps. We put in 8 years of service with the Navy. Eight years of war time service was no joke, it took its toll on us and especially on Violet and Ally. We had been through some shit, seen enough for a lifetime, we weren't going back. We had made it out relatively unscathed. Unlike some of our friends who either didn't make it home or, some that did make it home, became a shell of their former selves. Aside from a few nightmares and scars we made it through. I couldn't understand why he couldn't let go.

"Yeah, it's good money and flexible." James opened the cooler sitting between us and took out a beer, handing it to me. I shook my head at the offer.

"Why?" I asked, he just explained why but his explanation wasn't enough for me.

"I'm not ready to give it all up yet, maybe in a few years I will. I don't want to re-up, I want to try something else. I can't work a nine to five job right now. It's cake compared to the shit we do. It's mostly security details and deliveries." James sounded as if he was trying to reassure me but I wasn't biting.

"What do the girls think?" I nodded toward the cabin.

I saw a light turn on in one of the bedrooms. Violet was in the window drawing the curtains, I stared at her until she disappeared behind them.

"I haven't told them. I'm going to try it for a year then I'll talk to them about it." He shifted in his seat and I laughed.

"What are you gonna do, James, lie to them? You've gotta tell them."

I thought about Ally and Violet. Ally was just 16 when I first met her, Violet was eighteen. All they want is their brother home and safe. He made it through eight years of war, they would be heartbroken if he didn't give it up. "If Violet finds out she's gonna tear you apart. You *have* to tell them." I've never seen three siblings as close as this family. They hold nothing back from each other and they make most of their decisions as a family. Why would James keep this from them?

"I can't right now, I will but not now," he leaned back taking a pull from his bottle of beer, "I need you to do something, though." I didn't respond, I didn't have to, I would do anything for James who I considered my brother. "If something happens when I take this job…"

I held up my hand stopping him, "I already promised you years ago, I'll be here. That promise doesn't end when my contract with the Navy ends."

We locked eyes, he silently thanked me and I silently affirmed I would watch out for his family if he wasn't able to.

"I wanted to make sure we're on the same page," he exhaled and his smile returned, "Now, the next item." He raised his eyebrows telling me we were about to circle back to Violet. "Something I should know?"

"Something you wanna know?" I leaned back in the chair and turned to look at him.

"How long?" he asked.

"You're gonna have to be specific if you want to know something," I said.

I saw his jaw twitch, something he did when he was thinking.

"How long have you…" He couldn't say the word, "How long have you, ya know?"

"The time you brought me to your house for Thanksgiving that first year. If you're asking when I *really* knew, two years ago," I answered.

There was no point in lying to James, he would've known if I lied. I never lied to him before I wasn't about to start.

"Shit, man. I mean, I guess, I've noticed how you look at her." He laughed and it set me at ease. "But to be honest a lot of guys look at her. Those two girls drive me crazy. They drove me crazy their entire teenage years. "

"They're beautiful girls, they're good girls. Whatever you did, you did a great job." I was sincere, given their situation, Ally and Violet could have come away from their experiences very differently. They all deserved credit for what they had become.

"Ha, I ran away. It's all them, those girls are unbreakable, they're the strongest humans I know. Tougher than some of the guys we served with if you ask me."

I knew James felt guilty about leaving them when he came to training. When he first showed me a picture of his sisters, I thought he was crazy for leaving those two alone. I might have even told him so once, saying he should be home with a baseball bat fighting off all the hormone crazed teenage boys that must've been stalking around. It was a joke but after I told him he made sure to have his uncle check in at the house weekly.

"You think she knows? Does she know that you like her?" James asked the question but I didn't correct him. I didn't just like Violet, I loved her.

"Naw, man. She's too caught up with that asshole right now."

That's how we talked about Sam, James never used his name. Even the few times Sam had come around, James would never address him by his name. James wouldn't call Sam an "asshole" in front of him but we used the title when we talked about him.

"That won't last forever. Hopefully, it won't last much longer. Can't tell that girl anything," James said as he shook his head. Violet's relationship worried James, he shared his concerns with me about her on several occasions. .

Two out of the three things James put out there I knew for sure. There was only one I wasn't sure about. How long was Violet going to stay with the asshole? He treated her terribly and she always had an excuse for him. He definitely had a drinking problem which, I know, Violet thought she could help him with. It didn't seem like he wanted help, it didn't appear he even thought he had a problem.

"I'm gonna say a few things then I'm not talking about it anymore," he waited for me to look at him and nod in acknowledgement, "This asshole has done, is doing, a number on her. I tried everything to make her see but she has to see it for herself. She will one day and when she does she's going to need time." He used his eyes to check in with me, I nodded again. "I'd be happy if Violet had a guy like you, any guy other than him, really. You're a good guy, I trust you with my life. I trust you with my sisters." He sent me a teasing grin. "If it's you that's meant for her, you have to let her come to you." He stopped talking and we held our stare for a full minute.

"That's it?" I asked, sounding a little too relieved.

"Oh, if you hurt her I'll bury you and burn your cabin. I'm not talking figuratively either," his comment was firm and authoritative but there was humor in his eyes.

"Copy that, Sarge," I said as I sat back again to look up at the sky and wondered which stars Violet was looking at earlier.

After one stop for gas and a lot of memories later, I arrived at the Kelly house, it was close to one in the morning. I went to the back shed to retrieve the spare key, it had been in the same spot for years, I hoped Violet didn't decide to move it. I found the key under the garden gnome beside the shed. I went to the back door and unlocked it. Walking into the kitchen, I turn on the lights, I notice three boxes are piled on the kitchen table. I peer in and see they are Violet's things, work binders, pictures of her family, books and some vinyl albums. Who still listens to vinyl? There are two suitcases on the floor in the kitchen, most likely Violet's clothes from her condo. I walk through the living room and turn on the outside lights. I open the front door, half expecting to find a note taped to the door but there's nothing. I walk down the front path to the mailbox, it's full of flyers and mail. Violet must not have put a stop on the mail before she left. I grab all the mail and bring it to the living room. I spread out the papers and envelopes on the coffee table. There's a white envelope without a stamp, the name *Violet* written on the front. I turn it over in my hands wanting to tear it open but can't. I reach for my phone in my pocket and dial Violet again, she had two hours to cool down, maybe she'll answer this time. Six rings then voicemail.

"Violet, call me back," I left the message and put the phone back in my pocket.

I can't open this without Violet giving me the green light. Taking the envelope to the kitchen I put it on the table next to Violet's boxes. I take the two suitcases up the stairs to Violet's room, I don't linger in her room, I place them inside the door frame so when she comes home she can unpack. I'm happy Violet finally left the asshole. I'm worried she felt she had to go so far away to make sure she followed through with leaving him. I know that's why she left, she left because she has gone back to him before and she didn't want to do that again. I hope with everything inside me he didn't hurt her this last time, I do plan to talk to her about it but I need to give her time. I go across the hall to James' room and sit on the bed. The last time I sat here was the worst day of my life, it was also the first time I held Violet which made it one of the best days. I held her while she cried until she had nothing left and fell asleep in my arms. I felt her anger, her sadness, her confusion, her old grief for her parents and her new grief for James. I tried to take all those feelings radiating from her and swallow them into myself for her. After she fell asleep I laid with her for another hour, listening to her breathe, feeling the warmth of her body. I held her until I felt I was being selfish. When I got out of the bed I tucked her in the blankets. I kissed her cheek, I couldn't help it, it tasted salty and was cool from all the tears. I lie back on James' bed thinking of that night and the week that followed before the funeral. I take my phone from my pocket making sure the volume is all the way up and place the phone on my chest. She has to call me back, she will call me back, I just don't know when.

Chapter 26
Drew

I arrived back at the villa before three. I open the door and see Violet's laptop, mobile and a book on the coffee table in front of the sofa. I hear her call out my name when I close the door.

"Yeah, it's me," I called back, sitting on the sofa.

"I'm almost done, a few more minutes. Sorry," she apologizes for nothing again.

"We have time," I call back as I pick up the book on the table.

I flip through the pages without reading, I've read this title before in a literature class at university. *The Awakening*, it's incredibly depressing, I remember laboring through the story even though it's relatively short. I close up her laptop which is in sleep mode and pick up her mobile, bringing them back to the table in the kitchen to charge. When I place the mobile on the charger I see she has several missed calls from "Cullen". After plugging in each item I stand by the sofa waiting for Violet. The ceremony didn't start until 5, I dropped Davy off at the resort bar where my parents were getting ready for pictures with the photographer. Davy gave me an envelope to drop off with Mia, she's in a villa down the way getting ready. I thought I'd get Violet, drop off the envelope and head back to the bar to meet with my family for pictures.

Violet walks out from the bathroom as I'm turning around from pacing the length of the sitting area. My chin drops to my chest, my eyes grow wide, she looks absolutely amazing. Her blue dress is long, the slit in the side went up to the middle of her thigh. Her blonde hair is down in the loose curls I've come to love, a few curls are pinned back from her face. The tiny rhinestones on the pins sparkle as the sunlight hits them. She's the most beautiful creature I've ever seen.

"Wow," I whisper in a throaty voice. She laughs and spins around.

"You like it?" she asks when she turns to meet my eyes, taking a few steps closer.

"I more than like it." I reach out to take her hand and pull her close.

"You look handsome, I like this suit," she runs her hand down the lapel of my jacket, "It's the perfect color for a beach wedding, it looks like sand." Even though she's wearing heels she still has to reach up an inch or two to kiss me.

"I've got to drop this off with Mia, she's down the way. Then I have to take some pictures with my family," I explain as I hold up the envelope I pulled from my jacket pocket.

"Let's go then," she says as she reaches for the small clutch sitting on the chair next to the sofa.

"I don't have to worry about you jumping into the ocean at the end of this trip, do I?" I ask as I pick up the book, she laughs taking it from my hand.

"No, I'm not going to pull an Edna. I love this story. You've read it?" She flips through the pages and sets it back on the table.

"Yes, it's depressing." I raise a brow.

"The character is depressed but the story isn't. There are themes of comfort and restlessness, I think it's a beautiful story. If Edna had lived a hundred years later she would've had options. But she didn't." Violet shrugs as she looks down at the cover of the book. "Let's go, I don't want you to be late because of me."

"Do you want your mobile? You have a few missed calls." I want to ask her who Cullen is but it's not my place and I don't want her to think I'm jealous.

"I don't need it," she responds and I don't push.

When we arrive at Mia's villa, Violet smiles when she hears the sounds of giggling and shrieking children. I knock on the villa door, when it opens I don't see anyone in the doorway until I look down and see a tiny girl with a huge smile.

"Violet!" she screams and lunges toward Violet. Violet crouches down to greet the girl with a hug, "Wow, I like those diamonds in your hair! You look like a princess." The girl gently reaches for the rhinestones in Violet's hair.

"Do you really like them?" Violet asks and the girl nods her head vigorously. "Well, that's good because I brought some for you and your sisters."

Violet reaches into her small bag, bringing out a handful of bobby pins with tiny rhinestones attached. The girl cannot contain her excitement and runs into the villa calling for her sisters. When we walk in the villa, Mia sits at the table getting her hair done, it's in a low knot at the base of her neck, Lauren is holding a curling iron and curling strands of hair around Mia's face. Mia wears a robe and is looking at her reflection in the mirror on the table in front of her. When she looks up to see us her face lights up.

"Drew, Violet! What are you doing here?" Mia asks, standing when Lauren tells her it's okay to do so. She walks around the table to us and greets us with a hug.

"Davy wanted me to bring this to you." I hold out the envelope and step back when I feel a tug on my hand. It's the youngest girl, grinning up at me with a missing bottom tooth.

"Mia, you look beautiful." Violet says as she hugs Mia.

"You look amazing, Violet! Look at that dress, my God." She looks at Violet then back to me raising an eyebrow. "Drew, you're going to make a lot of men jealous tonight."

"I bet." I say as I allow the little girl to drag me to the sofa where she's playing with her dolls, covering them with stickers of unicorns and sparkles.

"Lauren, if it's okay with you, I brought these for the girls. I can put them in their hair." Violet holds out her hand full of the sparkly hair pins.

"They'd love that, thank you. That's very sweet of you," Lauren says, offering a warm smile.

"Girls, if you sit nice and still on the sofa I'll put these on." Violet doesn't finish the sentence before all three girls scurry to the sofa sitting pin straight, looking straight ahead. I laugh loudly and send Violet a wink. "Do we have five minutes to finish this?" she asks as I stand from the sofa allowing the girls to have the space.

"Of course." I place my hand on her lower back as she passes, feeling a bit of exposed skin from the open back of the dress.

Violet stands behind the sofa pinning the girls hair as they giggle. I watch her work, feeling something new inside. Similar to the feeling of seeing Violet in my bed, seeing her walking around my house, this too feels like home. In an instant from feeling that sense of home, an intense foreboding flashes through me when I remember the way Violet stood in my kitchen earlier sobbing in my arms.

"I'll be outside, take your time," I say with a soft smile.

"I'll be right out," she replies as she turns her attention back to the girls' hair.

I'm only waiting outside for two minutes when Violet emerges from the villa. She walks toward me and takes my hand. As we walk to the resort bar we talk about how happy Mia looked and how excited the little girls were about the wedding. Violet is charmed by Lauren's daughters. They're cute girls with strawberry blonde hair full of banana curls, they all have green eyes ranging from shades of jade to a deep forest green.

When we arrive at the bar, Davy and my parents are sitting at a high top table. I see a few of Davy and Mia's friends already sprinkled throughout the bar. Mia's friends from university sit at a table next to my family. Davy's friend Ethan, along with his wife, sit at the bar. Brian is talking with Tomas who sits next to Ethan. I scan the bar for Sean but I don't see him, I feel relieved I can leave Violet here without him swooping in.

"Wow, Violet! You look wonderful," Davy says as he stands to give Violet a hug.

"Thank you. You clean up nice as well," she kisses his cheek and he laughs at the comment.

"Beautiful," Mum says and goes to stand but Violet gestures for her to sit as she walks over to greet my mum.

They embrace, when they do Mum looks at me over Violet's shoulder sending me a wink. Dad stands next to greet Violet, they share a warm look before they shake hands. I laugh to myself, he's not the warm and fuzzy type but I can tell he really likes Violet.

"You look beautiful," Dad says as he shakes her hand.

"What a handsome bunch this is," Violet says as she looks around to each of us, "Good genes." She sits next to Davy and takes his hand, "Mia looks so beautiful, I can't wait for you to see her. This is going to be a wonderful day, thank you for including me."

"We both wanted you here." He gently rubs the top of Violet's hand then breaks free, clapping his hands together, "Let's get these photo's over with so I can come back and mingle."

"Can I get you a drink before I leave?" I ask as I bend my head to Violet's ear.

"I'm good, I'll go introduce myself to Ethan's wife over there." Violet nods toward the bar, "It's Sarah, right?" she asks, remembering the name from the conversation Thursday morning.

"Yes, that's Sarah." I kiss the side of her head before I follow Davy and my parents through the lobby.

As I exit the bar and walk into the lobby, I see Sean walk through the door. He's glancing down at his mobile, when he looks up a mischievous smile tugs at one side of his mouth. He holds out his hand as he walks toward me.

"Hey, mate," he says, still grinning, I stare down at his hand debating if I want to shake it. I don't want to antagonize him as I'm leaving Violet alone, I shake his hand firmly.

"Sean," I say, dropping my hand.

"Beautiful day." He's looking past me to the bar, I know the exact moment his eyes fix on Violet because his smile turns wicked. "Doesn't look like there are too many single women in there. Though, I think, I just saw one."

Sean winks as he sidesteps around me, laughing as walks into the bar. I shake my head and put my hands in my pockets to keep from grabbing him from the back. Violet will be fine, I won't be long, if she stays close to Ethan and Sarah she'll be fine. I turn, quickly, through the lobby to the exit where my family is under a gazebo waiting for me. This better not take long.

When I'm finally done with the pictures I check my watch and see it's 4:15. "We have time to get a drink before we head to the beach," I call over my shoulder to Davy who's talking to the photographer.

"Alright." Davy smiles and follows me back to the bar. "Slow down, mate. She's not going anywhere," he laughs as he jogs two paces to catch up.

The bar is filled with guests for the wedding, it's louder now. Conversations and laughter fill the air as I scan the area for Violet. I keep a look out for a sapphire dress and blonde hair but I don't see her. I walk toward the bar when my eye catches her, she's sitting on the patio, at a table with Ethan and Sarah. I order a drink for Davy and I at the bar, when the order is ready, I hand one glass off to Davy and motion toward the patio. As I get closer to the patio doors I see Sean sitting at the table as well, of course. I couldn't see him from the angle I was standing at the bar. I take a deep breath and open the patio doors. Violet turns her head and I see her smile brightly at me, Sean's face falls when she does.

"Hey, how did it go?" she asks as she goes to stand but I gently place a hand on her shoulder letting her know to stay seated.

I pull a chair from the table next to theirs and motion for Davy to sit. Then I pull a second chair, placing it between Sean and Violet and I sit. I hear a huff from Sean but I pretend not to notice.

"Went great, now we can remember the day forever," Davy sarcastically states, drawing a laugh from the table.

As we sit on the patio, several guests approach to wish Davy well and give thanks for the invitation. Violet reaches for my hand shortly after I sit down, she scoots her chair closer to mine, it's a small gesture but one I'm thankful for. Sean got quiet after that then excused himself a few minutes later. Conversation flows steadily between Sarah and Violet. Sarah had visited Boston when she was younger, she lived in Providence, Rhode Island which wasn't far from where Violet grew up. Sarah lived there as a preteen when her mother had a guest professorship at the Rhode Island School of Design. Sarah loved the seasonal changes of New England and was describing experiencing her first snowfall when Davy tapped me on the shoulder then pointed at his watch.

"We gotta go. I can't have Mia show up before me." We stand from the table and head to the beach for the ceremony.

Chapter 27
Violet

I walk to the beach with Ethan and Sarah, Tomas and Brian are close behind us. Sean had disappeared which I was thankful for, I didn't like the way he stared at me. Sean's presence didn't put me at ease, it put me on alert. As we approach the beach I see a makeshift valet table for shoes. Although there's a small wooden boardwalk outlining an aisle, most of the guest seats were on the sand. There's no way these shoes would be able to do anything in sand.

"What a cute idea." Sarah says wistfully as she hands her heels to a woman who hands her a small ticket.

"Mia's all about details." I laugh as we find a section of seats toward the middle of the aisle.

I take the end seat, I want to see Mia come down the aisle without an obstructed view. I'm excited for the ceremony, I feel a wave of anticipation roll through my stomach. I look in my purse for my phone to check the time but it's not there, I remember I left it in the villa. I don't need it but find myself wondering if Cullen had attempted to call me again and what our next conversation will be like. *Hi Violet, it's Emily.* Emily, who? *It's about James.* A thought comes to mind, maybe Emily worked with James out of Virgina. Maybe she had information on the investigation, maybe I'd finally get some answers as to where James died. My thoughts are interrupted by the playing of instrumental music. I push the thoughts down, remembering I promised myself I would put all of that out of my mind for tonight. I look around the crowd trying to refocus my attention on the present moment. When I look up to the altar I see Drew and Davy are already in their places, Drew's watching me curiously. He must have seen me deep in thought, I take a breath in, I give him a smile and a discrete wave. He smiles and turns his attention to Davy.

The brothers look handsome in their suits. They definitely look like brothers, yet they differ from each other as well. Drew with lighter hair and a larger frame. Davy with green eyes, Drew with blue but the eyes have the same shape and their brow is the same. Drew has sharper, more chiseled, features while Davy's are softer. The remainder of the guests take their seats. When the music fades out a hush falls over the crowd, this is it. Ian and Clare come down the aisle, arm in arm, followed by Mia's mother. Mia's mother is accompanied by Lauren's husband. Once they take their seats, Lauren comes down the aisle wearing a knee length navy blue dress that crosses over one shoulder. The three flower girls come next, Mia's nieces beam with smiles as they throw petals on the wooden planks.

As they pass me the oldest screams, "Hi, Violet!" She runs to give me a hug drawing a laugh from the crowd and causing the girl to flush with embarrassment.

I hug her, set her back on the path and motion for her to keep walking. When the girls make it up the aisle to sit with their father and grandmother the music stops. All the guests stand from their seats, *Canon in D* plays, Mia comes out from behind a screen that hid her. When I see her lock arms with the man about to walk her down the aisle my eyes fill with tears. Ian takes her arm, gives her a kiss on the cheek and the flood gates open. Tears spill down my cheeks and I wipe them quickly, telling myself to pull it together. As Mia walks by me, she turns and smiles, I turn to look at Davy who's wiping his eyes. I see him take a huge breath, his face red, a tear falls down his cheek. Then he smiles his one of a kind Davy-smile. My heart explodes for this family, for Davy and Mia's childhood love story. My heart is full of happiness for Mia, she has waited for this day since third grade, she's marrying her prince. Ian walking Mia down the aisle was something I hadn't prepared myself for, it made sense though. Mia's family has been very close with Davy's for many years. Drew said they always knew Mia would be a part of their family one day. Mia calls Clare and Ian, Mum and Dad, Ian was probably the closest thing to a father Mia has.

The ceremony is quick and traditional, when they kiss there's a loud whooping sound from the crowd, followed by clapping and cheers. Davy seems relieved it's over and looks more comfortable when he and Mia lead the recession down the aisle. Drew and Lauren follow Mia and Davy but are almost run over by the three little girls sprinting behind them, the crowd laughs again. I sit next to Sarah while the guests file out. I'm in no rush, Drew probably will be greeting people as the guests pass. I motion for the group to go ahead of me, I want to sit for a little while and take in the pure joy that clings in the air around me.

"You all go ahead, I'll be right behind. I'm going to take a walk over there," I say to Sarah as I gesture toward the altar with my hand.

I pass the altar and step down on the sand looking out to the ocean. *I want to talk to you about James.* The voice of Emily rings through my head as I try to concentrate on the ocean. *I left a note for you at your parents' house.* For some reason I want to scream, I want to run in the ocean and wash away the feelings tormenting me. I want the fear, grief, anger, confusion and frustration to leave my body. I want to feel freedom and escape as Edna had felt when she walked in but she never came back out. I want to come back out, I want to come out of this. I shake my head and ball my fists at my side, I tilt my head back and feel a scream at the top of my throat. I can't let it out, not here, not now. I close my eyes and concentrate on feeling the setting sun on my face, I listen to the movement of the ocean. I concentrate on feeling the sand under my feet, the feel of the satin dress on my body. I feel hands on my shoulders, they run down my arms then move to my waist. Arms wrap around my waist and pull me into a hard body behind me. I smell sandalwood.

"Hey," my voice is uneven.

"Hi," Drew's voice is calm. He kisses my neck and I open my eyes, the sky is turning yellow with the sunset. He turns me around to face him. "I thought I lost you."

"Just taking a minute," I say as my voice steadies.

I bring my hands to his neck and kiss him hard. If I can't go in the ocean I want Drew to be my ocean right now. I want him to take away all the intrusive thoughts penetrating my mind. I want him to take away the fear, anger and frustration coursing through my body. He kisses me as I want him to, commanding and strong. We kiss for a while before he pulls me away.

"We should get back, although I'm thoroughly enjoying this." His smile is cautious.

"Let's go." I take his arm in both my hands and walk with him toward the restaurant. "When your father walked Mia down the aisle, it did me in. I didn't know if I was going to come back from that." I smile up at Drew.

"I didn't know about that," his confession shocks me, "When Dad got up after he brought Mum to her seat, I thought she was going to kill him from the look she gave. I think Mia, Davy and Dad were the only ones that knew."

"That's so sweet," I say, bringing a hand to my chest.

When we walk back down the aisle I see my shoes sitting on a chair in the last row. Drew grabs them from the chair as we walk toward the patio of the bar. We stop on the patio, Drew places my shoes on the stones in front of my feet and I step into them. Walking into the restaurant on the second floor I'm greeted with sounds of laughter and chatter. The smell of dinner looms in the air making my stomach twitch with excitement. My body is less tense than it was on the beach, I scan the room to find Mia. She's standing with Davy in the back talking to a group of women. Her v-neck ivory gown is accented by lace and beading along the breast, it's a simple dress but on Mia it's stunning.

"If you have to mingle, I understand, I'm fine here," I say, falling into step with him.

"You don't want to mingle with me?" he asks as we approach the bar.

We order our drinks, a glass of wine for me and a gin and tonic for Drew. Taking our drinks we head toward Mia and Davy who are talking with Davy's friends seated at one of the round tables.

"There you are," Mia says as she steps in front of Davy to greet me.

"Mrs. Harris, you look beautiful, everything is perfect." I hug her, she kisses my cheek.

I sit next to Sarah at the table, I find out this is Sarah's first night out since having her baby. Her cheeks look flushed from the two drinks she had, I like Sarah. I sat there as I finished my glass of wine, Davy and Mia had moved on to another group of guests. The announcement dinner is about to be served comes over the speakers. I see Drew look at me expectantly. I give him a questioning look when he comes over to me.

"You're sitting with us." He stands behind me, ready to pull my chair out when I go to stand.

"Over there?" I point to the table where his parents and Mia's family sit, "No, I can't." I hold on to the bottom of the seat not wanting to get up.

He laughs and bends down to whisper in my ear, "You're my date, remember?"

"But that's the *family* table. I'm fine here." I grip the seat tighter as Drew starts to pull the chair out from the table. I give him a pleading look, he either ignores it or doesn't see it.

"C'mon." He reaches down for my hand which is sweaty now.

"Are you sure?" I whisper, taking my empty glass of wine. Drew laughs and guides me to the table with his family.

During dinner the conversation is guided by Clare and Mia's mother, reminiscing about young Davy and Mia. Lauren's daughters sit to my right and talk about flower fairies and princesses. The girls say they feel like fairies today in their lace flower girl dresses and gems in their hair. Drew sits to my left and occasionally rests his hand on my thigh, I don't shake it away tonight, I take his hand and hold it when he does. Davy and Mia join us at the table when they finish their meal and the girls have started to play on the dance floor.

Davy dances with his mother to start the night of music and dancing. Mia and Ian didn't have a dance and I wonder if Mia wanted to leave something for her father. When the first dance between Davy and Mia is finished, the three girls excitedly run to the dance floor. An hour into dancing, I notice two of the girls are fast asleep on their father's chest. Lauren set up a square playpen in the back of the dining room where they put the two sleeping girls. Around that time my feet start to ache from the shoes, I elect to only dance when Drew asks. When the DJ announces the last song, I sigh with relief. As the final song plays, my chest warms. I know the song well. It was one of my parents' favorite songs and their favorite band, *Long As I Can See The Light* by Creedence Clearwater Revival. It was such a fitting song for Davy and Mia.

Drew holds me close while we dance. When the song is over everyone claps and cheers for the newlyweds. The lights come on, signaling the night is over. I hold back at the table while Drew says his goodbyes to guests. I ask Lauren if she needs help with the girls, all three now asleep. Two girls are in the playpen and one is on a folding mat on the floor.

"Drew offered to help, thank you." She smiles down on her sleeping girls. "They had the time of their lives tonight."

"They sure did," I agree, I feel a hand on my shoulder and I turn to see Ian standing behind me.

"We're off, I wanted to wish you well, Violet," his voice is hoarse, his eyes look tired, it's a late night for a farmer. "I don't know if I'll see you again before you head back home. The offer still stands, anytime you want to come back to the farm and ride." He shifts on his feet, putting his hands in his pockets and his blue eyes stare into mine. "I wish you the best, I really do. I can't tell you how happy Clare was to see Drew enjoying himself."

"Thank you, Ian." There's so much I want to say but I can't find the words.

"I'm sorry for your losses, Drew told me about your situation." I nod my head because I'm unsure of my voice. "You're an amazing person to have been through all that and still be able to smile and put a smile on other people's faces. You're going to be alright, Violet." He takes his hands from his pockets and puts his arms around me. I'm shocked by the gesture and his words.

"Thank you, Ian. You should be very proud of what you have, your family is wonderful," I say shakily.

"I am and I know." When he steps back I see Drew watching us with a smile. "Drew's going to be fine, don't worry about that." He waits for me to nod my head then sets off toward Davy and Mia.

I turn back to look at the sleeping girls, Lauren's watching me with a huge smile.

"I have never heard that man say so many words at once before," she motions toward Ian with a nod.

I laugh, "We bonded over Johnny Cash and Fleetwood Mac."

Drew appears at my side and kisses my cheek. "What was that all about?"

"He was wishing me well. Lauren said you were going to help carry one of these fairy princesses to their room." Even though these girls slept through an hour and a half of blaring music, I kept my voice low not wanting to wake them.

"Yeah, when they're ready." Drew hands me his suit jacket and my clutch from the table.

"I'm ready, if you are," Lauren says as she lifts the smallest girl from the playpen. The girl is limp and doesn't stir in the slightest when Lauren hoists her up to her shoulder.

I laugh quietly as Drew kneels down by the mat to pick up the oldest. She, too, doesn't flinch at the transition. Lauren motions her husband toward the playpen to carry the remaining child. I lead the way to open the doors for the adults carrying the children. When I open the final door to the patio, I watch all three adults file out with the girls sleeping in their arms. Lauren opens the door to their villa and motions toward the back room, I head that way and turn down the blankets on the two beds.

"Where do you want this one?" Drew asks, quietly.

"Either bed," Lauren whispers.

Drew puts the girl into bed and gently pulls the blankets over her, Lauren puts the small girl in the opposite bed. Lauren's husband is the last to enter, Drew and I exit the girls' room so he can drop off the last sleeping girl. Lauren thanks us and we say goodnight. As we exit to the patio we see Mia and Davy walking up the pathway, we stop to wait.

"Tonight was so much fun, thank you both," I say when they're close.

"It was, I'm so glad you decided to stay and join us," Mia says in her bubbly voice, the long day and night showing slightly in her eyes.

"Come have breakfast with us tomorrow, if you're awake, eight o'clock on the restaurant's patio," Davy says as he takes Mia's hand.

"We will. Congratulations, you two." Drew hugs them both and takes my hand leading me toward our room.

Chapter 28

Violet

When I wake it is still dark, I reach for my phone on the bedside table. Lighting up the screen it reads 3:09 AM. I've only slept a few hours but I'm wide awake thinking about Emily. I get out of bed and put on a pair of sweatpants and sweatshirt. I need to make this call to settle my unease, I can't continue to let the stress of the unknown take over me. I don't know how long I'll be on the phone, I don't want Drew waking and panicking when I'm not here. I kiss the side of his head as I stand over him on the side of the bed and whisper his name until he stirs. He answers with a low hum and turns on his back to look up at me.

"What's wrong?" He tries to sit up but I gently press a hand on his chest.

"I have to make a phone call. I'll be back, I'm going outside to the patio." I kiss his temple before I step back.

"Call from inside, it's dark out there," Drew says as he turns on his side to face me.

"I'll be right outside, go back to sleep," I whisper before I turn toward the door and walk out to the patio.

I sit outside in the chair, it's cold and damp. I scroll through my phone, I see Cullen's number. He called me eight times yesterday. I need to call Emily first so I have something to tell him, maybe I'll have nothing to tell him. My finger hoovers above the number marked "unknown" for several minutes until my finger begins to feel cold. Taking a breath I tap on the number and wait for it to ring.

"Hello, Violet?" Emily answers on the second ring. Her voice is soft and shaky.

"Yes, is this Emily?" I try to keep my voice even as my heart begins to pound.

"Yes," she answers but doesn't go on, I guess I'm going to have to lead this even though this woman reached out to me.

"What can I do for you?" I ask, commanding my heart to slow down.

"Um, did you get my note?" she asks, her question full of unease.

"No, I didn't. I'm away," there is another pause, "Emily, you said you wanted to talk to me about James." I remind her as my patience starts to thin.

"Yes, I hoped you would have read the note," each word is spoken so quietly I have to strain to hear her.

"Emily, what can I do for you?" I ask, again, not regretting my annoyed tone.

"Well, okay, I hope you have a minute," she says, clearing her throat and I pinch the bridge of my nose with my thumb and index finger. "James and I met in January of last year, we met through a mutual friend he worked with. I'm from Delaware," she pauses again. "Did James ever tell you about me?" she asks, I can hear the disappointment in her voice.

"No, he never mentioned you," I say flatly and I hear her take a breath.

"Okay, well, we saw each other a few times when he came down to Virginia. I came up once and met him at your parents' house. We weren't serious, well, he wasn't serious. He didn't want a serious relationship at that time but we were close. I loved him, Violet." My heart sinks, I hear her sincerity and pain.

James never had a girlfriend for more than 6 months. Given his employment, he didn't want to leave for a deployment and have to worry about what a girl would be up to while he was gone. He didn't want to hurt anyone if something happened to him, this was something he told me.

"James wasn't one for long term relationships," I offer to her as a condolence but it comes out cold.

"The last time I saw him was before he left last July. I waited for him to reach out when he came back but I didn't hear from him. I called my friend and he told me James didn't make it back." Emily is crying now, gentle sobs leave her.

My heart aches, bringing me back to that July day when Cullen called. I try to keep calm, I have to keep calm. After a few seconds of Emily trying to regain her composure she continues, "I didn't go to the service because I didn't know there was one. I was really depressed after James died. There was so much I wanted to say to him, so much I wish he knew." Emily drew a few deep breaths. "I found out I was pregnant just after I found out he was gone."

I don't know if Emily says anything else because my world spins, ringing takes over in my ears and my hands shake. Pregnant. Emily is pregnant. I try to do the math in my head, James died 8 months ago, a baby is in the womb for 40 weeks.

"Violet?" Emily's voice echoes in my head from the receiver.

"Yes," the word is a croak at best.

"Did you hear me?"

I heard she was pregnant, I don't know if she said anything after.

"You're pregnant?" I ask and I stand up, I need to move my body and stay focused.

"I was pregnant," she answers back.

"You lost the baby?"

Maybe the grief and stress was too much for her and she miscarried.

"No, Violet. Please, listen. I know this is a lot," she pauses and I give her a hum of acknowledgement. "When I found out I was pregnant I was close to three months along. Twins run in my family, my mother was a twin."

I process her words in slow motion. Fucking twins, I continue to walk not having a destination. I walk around the patio to the path toward the beach.

"Twins," I echo, I feel the phone shaking in my hands. I feel a wave of heaviness settling on my body, I try to keep my mind focused on Emily's voice.

"There were complications toward the end of my pregnancy. I went in for a cesarean in November, I was thirty weeks but they couldn't wait anymore." I hear her holding back her tears trying to get through the details. "I had a little girl and a boy. My little girl…" There was a quick sob as I finally reached the beach. "She fought for three days before she left me." Now Emily's sobbing and I'm crying.

"I'm sorry," I whisper on the phone.

"My boy was strong, his name is Matthew," she explains.

Matthew. I cry harder when she says the name, my father's name. I pull the phone away from my ear and cry into my forearm. When I bring the phone back I hear Emily asking if I'm there.

"Yes, he's four months old?" I ask as I sit on the sand.

"Yes, he's healthy and happy, he's a good baby," her voice brightens when she talks about him. "But I'm not doing well, I'm having a really hard time. Losing James, losing my little girl, it's been a lot and I haven't handled it well," her voice drops, "I'm embarrassed but I need help," Emily's voice is a whisper now. I sit up straight and try to figure out what she needs.

"Do you need money?" I blurt it out, I can feel the tension come over the line.

"No. I need *help*, Violet. My mental health isn't good, it's affecting my physical health, it's starting to affect my everyday life," I hear the frustration in Emily's tone.

"What can I do? You need to tell me exactly what you need, Emily."

I don't know this woman, if there's any way she's the mother of my nephew, James would want me to help her.

"I need to go somewhere to get help. I found a place in Massachusetts, it has a bed available in two weeks. I thought you could help with Matthew and I could be close when I'm ready for visiting days," she sounds hopeful and unsure at the same time.

"Okay," I steady myself, my head is pounding, "Where are you now?"

"I'm in a hotel not far from your parents' house. I was hoping I could stay with you until I enter the program." She explains and alarm bells ring in my head. Program? She's in a hotel in Massachusetts. What kind of trouble is the woman in?

"What kind of program?" I ask, I've never sought help for mental health through means of a facility and I'm curious as to how this works.

"It's a rehab program," she answers.

My heart sinks and anger rises. She's a fucking addict?

"Rehab for what? Drugs? Alcohol?" I ask, memories flash in my mind, empty whisky bottles, beer cans littering my living room floor when I come home from work.

"Both," the word is soft and full of remorse.

"Is Matthew safe?"

My immediate thought is of the four month old baby in a hotel room while his mother does God knows what.

"Violet, I'm a good mother," she says with certainty but I don't believe her, "I'm trying to get help."

"Text me the name and address of the hotel, I can't get home for another day or two. I'll send someone to pick you up and take you to my house. Is there anything else you need from me, anything I can do now?" My words are clipped and icy.

"No," Emily cries.

I don't want to listen to her cry, I'm too angry to listen to it.

"I'm going to call you back in half an hour. Will you answer?" I try to sound warmer, I don't want Emily to regret reaching out to me. I don't want her to run away with Matthew and never hear from her again.

"Yes. Thank you," she sobs.

"I'll call you back shortly, Emily."

I disconnect and scroll through for Cullen's number. I receive a text from Emily with the hotel information within a minute of disconnecting with her.

Cullen answers on the first ring, "Violet," his voice is full of relief.

"Cullen, I need a favor and it's a big one," I don't wait for him to answer, I know what his answer will be. "Can you take a few days and stay at my parents' house? I'm working on a flight home but I need you to go there."

"What's going on? I'm already here," the relief in his voice is replaced with concern.

Of course he is, it shouldn't surprise me. What I know about Cullen is: he's always one step ahead of any situation, even if the situation is a surprise. I stand up from the sand and start walking back to get my laptop and search for flight information.

"I just talked with Emily, there's a lot of information. The short of it is James has a baby, Emily is staying at a hotel with the baby. She needs my help and I'm not there," I take in a breath when I hear Cullen exhale a huge sigh. "She needs to go to a program to help her, I think she's an addict."

"Fuck, Violet. Slow down. Please, I need a minute," there is a short pause. "James had a baby with Emily and didn't tell anyone?"

"Ugh, no. He didn't know Emily was pregnant, she found out after he died. They weren't serious, they only saw each other a few times," I'm talking fast as I pick up my pace toward the villa.

"Okay, and you believe this woman?" Cullen asks and I pause in my step.

"Why would she lie about this?" I'm asking the question more to myself than to Cullen on the other end. Is there anything to gain from her lying to me? I don't think so.

"I don't know." I hear him walking, I hear a door close and it sounds like he's stomping down stairs.

"If she's not lying and she has James' son in a hotel, while she's blowing lines off a coffee table or drinking bottles of vodka, I need to do something." I'm frantic now thinking about it. I feel panic rising and I try to keep my breathing steady.

"Don't go into catastrophic mode, Vi, breathe." Hearing the worry in his voice makes me confident I'm doing exactly what I need to do right now. "I got the letter she left for you, can I read it? Maybe it will give me the information I need and you can work on getting a flight back here."

"Read it, I'm going to text you the hotel address and room number. Can you pick them up and bring them back to the house? Make sure she doesn't leave until I get there." I reach the door to the villa and lower my voice not wanting to wake Drew.

"I can do that. Are you going to call Ally?" he asks.

I hadn't even gotten that far but of course I would call Ally.

"I'll call her. One more thing," I wait to hear him give me an "okay" before I continue, "Don't scare her, Cullen. Try to make her comfortable."

"I'm not scary, I'll be fine." He disconnects and I slowly open the door to the villa.

I hear Drew's slow breaths, I see Mia's wedding gift on the counter and my heart stills. This isn't how I wanted to leave. I want to cry but tears won't help now, they'll only slow me down. There will be plenty of time to cry later. It's so warm in the villa but I can't chance waking Drew right now, it's four in the morning. He'll sleep for a few more hours giving me time to collect my thoughts. I take the laptop off the counter and slip back out onto the patio. I get a message from Cullen,

Cullen: Read the note. I'm going to pick her up in an hour. She left her contact information in the note. Breathe.

Attached to the message are two pictures, I assume came from the note. One is of James and a woman, I conclude to be Emily. James is smiling, he looks handsome and happy. I know he's happy in this picture because his dimple is showing. James had a small dimple high on his right cheek, it only came out when his smile was genuine and it was usually accompanied by his laughter. My heart warms seeing James happy. Emily's leaning her head on his shoulder. She looks young, she has light brown eyes and dark hair thick with curls. The second picture takes my breath away, an infant with dull blue eyes that look like stone. He's smiling and looks to be chewing on his fist, droll slips down his chin onto his hands. He's beautiful and looks like James' baby picture hanging in my parents bedroom. James had a bit more hair as a baby, Matthew is almost completely bald. A single tear slips away and I swipe at it quickly reminding myself I can cry later.

I call Emily and tell her Cullen will be there in an hour to take her and Matthew to the house. I try to be reassuring but I notice flashes of anger and resentment fill me at times during the call. Emily's thankful and says James spoke very highly of Cullen and she's happy to be able to meet him. When I hung up from the call I wish I asked her about her family, maybe she has none. Maybe she does and they don't approve of her situation. Who would turn away a baby, though? I open the laptop and see my options for a flight home.

Sydney and Brisbane are the closest airports with international flight options. Brisbane is closest with a two hour drive, there's a flight tonight at 9:30 to Boston and one tomorrow morning at 7. I look over my shoulder at the villa door, not knowing what to do. I stay one more night with Drew or I rip the band aid and leave tonight. He's going to wake up to realize I'm leaving much sooner than expected and I have no idea how to handle that. But I have to go now, I have to help the mother of my brother's child, I have to go meet my nephew. He'll understand. An emotion rises inside me, close to anger more like annoyance. I'm tired of dealing with James's decisions, his secrets. As soon as the feeling comes it passes and guilt settles in.

I take a deep breath, I book the flight for tonight. I lean back in the chair and sob. I cry for James not knowing what he left behind. I cry for Matthew who will never meet his father and who doesn't know what's happening around him. I cry for myself because I want to be selfish, I want to stay here. I cry knowing Drew has changed me in the short time I've been here, he didn't take anything from me, he gave and he gave. I cry for Ally because she has no idea what's coming when I call her shortly. I cry for Emily because she has lost just as much, if not more than me. Emily lost a child, that has to be the worst heartbreak a human can experience. Whether she had her demons before James or whether she gained them after, it doesn't matter because there's a child involved now. As much as I want to judge Emily for her challenges, I have to keep that in check. Now that I know about Matthew, I won't allow my behavior toward Emily to interfere with me being a part of his life. I'm still crying when the door opens and Drew steps out wearing only a pair of sweatpants, fear and worry fill his entire body. He slowly moves toward me and sits down next to me. I see him glance at the laptop screen, his shoulders sag and I hear him take in a sharp breath. He registered that I've booked a flight home.

"Violet?"

He shuts the laptop and turns the entire chair I'm sitting in toward him.

"I'm sorry," I choke out, my nose is running, my face is soaked with tears, I'm full on ugly crying now. I take deep breaths as I wipe the snot and tears on the sleeve on my shirt.

"Come inside," I hear the hurt and anxiety in his voice and it's agonizing.

I do as he says and I go inside. I go to the bed and crawl in, I want the bed to swallow me. I want to feel the warmth of the blankets against my cold body. Drew doesn't get in the bed, he sits on the side looking down on me. He brushes the hair out of my eyes and face, I see tears in his eyes and it makes me want to unleash the river of tears inside me. But I don't, I need to tell him, he needs to understand. The pillow feels so good against my pounding head, I can feel my eyes are already swollen.

"I have to go," my whisper is raspy, Drew stiffens and stands.

"Go where?" he asks but he knows the answer. He knew the answer as soon as he saw the laptop screen.

I sit up, "I'm going home tonight."

He's stunned and takes a step back. I reach for his hand and pull him back to sitting. I tell him everything that transpired in the past hour and a half, it's a lot given the time frame. He nods as I work through the details of the conversation with Emily. He rubs my hand at times, he wipes tears that fall from my eyes. I can't look at him as I explain, I keep my eyes on the comforter and on our hands when they clasp together. When I'm finished I look up and my heart wrenches in my chest. His face is covered in defeat, I feel his crippling disappointment.

"You have to go." Those four words are spoken with such sadness my stomach heaves when I hold in a sob. "It's amazing you found a piece of your brother." He looks into my eyes and tries to smile which makes me adore him even more.

"I'm so sorry," I barely finish the sentence before Drew takes my face in his hands and pulls me toward him, taking over my lips.

"What time is your flight and where?" he asks, his lips lingering on mine.

"Tonight, nine-thirty in Brisbane." I kiss him again and again, hoping this is all a dream.

"I'll take you," he says as he lies down next to me on the bed.

I want to decline his offer, I don't want to make this harder than it already is for him. The words don't come out though, instead I whisper, "Okay." I settle into his chest and he holds me in his arms so tight it's almost uncomfortable.

"Violet, I…"

I reach up and cover his mouth with mine before he can say anything more, "Please, don't. I can't hear you say it." Tears stream down my cheeks and Drew nods his head.

We lie on the bed for a while in silence. I allow the moment to carry on until the creeping anxiety of what I have to do next sets in. I have to call Ally, I have to pack, I have to tell Mia and Davy, I have to go. When I shift in the bed to look at Drew, his eyes are closed but he's not asleep.

"No more tears for me today. Let's enjoy these last few hours, if that's okay with you," I say, putting a smile on my face.

"That's okay with me."

He pulls me on top of him and he slowly and tenderly makes love to me. This time is different from any other time we've had sex. I feel his angst, his worry, his adoration. I feel his love. You can fall in love with someone in a few days, Drew's proving it to me. He washes away the fear and restlessness, only for a few moments but I take the relief. I allow myself to fully commit to this moment. The moment I have with someone who adores me, loves me, someone who's in the present with me. This may be the last time I'm in the arms of a man who gave me things I didn't know I needed. He gave me things and never took anything away from me. The last moments I had with the ones I loved were moments I didn't know were my last with them. I'm conscious of the fact these may be my last moments with Drew. I'm not going to be sad about that, I'm going to relish in them. And when it's time to go I'm going to be able to watch him walk away, knowing I'm happy with all the decisions I've made here. I will not let the image of Drew walking away haunt my dreams as so many others have.

Chapter 29
Drew

Violet went to take a shower and I can't make myself get up from the bed. The last hour has been a whirlwind of emotions. When I heard crying outside on the patio this morning I couldn't have prepared myself for what was about to unfold. Selfishly, I thought she might have been crying because she knew her time in Byron was ending and she was conflicted on staying here for the rest of her trip or moving on. Then I saw confirmation of an airline reservation on her computer screen and my heart dropped in a nanosecond. The air left my lungs and I replayed the entirety of last night's events trying to see if I had missed something. But her tears and her eyes told me she didn't want to leave. Whatever had transpired in the call she made earlier shifted Violet's plans on staying in Australia. Now she's leaving, she was always leaving, she's leaving today. My stomach lurches with nausea and frustration. I thought I'd have a few more days with her, I guess it doesn't matter whether it's a few more days or a few more hours. It's going to hurt either way. I've never been with someone like Violet, I've never felt this for another person. Violet may not love me as I do her but there's something between us that cannot be put into words. I remind myself, if Violet and I are truly meant to be we'll find our way back to one another. In the pit of my stomach I feel this is the end of us and it's soul crushing.

I stand from the bed and make my way to the bathroom. Violet said she wasn't going to cry today but I hear whimpers escaping her in the shower. I close the bathroom door to let her know I'm here. I step in the shower behind her and turn her toward me. I smile at her because that's what she needs. She doesn't need to see my pain or my torment.

"I need to say something," I pause and wait for her to look at me, "You're doing the right thing, you're going to do right by your brother. You're going to meet your nephew and make sure he's safe and his mother gets the help she needs. They're lucky to have you. I'll be here and if there's a time you want me to come to you I will." Violet shakes her head, I place her head in my hands, "I would leave here to be with you but that's something you have to decide, in time."

"Drew," she whispers my name.

"I know you can't tell me exactly what you feel right now. But I need you to know I've fallen in love with you and it's not momentary. I know I have to let you go, Violet. I have to because it's the right thing to do." She reaches up to kiss me, she can't answer me because I asked no question.

"Thank you, for everything." She wraps her hands around my waist and we stand there for a full minute before she pulls back. "I need to get dressed and call my sister." I open the shower door for her to leave.

I finish my shower and get dressed. I sent Davy and Mia a text, briefly, explaining what's happening and telling them we won't be at breakfast. I silence my mobile because I don't want to answer any questions they send me. I pick up around the villa while Violet's on the patio talking with her sister. I give her space. When everything is packed up and the bags are by the door I sit on the sofa staring at the cup of coffee I can't manage to drink. Violet comes in later looking more composed than I anticipated, she's strong and I can imagine her sister is as well.

"How'd that go?" I ask hesitantly.

"I managed to get through it without crying. Ally's going to the house first thing in the morning. She's confused and shocked." Violet sits down next to me releasing a sigh, "Ally doesn't trust Emily. I can't think of a reason for her to lie about anything. There's no benefit to her, it's not like she and James were married, she isn't entitled to anything. I don't have any reason not to believe her."

"You'll figure it out, you and your sister. It sounds like Emily's in a bad spot and needs help to get on her feet." I kiss her hand when I hear a knock at the door.

Violet shifts her stare to me then the door and back to me. I stand to answer it. Mia and Davy are there wearing brave smiles. I widen the door to allow them entrance. Mia goes to Violet and hugs her from the sofa. Davy shakes my hand and offers me a sympathetic look.

"How are you?" Mia asks Violet, holding her at arm's length.

"I don't know," Violet answers softly while shifting her gaze to the floor and Mia hugs her again. "I have something for you." Violet walks over to the counter and takes the gift bag, handing it out to Mia.

"Not necessary," Davy says as he leans against the counter watching Mia open the gift.

"I wanted to give you something for your wedding and as a thank you for all your hospitality." Violet shrugs and I see a smile, a real smile with no sadness or fear, I smile with her.

Mia pulls out a wooden box with a glass cover, inside the box is a horseshoe. "Violet, it's perfect. Look, love, it has our initials. Look M.H.!" Mia holds the box to her chest then out to Davy to look at.

"I know you two don't need luck but I do wish you all the luck in the world." Violet cheeks redden and she watches Davy take in the gift.

"Everyone could use a bit of luck. It's beautiful, thank you." Davy places the box on the counter and takes Violet in an embrace. "Thank you," I hear him whisper again.

"Take care of that girl, she's something special," Violet whispers back.

"You take care, it was truly a pleasure to meet you, Violet. Let's make sure you keep in touch with my wife." Davy steps back putting his hands in his pockets.

"I will. I'm going to follow your love story for as long as I can." She glances at me when she says it and I have no doubt Mia and Violet will continue their friendship. I don't know how or if I figure into any of it.

"Do you have time for a walk, Violet?" Mia asks, looking at me then to Violet.

"Sure," Violet says and she takes Mia's outstretched hand and heads out the door.

When the women exit the villa Davy's exhales with a whistle. He walks toward the sofa and takes a seat. "I'm sorry, mate. This is a tough one." He shakes his head and leans back against the couch.

"She had to leave sometime," I say as I take a seat in the chair next to Davy.

"Don't fight it. I'm here offering you my shoulder, take it," he offers with a sly smile.

"Yeah, maybe later. Right now, I want to get through these next few hours," I say feeling incredibly deflated.

"Do you want to go with her?" I laugh at Davy's question because of course I want to go with her but I can't.

"I told her how I felt. She needs to go and I need to give her time to settle things on her end. I can't be a part of that. She knows I'll be there if she asks me to," I say.

"Maybe she doesn't want to ask you."

"She doesn't want me to go there now, I know that. Let's change the subject. Or do one better and help me take these out to my car." I gesture to the bags at the door. "Do you think you and Mia could drop off Violet's rental at the shop, by Tallow beach, today? I'm going to take her to the airport, one less thing she has to worry about."

"Of course, give me the keys before you leave." Davy leads the way to the parking lot.

Davy and I sit in silence on the patio after we load the car with the bags, waiting for Mia and Violet to return from their walk

"Do you want me to drive you and Violet to the airport? You could have someone to ride back with." I shake my head at his question but offer no words. "I'll chauffeur, you and Violet can sit in the back and make out the whole way, I won't even look." He holds up his right hand as if saying a vow of honor.

"No, Davy."

I see Mia and Violet emerge from the beach. They're holding hands, as they get closer, I see they both have red rimmed eyes but they're smiling.

"Beautiful, girls, those two." Davy quietly says to me, standing to greet them as they approach.

"Sure are," I say but I can't stand with him, my legs are gelatin.

"We're going to take Violet's rental to the shop for her." Mia says to Davy.

"I know, I've arranged that with Drew," Davy says, wrapping an arm around Mia's shoulder.

Violet looks at me and smiles because we had the same idea. I reach for her hand and gently rub my thumb along her knuckles.

"We've got to go. Mum and Dad are waiting for us at the house. They want to say goodbye before they head back home," Davy says. He knows this is hard for Mia and Violet, I can tell by the way he shifts on his feet.

"Alright, Violet, let me know when you land. Call me when you're settled. I want to hear how you're doing," Mia says with a shaky and uneven voice.

"I will. Thank you, Mia," they hug once more for a long moment when they pull away Violet whispers, "I love you. I hope we can be friends forever."

I hope they do remain friends even if it's hard for me. After Davy and Mia say their goodbyes, Violet and I head to my car.

"I have to stop by my house before we head to the airport. What time is check in for your flight?" I already know she has to be there by 7 PM, I don't know why I asked.

"Seven," Violet says as she puts on her seat belt. Looking at the clock, it was only 9:30, the countdown begins, nine more hours.

Chapter 30
Cullen

I arrived at the hotel an hour after I got off the phone with Violet. Before I left the house I set up the guest room on the first floor. I emptied the dresser of spare linens and towels, stuffing them in a storage closet. I don't know if Emily has a lot of stuff but I want her to feel comfortable. After reading Emily's note and talking to Violet, it appeared Emily would be staying at the house until the rehabilitation center had an open bed for her in two weeks time. I'm still reeling from the information that has been laid out before me in the last few hours. James possibly has a baby, I say possibly because I'm not fully ready to commit to the idea until I get more information. Emily's note said she found out she was three months pregnant at the end of July, she went into a deep depression around that time. Finding out your boyfriend is dead, then finding out your pregnant would do something to your psyche. Emily also wrote her pregnancy was difficult. After she had an emergency c-section and lost her baby girl, she went deeper into her sadness. The doctors prescribed her pain medication after her c-section and she used them not only for her physical pain but her emotional pain as well. In the letter, Emily stated she doesn't have a relationship with her parents and has no siblings, she didn't go into detail about her family. She didn't have anyone to reach out to, she was alone with an infant and grief. I'm not sure how much Violet got from Emily on the phone so I kept the letter, putting it on Violet's bed for when she returns.

I sit in the hotel parking lot taking in the surroundings. It's a nice town, situated between Violet's office and the Kelly house. The hotel is seedy though, most of the rooms are reserved for temporary government housing. Families and single people are placed here while they wait for permanent housing. I take out my phone to text Emily I've arrived and on my way to her room. I take a deep breath and exit my truck. When I reach room 223, I knock at the door, I take a step back and wait for the door to open.

"Cullen?"

A short woman, dark hair full of unruly curls, answers the door.

"Hi, Emily. Nice to meet you," I say as I peer over her shoulder, trying to get a look in the room, seeing if there's anyone else inside.

"Yes, come in. I'm getting my things together." She steps back and motions for me to come in with her hand.

I see a sleeping baby on the bed surrounded by pillows to keep him from rolling off. He's lying on his side, I can't see his face but it looks like the child in the picture Emily left inside the note. I quietly peer at him as I walk closer.

"That's Matthew," Emily says softly.

I turn from the bed and look around the room. It's messy but not any more than I would assume when a small child and adult are living in a small space. There are two small suitcases on the second bed and one on the small round table that Emily is stuffing things into.

"Can I take anything out for you? I have my truck in the back lot."

I continue to look around, there are five empty wine bottles lined next to the trash. There's a stroller collapsed in the closet along with a large plastic bin with toys inside. I remove the items from the closet and place them next to the packed suitcase on the bed.

"Sure, all that can go." Emily is despondent now, she knows I'm assessing. I try to remember what Violet said, make her feel comfortable and not to scare her.

"Great, I'll take this out and be right back."

I take the two suitcases and the stroller out to my truck. When I finish loading the items in the bed of my truck I hear a ping from my phone. I pull it out of my pocket and read the message.

Ally: On the first boat in the morning. Call me when you can. Is this really happening?

Me: Just got to the hotel, call you when I get Emily settled at the

house. Yes, it is.

I place my phone in my pocket and head back to the room. When Emily answers the door this time I try to send her a reassuring smile. This must be awkward for her, maybe even a bit demoralizing. It seems all the personal items have been packed, Emily lifts the sleeping boy from the bed. Matthew shifts slightly, nuzzling into his mother's neck while she puts him on her shoulder.

"That's everything." Emily's eyes shift to the floor, "Thank you, Cullen. I appreciate this."

"It's nothing, Violet's sorry she's not home right now. I'm happy to help any way I can." I smile at her again as I take the last suitcase from the table.

"James always spoke so fondly of you, he really loved you," she says softly as to not wake Matthew.

"I know," my response is quick and I don't offer anything more.

I wish I could have told her that James spoke fondly of her but I can't because it would be a lie. James never told me about Emily and my only question is, why? When we exit the back of the hotel toward my truck I realize I don't have a car seat and wonder if one of these cars belongs to Emily.

"I didn't think to get a car seat. Do you have one?" I turn to look at her as I push the suitcase into the bed of the truck and close the tailgate.

"My car is over there," she nods toward a row of cars in the back of the lot, "I can grab it."

"I'll get it, do you have the keys?" I ask as she shifts Matthew slightly to reach in her pocket for a set of car keys. "Which one is it? Do you want to follow me or ride with me?" I ask her because she may want her car at some point and considering I have all her belongings in my truck she isn't a flight risk. I see a hesitant look cross her face, "It's whatever you want. We can come back for your car later or you can follow," I try to make my voice as pleasant as possible.

"The battery is dead." Her eyes fill with tears, she stares at the ground.

"No problem, I can jump it." I turn back toward the bed of the truck, I have cables in the cargo box.

"It's out of gas, too," her voice is steady but the tears leave her eyes.

"That's fine. How about this? I'll get the seat, we can come back for the car after you're settled in at the house. No big deal," I offer as I open the cab door of the truck, I hear her sigh with appreciation.

After managing to figure out how to get the damned seat unclipped I brought it to the truck. Emily instructs me how to install it in the backseat and once it's secure she gently places Matthew in the seat and straps him in. He's a solid sleeper and only flutters his eyes once before he drifts off again. I open the passenger door for Emily and wait for her to get inside.

Once Emily is in the passenger's seat I close the door and silently sigh with relief. The ride back to the Kelly house is quiet, I have so many questions but now isn't the time. I park in the driveway and go ahead to the front door unlocking it with the spare key I placed on my keychain. I leave the door open as I head back to the truck to gather the bags. Emily carries Matthew inside the house and I follow behind with the three suitcases.

"Your room is through here." I see Emily looking at the pictures of the Kelly clan sitting on the mantle of the fireplace.

I pass by her as I head to the hall separating the kitchen from the living room. I put the suitcases on the floor at the foot of the bed in case she wants to put Matthew on the bed. I make a mental note to find a few more pillows for the bed. I hear Emily enter the room behind me.

"This is perfect, thank you." She looks around the room and smiles at me.

"There's only a half bathroom here. There's a shower and tub upstairs. I was going to give you James's room but…" I don't finish the sentence because if I had I would've told her Violet might not want her in James' room. So, I clear my throat and say, "Ally's coming tomorrow and Violet will be back the day after, hopefully. I thought you'd be more comfortable down here." It's a solid recovery, I think.

"This is very generous, thank you." Emily sits on the bed, Matthew still asleep in her arms, "He will be awake soon. I'm going to rest here until he's awake."

"Great. Are you hungry? I'm going to the market to get some things for the house. Is there anything you want or need?" I put my hands in my pockets as my eyes shifted from Matthew to Emily.

I feel awkward leaving her alone but I need food for them. I don't want to treat her like a prisoner but I'm happy she decided to leave her car at the hotel. If I left and she spooked and took off, Violet would kill me. Emily doesn't seem like she wants to leave though, she reached out for a reason. She wants help, she wants somewhere safe for Matthew and this is her best option.

"I am hungry. I need diapers, size two. And maybe a few jars of baby food, bananas and sweet potatoes. I've started introducing food, he loves bananas. Thank you, Cullen." She looks down and kisses Matthew's cheek.

"Baby food, banana and sweet potato, size two diapers. That it? Milk or formula?" I ask.
"He can't have milk yet, I have formula for him in my bag," she answers as she places Matthew down on the bed.
"Alright, relax and get comfortable. You have my number if you think of anything. I'll be back soon."
I turn to leave and gently close the door behind me. When I get in the truck I call Ally.
"Hey, Cullen. How'd it go?" Ally sounds eager for information.
"Good, Emily and Matthew are settling in. I set them up in the downstairs bedroom. I'm going to the market to get some things now." I sit in the driveway and start my truck.
"You're leaving her alone?" Ally sounds more nervous now.
"Ally, there's nothing in the house for her to eat. She doesn't have a car, she's not going anywhere. I'll be back in less than an hour." I try to reassure Ally and myself.
"Alight. Thank you, Violet and I really appreciate this," she sighs into the phone. Ally doesn't have to thank me or think I'd rather be anywhere else but here.
"I'm glad to be here, Ally. What about Violet? Have you heard when she will be back?" I hear Ally shuffling papers and exhale a sigh again.
"I have her flight information somewhere here, let me check," Ally says as I put the call on speaker and pull out of the driveway. "Ah, here. She leaves Brisbane at six thirty in the morning, that's our time tomorrow, stopping in San Francisco for a layover. Leaving California around midnight and arriving in Boston at five forty-two AM Monday morning."
"I'll pick her up, text me the flight number," I say as I turn off the cul-de-sac onto the main road toward the shopping plaza.
"How does Emily seem? What about the baby?" Ally asks with a soft voice.
"She seems sad and embarrassed. Matthew seems fine, I haven't seen him awake yet. There were a lot of empty wine bottles in the hotel room, as for the other stuff I don't know," I tell Ally what I know and nothing I assume. If I were to tell her what I assume I would tell her I think Emily is on to something by the size of her pupils but I don't say anything about that yet.
"When you get back to the house, put away any liquor that might be around. There's a cabinet in the basement with a lock, put

it in there for now," Ally explains but I already put all the alcohol away not in the basement but outside in the shed.

"Done," I say then continue, "If they're going to stay here for the next two weeks, if Matthew stays longer, I think we might need some things. Starting with a safe place for him to sleep. A crib maybe? I don't know what else but maybe you can assess when you get here, I can get whatever you need." I have no idea what a 4 month old baby needs but I think a crib is a good place to start.

"Does she have a pack-and-play or anything for tonight?" Ally asks.

"I have no idea what that is, Ally. She puts him on the bed surrounded by pillows so he doesn't roll over. Maybe she sleeps with him at night, I didn't ask." I pull into the grocery store parking lot and exit the truck trying to make this as quick as possible.

"Alright. I'll pick one up on my way there tomorrow. Call me tonight after they go to sleep, keep me updated." Ally's going into planning mode, her tone has shifted from anxious to determined.

"You got it."

I disconnect, take a shopping cart from the bay and head into the store. I decided to cook a comfort meal for tonight, spaghetti with meatballs and sausage. I pick out some sugary snacks, I read it can help with withdrawal to some degree. Sugar increases the natural levels of opioid and dopamine. I get breakfast food for the morning and everything Emily asked for. While I stand in the baby section I'm overloaded with diaper options, from the sizes to the leak protection. I'm overwhelmed by all the options, overnight protection, 12 hour protection, hypoallergenic, little snugglers, little swaddlers, leak proof, BPA-free, chlorine-free, hospital recommended, pediatrician recommended. When the fuck did choosing a diaper become so difficult? I've never bought diapers before but this is ludicrous. Just when I'm about to pick one of every variety I'm interrupted.

"First time?" A woman stops her cart with a smile like she has been watching me stare at the shelf for the past 10 minutes.

"Yeah, aren't they all the same?" I turn to ask her.

"Definitely not. What size do you need?" she asks with a laugh.

"Size two, a four month old boy." I continue looking at the shelf.

“Pampers or Huggies is what I recommend,” she says, pointing to the brands in the middle of the shelf. “Get the big box, babies that age go through a lot of diapers and it’s better to buy in bulk.”

I want to hug this woman but instead I grab a large box of each brand she mentioned and toss them into the cart. Standing in the check out I send Violet a text.

Me: I’ll pick you up Monday morning after your flight. Call me.

I want to add I can’t wait to see her and I miss her, but that’s not appropriate given the current situation, especially given she has no idea how I really feel about her. I haven’t seen Violet since Christmas, three months ago. She came up to the cabin with Ally and Nate for the holiday. We had Christmas dinner together and spent the four days she was there hiking around the property. She read books by the fire and baked something everyday. She didn’t talk about Sam but I saw she was content and happy at the cabin. I would spend a few hours a day at the cabin visiting with them then I would head back to my cabin for the night. One night I heard someone walking up my porch steps, when I opened the door I saw Violet about to knock.

“Can’t sneak up on you,” she said as the warm air leaving her mouth turned to vapor in the cold air.

“You walked here?” It was only half a mile but it was dark and the temperature was only 5 degrees that night. “Come inside.”

I opened the cabin door as she hesitantly crossed the threshold. She rubbed her gloved hands together and took off her coat. I went to the stove to put a kettle of water on the burner.

“What’s up?” I asked her, waiting to hear why she had walked here at midnight.

“Do you ever sleep?” she asked, looking around the cabin.

I gave a huff of a laugh, “Sometimes.” I placed my hands on either side of the stove as I waited for the water to boil.

“Have anything stronger than tea?” She asked as she glanced over the books on the shelf behind my recliner.

“Whiskey?” I asked as I turned behind be to a cabinet holding liquor.

“No, not whiskey. Never whiskey.” She turned to look at me with a disgusted look on her face as if I offended her by offering her whiskey.

“Schnapps? Wine? Scotch?” I read the labels of the bottles in the cabinet.

"Schnapps, with ice if you have it." She turned back to the bookshelf and I took down two glasses. I poured out two fingers in each glass and added ice.

"Happy New Year, Vi," I said as we tapped the glasses together, New Year's Eve was two days away.

"Happy New Year, Cullen."

She sipped and sat down on the couch looking at the fire. I sat in my chair and watched her staring at the flames, the reflection of the fire flickered in her eyes. I waited patiently, I knew she was there for something but I didn't rush her. Violet talks when she's ready and I enjoyed seeing her inside my cabin.

"I miss him." Her eyes stayed on the fire and she sipped again. I saw her throat shift as she swallowed the clear liquor and the grief.

"Me too," I said, taking a sip of the peppermint flavored liquid. I hated schnapps.

"Sometimes, I'm so angry," her hands gripped the tumbler so tight I saw the white of her knuckles, "Sometimes, I'm so angry, I hate him." She finally shifted her stare from the fire to me. "Do you ever hate him?"

"No," I replied, honestly, in a whisper. "James saved my life more than once when we were over there. I could never hate him but I understand how you might feel." I leaned forward in the chair wanting to be closer to her.

"Have you read your letter?" she asked, leaning back on the couch.

"The letter from James?" I knew what she was talking about but I wanted to be sure there wasn't another letter out there she may have been referring to. When she nodded I told her, "Yeah, I read it the night Theo gave it to me."

"Did it make you feel better? Did it offer you anything?"

She stared back to the fire and I understood she hadn't read hers yet and I was curious as to why she had waited five months.

"It gave me comfort reading his words. He didn't say anything I didn't already know. It made me feel good knowing he didn't want to leave anything unsaid." I searched her face to see if I was offering her any relief. "You haven't read yours yet," it wasn't a question because I knew the answer.

She took a sip and exhaled, not responding to my non-question. We sat in silence until her drink was finished. She stood and went to the kitchen, placing her glass in the sink.

"Thanks, Cullen," she said as she put her coat on. I laughed because I knew she wasn't thanking me for the drink, she was thanking me for the company and she never had to thank me for that. "Get some sleep, you look terrible," her tone was sarcastic and I knew it wasn't the schnapps that warmed my chest.

"I'll walk you back."

I took my coat off the wall by the front door and grabbed two hats. I couldn't believe she walked there without one. I handed her the hat and she put it on.

"I know the way," she said, opening the door and stepping out onto the porch.

"Shut up, I'm walking you back," I said, closing the door behind me, I turned on the flashlight I had hanging next to my jacket on the wall.

The half mile walk was in complete silence. The only sounds were our breaths and the crunching of ice and snow beneath our feet. When the cabin came into sight from the tree line, I thought it might be my chance to unleash the feelings and words that had been pent up inside me for years. I stopped with the cabin a hundred yards away, Violet stopped when she didn't hear me walking beside her.

"Good night, Cullen," she said when she turned to face me. Her smile replaced the sadness and anger she showed in the cabin. "I've got a letter to read."

She stepped toward me and kissed my cheek. Her lips were cold and her cheek was colder when it brushed against my face. The icy temperature of her skin didn't feel cold, it warmed me, it made the blood pump faster in my body.

"Good night," I said as she turned to walk to the cabin, I held the flashlight on her until she reached the porch and opened the door.

Before she closed the door she waved and I clicked the light off, on, off then back on before I turned to walk back home. When I got home I washed the glasses that held our schnapps. I paused over the sink, I reached above, and took down the bottle of whiskey from the cabinet. I took off the cap and upturned the bottle over the sink, dumping the contents down the drain.

"Never whiskey," I mumbled as I watched the amber liquid fall down the drain.

I'm completely wrapped up in my thoughts as I check out at the market and load up the truck. When I arrive back at the house, I bring in the bags and leave them on the counter in the kitchen. I stop and listen for movement or sounds of Emily or Matthew. I hear something coming from the living room so I head that way. Emily's sitting on the couch looking at a family photo album she found on the bookshelf. There's a quilt on the floor and Matthew is on his back gumming a toy, he rolls over to this belly and reaches for another. His eyes are blue like the Kelly siblings. When his head turns and he sees me, his face changes, worry comes over him. He turns to find his mother, his head can't turn far enough to get her in his line of sight, he starts to cry and I take a step back.

"Matthew, it's okay. That's Cullen, Daddy's friend." She picks him up and bounces him in her arms, soothing him with her voice and touch. He calms down once he's in her arms, he feels safe with her.

"I'm going to start dinner." I gesture toward the kitchen behind me. "I'll put the diapers in your room."

"Sure, I'll get you some money from my purse." Emily starts toward the hall.

"No, please." I hold up my hands.

"You've already done enough, I can pay you for the diapers," she sounds insistent.

"Consider it a baby gift." I'm relieved when Emily laughs softly and seems okay with the exchange.

After I put the two boxes of diapers in the closet of Emily's room I go back to the kitchen and start the dinner prep. I glance at my phone hoping to see a response from Violet but there are no messages. As I prep the meat I check the clock, 6:08 PM, Violet will be on a plane in 12 hours. I will see her in 36 hours, the countdown begins.

Chapter 31
Drew

The short ride to my house was in silence, Violet holding on to my hand tightly as if something was attempting to rip her away from me. When we arrived, I put my bags in my bedroom and laid on the bed with Violet. I've been holding her for the past hour. She talks about her family home and tells me about her brother's best friend and team member, Cullen. From the way Violet explains it, he's a family friend charged with checking in on the sisters. One of James' last wishes was to make sure his sisters were looked after and Cullen was the man for the job. She speaks of him with the fondness a sister would speak of a brother but there's no man in the world who could view Violet as a sister if there was no blood relation. My heart pumps with jealousy. There is a man waiting for her return, waiting to help her through a stressful situation. When I asked Violet last week if there was someone waiting for her, she answered me honestly with a "no". I wonder if he's waiting for her with hopes of a connection one day, I try to push it down, jealousy isn't what I want to feel in my last moments with Violet. I'm happy when she changes the subject. We talk about baby Matthew, Violet shows me a picture of a bubbly boy with blue eyes that resemble Violet's eyes. The shape and long lashes look just like hers. I'm happy she found a connection to her brother, a living connection, that may be able to heal some of her grief.

After a few moments of silence from Violet, I feel the change in her breathing as I hold her against me, I realize she's asleep. I don't blame her, the late night and very early morning, the tears and emotional roller coaster have left her exhausted. I kiss her head and let her sleep. I gently shift my body from under her and slip away from the bed. I cover her with a blanket and head to the kitchen. I make two sandwiches, wrapping one for Violet to have when she wakes. I sit at the table and eat while I reflect on the time I've had with Violet. I have no regrets about the time we've spent together. The only regret I have is that she's leaving suddenly, with little warning. I console myself with the fact that although the situation may be stressful to her now, I think it will become a blessing for her and her family.

I offer myself two best case scenarios for what might become of Violet and I. First best case, she gets through this time with her family and finds she does love me, knowing what we've shared is special. Violet will tell me she can't be without me and I'll go to her. I'd give it all up if she asked. I would move there to be with her, my family would understand. They've met her, they know how special she is. I could relocate, find a job with an American company or an international company. We could travel back here to visit my family for a month out of the year. I think we could both live with that.

Second best case, she goes back to America and finds someone to love her as she deserves. Someone who knows she's the best thing to happen to them. She falls blissfully in love and makes a houseful of babies and lives happily-ever-after. I could live with this second case if it was truly what she wanted and deserved. If the man gave her unconditional love and affection. I don't know if you can find two loves in a lifetime, I know you can love more than once. Do we really only have *one* true love? With all the possibilities of matches in the world, is there only one that's true?

I can't go over the worst case scenarios in my mind right now, they're too depressing to bear at this moment. I'll worry about those another time. I told Violet how I felt, I left it all there for her. I didn't do it so she could tell me she loved me. I know she's battling with the idea of love because she has lost most of the people she loved. She spent years with someone she wanted to love, someone she wanted to love her, it didn't work. She's confused if what she feels with me is love or if she's romanticizing the relationship because she's finally with a man who gives her the attention and affection she didn't realize she was lacking. She knows I love her, she knows if she asks me I'll wait for her. If I didn't tell her I'd have regretted it and I don't want there to be any regrets at the end of this day. I hear Violet enter the kitchen, her bare feet are quiet but I'm already familiar with the sound. I glance up and watch her walk toward me.

"You should have woken me," she says as she pulls out a chair to join me at the table.

"You needed to rest, you only slept about an hour. I made you a sandwich." I go to the fridge and pull out the wrapped sandwich from the shelf.

"Thank you." She takes a bite while I pour her a glass of water.

"I thought we could head to Brisbane early, walk around and get an early dinner before your flight." I keep my tone upbeat.

"Sounds great." I place the water in front of her plate as she takes another bite.

The ride to Brisbane is light and conversation flows easily. Violet seems to be in good spirits and I try to keep my emotions in check. We replay the events of the wedding, Violet talks about meeting Sarah and talks fondly of Lauren's three girls. She only gets emotional once, about halfway through the drive, when she says she's going to miss me. She asks me if I'll be okay and I laugh, of course I will be okay, I lie. Then I tell her my best case scenarios. If I didn't look over and see the tear fall onto her right cheek I wouldn't have known she was crying.

"You're a very good man, Drew." She squeezes my hand.

I change the subject and tell her next time she comes to Australia I'll make sure she gets to Whian Whian National Forest. I'm not certain she'll come back, it's nice hoping she will one day. When we arrive in Brisbane I find parking between the airport and a shopping strip with a few restaurants. Violet wants to walk around as much as possible, she's not looking forward to the flight. As we walk around the shops, hands holding tightly, she smiles and laughs at stories I tell of Davy and I as children. It's a good sound, a good feeling. Sometimes Violet gets really quiet and I can see her processing everything unfolding before her, I give her time to do that when she does. I put my arm around her and kiss her a lot in those moments. When I see the time is close to five I ask her what she wants to eat, she says she wants pasta. I know of a good Italian restaurant by the airport so we head back down the street that way.

The restaurant is quiet, it's early for dinner, we have the place almost to ourselves. We eat our salads as Violet talks about her parents and memories from her childhood on the beaches of Cape Cod. It sounds like a lovely place and I wonder if I'll ever see it. I tell her about the first time my parents took Davy and I to the ocean for a holiday. I was about ten years old and Davy was seven. I was taken with the ocean and couldn't believe how powerful the waves were. Mum was riddled with anxiety, we knew how to swim because we swam in the lakes and rivers but we were new to the ways of ocean currents.

Violet starts playing with her noodles, shifting them from one side of the plate to the other and stops eating. I ask if she's ready to go. She says she wasn't but she has to check in soon. I pay the tab and we walk toward the airport, the sun is low in the sky.

I stop at my car which is parked in the lot by the airport, I gather her suitcase and backpack from the boot. I carry her luggage while we enter the airport. We stopped in front of the airport bar where we first saw each other.

"Feel like ages ago but at the same time just yesterday," I say to her as we smile at the memory.

"What if I never dropped my phone that day?" She looks up at me with her brow furrowed.

"I think we still would've found each other. Now, if you never went to Pottsville, if you never met Mia on the beach in Byron, then we might have a different story. Too many things aligned in my favor for me not to have seen you again." I bend down and kiss her.

We walk further into the airport and Violet checks in.

"I don't think you can go any further than this point but I have some time before we board. We could sit over there if you have time," she says after returning from the check in counter.

I walk over to the attendant, Violet watches with confusion.

"Hey, Jim. I'm making sure she gets on her flight without issue. Can I go through?" I ask.

"Of course, Mr. Harris. Here," Jim hands me an airline badge which I place around my neck and walk toward Violet who's smiling with amusement.

"I guess you have some pull around here," Violet says and I laugh as I take her bags and motion toward the ticket holder waiting area.

Violet and I kiss but we're conscious to not make a full on public display of our affection. We sit for a little while then stand up, taking laps around the waiting area, we look out the windows at the planes landing and taking off. Around 8 o'clock Violet goes to the women's room to change into joggers and a sweatshirt for more comfort on the long flight. It's dark outside now and the airport runways are lit up. I check my watch just as they make an announcement for boarding of Violet's flight, my stomach rolls and my chest heaves. This is it. I hold Violet for a while until they make the second boarding call. I kiss her as tears fall from her eyes but I remain stoic, I try anyway. My heart pounds and my palms sweat, I rub my hands up and down her arms.

"Thank you, Drew. For everything, I really mean it. I wish I could say everything but..." I stop her by kissing her again.

"I know," I say as the final boarding call echoes over the PA, shaking my insides into reality. "Call or text me when you land," I whisper in her ear. "Safe travels, Violet."

"Drew," my name is a cross between a plea and a demand.

I pull her from my hold and kiss her for the final time. "Get on the plane, Violet. I love you, let me know when you arrive safely."

She nods and I bring my arms over my chest to keep my heart from exploding or falling to the floor, I don't know which. I watch her walk toward the terminal entrance, I don't move from my spot. I won't allow her to turn around and see me walking away from her. I want her to see I'm here, I'm right here. She turns when she gives the attendant her ticket. She puts on a brave smile and waves goodbye. I raise my hand from my chest and give her a wave. When she's through the gate I collapse on the chair and hold my head in my hands. I sit there for a full half hour until I hear the gates close and the engine on the plane start.

The drive home is much like the one I took after my first encounter with Violet, autopilot. When I pull into the driveway of my house I see Mia's car parked on the side. I open the garage door and step into the house. Mia is settled on the sectional reading a magazine with an afghan covering her. I check the time, it's after midnight. I hear shuffling in the hall and see Davy coming from the guest room.

"Hey," Mia says as jumps up from the couch and carefully approaches me.

"What are you doing here?" I ask, tossing my keys on the counter. "Not really up for company," I say as I run my hand through my hair and rub my tension filled neck.

"We wanted to be here if you needed anything." Mia hugs me tightly and I almost break in her arms.

"Are you alright, mate?" Davy asks, searching my eyes for reassurance that I can't give him.

"I need to sleep," I say as I move past them to the couch. I stop when I see a large rectangular package wrapped in brown paper. "What's that?"

"Violet left it and asked me to give it to you after she left." Mia shrugs her shoulders.

"Thanks," I say as I walk over to the package.

"Well, we wanted to make sure you made it home safe. Dinner at our house tomorrow at six, we really want you to come," Mia says as she gives Davy a look telling him it's time to leave.

They each give me a hug before they leave but I can't take my eyes off the large rectangle resting on my couch. When they leave I pick up the thin box, I turn it over to find a point where I can rip the paper free. It's the back of a canvas, I take the wrapping off and turn it around and when I do I smile. It's a large canvas print of the sunrise I watched with Violet that morning before we walked Cape Byron. I place it on the couch and step back to look. I love it, I love her. I sit on the coffee table, letting all of the emotions of the day fill my body and I break.

Chapter 32
Violet

An hour into the flight I feel my swollen eyes, I can't hold them open any more. The tears don't stop even through my closed eyes. I'm thankful the woman next to me left the seat between us open and elected to sit in the aisle seat. The woman asked me if I was okay once, a half hour ago, I nodded and continued to silently cry. The sobs stuck in my chest are fighting to be unleashed, I won't allow them to be free. I put my head against the window and tell myself after I count to 20 I'll stop crying, I've done that ten times now. I try it again, I reach 14 when I feel sleep overtake me.

I wake up from a dreamless sleep four hours later. Eight more hours until I land in San Francisco for a short layover. I feel the skin on my cheeks and under my eyes is tight from the salty tears. I go to the restroom and wash my face with cold water. Sitting back in my seat I reach for my backpack and pull out James's letter from the bag. The envelope is worn and the page is close to tearing because I've opened and closed the letter so many times. I've read the letter from James enough times that I have it memorized but I still like to read it. Seeing his handwriting and hearing his voice come off the page to me is soothing. It took me over five months to read this letter because I was afraid of what was inside. I was afraid to forgive James, I was afraid what he might tell me would make me hate him, I was afraid I'd only have more questions after I read it. I gently pull the paper from the envelope and open it on my lap.

Violet,

If you are reading this it means you're pretty pissed off at me. I've written this letter to you so many times over the years I spent in the Navy. Sometimes I'd write it after a dangerous mission, sometimes after I lost someone in our unit. I threw most of them away, they were terrible anyway. As you may have figured out, I left the Marines. I was recruited by a contracting company, the work has been easy. I don't know why I wasn't honest with you and Ally about it other than I knew you wouldn't be happy with the decision. I knew you wanted me to leave military life completely. I was really good at what I did, it might be hard to believe especially after getting this letter. I understood the risks when joining the Navy and this unit, that's why I worked hard to be the best I could. I'm sorry it didn't work out this time.

I love you, Violet. I never wanted to leave you or Ally. You girls mean the world to me and I tried, really hard, to do right by both of you despite my decisions. There are a few things I want to leave you with before I end with my last wishes.

You're strong and resilient, you're loyal and unwavering, you make me proud everyday. Despite everything the three of us have been through, we stuck together and became strong individuals and stronger as a family. I know you're caught up in a relationship, I really don't want to talk about him, I've told you enough times how I feel about it. One day you'll leave him, you just have to be ready to do it. I couldn't make you, Ally couldn't make you, only you can be the one to decide when it's time. But there will be a time and when that time comes, please don't look back, move forward. Violet, some people can't be saved, they'll only drag you down with them. Love yourself, be happy with yourself and forgive yourself. You have to do all of these things before you can find love and happiness with someone else.

Just because we experienced sad things in our lives, incredibly difficult things, it doesn't mean you have to live a sad, difficult life. Find happiness, find love, find joy in life. This ride is short and you never know when your time is up. Be the happy, confident woman I know you to be. When you find something or someone that makes you happy, hold on to it. Find someone that lifts you up and doesn't tear you down, find someone who helps you gain confidence not someone who takes it away.

You and Ally are all that remains of our family, I know you'll support each other. You two are so close and I hope you don't let anything come between that. This will not break you, nothing can break you.

That leaves me with my last wishes, I guess. I want you to keep the cabin for three years. I've set aside money for taxes and expenses, enough for 5 years. If there comes a time you and Ally want to sell, please, allow Cullen to buy you out before you open it to market. It's in my paperwork with the lawyer. If you wish to keep it in the family I'd be very happy but it's up to both you girls. I want to be buried with Mom and Dad, again this is all arranged. Don't feel you have to visit me, I won't be there. I'll be in the mountains, the wind, the rivers, I'll be with you and Ally always. I love you, Violet. Please remember how strong you are.

Love Always,

James

I read through the letter three times and gently folded it back in the envelope. I remember the night I read this, I was at James' cabin for the Christmas holiday with Ally and Nate. I had brought the letter thinking I could read it while I went on a hike but Cullen didn't want me hiking alone in the woods with the snow and ice. Cullen came with me on the hikes and the one time I tried to sneak away to hike alone I ended up stumbling on him shortly after I got on the trail. I'm sure if I told him what I was up to he would have given me the privacy I wanted. I went to Cullen's cabin late one night hoping to gain some courage. Cullen always made me feel I could be brave even when I was crumbling. I drew strength from him because he was always so calm in any situation, I don't know if they trained him for that in the Marines or if it came natural to him.

Before I went to Cullen's cabin I saw Ally reading a book by the fireplace. It was late for Ally but she had taken a nap earlier in the day and was anxious to finish the book she started the day before.

"Ally?" I sat down on the stone hearth letting the fire heat my back. She hummed at me before she put her book on her lap. "The letter James wrote, when did you read yours?"

Ally didn't hesitate with her answer, "The day of the funeral."

I hummed and stood up, I went to the door and took my jacket from the peg on the wall. Before I opened the door Ally said, "Maybe if you read yours you'll be able to forgive him." When I turned around Ally was already back to reading her book.

"I don't blame him," I said before Ally hummed at me again without bringing her eyes from the pages. I let out an annoyed huff and went out the door.

The walk to Cullen cabin was less than ten minutes on a regular day but the night was so cold and dark, I made it there in six minutes. It was late, I knew Cullen would be awake. I saw the lights on inside as I approached, before I could bring my fist to knock, the door opened. Cullen was dressed as he was earlier, jeans with a long sleeve flannel shirt. The green and gray shirt matched his eyes but I doubted if that was the reason he wore the shirt. There was a white thermal shirt under the flannel, I could see it because the top three buttons on the flannel were undone. His hair was windblown or maybe he was sleeping before I arrived and it was bedhead. I wanted to rustle it more or put my fingers through it to straighten it, whichever one would annoy him more.

It was the first time I'd been inside the cabin since it was completely finished. I took in everything around the cabin, the wood was stained darker than James' cabin. The fire light from the wood stove made everything in the cabin glow amber and gold. I paused at his bookshelf reading through the titles. The books were mostly nonfiction, guides of New Hampshire, hunting and survival books, and a few classic novels. Cullen offered me a drink and poured peppermint schnapps with ice. I sat on the couch, staring through the glass of the woodstove watching the flames dance. I asked him about his letter, asking if it comforted him. I asked if he was mad at James. James was a brother, a fellow soldier, they needed the best from each other to survive. Maybe Cullen got the best of James and there was nothing to resent him for or be angry about. I'm sure James gave me his best and when I felt anger toward him I knew it wasn't fully James' fault. I was angry with myself and sometimes I directed my anger toward James.

I sat in Cullen's cabin for a long while, most of the time in silence, listening to the fire hiss and pop. I tried to draw something from Cullen I had felt months ago, I didn't know if I was going to find it but I found comfort and support in his presence. After some time of sitting in that comfort I stood to leave, Cullen walked me back to the cabin and I went inside to finally read the letter my brother wrote months before. A letter my brother wanted me to read when he wasn't able to come back to me.

As I read the words today on the plane, knowing what I just came from and knowing what I have waiting for me at home, I ask if I've forgiven myself. I ask if I love myself and if I'm happy. For the first time in a long time I am happy. Despite all the tears I've cried over the past day, I'm happy. I removed myself from a toxic relationship, traveled to a foreign place where I found boundless beauty and contentment, I am happy. I left that place of beauty to help someone in need which also brings me happiness. I'm terribly afraid of what's waiting for me at home but I'm happy with my decision to go home. Finding new friends in Mia and her family made me happy. Being able to spend time with a close family who had normal family relationships made me happy. Spending my time with a man who made me feel worthy and desirable made me incredibly happy.

I'm still working on forgiving myself, I'm still angry with the decisions I made over the years, not just with Sam but with other parts of my life as well. I'm angry for allowing myself to become lost, Sam had very little part in that. It's going to take time but I'll one day forgive myself. When I do, maybe I can love myself. Until then, I couldn't have fallen in love with Drew. I loved the time I spent with him, I loved the way he made me feel, I loved the confidence and affection he brought out in me. If I had told Drew I loved him, I would have been lying to myself and to him. I couldn't ask Drew to leave his family. I would never ask someone to separate from their loving, caring, nurturing family, that would never make me happy.

Drew offered his heart to me, couldn't have taken it. We lived too far away from each other, maybe my time with Drew was meant to be brief. What I love most about Drew is how he allowed himself to be vulnerable with me. The man stood before me, naked in a shower, and told me his feelings and thoughts. He did that knowing I was not able to reciprocate. Something brought me to Drew, something brought me to Mia and I'm thankful for that. Drew gave me his best case scenarios as we drove to the airport, I didn't ask for the worst case because I know those. The bottom line is that Drew wants love and happiness for me. I'll have it, I'll find it, within myself. Then I'll find someone to share it with. I don't know if our story is done, I won't know until I work through some things. My story with Mia will not end, from the talk Mia and I had on the beach, I know we'll be lifelong friends.

As I stare out the window, I wonder if James forgave himself. James carried a lot of guilt for the decisions he made for our family and for situations that happened overseas. He talked very little about what happened while he was deployed but I know he carried a lot. I wonder if I have to forgive myself for all the single things I'm angry about or if forgiveness comes and absolves everything once you find it in one thing.

Maybe helping Emily get through this difficult time will be a good start in helping me. Matthew's going to need a lot of attention and it's going to be a lot of work when his mother goes away to start her program. I know very little about babies but I'm not running away from this challenge. I'm going to meet this challenge and I'm going to ask for help if I need it. Ally will be there to help and Cullen will help. From here on, I won't look back. I'll move forward. I'll forgive myself and forgive others. I'll love myself and allow myself to be loved because, damn it, I deserve it. I take out my book and finish the story of Enda. After reading the book I realize I'm less than an hour away from landing in California. I pack up the book and the letter and gaze out the window until I see the lights of the city below me. I'm one step closer to home, one step closer to meeting my nephew.

The layover in San Francisco is three hours, I freshen up in the ladies room and check the time. I traveled a 13 hour flight and somehow managed to go back in time. I left Brisbane Sunday at 9:30 PM, after a 13 hour flight, I landed in California on Sunday at 4:30 PM. I wish there was a time zone out there that could bring you back a year, or 12. I power on my phone and check my messages. I see a message from Cullen I didn't respond to.

I want to call him and get some information but I don't know if he can talk. Then, as if he can read my mind from three thousand miles away, my phone rings.

"Hi, Cullen," I say the tiredness is blatant in my voice.

"How was the flight?" he asks as I hear a door close on his end.

"Long. How's Ally and Emily?" I ask to get right to the point.

"Getting to know each other. Ally's asking all kinds of questions and getting to know Matthew. I don't think Emily minds but I think…" He trails off, I bite the nail on my thumb and when I realize I'm doing it I sit on my hand.

"You think what?" I ask, holding my breath.

"I think Emily is using, she disappears sometimes and when she comes back her pupils are different. I'm trying not to say anything to Ally but if Ally picks up on it…" He doesn't finish and he doesn't have to. Ally will come down hard on Emily.

"Maybe she knows and she's trying to keep calm until we can all be together and talk with her."

I hope Ally wouldn't do anything to scare Emily off, she wouldn't do it knowingly but Ally's tough. She says exactly what she thinks and it's not different with strangers.

"I'll be at Logan to pick you up in the morning. I'm going to get back inside, Emily's getting Matthew ready for bed. I'll talk with Ally tonight when they go to bed," Cullen sounds as tired as I feel and it makes me feel guilty he's shouldering my load right now. It makes me more anxious to get home.

"Thanks, again. See you in the morning."

I take out my notebook and pen from my bag thinking I need to write down some questions for Emily and for Google.

"I'll see you soon, Vi." Cullen hangs up and knowing he's there puts my mind at ease.

I start walking laps around the seating area while I wait for the boarding call for my next and final leg of the journey back to Massachusetts. I wrote down some questions for Emily. I also wrote questions about addiction and ideas on some ground rules for Emily while she stays at the house. I'm in way over my head here and hope Ally, being the planner she is, has come up with some ideas as well. I pull up my text messages and tap Drew's thread.

Me: Landed in San Fran. I left something for you with Mia, I hope you like it.

After three laps I get a response.

Drew: I love it, thank you. Text me when you land (again).

He sent me a picture of the canvas printed for him, he hung it in his living room across from his sectional.

I boarded the flight back home after 9 PM, PST. I sleep for the last three hours of the flight, I wake with the pilot telling the passengers he's starting the descent. I stretch and take my hair out of the bun, shaking it loose and running my fingers through it. I feel dirty from the recirculating airplane air, I want a shower. My stomach rumbles, I want food. I smile to myself thinking of how I felt when I landed in Brisbane two weeks ago. After I exit the plane I go to baggage claim and wait for my suitcase. Thankfully, I don't have to wait too long, my section was the last to exit so the baggage is already waiting on the carousel. I grab my bag and head toward the pickup. I take my phone and call Cullen.

"Through the doors, two o'clock," he says when he answers.

I walk through the doors and sure enough I see Cullen leaning against his truck in the pick up lane at the clock position he stated he would be. He pushes off his truck and walks toward me, he looks good as he always does. His hair is shorter from the last time I saw him but not short by Marine standards. His beard is neat and trimmed. When he gets close he takes my suitcase.

"You good?" he asks with a humorous smile.

"I'm fine. I know, I'm a mess. I'd like to see what you look like after twenty hours on a plane." I toss the backpack at him because my back is killing me.

"I was going to say you look good. Single suits you." He opens the back door of the cab and tosses in my bags.

When Cullen pulls out of the airport he fills me in on the happenings at the house. Emily and Matthrew are starting to get comfortable. When Cullen and Ally spoke last night Ally talked about the possibility of getting a DNA test to make sure Matthew was James' son. While Ally is concerned about Emily's motives and Matthew's legitimacy, Cullen believes Emily's doing exactly what she says. Which is recognizing her problem and reaching out for help. Cullen thinks Emily is using while in the house but says he hasn't seen her drink. He noticed Emily's hands were shaking a lot last night and thinks alcohol withdrawal is setting in. I know the signs of withdrawal from alcohol. Sam would sometimes shake when he tried to stop after a few days, he always went back to drinking.

"Ally took the week off. I've got to get home and take care of a few things. I'm going to come back and help with whatever I can. Emily leaves for rehab a week from Wednesday. She's hoping to leave Matthew with you."

Cullen's overloading me with information right now. I can't concentrate because my stomach is roaring with hunger.

"I can't concentrate until I get food. Can we stop and get a burger?" I look around and notice we're still a half hour from the house and I don't know if I can make it.

"A burger? Violet, it's five thirty in the morning," he laughs.

"I'm still on Australian time, it feels like dinner time. I haven't eaten in over twenty four hours. I need food before I lose it," I warn as I try to think of where we are. "That breakfast place we went to after I picked you and James up from the airport a few years ago. When you came home for Christmas, remember?" I ask him as I pull out my phone.

"I remember, it's in Braintree." He does remember and I'm thankful it's only two exits away.

"Second exit, take a right." I sink back into the seat as Cullen laughs again.

When we get to the restaurant I order a breakfast burger with french fries and Cullen looks at me like I have a third eye. He orders an omelet and a milkshake. I tear into the burger not caring what Cullen thinks of my table manners. It's the best burger I've tasted. When I'm three quarters of the way through I finally look up and see him watching me with absolute amusement. I slowly reach for the napkin and wipe my mouth.

"Wow," he says as he takes his eyes off me and takes a bite of his omelet. "I've eaten with lots of men in my life. Men that haven't eaten for days and let me tell you something." He lifts his fork and points it at me. "That was…"

I toss a piece of ice at him from my glass of water before he can finish but he catches it with his other hand.

"Don't judge me." I take a sip of my water then I'm hit in the cheek with the ice cube I just threw, "Jesus."

"Feel better now that you inhaled a quarter pound of meat in thirty seconds? That's not gonna feel good in," Cullen looks at his watch, "ten minutes."

I yawn, "You better eat up, I want to go meet my nephew."

I stand from the booth and head to the ladies room. I look in the mirror of the rest room and laugh. My eyes have bags from all the crying and sporadic sleep. My skin is pale as it gets when I'm overtired. My hair, my hair actually looks alright. I wash my hands and face in the sink. When I exit the bathroom I find the waitress and pay the bill before she can bring it to the table. When I return to the table I see Cullen finished his omelet and starting eating the french fries off my plate.

"Those are mine," I say when I sit down.

"You can't eat another thing. I don't need you throwing up in my truck. Are you ready?" He asks, looking over his shoulder for the waitress.

"It's all set, I paid the bill. Ready when you are." I say and then take a sip of water.

"You didn't have to do that." Cullen stands from the booth as he takes one more french fry from my plate.

"It's the least I could do." I walk behind Cullen as we exit the restaurant.

As we walk to the truck I hear a ping on my phone. I pull it from my back pocket and see a new text message.

Drew: Did you land in Boston?

Me: I did. Almost home. Can I call you later?

I get in the truck and put my seat belt on when the phone pings again.

Drew: Of course. I'd love to hear your voice.

I smile as I put the phone in the cup holder. I turn to look at Cullen watching me with curiosity. I smile but don't explain anything. With my hunger gone, I lean back in the seat and watch the highway. As we near the house I felt a heaviness in my stomach, I ate too fast. I want to double over to help with the cramping but then Cullen will know he was right. I shift in my seat and loosen the seat belt around my stomach. I hear Cullen laugh under his breath.

"How's your stomach?" He turns to me with a smile.

"It's fine," I breathe through an awful cramp, "I just need to walk around."

He laughs again, "We're almost there, don't puke in my truck."

Cullen pulls in the driveway behind Ally's car. He takes my bags from the backseat as I stand next to the passenger's door. I'm finally here. I'm nervous about what's waiting for me inside, it makes my stomach ache more.

"Are you coming?" Cullen asks as he walks past me with my bags.

I take a deep breath and follow Cullen through the side door of the house. When I walk in I see Ally at the kitchen table, her laptop open, the house is quiet. Ally sees us walk in and stands from the table. I greet her with a hug that lasts longer than most hugs from Ally.

"Glad you're home," she says when she pulls away. "Thanks, Cullen." She turns her attention to Cullen who's standing in front of the fridge and takes out several water bottles.

"Where's Emily? Matthew?" I ask, looking around as Cullen hands me a water.

"They're asleep. Should we go upstairs to talk?" Ally shuts her laptop and heads out of the kitchen toward the living room where the stairs lead to the second floor bedrooms. That's when I realized she wasn't asking, it wasn't a question.

I look back at Cullen as he sits at the table and ask, "Aren't you coming?"

"Maybe you two should talk, fill me in later." He takes a drink from his water bottle.

"C'mon, I'm not repeating everything she says. Let's go." I don't wait for him to respond and when I hear the chair scape against the tile floor I know he's behind me.

I know where to find Ally when I get upstairs, not in her room or mine but she's in my parents' bedroom. This is the room where we held most of our family discussions after they passed. We planned their funeral in this room, we planned James' funeral in here. There were also happy family discussions in here, this is the room where James told us he was building the cabin and this is the room James and I planned for Ally's college graduation party. I still preferred the living room but since Emily and Matthew were staying down there, upstairs would offer us more privacy.

"Catch me up," I say as I sit on the upholstered chair on the far side of the room by the window that overlooks the backyard.

"Emily's leaving for her program a week from Wednesday. The program runs seven to eight weeks. The facility is on the Cape, they have good reviews and I spoke with a counselor last night. They like the patient to establish a routine before they start having visitors, she recommended we let Emily settle in and maybe visit on the second or third week." Ally's on top of everything it seems, I'm not surprised, she opens her laptop, "The counselor said Emily won't have contact with anyone but facility staff for the first five to seven days, they call it a blackout period. The withdrawal process is different for everyone but during this time they don't allow calls or visitors." My stomach hurts but it's not from the greasy burger. This is going to be hard for Emily, I don't even know her yet but not having contact with your child must be very difficult.

"Okay. What about from now until she checks in?" I scan around the room, Cullen's leaning on my father's desk and Ally sits on the bed.

"Well, I think we get to know Matthew's routine and allow her time with him. Let her get to know us." Ally finally looks up at me for the first time since she started talking. "I think we need to call Tom."

"Why?" I ask, Tom is our family lawyer, conversations with Tom never go well.

"*Why*? Because we're about to be the caretakers of a baby. What if Matthew gets sick and we need to take him to the hospital? What if he has an accident and needs medical attention? What if we want to take him to the cabin while he's in our care, can we take him across state lines? I don't know the rules on all this stuff. I think we need to cover all our bases. I've looked into a temporary custody agreement, I think this is our best option. Emily doesn't sign away her parental rights but it gives us the ability to make decisions when she can't," Ally explains as my head spins, she's thought of so much over the last 24 hours.

"Okay, we have to talk to Emily about all this. I can call Tom today when the office opens. What else?" I look at Ally and she sighs, there's more.

"I think we should get a DNA test to be sure Matthew is, in fact, James' child." She looks at me with a stone face, "I'm not saying Emily is lying but we don't know her situation. She may believe Matthew is James' but we don't know if she was with anyone else during the time she was with James."

"Ally, she named her baby after our father. He looks just like James." I point to the baby picture of James on the desk Cullen is leaning against.

"I'm not negotiating on this one, Vi." She turns her stare back to her laptop and I look to Cullen who stares at the floor in front of him.

"And how do we get DNA from James?" I'm sure Ally has it all figured out, she has already done the research, I'm positive.

"We don't have his DNA, I don't think we want to exhume him. We can test our DNA to Matthew's, it's the next best thing." She closes her computer screen and leans back against the pillow, she looks pale.

"Okay," I sigh, this is so much more than I thought. "So, you're here this week. I'm home now so we can work out a schedule. If I can get into the office this week I'll be able to take next week off or I could work from home. I don't want you to take too much time off." Ally had a week off in April for her spring break. I'd have to look into getting help around here if I wanted to work and tend to Matthew.

"I can look into taking a leave but…" Her voice trails off as she puts her head back, she is looking more pale.

"Ally?" I stood from the chair and went to the side of the bed.

"I'm fine, just dizzy." Ally sat up and brought her legs over the side of the bed.

"Here," I hold out the water bottle in my hand.

"Thanks." Ally takes the bottle with shaking hands. Cullen is now standing over me as I crouch on the floor in front of Ally. "I'm fine," she says.

I stand up and look at Cullen who keeps his eyes on my sister, assessing her condition. We wait a few minutes and watch Ally take a few small sip of water, the color slowly returning to her face. I thought she might be having a panic attack, I've had enough experiences with those and my body acted similar to what I was seeing with Ally now. A wave of guilt washes over me, if I had been home Ally would not have had to do so much over the past 36 hours.

"I'm sorry, Ally. I wish I was here to help you with all this." I sit next to her on the bed and rub her back.

"I'm fine. Like I was saying, I was going to look into taking a leave from work but I was hoping to hold off and use it in the fall." Ally turned to look at me, her face less pale but a tiredness had set in her eyes.

"In the fall? Emily will be back by June." I'm confused as to why Ally thinks taking a leave in the fall would be helpful.

"I'm going to need to take time off because I'm pregnant." She smiles and then turns pale again.

"Really?" I ask in an exhale as I stand up from the bed. "You're having a baby?"

"It's still early, we haven't told anyone yet. I've been so sick in the mornings it's hard to hide. I'm due in early October." She takes another sip of water as she watches me.

"Ally!" I hug her and she laughs when I do, "Congratulations!" Cullen laughs at my excitement from behind me.

"Congratulations, Ally." Cullen hugs Ally when she stands.

"Again, it's early and we haven't told anyone." She looks at me then to Cullen. Cullen nods letting her know her secret is safe.

"I won't say anything," I say before I hug her again. "This is amazing. How did Nate take it? He must be so happy."

"He's very excited." Ally sits back on the bed and drinks more water.

I turn around and smile at Cullen who looks much more relaxed now knowing what was making Ally sick. He smiles at me and takes his place back in front of the desk. He crosses his feet at the ankles then crosses his arms over his chest as he leans back on the desk.

"I'll be going home tomorrow night. I'll be back Sunday to help you with anything you might need next week. I can bring Emily to the center and then help with Matthew if you need to go into work," Cullen says, bringing us back to the task at hand.

"You've done so much already. I'll be okay," I say, sitting next to Ally on the bed again.

"Think about it, Violet. You're going to need help with Matthew. A baby is a lot of work. I can come back on the weekends. I have a week off in April too, the week we go up to the cabin. May is going to be tough, it's a long month for me at work." Ally lays back on the pillows again looking from me to Cullen.

"I'll be fine. Cullen shouldn't have to upend his life for this," I say flatly, looking to Ally for confirmation.

"I'll be back Sunday. Do you want some tea, Ally?" Cullen walks to the door and waits for Ally to answer.

"Sure, thank you," Ally says before Cullen leaves the room. There are a few moments of quiet before Ally speaks again. "How was the rest of your trip? How was the wedding?"

"The wedding was beautiful. I had a great time." I keep it simple, I feel the tears forming and before Ally can see I stand up and go back to the chair I was sitting in earlier.

"How'd the handsome Aussie take to you leaving so abruptly?" she asks, I feel Ally looking at me but I can't look up to meet her eyes.

"He was great," the last word is half a sob as I bring my hands over my face, "I can't talk about this right now."

"Alright, fill me in later. You look like you need some rest." Ally gets up from the bed and walks out the bedroom door.

I sit with my head in my hands for several minutes before I go down the hall to my bedroom. I see the suitcases I packed up from my condo two weeks ago standing by the door. I go to my dresser and pull out a clean pair of sweatpants and a t-shirt. I go down the hall to the bathroom and turn on the shower. When the water starts to steam I step in, I allow myself to cry. I let the sobs I held in my chest during the flight free. When I feel I set them all free I turn off the shower and towel off. I slowly get dressed and brush my hair. When I look at my reflection I see my red puffy eyes and red face. I lotion my face and then head back to my bedroom. Before I enter my bedroom I stand on the top of the stairs and listen, I don't hear Emily or Matthew, I don't hear Ally or Cullen but I smell bacon and coffee. I go to my bedroom and move my suitcases in front of the bed, I'll unpack later. I lie on my bed and exhale, I'm finally home. I check the clock and see it's almost 8, I'll take a short nap before I go downstairs to meet Emily and Matthew. It doesn't take me long to drift off.

Chapter 33
Violet

"Violet, wake up," Ally says as she gently pushes on my shoulder.

"I'm awake," I say, my eyes feel heavy, I'm still so tired. "What time is it?" I sit up on my bed and look around the room.

"It's two." Ally gets up from the bed and opens the curtains on my bedroom window. I slept the entire morning into the afternoon.

"What? I didn't mean to sleep that long." I stand up and run my hands over my hair, it's dry and matted.

"You needed it. You have to readjust to the time difference." Ally sits in the desk chair in front of the window. "How are you feeling?" she asks, looking at me with concern.

"I'm fine, just tired." I go to my closet to look for a pair of sneakers.

"Do you want to talk about anything? About Drew?" I hear hesitation in her voice.

"Not today, I want to meet Emily and Matthew. I can't believe I slept so long." I tie my sneakers and head toward the bedroom door. When I see Ally still sitting in the chair I ask, "Are you coming?" She nods and stands, following me down the stairs.

I walk down the staircase feeling anxious, I turn to make sure Ally's close behind me. When I enter the living room I see Emily on the couch with a mug in her hand looking to the floor. I look at the floor and I see a baby dressed in a blue onesie pajama outfit. He's lying on his back playing with a giraffe that squeaks when he bites down on it. Each time the squeak comes from the toy, Matthew flinches in surprise then laughs. I see Emily stand up from the corner of my eye but I can't take my eyes off Matthew. I slowly walk closer, I get down to my knees in front of the blanket Matthew's playing on. When he sees me he freezes and stares at me. I smile down at him, his eyes curiously scan my face as his feet kick the air.

"Hi, Matthew," I say as I bring my hand to his, he grabs one of my fingers and squeezes tight. "Aren't you a strong boy," I say as he roughly shakes my finger, I laugh.

The sound catches him and he stills but then he smiles at me. I see a dimple high on Matthew's right cheek when he smiles, just like James. My heart sinks and tears fill my eyes.

"He has the dimple," I say as I turn to Ally, she nods. I turn to Emily and ask, "Can I pick him up?"

"Of course," she says, smiling.

When I pick up Matthew his legs kick wildly, he doesn't take his eyes off me. When I settle him in my arms he drops the giraffe and makes a grab for my hair. He catches a piece and pulls hard, I laugh. I gently pull the strands of hair from his grasp and flip my hair behind my shoulder. Walking with Matthew to the couch I sit down and place him on my lap. Matthew continues to stare at my face, I smile down at him and bounce him gently on my lap. He smiles and I hear a giggle which makes my heart leap.

"I thought we might talk about a few things now that we're all together." Ally gets right to business. I glance at Emily who puts her mug down on the table with shaky hands.

"Sure," I say.

I haven't even introduced myself yet and jumping into heavy conversation wasn't the way I wanted to start off. I shouldn't have let myself sleep all day. I hear movement coming from behind me and turn to see Cullen come into the room. He meets my eyes and smiles, he has a nice smile and it sets me at ease.

"I can take this guy for a walk if you'd like," Cullen says, looking at Emily now.

My heart sinks along with my stomach, I thought he would stay while we talked with Emily. Having Cullen around for the conversation would have brought me comfort. Emily nods her head and stands up.

"I'll bundle him up and get the stroller ready, if you're sure. He might fall asleep, it's close to his nap time." Emily heads down the hall toward her bedroom.

"You're not staying?" I ask Cullen then look to Ally for assistance, hoping she'd want him here as well.

"No, you girls got this." He takes his jacket from the closet and pulls it over his broad shoulders.

While Matthew sits on my lap Emily puts a puffy green jacket on him with a knitted hat. She adds a second pair of socks to his feet and covers them with fleece booties. She takes him from my lap as he squirms in her arms and wraps him in a blanket. Emily and Cullen walk through the kitchen to the side door.

"I talked with Tom and he's drafting a temporary custody agreement, he said he'd email us a copy by tomorrow morning," Ally quietly relays.

"I'm sorry I slept so long. I should've helped you with that." I nervously grasp my hands together on my lap, they're already sweating with anticipation.

"It's fine. You're gonna have plenty of opportunities to help me with other things in the next few weeks," Ally offers with a reassuring smile, I hear the side door open and close.

Emily sits next to me on the sofa looking nervously around the room. I hope she's tough because Ally can be harsh. I resign myself to be the good cop in this situation even though I'm concerned about Emily's challenges and their consequences.

"Emily, I'm happy you reached out to us. Matthew's beautiful, thank you for bringing him here," I break the ice, trying to take the edge off of how she might be feeling.

"Thank you for having us. It's so great to finally meet you, Violet. James spoke of you, both of you, a lot. I'm sorry it took me so long to reach out, I feel awful these are the circumstances but I have no one," her last sentence is a whispered confession.

"James never told us about you, I hope you can understand our surprise," Ally cuts in and I think: here we go.

"We weren't very serious, as I told both of you, we saw each other only a handful of times." Emily keeps her eyes downcast, "Maybe seven times from January to July."

"We want to help you and Matthew in any way we can. James would want us to help you both," I say as I look at Ally, trying to tell her with my eyes to keep things civil.

"Yes, he would," Ally confirms, giving me a look of her own that I translate into: I got this.

"I know this must be hard for you, Violet. But I want you to know I want help because I want to be a good mother and I want to be the best version of myself for my son." Emily takes her eyes from inspecting the hardwood floor to meet mine.

"Hard for me?" My voice is uneven as I repeat her words.

I know what she means and I'm both shocked and angry. I'm shocked she knows details about my past relationship. I'm angry because, obviously, I was a topic of conversation between James and a woman I had no idea existed. I'm angry she would try to make this about anything except her and Matthew.

"James mentioned that..."

Before she can finish I put up my hand and close my eyes and interrupt, "Emily, I don't know what James told you and I don't want to know. This is hard for me because in the last thirty-six hours I found out I have a four month old nephew that I've never known about. This is hard for me because I got a call from a woman my brother never told me about, telling me she and her child need my help." I feel the anger seeping through my words and try to remember I'm supposed to be the good cop here. "Let's not make this about me and whatever happened in my past, I'm trying to move on from that. Everyone has their own issues and I would never put you in a box with anyone I may have had experiences with."

I don't take my eyes from Emily, her face reddens and her lips purse together as if she's holding something in or regretting saying anything. I wait to see if she has something to say before I go on, reminding myself I cannot alienate this woman if I want any kind of relationship with my nephew.

"I'm happy to help in any way I can. I'm glad you want help, this is the first step. I hope you take this opportunity to become the things you mentioned. Matthew doesn't have a father and he needs his mother. Every child needs a mother, Emily," I try to keep my voice even but the last few sentences are choppy at best.

"Okay," Emily says, "I'm sorry."

"Ally and I have come up with some ideas to help you and Matthew during the next few weeks. It's important to us that we get to know you and Matthew. It's important that Matthew gets to know us. Hopefully, he'll become comfortable enough with us and this situation won't be stressful for him or you. The more we learn about Matthew and his needs the better we can be for him." I turn my attention toward Ally signaling I'm letting her take it from here.

In the next hour Ally gets a full medical history for Matthew, allergies, hospitalizations, reactions to anything from medications to brands of diaper cream. I sit in awe of my little sister, she never fails to surprise me. I'm happy to learn Matthew's a very healthy, happy baby with no major concerns we need to be made aware of. The only things Emily mentioned was a reaction to a certain brand of laundry detergent and Matthew has shown signs of acid reflux.

Emily shares she's looking into a new pediatrician, considering Matthew's current doctor is based out of Delaware. We add the item on our list of things to do before Emily leaves for the rehabilitation facility. When Ally brought up the temporary custody agreement I was ready for things to unravel quickly but Emily remained stoic and agreed some measurement should be put into place. She was adamant she would not be relinquishing her parental rights but open to the idea of reviewing the document our lawyer would come up with. I was relieved and satisfied with how Emily handled that part of the conversation. She asked important questions and stated her thoughts clearly to Ally, Emily was bright and well educated. I could tell from her thoughtfulness she was already expecting that part of the conversation.

Cullen came in with Matthew after we talked about temporary custody, we heard clattering and low mumbling coming from the kitchen. When all three of us went to the kitchen to see what was happening, we saw Cullen struggling with the stroller. He was attempting to bring the stroller through the door, mumbling to himself as he did.

"What are you doing?" I ask in a hushed tone, I see Matthew sleeping in the car seat that's clipped into the stroller base.

"I can't get him out, what the hell is this thing?" he asks in exacerbation as all three of us quietly share a laugh. "You all gonna stand around laughing or get this kid outta here?"

I readily admit I have no idea what to do either, I would've unclipped him from the seat and carried him in but I don't say anything out loud. Instead I watch Emily carefully as she reaches to the back of the car seat and holds a release button, lifting the seat from the base. Then with one hand she holds another button in the center of the stroller's handle while twisting and the stroller instantly collapses. She places the car seat on the kitchen table and gently unbuckles the straps, slowly taking Matthew out of the seat, she brings him to the bedroom.

"Well, that looked easy," I say, smirking at Cullen.

"Bullshit. Like to have seen you do that." He tries to look annoyed but I see a sly smile tugging at the corner of his mouth. "How's everything in here?" His face grows serious as he looks to Ally then back to me.

"Good, I think. Almost finished," Ally says with a smile and I see Cullen's posture relax knowing things aren't as uncomfortable as he may have thought.

When Emily returns to the kitchen we sit at the kitchen table while Cullen makes coffee at the counter. Ally and I sit across from one another and Emily sits at the end of the table. I look to Ally wondering what else we have to cover because the last hour and a half was filled with so much information, I can't imagine there being much more. I hope Ally doesn't bring up the DNA test today, I think that might be too much right now. I'm relieved when Emily breaks the silence.

"I know you both work and will need help with childcare, I have some money saved but I haven't been able to work the past few months. I want you to take what I have saved." Emily turns her mug in slow circles on the table.

"That's not necessary. You should focus on getting better and you're going to need whatever you have saved when you come back. You're welcome to come here after your program and stay as long as you need." I look to Ally for confirmation because the financial end of this situation is something neither of us has previously talked about.

"We don't have to worry about that now. Violet's right, let's get through the next few weeks first," Ally gives the confirmation I was hoping for.

"I'd like to go get my car from the hotel. Matthew will sleep for a few hours now, would you mind watching him? Maybe someone could bring me to get the car, it needs a jump," Emily asks, looking from Ally to me, her eyes wide and hopeful.

"I can bring you. Not a problem," Cullen offers as he pours coffee into a mug.

"Thank you," Emily whispers as she stands and brings her mug to the sink.

Ally and I look at each other, searching to see if there's anything else the other would like to add. If Cullen takes Emily to get her car, Ally and I can reconvene to talk about anything else we want to discuss with Emily at a later time. Ally nods slowly as if reading my mind. I move to the coffee pot to pour a cup of coffee while asking Ally if she wants a cup of tea. Ally says she's going upstairs to take a rest and to call Nate. Emily goes to her room to get ready to go back to the hotel to get her car, leaving Cullen and I alone in the kitchen.

"You good?" Cullen asks, taking the cream from the fridge.

"I think so," I exhale as I sit at the table again, "I don't think I really know what I'm in for but I'm up for the challenge."

"You two will be fine. I'm here to help, too." Cullen takes the seat across from me, his green eyes search my face but my face is blank of all emotion.

"This isn't your problem, Cullen. You have things to do, I'm sure. Ally and I can handle it." I don't want Cullen to feel this is another problem James has dumped on him.

"Stop it, I want to help." He takes a sip of his coffee and leans back in the chair.

"Why?" I ask in confusion.

Cullen's a 30 year old man with a business, property and a life 200 miles away. Cullen owns a small business, a sporting goods store. He sells and rents skiing equipment during the winter, in the spring and summer months the store sells hiking gear and offers kayak rentals. He's done well since he opened the store three years ago. When I called Cullen two days ago I heard a woman in his house late at night, he probably had someone at home waiting for him.

"Why?" he repeats in a scoff, "Because I want to help, I just said it."

"You have other things to worry about. I can't ask you to take time away from your job and life to help us. We're fine, we can work it out," I explain as I stare back at him, his face hardens, he starts to chew on the inside of his cheek.

"The store is fine without me for a little while. I have a store manager now, I've taken a step back this year. I want to be here," Cullen explains.

"You don't owe us anything. What about your girlfriend? She probably won't appreciate you leaving to come stay with two women for weeks at a time." I don't mean for the comment to sound as severe as it does. Between the emotional roller coaster the last few days have been and the anger that keeps rising inside of me out of nowhere, I can't help sounding short.

"Girlfriend?" His face becomes full of bewilderment and doubt. His brow furrows and one side of his face scrunches up.

"The woman, on the phone the other…" Just then Emily appears from the hallway and pauses before she enters the kitchen looking at me, possibly picking up on the tension in the room. She has her jacket in her hands and slowly starts walking toward us when Cullen turns in his chair.

"Sorry, I can wait in the other room." Emily gestures with her thumb over her shoulder toward the living room.

"No, it's fine." I stand from the table and I hear Cullen whisper my name but I pretend not to hear. "I'll stay down here and read while Matthew sleeps." I walk toward the living room without looking back.

When I settle into the couch with a book I hear the kitchen door shut, a minute later I hear Cullen's truck start and leave the driveway. I sigh with relief. I don't want Cullen to feel like he has to be here. We're grown women and his promise to James' shouldn't interfere with his life. He helped us through James' death and he always checks in every few weeks to see how we're doing but this was different. This was something that didn't involve any promise Cullen made. I regretted calling Cullen when I got Emily's voicemail, I wish I had kept it between Ally and I. But I wanted to call him, I wanted to talk to him because any time I felt anxious Cullen comforted me. He was calm and reassuring when I felt out of control or scared. Cullen told me to breathe, he helped me find air when my fear took the air away. That wasn't fair to him, I shouldn't put that on him. I need to figure things out myself, I need to put on my big girl pants and let him live his life without burdening him with his dead best friend's family drama. I don't need to be taken care of, I can take care of myself. I can take care of Matthew. Cullen is loyal, trustworthy and unwavering. He also drives me crazy because he's headstrong and usually always right, especially when I don't want him to be. As I'm wondering how to tell Cullen he's discharged from his duty to James I hear Ally descend the stairs.

"Hey, how are you feeling?" I ask moving down the couch to make room for Ally to sit next to me.

"Tired, overwhelmed but overall I feel pretty good about how things went today." Ally leans against the arm of the couch and brings her legs up stretching out so the bottom of her feet are touching my thigh. "How about you?"

"Same. I can't believe how much thought you put into the details of taking care of Matthew." I place my book down on the coffee table and notice a chill in the air. I go to the wood stove and see it is already prepped for a fire, it had to be Cullen.

"You can't?" Ally asks sarcastically, raising her brow, it makes me laugh. It feels good to laugh.

"Well, I guess I should have known. Really though, thank you." I take the box of matches off the mantle and strike the match which emits the smell of sulfur in the air. I toss the match in the fire and watch as the flame catches to the kindling.

"We make a good team, ya know?" There's a moment of silence as I watch the fire catch, I feel Ally watching me but I don't turn around. "Have you heard from the Australian?" she asks.

"No, I said I would call him today but I haven't yet." She doesn't ask anymore questions which I'm thankful for. My thoughts drift to what I had been thinking about on the couch. "Ally?" I finally turn around, once I'm satisfied the fire is going strong, and take my seat on the couch.

"Yeah." Ally says quietly, she tilts her head to look at the fire.

"Maybe we should talk to Cullen and let him know we're good. He has a life and other responsibilities. He doesn't need to be here," I say.

Ally looks at me, I see a flash of something in her face. Almost too many emotions to name, curiosity, question, sadness, knowing, I even see a flash of humor. She doesn't respond so I go on. "He doesn't owe us anything. You have Nate and I'm going to be fine. Matthew will be a lot of work but I'm pretty sure I can handle it." Ally smiles, knowingly. "What?" I ask just before she laughs.

"A baby is a lot of work. I think it'll be great practice for Nate and I. You have work and you're alone here, it's going to be a lot. Are you sure you want to willingly let someone go who's offering help, free help at that?" Ally stands from the couch and walks toward the front windows

"I don't want him to feel he has to be here out of some duty to James." I pick up my coffee mug and take a sip. It's cold now so I place it back on the table.

"That's not why he's here," Ally says flatly as she closes the blinds.

I think of all the years we've known Cullen. He came home with James a year after James joined the Navy. Cullen didn't talk much about his family but from what I've put together his father left when Cullen was young. Cullen's mother had a series of bad relationships and worked a lot when she became a single mother. Cullen had an older sister who lived somewhere on the west coast, she got married young and had two kids. I know they keep in touch and he goes out there to visit with her several times a year. Maybe Cullen had found a family with us, I never thought of Cullen as a brother but James did. I thought of Cullen as exactly what he was, my brother's best friend.

"You don't think he's here because he promised James?" I ask when Ally turns around to face me. She's withholding, I see it all over her. Her stance is straight with her hands on her hips, her head is tilted and her mouth is a tight line. "What?"

"Honestly, Violet. Sometimes I can't believe how oblivious you can be."

Ally puts her hands up in the air and shakes her head, a laugh escapes her. The comment stung, I recoiled. Ally thinks everyone should know what she's thinking but it's honestly an impossible task.

"Ally, I'm just asking if we should let Cullen know we're okay with handling this situation and let him go home without having to feel he needs to come down here and check in with us." I'm angry with her hurtful comment but at the same time I'm concerned this might be some hormonal pregnancy behavior I'm not familiar with. She did mention she's overwhelmed, maybe she's projecting.

"That's not what you're asking. You're asking why Cullen's here and that's something you have to ask him." Just then we hear a cry come from the back bedroom, Matthew is waking. "I'll get him, they should be back any time now." Ally starts toward Matthew and I follow behind her.

Ally picks Matthew up from a square pack-and-play on the side of the bed. She takes a diaper off the bureau and heads back out toward the living room. I watch as Ally changes his diaper and redresses him, he's a squirmy baby and it takes her a few tries to snap up his onesie. Every time he kicks his legs a button unsnaps, it's cute. Matthew seems content with Ally. He smiles up at her and Ally speaks gently and quietly to him. She moves the coffee table in front of the woodstove to prevent Matthew from becoming interested in the fire. Ally pulls the afghan from the back of the couch and places it on the floor. There's a small bin of toys by the couch and she dumps them on the blanket for Matthew to play with. Ally talks about something called “tummy time” and motor development. She tells me he likes the floor, because he rolls, we have to be mindful of his movements. Emily had filled Ally in about Matthew’s nap and feeding routine, Ally said it’s almost his dinner time. I hope Emily will be back soon because I’m a visual learner and all of Ally’s explanations are leaving my head spinning. I hear the kitchen door open and exhale in relief, I see Cullen come into the living room and look around expectantly.

“Emily isn’t back yet?” he asks as he sits on the couch looking at Matthew.

“No, she didn’t follow you?” Ally asks, not taking her eyes off Matthew, she’s playing peek-a-boo using a burp cloth to hide her face.

“She said she had a few errands, needed baby formula.” Cullen wraps his arm over the back of the couch and scratches his chin under his beard.

“I brought three cans when I came yesterday.” As soon as Ally finishes her statement I’m hit with memories.

Sam needed to go out for aspirin or saying we were out of milk and the laundry list of items he went out for but never came home with. They were excuses for liquor runs, as I called them. It came to the point in our relationship I didn’t even ask why he was coming home empty handed, I was more angry he was out driving around than lying to me about what he was doing. But I told Emily I wasn’t going to judge her by what I experienced with Sam. How could I not right now?

“Did Emily know you brought formula?” I ask, reaching for my phone in my pocket.

“Yes, I called her to make sure I bought the right kind before I checked out.” Ally looks up at me and I look at Cullen, “What?” Ally asks as Cullen stiffens and I start dialing.

“She’s not going out for formula,” I utter as I bring the phone to my ear and listen to the line ring until it goes to voicemail. I guess I’m not as oblivious as Ally might think.

“Violet, she’s not a prisoner. She’s an adult, she can make her own decisions,” Cullen says calmly as he stands, “Matthew’s here, he’s safe.”

“What?” Ally asks, picking up Matthew, her eyes flashing to Cullen then to me.

"She might have gone to get a drink or maybe something else." Cullen answers, maintaining a calm voice not wanting to upset Ally, Matthew or me.

Ally and I look at each other, I don't know what to say. Ally either thinks Cullen and I are spot on or she thinks we're overreacting.

"Come to the kitchen I'll show you how to mix his food with the baby cereal and how to make him a bottle." She motions toward the kitchen and I follow, still holding my phone.

I watch Ally feed Matthew sweet potatoes and rice cereal. He spits out more than he takes in but he likes the food. Matthew's a complete mess after he's done eating. Ally comments we need to find a high chair for him and mentions the name of a local thrift store specializing in baby resale items. As Ally feeds Matthew I glance at Cullen a few times as he stands by the kitchen island watching Ally. He doesn't meet my eyes, his brow is wrinkled, his arms are folded across his chest. He looks upset and I don't know if he's bothered that Emily took off or if it's because of our conversation earlier. Ally tells me she's going to show me how to bathe Matthew next. My brain is on the verge of exploding with the events and information I'm expected to process today. I don't argue with Ally, if you know what's good for you, you never argue with Ally.

Matthew loves the bath, he splashes and laughs when the water droplets fly in the air. He likes the bath toys Ally put in the tub with him. Watching as Ally bathes Mathew, I can picture her with a baby of her own. She's going to be a great mom, all those years of babysitting really paid off for her. When Matthew's bathed and dressed, in the cutest full body pajamas, Ally dismisses me saying she'll stay up with him for another hour or so. Emily still hasn't arrived back and I'm growing more concerned and angry with each passing minute. Ally doesn't seem too worried, I go upstairs to relax before Ally turns in for the night and I'd take over baby duty if Emily wasn't back. I call Emily once more when I get to my room. It had been over an hour since Cullen returned from the hotel parking lot. The call goes unanswered so I decide to call Drew. My heart races as I hear the line ring and then it sinks when it goes to voicemail. I listen to his message and smile when I hear his voice but I don't leave a message. Soon after I hang up I receive a text.

Drew: Heading into a meeting. Can I call you later?

I'm hesitant with my reply. Do I tell him I miss him? Do I tell him I wish he was with me when I go to bed tonight because sleeping alone is awful? Considering he's going into a meeting, I keep it short.

Me: Yes, looking forward to it.

I have several missed calls from Beth and wonder if she knows I'm home. I wonder if Ally has connected with her during the last few days to fill her in. I text her letting her know I'm home and will call her in the morning, there's a response within seconds.

Beth: I talked with Ally yesterday and have been thinking about you since. Call me if you need anything, check in when you can. I want to come over but if it's too much I get it.

Maybe I'll meet Beth for lunch or dinner this week while Ally's here to hold things together but I don't want to sneak away when I just got back. I could really use a few hours with Beth to help me work things out. I sit on my bed and stare at my phone, I place it on the charger by my bed and start unpacking my suitcase.

After I unpack all the clothes from my trip and the two suitcases stuffed full of clothes from my old condo, I feel a bit accomplished. There's a faint knock on the door, when I look up it's already opening.

"Matthew's asleep. I put the portable sleeper in the living room, if Emily doesn't come back soon Cullen said he would stay with Matthew down stairs." Ally sits on my bed zipping up the, now empty, suitcases. "Wow, you did a lot."

"I'll go down and sit with Matthew for a little while. I'm not going to be able to sleep for a few more hours." I pause and then ask, "You're not upset she took off? Not even a call or text?"

"Like Cullen said, she's not a prisoner. Matthew's safe, she knows he's safe with us. Today was a lot for her, I'm sure. I'm not excusing her behavior, Violet. Don't look at me like that," she says when I shoot her a glaring look filled with frustration. "She's about to get proper help, I'm not a counselor and have no experience with this type of thing. I can only hope she comes home soon or calls if she needs a ride."

I try to take Ally's attitude on the situation and shake out the anger and resentment building inside of me. "I'll go downstairs." I take the laundry tote from the foot of the bed as I exit the room.

"Good night," Ally says as she walks the opposite way down the hall to her bedroom and I take the route to the stairs.

I walk quietly down the stairs, I don't want to wake Matthew. When I get on the landing and turn toward the living room, I see the fire is still aflame and Matthew is sleeping on his belly in the playpen. Cullen's lying on the couch reading a book. I can't see the title, the paperback book is folded so Cullen can hold it in one hand as he reads. He glances up at me as I pass.

"I'm going to start this, be back in a minute. Can we talk?" I hold up the laundry tote as I look down at him from the back of the couch.

His eyebrows raise and a smile hints on his lips but he tries to stop it from fully forming, it's too bad because when Cullen smiles it's such a nice thing to see. Cullen smiles often but when he really smiles, with his whole face and eyes, it's hard not to smile with him.

"Am I in trouble, Ms. Kelly?" He tries to look serious but when my smile doesn't come his face becomes serious and he sits up. "I didn't know she was going to take off. If I had, I would've followed her." He tosses the book on the cushion next to him.

"I'm not mad about that." When he looks at me with confusion I continue, "I'm not mad about anything. I just want to talk."

"Sure," he says quietly and points to the kitchen, silently asking if he should meet me there. I nod as I set off to the laundry room across from Emily and Matthew's room.

I take longer than I need to start the laundry, trying to gather my thoughts on approaching Cullen. When I have an idea on where to start I take a deep breath, press start on the machine and make my way toward the kitchen. When I enter the kitchen I see Cullen sitting at the table, he has a bottle of water, a second bottle of water is across from him on the table. I take a seat, he smiles warmly at me, he tilts his head and raises his brows in question.

"So?" he asks as he crosses his arms across his chest. "Give it to me." He takes one hand from his chest and with a placating gesture he waves his hand toward him.

"I appreciate everything you've done the past few days. Ally and I can take it from here. You shouldn't have to take time away from work or your life to come down and help us," I say as I watch Cullen chew on the inside of his cheek, something he does when he's annoyed or frustrated. "We can handle things, you don't owe us anything." He laughs and brings his hands to the table, folding them in front of him.

"What do you know about taking care of babies? When Ally leaves you're going to need help. You're going to need to go back to work, I can help. There's nothing at home that can't wait for me." He leans forward resting his forearms on the table.

"What do *you* know about taking care of a baby? I may not know a lot but I can learn. I can do this, I don't need your help." I meet his stare and narrow my eyes, "Don't you have someone waiting for you?"

"What? No. Is that what this is about? Because you heard someone the other night while we were on the phone," he looks expectantly at me.

"No, that's not what this is about. I'm trying to let you know you don't owe us anything, we can do this." My face flushes when I see Cullen give me a knowing smirk. He knows I'll be in over my head when Ally leaves and although he doesn't know anything about child rearing he knows having an extra set of hands would be helpful.

"I'm going to say this one more time, I'm not going anywhere. I want to help, I want to be here. Stop being so stubborn and accept the fact I'll be here to help and accept you can ask me for help. I'm not doing this for James." Cullen leans back in his seat with an exhale.

"If not for James, why?" I search his face as I see sadness, hope, and something I don't recognize enter his eyes, fear maybe. I've never seen Cullen afraid. "Ally says you're not here because you promised James. You're a successful, handsome thirty year old man with a life up there, why are you here?" I continue to look at Cullen but he doesn't raise his head to meet my eyes, he continues to look down at the table.

"You think I'm handsome?" Cullen finally looks up at me with a roguish smile, when I roll my eyes he continues, "What did Ally say?"

"She said I should ask you why you're here. She told me to ask you after she said I was completely oblivious, like I should know why…" I don't finish because a wave of unease floods my stomach.

No, it can't be. I'm hit with realization or ignorance. Cullen might be here because of me. No. It can't be that, Cullen is James' best friend, I've known him for 10 years. I'm being too confident, I'm not the reason. Cullen thinks of us as family, he has come to every Thanksgiving and Christmas with us when he and James weren't deployed. I see Cullen looking at me as I stare at him but there's a long while of silence. I wait because I said all I need to say and now I need answers. But I'm afraid of the answer.

Chapter 34
Cullen

So, I guess Ally knows. Ally knows and didn't tell Violet, I take that as a sign Ally's routing for me. I see a wave of realization cross Violet's face as she asks why I'm here. I don't know if I should confirm or deny her thoughts. If I'm honest and tell her I'm here because I love her, I want to be with her in any capacity I can, she'll definitely send me away. She'll think I'm being disloyal to James, she'll think it's a betrayal to James, she'll deny any feelings she may have for me. Violet doesn't know James knew how I felt about her and gave his blessing. If I deny it, I'll have to lie to her. I promised her I would never keep anything from her again. James told me if anything was going to come of Violet and I, she had to be the one who came to me. She has to be the one to see there's something between us. There *is* something between us but she can't see past the "brother's best friend" issue.

As the silence starts to stretch out toward an uncomfortable amount of time, when I know I have to respond to Violet's question and the unspoken realization, I hear the door to the kitchen open behind me. Violet's eyes scan past me to the door and I watch as relief and anger flood her eyes. It's Emily, I know Violet's happy she's back but angered at Emily for taking off. I turn to look at Emily, in an instant I know Emily isn't sober. Her eyes are glassy and bloodshot, her face is pale. I look back at Violet as I hear her stand from the table, I give her a look trying to communicate to her to stay calm.

"Give me a minute, I want to finish this," Violet whispers to me as she walks toward Emily who's attempting to take off her coat. I sigh, Violet means business tonight, and nod to her letting her know I'm not going anywhere.

I watch as Violet helps Emily with her coat and leads her down the hall whispering calmly as she guides her. I remain sitting, trying to focus my thoughts as to how I'm going to answer Violet's question. I need to make her see there is something here worth exploring. She's fresh off a bad relationship and I want to give her the time she may need to get over that. There has to be a way to communicate to her all the feelings and interactions we've had over the years that are so much more than a friendship without overwhelming her.

I could remind her about the time she took my hand at James' funeral. She took my hand as we sat in the chairs at the cemetery, she took my hand as Sam sat on her other side. It was a reflex, her reaching for me, she held my hand tight and stared ahead at the coffin in front of her. Sam stared at our clasped hands for a full minute and I stared at Sam waiting for him to say something but he didn't. She reached for me, not him, at that moment and it had to mean something. In the weeks following James' funeral Violet called me almost everyday, she cried on the phone sometimes, other times she wanted a distraction from her sadness. I brought her comfort, I knew, I brought her relief. The night she came to my cabin at midnight looking for courage to open James' letter, I didn't give her that, she found that on her own but she came to me. It had to mean something.

Violet didn't think of me as a brother, I knew this. Over the years, I've seen how Violet and James interacted. She never took his hand the way she took mine. She never melted into him when he hugged or held her the way she has done with me. One winter, we went snowmobiling. Violet rode on the back of the snowmobile with James, when she did she held his shoulders or put two hands on his waist for support. When she rode with me later that day she wrapped her arms around my waist and rested her head on my back. It meant something. Violet visited the cabin after a fight with the asshole two years ago. She arrived late at night, James and I were playing cards with two former team members that had come to visit. She was happy James had company and couldn't talk about why she was there, we knew why she was there. When the guys had gone to bed, Violet stayed up reading on the couch. I sat down next to her, I asked if she was okay or if she was hurt. She shook her head and said she was fine, a lie. I sat back and placed my arm on the back of the couch. She changed her position and leaned on me, resting her head on my chest and her back against my ribs. We sat in silence like that for a long time, watching the fire and listening to each other breathe. It all had to mean something, why couldn't she see that? Either, Ally was right and Violet was oblivious to the meaning behind our interactions or Violet knew. And if Violet knew she either wanted me to confirm it or she felt she couldn't act on it because she thought James wouldn't approve. I hear movement come into the kitchen and I'm surprised when I see Ally enter.

She's in her pajamas, a flannel pants set with a terry cloth robe. She looks at the clock above the stove and then to me sitting at the table.

"Everything all right? I thought I heard the door." Ally's eyes look sleepy and her long brown hair is tousled on one side of her head from sleep.

Ally's someone I think of as a sister, one hundred percent. I watched her grow up and during that time I always wanted the best for her. I watched her graduate high school and college. I watched her fall in love and get married. Now I'll see her become a mother. I always wanted Ally to find someone to make her happy and she did. With Violet I want to be the one best for her, I don't want to watch her fall in love with anyone but me. Violet isn't some girl I think of a sister, I never have and I never would.

"Emily's back, Violet's helping her settle in." I nod toward the hallway.

Ally hums in acknowledgement and walks toward the fridge taking a bottle of water. She stands behind the chair Violet vacated a few minutes ago.

"So, you two working things out?" Ally raises her brows and takes a sip of the water.

"Trying to. She says you two don't need me here to help." I lean back and place my hands behind my head.

"She's stubborn and doesn't want you to feel obligated." Ally shrugs her shoulders and takes a seat. "Has she asked you?" It's a broad question but I know exactly what she's asking.

"Asked me what?" I play dumb because I want to see how Ally has figured it out. She doesn't answer, instead she sends me a sly smile and tilts her head waiting for me to go on so I do, "I told her I'm here to help because I want to be here."

I look into Ally's bright eyes and wait for her to scold me or laugh at me. She does neither, she continues to look at me in the way only Ally can. Ally has a stare that can make a mute man speak.

I quiet my voice not wanting my words to travel through the silent house, "I can't tell her yet, she's not ready to hear it. James said she had to be the one to come to me. I'm hoping it happens in time."

"You and James talked about it?" Ally looks confused and in typical Ally fashion she doesn't wait for a response. "Maybe you should tell her, Cullen. Tell her everything because she'll never act on anything she may feel toward you if she thinks James wouldn't approve," she pauses briefly, "I've been pulling for you for years now, waiting for you to get up off your ass and do something about it." She smiles and her comment makes my chest inflate with warmth, she is routing for me.

"I didn't know you suspected anything." I smile back at her and she rolls her eyes.

"It's hard not to notice. I'm certainly routing for you over the Australian living half a world away."

As soon as she finishes her sentence, Ally's eyes widen and her lips pull together in a tight line, an apparent regretful gesture. In that second all the warmth in my chest is replaced by ice filling my lungs. What Australian? She was only gone for two damn weeks, she couldn't possibly have met someone.

"What?" I whisper to Ally as she starts to stare at something on the table but there's nothing there. "What Australian?"

"She had a fling with a guy while she was away, it's not serious. They're from two different worlds, nothing can come of it," Ally sounds like she's trying to reassure herself more than me.

Of course Violet would be noticed by men, she's charming and beautiful but I never would've guessed she'd move on so quickly. Maybe Ally's right and it was just a fling. I had plenty of those over the years and nothing came of them. Nothing could come of them because Violet was the only one worth starting anything with. Frustration rises inside me, frustration I missed a chance and anger that a guy halfway around the world had a chance with her before I could have an opportunity to tell her how I felt. I try to control the rapid beating of my heart and the accelerated breaths taking over.

"Cullen, relax." Ally reaches for my hand across the table. "Just tell her. Tell her sooner than later. You can still let her come to you when and if she's ready but she won't know to do that if she doesn't know how you feel."

I focus on Ally's warm hand and my breathing to divert the feeling of my insides crumbling. I admit I knew Violet couldn't be single for long, she has too much going for her not to be a prize to most men. I foolishly thought she would need more time to get over her relationship. It was stupid to think that because she was over Sam before she left him, that much was obvious. She was months ahead of getting over the relationship before she even left. Stupid. I feel Ally remove her hand and shift in her seat, I look up and see Violet enter the kitchen looking at Ally's hand resting on mine.

"Everything good?" Ally asks as she withdraws her hand and before Violet can question what we're talking about.

"She's in bed. I told her I'd listen for Matthew tonight. I'll talk to her in the morning, she should've let us know where she was. But I can't talk to her about that now, later when she's sober." Violet shakes her head and fills a kettle with water at the sink.

"Glad she's okay. I wanted to talk to Emily about a DNA test, maybe we can do that tomorrow, I found a local lab. If she's open to the idea, we can get the samples this week." Ally stands and doesn't wait for any responses. She looks at me with sympathetic eyes and says, "Good night, guys. See you in the morning." She turns toward the livingroom and after a moment I hear her go up the stairs.

I stand from the table and go to the kitchen island where Violet's placing a tea bag into a mug. I stand opposite her, keeping the island between us.

"That woman you heard on the phone the other night was no one. I met her at a bar that night and I took her right back to the bar after our conversation. I haven't heard from her since." I see Violet flinch at my explanation and I wonder if it's out of jealousy or because of my matter of fact tone.

"You pick up random women at bars and take them home?" Violet's voice is full of disgust and definitely a hint of jealousy, it makes me smile. When she sees me smile she holds up her hand and closes her eyes. "Nevermind, you're a big boy, I don't care what you do."

"You don't?" I ask as I fold my arms across my chest. Maybe we could get somewhere with this.

"Of course not. You're an adult, sleep with whoever you want, sleeping with a complete stranger is a great life choice," her tone drips with sarcasm and bitterness. Now we're getting somewhere.

"I could tell you the same thing, it seems I'm not the only one who sleeps with strangers," I immediately regret the words as they leave my mouth when I see the anger and hurt in Violet's face. She looks past me toward the living room where Ally retreated a few minutes ago. I take a calming breath and put my hands up in the air. "Violet, I don't want to fight with you. I need to tell you something, please sit." I gesture to the stool next to me at the island.

Violet, defiantly, puts her hands on her hips and narrows her eyes, "I'm fine standing."

"Fine," I take one more breath to sort out the thoughts running inside my head. "I came from a very dysfunctional home. My father was an alcoholic, a womanizer, my mother put up with a lot of shit while working to support us and his habit. She stayed with him because she thought breaking up the family would've been worse on my sister and I. I watched her become a shell of the vibrant, beautiful woman she had been when I was young. She stopped thriving and started surviving. My father left us when I was ten, one of those, 'I'm going out for cigarettes' scenarios. My mother worked even harder to support us, the little help my father provided was gone. When I was finally old enough to leave I didn't know what to do or where to go, so I enlisted." I see Violet watching me intently, a look of confusion crosses her face, she doesn't know why I'm telling her all this.

"The military was my way out. I wasn't college material, I had to work full time in high school to help my mom, school wasn't a priority for me. I met James during basic training, we clicked. We became great friends, he talked a lot about his family and I told him about mine. I heard from his stories what a real, solid family was like. The family you had before your parents passed away was something I had dreamed about as a child. I came home with him for Thanksgiving after training, do you remember that?"

"Yes," her voice is a whisper and I move to the stove to shut off the steaming kettle. I pour the water into her mug and place the kettle back on the stove before I return to my place opposite her at the island.

"I came here that weekend thinking I'd find a broken family. A family that was barely holding themselves together. I thought I'd feel better about my family knowing most families were broken and full of dysfunction. But I found the opposite, the three of you laughed as you cooked an entire Thanksgiving meal. You all supported each other, there was so much love here. Sure, there was sadness and grief. The happiness and love was something that overwhelmed this small town, mid-western boy. I knew then, four hours after being in this house, this was what I wanted to be a part of. I wanted to be a part of this family." I sighed and watched Violet's eyes well with tears.

"We're family," Violet says with a hint of question.

"James was a brother to me, we went through hell and back several times over. We came out of it brothers, I knew James better than anyone. If he was alive today, if he knew about Matthew, I would be here for him, Matthew and Emily. That's why I'm here with you, I want to be here. Please, stop pushing me out. That boy is a blessing, a piece of James we now know about. I wouldn't miss this for anything," I finish and watch as Violet places her hands on the counter, a few tears slip down her cheeks. I want to brush them away but I stay still.

If I know anything about Violet it is, when you confront her with something she's not ready for she retreats. If you tell her what to see or what to do, she'll dig her heels in and try to prove you wrong. We all learned that from her relationship with Sam, as much as we told her to leave him she continued to stay attempting to prove us all wrong. I can't tell her how I feel right now, I can't do what Ally said, if I do she'll push me away. She'll tell me to leave and then I'll have no chance. If I can stay close to her now, maybe in time I can make her see there's something between us. I decide at this moment I must break my promise to Violet and keep a secret from her. I resolve, I've kept this secret for this long, she'll be able to forgive me when she realizes why I'm keeping it. I have to allow her to come to me.

I decide to leave Violet with a choice, "If you want me to go home, leave you to tend to Matthew while you go to work and find childcare, I'll do that. If you want I can come back next week and help you, I have nothing keeping me from being here with you." I choose my words carefully, "If you can try to be less stubborn and more willing to accept help, I think we could be a good team. With Ally, we can make sure Matthew gets what he needs while Emily gets help. I know you don't like asking for help. If you think me being here is some kind of burden, I need you to know you are wrong." I take a step back while I watch Violet drink her tea.

There's a long silence and then Violet asks, "Do you talk to your mother?"

I wasn't expecting that question after everything I said but I'm thankful she didn't tell me to leave. "I talk to her a couple times a week. She's in a good place now. She lives in Colorado with her new husband. He's a decent guy, I like him." I sit down on the stool across from her. "I went out to visit her last month. I visit her every few months." There's another long pause as Violet processes her thoughts.

"I have some things I need to do, things to work out," she looks over my face as she explains, "I'm not sure where to start."

"Anything I can help with?" I ask, hoping I can be useful in some way.

"I don't think so." Violet picks at a piece of nonexistent lint from her shirt sleeve. "I'm trying to learn how to trust myself again. There are so many choices and decisions I've made over the years that I hate myself for. I'm trying to forgive myself and others. I'll ask for help when I need it." I try to remain as still and quiet as possible, Violet's giving me a piece of her and I live for these moments. "I'm afraid I'm not going to be good with Matthew. You're right, I know nothing about babies and how to care for them. Making decisions for myself is difficult enough right now, never mind having a baby to care for." The apprehension on her face and in her voice makes me wish I had never made the comment earlier.

"You're going to be fine, you'll learn as you go and you'll have Ally and me. As for the other stuff, we all make mistakes, no one is perfect. No one out there has made all the right choices in life. It's how we grow and become who we are." I want to be closer to her, the island between us feels like thousands of miles of open ocean. "The decisions you've made recently have been good. You left an asshole," I hold up one finger and offer a smile. "You went on a trip by yourself, that took courage," I held up a second finger then a third. "You came home when you found out someone needed your help." I pause and wait for her to look at me before I hold up the fourth finger, "You're helping Emily and Matthew so they can have a chance of being a healthy family."

"Those are common sense decisions," she responds.

The way she brushes it off makes me huff in annoyance. She can't give herself any credit, maybe from lack of confidence.

"Give yourself some credit, Violet. Stop doubting yourself. We all have stuff we need to forgive. It's more about moving forward and not repeating those mistakes. If you're moving forward you're, in turn, forgiving yourself." I watch as she leans against the sink with her lower back, holding the tea between her hands.

"I'll be fine," Violet sighs and I laugh.

"Of course you'll be fine. Don't be so hard on yourself." I watch as she moves toward the living room and stands over a sleeping Matthew. Before I take a seat on the couch I add another log to the wood stove.

"You can sleep upstairs tonight, I told Emily I'd watch over Matthew. I'm going to be up for a while anyway, I slept too much today," Violet whispers as she sits next to me on the couch.

"I'm going to be up for a while, too." I reach for the book I was reading earlier but Violet grabs it before I can get my hand on it.

"There are five beds in this house, why do you always sleep on the couch?" She flips through the pages, keeping her thumb on the page it was open to, she studies the cover.

"Compared to some of the places I've slept while active, this is five stars." I watched her study the book.

"Beekeeping for Beginners?" she whispers looking at me, raising a single eyebrow.

I take the book from her and open it to the page I left off on. "I'm thinking of getting a hive or two. I've always wanted to try it." I keep my voice low and soft, I don't want to wake Matthew.

"Sounds great. Tell me more."

I think she's joking but when she settles into the couch getting comfortable she looks expectantly at me.

"You want me to tell you about beekeeping?" I ask, trying to suppress a laugh.

"You don't have to," she shrugs her shoulders, the way she whispers makes my heart pound.

I settle in next to her and flip through the first few chapters I read earlier, I gather my thoughts on the information I've gotten from the book. I whisper to her what I've learned about bee colonies, the structure and hierarchy. She watches me, I see interest fill her face. I tell her about the construction of the hive, about how the bees maintain the hive and make honey. When I start to tell her about potential pests and disease, Matthew stirs. When he moves we freeze and watch to see if he wakes or goes back to sleep. Matthew rolls over with a few whines, without opening his eyes, he reaches around to feel for his pacifier. When Matthew places the pacifier in his mouth I hear him sucking on it, the sucking sound settles and his light breathing starts again. Violet and I looked at each other with relief he didn't wake. Violet pinches her thumb and index finger together drawing them over her lips making a zipping motion, her eyes are wide. I smile and nod at her, no more talking.

I quietly stand and bring the book with me to the recliner, I sit and try to read but I'm watching Violet from my peripheral. She watches Matthew for a few minutes then stares at the flames in the stove. The flames are low now, soon only burning red embers will remain. I nod toward the stack of wood by the side of the stove, silently asking if she wants me to add another log, but she shakes her head. She lies down on the couch and draws the blanket hanging off the back over her. I continue pretending to read by turning a page. I wonder what Violet's thinking. Her stare moves from the pictures on the mantle, to the stove, then to Matthew continuously over the next several minutes. Occasionally I hear her sigh.

After what feels like hours pretending to read I stand from the recliner and stand over Violet on the couch. She shifts her gaze to me and smiles. I want to scoop her up and take her upstairs, my heart pounds as I try to get a grip on the situation. I don't know how long I stand over her but when she sits up her smile is gone.

"What?" Violet whispers as she looks around the room then back to me.

"What are you thinking about?" I reach out for her and she looks at my empty palm.

"Everything," she whispers, still not taking my hand to stand up.

"Do you remember the weekend we spent camping near Hampton Beach?" I still have my hand out, Violet looks to my open hand and to my face in intervals.

"Yes." She brings her legs from the couch to the floor now looking up at me, "What about it?"

She continues to look toward my open hand debating if she wants to take it.

"Your tent started leaking when that sudden downpour came." She nods so I continue, "You unzipped my tent and told me to move over. You were shivering and damp." I see the memory cross her face and her eyes jump to mine.

"I was soaked, not damp." She smiles and I see she puts her hands on the couch getting ready to stand.

"Why didn't you wake up James? Why didn't you go to his tent?" When I finish, she looks away and her face turns a deep red.

She holds her palms to her cheeks, not making eye contact, "I, uh, I didn't want to wake him." She finally looks back to me and there's defeat in her eyes. "I knew you'd be awake, you never sleep," she tries to laugh off the answer.

"Lie." My hand is still out to her even though she no longer looks at it. "Why did you come to my tent, Violet?" My voice is calm and controlled but I'm shaking on the inside.

"I don't..." Violet voice sounds like my insides, trembling.

"Tell me," I plead, begging her to be honest with herself. Even if she can't say it out loud, I hope she can be honest with herself.

Her eyes change in a second. They were soft before, about to concede, then a flash of defiance fills them. I've confronted her with something she's not ready for, she feels I'm challenging her. I finally removed my open hand, knowing she won't take the offer now. She stands up in front of me, our bodies are inches from each other. The blanket covering Violet falls to the floor between us landing on our feet.

"What are you doing?" Violet's eyes are narrow and full of opposition. I smile, a bad move, when I do she becomes irate and that makes me smile more. "What are you smiling about?" she hisses at me.

"Waiting for an answer." I shrug my shoulders and put my hands in my pockets to keep from grabbing her and pulling her into me.

"That was like five years ago, Cullen. I don't remember," she lies, she remembers. She remembers everything about that night, I feel it in my bones.

"If you don't want to tell me then fine but don't lie to yourself," I lean in to whisper in her ear.

She stiffens, if she wasn't on Matthew-duty I know she would have stormed upstairs about now. She stares up at me, her blue eyes bright with emotion.

"How about this?" She puts a hand on her hip, "I'll give you an answer if you give me an answer."

"An honest answer," I add before I take a step back and cross my arms over my chest.

"Of course," she tilts her head, "I'm always honest with you, Cullen."

I refrain from rolling my eyes and gesture with my hand for her to go on. She takes a few deep breaths, I see the apprehension in her every fiber. I give her the time she needs because I want to hear her answer so badly I can hardly keep my body from shaking with anticipation.

"You comfort me," she thinks that answer is enough but it's not. I raise my eyebrows and tilt my head, cueing her to continue.

When she doesn't continue I softly clear my throat, "That's not an answer, if you want me to answer your question you have to fully answer mine."

"I went into your tent that night because I was cold and wet and I wanted to be warm and dry," her tone is abrasive but then softens. "When I'm annoyed, or sad, or upset. When I'm frustrated, scared or confused," Violet takes another breath, "I like it when you're with me in those moments. You bring me a sense of calm, you help me relax," she whispers her explanation and my insides soar with pleasure. She keeps her eyes on mine the entire time and I see her struggle sharing the confession with me, "You help me breathe, Cullen." Tears fill her eyes, "You help me to breathe when I can't find air."

I take a step toward her but she brings up her hand signaling me to stop. I stop and turn when I hear Matthew grunt. We stare at Matthew for a moment watching as he settles into a new sleeping position, his bottom lifts in the air and he lies with his chest on the mat. I see Violet smile at his new position and I smile too.

"You were James' best friend, I was with Sam. I didn't mean for you to think anything would become of this." She motions toward herself then to me, "You just said you think of us as family. I'm sorry if I was inappropriate with anything that happened over the years to make you think…" she doesn't finish, instead she allows her voice to fade out.

"There *is* something, Vi. You've done nothing wrong. Think about all the moments we've shared, small moments you may not have noticed. Think about those times and then you tell me if I'm imagining things to be different from what they are. Those moments mean something. Yes, I bring you comfort but that's not all. It would be wrong if you tried to lie to yourself about this, if you tried to convince yourself I'm wrong, you'd be hurting more than me. You're not with Sam and I'm not going to wait around anymore while you get swooped up by someone else," I watch Violet as shock and surprise take over her. "James knew about all this, Ally knows. It killed me, maybe even more than James, to see you in that relationship. As much as James told me it wouldn't last forever, one day you would wise up and leave, I was scared you'd stay too long. I was afraid you'd stay as long as my mom had and you'd lose yourself completely. It took all I had to let that play out for all those years. James told me you'd leave him when you were ready and when you did I had to give you time and space before anything could happen between us. I'm going to give you time and space to work out all this but I'm not going anywhere. I'm going to be here when and if you are ready to trust yourself to see what I see. If I'm wrong then I can face it," I tentatively take another step toward her, a sense of relief passes through me when she doesn't signal me to stop.

"I can't do this right now," she says as the fear and panic return to her face.

"I know, I'm not asking for anything. I said I'm giving you time and space. But I won't walk away from you while I do that." I wait for the worry to leave her face before I continue, "What's your question?"

Violet shakes her head as if she forgot we agreed to an honest answer for an honest answer. When she gathers herself she answers, "Nothing, everything you just said negates my question."

She sinks to the couch, looking at her hands on her lap. There's a long silence between us. The only sounds I can hear is Matthew's light breathing, the occasional pop of the fire and my rapid heartbeat. I'll continue to share with Violet the moments like camping, the funeral and so many more until she sees there's something here. If she doesn't push me away first, I'll be able to share with her all the memories and moments I have of falling in love with her. There's a buzzing sound breaking the silence, Violet's phone shakes on the coffee table in front of us. I'm still standing over her when I glance down to the phone. A picture of Violet smiling a pure smile, something I don't see often, behind her is a broad shouldered man with an equally wide smile. My stomach turns, the name on the call display reads "Drew". She reaches for the phone but instead of taking the call she taps the ignore icon and puts the phone face down on her lap.

"Good night, Violet," I say as I turn and go upstairs.

I've never slept upstairs at the Kelly house but Violet needs space and she'll insist on staying with Matthew tonight. I've come to James' room sometimes to look around, when I came here the other day I laid on his bed willing Violet to call me back. I remember the night I held Violet in this bed, I'll sleep there tonight. I won't sleep, I'll replay the conversation tonight, I'll remember all the moments I've had with Violet of the years. I could keep things casual with Violet if that's what she wanted. I might even be able to move on from this one day but I would always wonder what a life with Violet Kelly would be like.

Epilogue
Violet

It's been one week since I came home from Australia. Ally went home last night after a long week at our childhood home. We got to know Matthew and his routines really well. I've come to understand that a four month old baby is a creature of habit. His naps, bath time and mealtimes are structured, the rest of the day is filled with playtime, park visits and long walks in the stroller. I've learned so much in the past week, things I never thought I would need to know. I've learned how to attach a car seat to the mysterious latch hooks I found tucked in the backseat of my car. I can change a diaper in under a minute now, unless it's poo then it takes me longer. I've also learned baby boys will pee on you if you're not careful when you first take off their diaper. I've learned how to make a bottle and check the temperature of the bathwater. I can break down and pop up a pack-and-play. I've also learned a lot about Emily. After that first night, when Emily came home late and not sober, we had a sit down the next morning. I tried to keep my anger and resentment in check during the conversation. I laid down ground rules for Emily while she stayed here. Cullen was right, she can't be treated like a prisoner during her time here. I told her she had to answer my call or texts when she was out of the house, she couldn't drive if she had been drinking or under any influence. I told her I would pick her up and not ask questions if she called for a ride. During the conversation Emily kept her head down and her eyes low. She agreed to my rules and hasn't pulled a disappearing stunt since. Sometimes I find tiny bottles of alcohol in the trash, I don't ask questions because Emily never appears to be drunk at the house. She goes to rehab in two days and I'm hoping, with all I have, she can get past this challenge.

Emily shared she grew up in foster care since the age of four. My heart broke for her as she opened up about her life. The longest she had a home growing up was four years from the ages of six to ten. It was a life of constant change, new schools, new homes, new parents, new siblings. When she turned 18, she started working and taking classes part time at a local community college. She got her associates degree in four years then moved to Delaware. The roommate she found in Delaware was Theo's girlfriend and now wife. That's how she met James two years after moving to

Delaware. She started online classes for her Bachelors degree but hasn't finished, she plans to re enroll after she gets out of the rehab program. Emily was kind and smart, I was thankful she shared her story with me.

I was able to go into work everyday last week and it felt good to get back into a rhythm. People at work commented on how happy and relaxed I looked but I laughed it off. I was completely stressed inside but I'll admit the trip to Australia was good for me. I talk to Drew most days, it's nice to hear his voice, we keep the conversation light talking about our day and he listens to my worries about Matthew and Emily. Sometimes we video chat and I see the tiredness and hurt in his eyes. He ends every call saying he misses me but he doesn't push or ask where my thoughts are with him. Yesterday afternoon during our video chat I saw him lying in his bed. I loved his bed. When I commented he said it was his first night back in his bed and he had been sleeping in his spare room, my heart sank and tears filled my eyes. After he told me I saw he regretted sharing that piece of information and he quickly changed the subject.

Mia and I spoke regularly, she's a great listener and friend. She's excited for me to have time with Matthew, she listens to all my concerns about being a primary caretaker and offers reassurance. I miss the Harris family, they were all so good to me during my stay. In the past when I met a family I always resented them. When I saw a family together as a unit, a father, mother, children, I resented them with all my being. I was angry seeing people with their families because I didn't have mine. Why were they allowed to be happy with all their loved ones and I was forced to live without my family? It was irrational but it happened for many years. I thought of those families as entitled and allowed the resentment to fill myself. When I met the Harris family I felt differently, I was happy for them, I wished them a lifetime of togetherness.

Cullen left last week allowing Ally and I to have time with Emily and Matthew. He said he would come back today to help with Matthew and Emily. But I told him I didn't need him here right now. He didn't push me, which I was thankful for. After our conversation last week I tried to keep my distance from Cullen. I don't want to give him the wrong idea about what I might feel for him. I'd be lying if I said I wasn't thinking about him and the conversation we had that night. Why do I feel a need for him? Was it because of comfort? Was it the security I felt when he was around? Was it because he has been a part of my family for so many years? I had no idea yet but I had to find the answers in order to put him and me at ease.

I talked Ally into holding off on the DNA test conversation for a few days after Emily disappeared, I didn't want her to think of the DNA test as a punishment for her leaving that day. We spent the next few days shopping at local thrift stores for items Matthew would need for the house. We bought him a crib, a bath seat, clothes, a highchair and my favorite item was a baby carrier. It was a carrier you wore like a front backpack and put the baby in when you went on walks or around the house. Matthew loved it and so did I. It was nice being able to hold him without my arms starting to ache. I thought it would be great for our upcoming trip to the cabin, I could hike with him on my chest or back. I was excited to show Matthew his father's cabin. After a few days we brought up the idea for a DNA test to Emily. She was willing to prove Matthew was in fact James'. I think we all know in our hearts but Ally needs to see it in black and white.

I had lunch with Beth last week to fill her in on all the happenings, we spent four hours at the restaurant. Beth took the afternoon off and listened to everything I told her about leaving Drew, returning home to meet Emily and Matthew, Emily's disappearing act and Cullen's question to me the night before he left to go back home. She was enthralled and even giddy at times telling me "boring" would never be a description of my life. She offered to help with Matthew when she could, even if I went into the office in the evenings when she got out of work. I was thankful for her, I've always been thankful for her. During our lunch she asked about my thoughts on Cullen but I didn't have answers. She, like Ally, said it was obvious he held feelings for me. When I wore a look of surprise she rolled her eyes, like Ally had.

"It's obvious by the way he looks at you, Violet. Honestly, I don't know how you can't see that. You're an attractive woman, successful, funny, many guys see that. I don't know what Sam said or did to you to make you unsee the fact you are a bombshell waiting to be worshiped," Beth said with a tone of unsubtle frustration in her voice.

Beth never held back her thoughts and she knew me very well. She always had a way to keep even the heaviest of conversations light and added humor to release the tension. Although the conversation left me with more to think about, it also left me relaxed. I find myself wanting to make a plan for myself, for my life, but given my current situation I have to take things one day at a time right now.

As I pull in the driveway after a few hours at the office this afternoon, I see Emily pushing Matthew in his stroller up the driveway. I wait for her to reach the back of the driveway before I pull up. I exit the car taking the ingredients for the lasagna I picked up at the market after I left the office.

The crib we bought for Matthew hasn't been put together yet. I was thinking of cleaning out James' room and setting the crib up in there, which is right across the hall from my room. Having Matthew upstairs with me would give me peace of mind knowing he's across the hall rather than downstairs alone. Ally and I talked about cleaning James' room several times since James has been gone but neither of us can bring ourselves to do it. My phone rings as I place the items I bought at the store on the counter. I look at the screen, Cullen. My heart beat escalates and I take a deep breath before I answer. Before Cullen left he made me promise to keep in touch and answer his calls while he was away. He said if I didn't want to talk to him that was fine but I had to answer the phone and tell him.

"Hey, Cullen." I hold the phone to my cheek with my shoulder as I grab a pan from the cabinet.

"Violet, how are you?" he asks, his voice soft and smooth.

"Good, you?" I try to keep things simple with Cullen, hoping we can get back to how things were before that night.

What was our relationship before that night? We were friends, our conversations were full of banter and teasing. We laughed together, we had serious conversations and light conversations. I want to go back to that without feeling the tension of things unsaid or things undiscovered.

"Great, can't believe how cold it's been. Do you have enough wood over there?" he asks.

Weather talk, simple enough. We have had a cold snap this week and have used the wood stove many times over the past week.

"Yeah, there's enough to get us through another week," I answered.

"Did you get the crib set up yet? How does Matthew like a big boy bed?" I hear a car door close on the other end and hear Cullen's truck engine roar to life.

"I haven't yet, I'm thinking of setting it up in James' room so I can hear him better at night while Emily's away. I have to get up there and do that this week," I explain to him. Emily leaves in two days, I need to do it soon.

"I can come down if you need a hand," he offers. Cullen wants to come and help, I know he does but I can't have him here right now.

"I'm fine, Cullen," I say quietly.

"Alright, well, call me if you need me. I'm available, Violet," his last sentence sends a shiver down my spine. I know what he's doing, I know what he means when he says it.

"I'll be in touch." I wait for Cullen to say goodbye before I disconnect.

While Matthew naps I start layering the lasagna and Emily works on making a salad. Beth comes over for dinner and the three of us sit in the living room while the food cooks. Matthew wakes up and joins us at the table in his new highchair. During dinner I mention to Emily I have a long day at the office tomorrow, I really don't. I want her to have a full day with her son before we leave the following day to drop her off. I have things at the office I can busy myself with to allow Emily time with Matthew.

I wake up Tuesday morning early and leave the house before 7 AM. We should be getting the DNA results today which is another reason I didn't want to be at the house. When Ally calls with the results I want to be by myself, as much as I feel Matthew is James', I know nothing is certain until we get the confirmation. It's just after one when my phone rings and I see Ally's name flash on my phone.

"Hi," I answer the phone with one word, I can't trust the shakiness I feel in my core.

"Hey, I got the test back. Matthew's a close relative to you and I. He's James' son," I feel relief wash over me with her words. My eyes fill with tears and a sob lingers in my throat.

"Glad we could confirm," I choke out the words.

"Yes, me too. Thank you for supporting me with this."

I want to respond but I can't speak. Matthew is James' son, I knew it in my heart but hearing the words brings so much emotion.

"Okay," I say as the tears spill down my cheeks.

"I love you. See you soon." With that Ally hangs up and the flood gates open.

I sit at my desk and cry for a while. I take a few moments to pull myself together in the small bathroom inside my office. I wash my face and take long deep breaths. My face is red and my eyes are puffy. I take my coat, purse and keys off the hook hanging on the back of my office door. It's after three when I pass Stacy at her desk and tell her I'm off for the day and will be available by phone if she needs me. She looks at my face but doesn't ask, she offers me a look of sympathy and says she'll call if she needs me.

I get in my car and start driving, not knowing where to go or what to do. I want to give Emily a few more hours with Matthew so I drive through back road neighborhoods thinking about James and Matthew. The anger rises again. James would never be with his son, Matthew will never know his father. Why? It's not right, it's not fair. I don't realize I've stopped the car until my mind starts to calm and the anger fades. Where am I? I look around, tall oak trees surround the property, a stone wall surrounds the border. I'm at the cemetery. I take a deep breath and exit my car. My heels sink into the dirt path, the spring thaw is coming, even though the temperatures have been colder than a typical early spring in New England. I walk around the cemetery, it's cold and crisp, I bring my jacket into me and zip it up. I find the grave site, three headstones all with the name KELLY. I haven't been here since James' funeral. I rarely visited my parents before James died. I don't feel them here, I feel them more at the house, I feel them at the beach or in the mountains. I feel James at the cabin. I don't like to think of them below me in the ground, cold and decomposing. The thought brings rise to bile from my stomach. I push it down and sit on the cold ground. The grass is wet and I instantly feel my pants dampen.

"You have a son, James. Mom and Dad, you have a grandson."

I don't know why I'm talking out loud, I've ever done this before. Maybe I'm saying it out loud for myself.

"His name is Matthew and he's the most beautiful baby I've ever seen. He looks just like you, James," I take a breath and look up at the tree above me.

The tree is still bare but I see signs of the tree coming out of dormancy. I see tiny buds along some of the branches. The tree looks dead but soon it will spring to life, bringing new leaves and acorns to the bare branches. The tree is large and healthy, it's strong, undefeated by the cold winter. I feel the cold of the ground penetrating the back of my thighs and bottom. I bring my knees to my chest and continue looking at the tree then back to the stones.

Spring is coming, a time for new growth. All the bare trees around this cemetery will form new growth, new life. They'll create acorns and the maples will create those helicopter seeds we used to throw in the air and watch as they spun to the ground. The idea fills me with hope, things will grow. I'll grow, the parts of me that lie dormant will spring to life. I have to believe that, I have to allow that. I'll start my garden soon, from one small seed I'll grow a pumpkin for Matthew to paint or carve in the fall. I'll grow carrots and puree them for Matthew to eat. Where will Emily and Matthew end up? Will she go back to Delaware? God, the idea makes me sick. I hope they stay close, I hope I get to be a part of Matthew's life for the rest of mine. The sky starts to darken and I look at my watch, it's close to 5, my body is cold from sitting on the ground. I stand up and look at the headstones one more time.

The drive home isn't long. My legs finally thaw out with help from the heated seats. I pull in the driveway and take a moment to gather myself before I enter the house. I hear the tub running upstairs when I enter the kitchen, I toss my keys on the counter and go upstairs.

"Hey, Emily," I call out letting her know I'm home, I don't want to sneak up on her.

"I'm here," She calls back but her voice is different.

As I reach the top of the stairs to the landing I look toward the bathroom when I notice the light is on in James' room. I look inside his room, I see the crib assembled and sitting in the middle of his room. There's a piece of paper attached to the side of the crib. I go to it and read it.

Violet,

I didn't know where you wanted it. If you need help moving things around here or anything else CALL ME.

Cullen

I'm shocked, I didn't see his truck when I pulled into the driveway. Did he step out, maybe to get dinner? I walk toward the bathroom and see Emily leaning over the tub washing Matthew with a cloth.

"Hey. Is Cullen here?" I ask, holding up the note.

"He left about an hour ago," Emily doesn't turn to look at me but I can hear her voice shaking.

"Are you okay?" I kneel down in the doorway trying to get Emily to look over at me.

When she turns her eyes are red and tears are on the verge of spilling over.

"No, I'm not okay," a hint of anger fills her tone.

"I'm sorry, Emily. Is there anything I can do?" Now my voice shakes.

She sniffs and smiles down at Matthew, he looks up with concern. Matthew's a perceptive baby, maybe all babies can pick up on emotions and feelings but Matthew is in tune with others emotions, especially his mother's.

"I know he'll be okay with you and Ally. I'm just so scared to leave him," she starts to cry, her hands shake. Then Matthew starts to cry and I know I have to pull it together.

"Emily, I know it's hard, Matthew will be fine. I promise you, I'll check in everyday when you can, we can FaceTime and visit anytime you want." I put my arm around her as I grab a towel from the bathroom counter. I whisper, "Let's try not to upset Matthew." I hand her the towel, she nods and wipes her eyes.

"Okay, okay. Just give me a minute with him, let me finish this," Emily says as she rinses Matthew off.

I do as she asks and go to my bedroom to change out of my damp pants. When I've changed I pick up my phone and open my message app, I tap on Cullen's message thread.

Me: Thank you.

I see the thought bubble appear with three dots and I watch and wait for his response.

Cullen: For what?

I roll my eyes and respond.

Me: For the crib, dummy.

Instantly there's a response once again.

Cullen: Happy to help.

I thought about asking him why he didn't stay, why he didn't wait for me to come home from work but I thought it was best to leave it alone. I know why he didn't stay, I didn't ask him to come and he was waiting for me to let him know when I needed him. I still thought his gesture was sweet, driving all the way to assemble a crib just to hop back in his truck and drive back to New Hampshire.

When Emily was finished with Matthew's bath and he was dressed in his pajamas we sat in the living room watching Matthew play on the play mat in the middle of the floor. He was a happy baby, I wonder if he suspected how different things would become in just a few hours. I hoped Matthew would adjust to living with me with little stress. I know he'll miss his mother, she's the only constant he knows. I take a deep breath, I'll be fine. I tell myself over and over in my head: I will be fine. Just like Matthew will have an adjustment period, so will I. I'm up for the challenge. I'm ready to watch Matthew grow, I'm ready to grow. Like the trees outside, the dormancy inside me is waking and ready to awake. I'm ready to meet these new challenges and see myself come to life. I go to the floor and lie down beside Matthew, he turns to look at me, he reaches for my face. He takes a swipe at my cheek and I smile. He smiles at me with that dimple high on his cheek showing, I look him in the eyes. When his eyes meet mine it's as if he's staring into my soul, I silently tell him: I've got you, you've got me, we can do this.

Made in the USA
Middletown, DE
30 September 2023

39716284R00209